Immigrants

Volume 1

Dragon Tooth Gold Series

By

Kent J. McGrew

Dragon Tooth Gold – Volume 1 - Immigrants

Copyright © 2018 by Kent J. McGrew

ISBN 978-1-7336650-0-1

Cover Image by Night Raven Illustrations
www.deviantart.com/nightravenillust
nightravenillustration@gmail.com

Kent J. McGrew

Meet and Contact the Author @

https://dragonstoothpublishing.com/
Printed in the United States of America

2nd Edition: November, 2019
Dragon Tooth Publishing

Considerations, Dedications, Acknowledgements & Thanks

*Consider this saga of gold mining in the American West as
penance for 60 years of technical writing – excruciating
boredom lining the walls of mining company boardrooms and
forgotten archives.*

*Dedicated to the droves of want-a-be gold miners near Congress,
AZ. Intrepid folks who flock to the streambeds and hillsides of
our famous mountain range in search of the yellow metal,
dreaming of riches and laboring like the damned.*

For my wife Sally – Morals, and Ethics Editor
For my daughter Tahtim – Creative Writer/Editor
*For my Sister-in-Law Terry – Fun and Enthusiasm Director and
Reader/Editor*
Cousin Loretta – Punctuation Director and Reader

*Thanks to all my teachers, mentors and associates. It has been a
great ride.*

Table of Contents

Prologue 1

First Nanosecond and Beyond..3

Proterozoic Pandemonium...5

190 Million Years Ago 7

THE Extinction...11

The First Find 15

Immigrants..31

The Departure 43

Delaware Bay...65

Pamlico Sound 75

Ports of Call...87

Trial by Storm 95

Revelations and Repairs 103

Jamaica 111

Cuba...123

New Orleans..131

Vicksburg 145

Saint Louis...155

Independence...169

The FirstBorn 181

The Assassin...191

Marriage and Celebration 205

The Professor..215

The Christmas Horse..227

Suzette...243

Farewell Brothers.. 257

Runaway.. 267

Epilogue... 277

PROLOGUE

Gold, the strength of kings, empires, and governments from ancient times to the present day, is also coveted and sought for by the common peoples of the earth. While the history of empires, currencies, and impact on the economy of our species is of interest, it is nowhere close to the romance, intrigue, and lore that the yellow metal has inspired in the art, literature, and the darker alleys of human consciousness.

While gold is relatively scarce, its high density and brilliant luster made it discoverable in streambeds worldwide by primitive peoples. The yellow metal, coveted for its beauty and immunity to corrosion, was hoarded as a symbol of strength and even revered as a sacred metal by the earliest of men. Gold's easy workability facilitated jewelry making as early as 2450 B.C., as evidenced by the excavation of the treasure trove known as The Gold of Troy discovered in Turkey by the classical archeologist Heinrich Schliemann at Hissarlik in 1873. Easily melted and formed into coins, gold assumed its role of money in Greece around 700 B.C. The Greeks greatly improved mining methods and employed slaves, convicts, and prisoners of war to feed the gold economy of their society. By the height of the Roman Empire, gold coins circulated throughout Britain, Egypt, and North Africa. As trading increased, Roman gold and silver flowed to India for spices and far east to China for silk.

But this work is not about Europe and its quest for gold. It is about a unique and poorly understood gold deposit in the desert southwest of North America. Here was an area of the world awaiting the arrival of Europeans to take the stage in the gold history of the world. Come with us now on this imaginative journey that wraps us in the mystery and excitement of discovery along with the shenanigans of promoters, thieves, and killers that always overlay the efforts of hard-working prospectors and miners. *Gold Fever*, a nonscientific property of gold, instills lust, greed, and all the negative emotions and madness of humanity in all who contract the disease.

FIRST NANOSECOND AND BEYOND

Science cannot see back beyond 13.8 billion years ago, where the event known as the "Singularity" is calculated to have occurred. Extrapolating back in time from measurements of the expanding universe and the red-shift in the light of distant galaxies indicates that before the *Big Bang,* there was a *Singularity*. What that means to the non-scientific community is that a dense, super-hot primordial mass of electrons, protons, and neutrons existed in one super-dense-homogeneous mass. Where that matter came from is still a mystery to science and lends itself to the religious interpretation that has dominated most of humanity's existence. Religion has accommodated those who need a quick answer as to where their species came from rather than wait for science to unravel the secrets of the universe. Consider for a moment that perhaps our *Big Bang* wasn't the first *Bang* but a cycle of expansion and contraction of the universe that encompasses trillions of years or longer, unfathomable to the finite mind of humanity.

Science puts forth that in less time than it takes for an electron to circle the proton in the nucleus of a hydrogen atom, the dense mass expanded, thus the term *Big Bang*. Within minutes, hydrogen, helium, and traces of lithium formed and continued to expand their dense cloud to form the building blocks of the universe as it appears today. The universe continued to grow, to coalesce into clouds, then forming stars, planets, solar systems, and galaxies. Through a process of nucleosynthesis, elements heavier than lithium were generated to include gold, iron, silica, and every metal up to uranium and including uranium in the Periodic Table. Nucleosynthesis is believed to occur within supernovas, the explosion of which scatters the heavier elements throughout the cosmos to re-coalesce into new stars and planets. Such are the workings of the universe, and 4.54 billion years ago, the earth and its solar system formed from the dust and debris of previous supernovas. Earth is likely a second or third-generation solar system reforming from the scattered remains of long-gone supernovas.

Blessed with an abundance of iron and nickel in its core, and lighter elements making up its crust, the mass to become known as Earth to its inhabitants was likely a molten stew, cooking water and carbon dioxide out of the cosmic dust that formed it. Cooling and condensation were to form oceans, create weather, and an environment where life could start and progress forward until our part of the universe became aware of itself. Consciousness, an interesting journey in itself, with which the modern thinking and investigating human mind has only shared the universe for a very short time, is relentless in its quest to understand the nature of itself. Time, the enemy of the living, is the friend of that quest.

Measured in meters, the distance from the spire of the Empire State Building in New York City to the summit of Mount Whitney in California is on the order of 3,842,864 meters. If we equate the age of our planet to the distance from the spire to Mount Whitney, modern man's presence on that timeline would only be 169 meters; not even far enough to cross 6th Avenue on the journey west.

Despite humanity's short existence in the world, the constant forward motion of science has accelerated at an exponential and exhilarating rate. In 1982 Buckminister Fuller estimated that before 1900, human knowledge doubled every century. By the end of WWII, it accelerated to every twenty-five years. In our present time, the estimated time for doubling has shortened to only thirteen months. Now the expectation is that with the invention and construction of even larger computers and interaction with artificial intelligence, the rate of doubling could decrease to once every twelve hours. Considering that it has only been 544 years since Copernicus figured out that the Earth wasn't the center of the universe. It is mind-boggling to wonder what we will know in thirteen months or eventually in the next twelve hours. Consider asking the question, "Where did the universe come from?" and only having to wait twelve hours for the answer.

Science will progress, superstitions and darkness will continue to be replaced by knowledge, but man's need for gold will keep the mystique and excitement of hunting, finding, and possessing it alive forever.

PROTEROZOIC PANDEMONIUM

Let's defeat time with our imagination and return to the earth 2.5 billion years ago. Let's stop in orbit and look down at the part of the that will become Arizona. Now, we take a picture of the earth every million years. If we could run our pictures like a slow-motion movie, we would see a dynamic and ever-changing landscape. Run the movie at one second per million years; in less than an hour, our landscape would unfold. What we would see would be a landscape that was alive with crashing waves of molten rhyolite and basalt; great molten masses of granite intrusives pushed up by heat and tectonic movement deep within the earth. We would see volcanoes erupting, ash clouds covering the land, massive wildfires, and rampaging storms eroding the mountains and filling the valleys with sand, silt, and gravel.

From 2.5 billion to 500 million years before the present, the land that was to become Arizona lay under a tropical jungle, further to the west and closer to the equator. Continental drift would much later, and very slowly, move the land to its present-day position on the globe. The change of the atmosphere from the early carbon dioxide gases to oxygen had started around 1.8 billion years before the tectonics that would mold the final form of Arizona. The oxygen atmosphere resulting from the earliest single-celled life in the oceans supported a wide variety of life, and photosynthesis had been at work since the evolution of the oxygen atmosphere. Rainforests, swamps, bogs, and mud covered much of the lowlands with the process of orogenesis forming mountain ranges with colossal sources of heat working on the surrounding rocks and sediments.

Deep in the crust of the earth, molten magma was melting its way to the surface. Unlike its violent cousin, the volcano, the process was slow and painstakingly eating away at the rock and sediments above it. The surrounding area was also affected by the heat from the rising magma changing to shale, mudstone, and a multitude of other hardened, resilient rocks. Such was the geologic action where granite diorite pushed up to form Lyon Peak and the not yet rich, *Rich Hill*, but *Mother Earth* prepared to do her magic.

Rich Hill, now a 5,300-foot-high prominence on the west side of a valley that was to become known as Weaver Creek, dominated the local skyline as a rugged granite mountain. To the east of the valley was another mountain that would become known as *Weaver Mountain*, a large block of schist, a mountain of metamorphic rock rich in organics and bedding planes that were later to become hosts for mineralization.

Rich Hill and Weaver Mountain would have to wait for their turns to become important mining areas in the geological sequences that were to follow. But the genesis of the gold deposit had begun. Deep under the area, the massive pluton of molten magma started to cool. Not an uncommon geological event worldwide; however, this particular pluton was rich in gold, silver, lead, and other heavy metals. The process of forming veins of quartz, iron pyrite and gold was at work with meteoric water penetrating down deep into the earth to leach minerals and carry them to the surface. From hundreds of miles down in the crust of the earth, the migration of the minerals upward in thermal waters would take eons before manifesting close to the surface.

The earth, however, is a patient place on its travel through space. As always in nature, the inevitable would happen to result in gold, silver, lead, iron, and uranium enrichment of relatively small localized areas. It was just a matter of another billion years or so to finish the process and make the area interesting to the humans who still had to wait many more millions of years to walk the planet.

190 MILLION YEARS AGO

As the darkness subsided over an arid landscape, a wide variety of life started a slow and careful migration off of the surrounding savannah to a waterhole on the edge of the remnant forest. Life was safer in the open where larger predator dinosaurs could be seen from a distance and avoided. Back then, the mega-continent Pangaea had not yet started to break up, and virtually every species could roam the lands, literally having access to anywhere on earth. The area that would become Arizona was excessively harsh with wildfires and climate swings that made life and a steady food supply for large dinosaurs impossible. The landscape teemed with smaller theropods ranging from three to one thousand pounds. These animals preyed upon each other, constantly hunting in the daily challenge to survive.

A pack of segisaurus stir in the first dim light of dawn and as always immediately look around in the dim light to see if any predators had moved in during the night. Weighing only ten pounds and measuring three feet long, the small and fast segisaurus can rarely be taken except by surprise or accident. Resting in the open and sleeping like a crocodile with one-eye opened, the pack would scatter in every direction if threatened. This morning there were no nearby threats, and the pack rose and slowly and carefully started to move to a waterhole several miles away.

In the distance, there were several larger dinosaurs. Several chindesaurus were moving in the same direction, but the pack didn't feel threatened by them. Larger and heavier at ten feet and weighing twenty to thirty pounds, a pack of segisaurus could easily take down one of the larger animals if it was hungry enough or chose to exercise a territorial defense. The pack was generally non-aggressive, easily catching small mammals, snakes, and even large cockroaches that made easy prey for their long necks and lightning strikes with sharp teeth and strong claw-like hands.

The waterhole was on the edge of the small remnant of forest, and the pack approached cautiously, expecting to find larger predators lurking nearby waiting for prey. Caution, the trademark of the predator and prey, rewards the pack well because standing at the edge of the forest was a dilophosaurus, a twenty-foot-long monster weighing one thousand pounds and the largest dinosaur in the area; a virtual giant compared to the diminutive members of the pack. The larger dinosaur could eat six or seven of the little guys if he could catch them, but the pack's reaction was more based on territoriality than fear. The alpha male started to approach, and the pack, about six dozen strong, flowed like one green mass behind him. The effect of a large green body moving towards the dilophosaurus was mildly disturbing, but he had seen this tactic before, and he was going to stand his ground, not because of his territorial instinct but because inside the tree line was a female of his species and he was ready to start his mating ritual.

Ever watchful and silent as a snake, the pack advanced as one, slowly to within twenty feet of the larger animal. A stare-down was in the making, and tension hung heavy in the air. Without warning, the female dilophosaurus burst out of the forest and made a lunging attempt with snapping teeth to catch one of the segisaurus. With speed faster than the reptilian eye of the male could perceive, the pack broke formation and scattered in every direction. Startled, the male whipped around and, quite by accident, hit one of the smaller animals with a sweep of his tail. Flying through the air and tumbling to a stop, the small animal was slow to recoup his senses and get up. The male was on him in a second and had his prey firmly held in his jaws lifting the screaming segisaurus high in the air before crushing out its life in his strong jaws.

With his best dinosaur invitation to breakfast, the male dropped the dead animal in front of the female and backed off to start his mating ritual. The female tore into the dead body offered by the male, more interested in eating than mating. Undaunted the male started his complicated ritual of making quiet clucking noises deep in his throat and bobbing his head up and down and back and forth to entice the female. Making quick work of her breakfast, she started to watch with more interest. Encouraged by the female, the male quickened the pace of the dance. The scene would have likely resulted in a successful mating if *Mother Nature* hadn't stepped in with other plans.

It began with a quiet rumbling like a distant freight train and grew louder as the ground started first to vibrate and then shake violently, side-to-side and up and down. The two dinosaurs broke off the mating ritual and experienced a deep fear of the unknown; the strange movement of the earth that had been nothing but terrafirma all their lives. Soon they were crouching down and held on with their strong front claws as the shaking became even more violent.

The female broke loose from her grip on the earth and rolled into the water. Even though the water was relatively shallow, she was unable to gain her feet to stand up and quickly drowned. The shaking continued as violent as ever, and then there was a tremendous ripping sound and the earth tore in two and a rift, forty miles long formed from up in the mountains to down across the arid plane below.

When the ground stopped moving the male was left on the side of the chasm several hundred feet deep. Much of the forest behind the male was flattened and dead animals, dinosaurs and mammals alike littered the landscape. The chasm quickly filled with steam from thermal waters below the hard rock surface of the earth.

The male dilophosaurus rose from the ground, and while in his limited mental capacity could not likely experience a feeling of luck or relief, it was obvious that something major had happened and the riff created swallowed the waterhole and his would-be mate. As he rose to walk away, an aftershock in itself stronger than killer earthquakes of modern times, hit and broke off a good piece of the ledge he was standing on. Now his reptilian brain experienced fear, and his scream echoed up and down the newly opened rift. The haplass male falls several hundred feet to the bottom of the chasm, he joins the female in death. Eroded material quickly buries the two bodies, and over eons, the thermal waters from below cement the scree and fossilize the remains.

Buried far below the surface of the earth and frozen into the geological record of the earthquake event, the pair of dilophosaurus will remain for nearly two hundred million years before playing their role in the drama of the Dragon Tooth Gold Mine. All along the riff created by the ancient earthquake, thermal waters laden with silica and heavy metals continued to migrate upwards. The surge of minerals that would build the gold mine was still only halfway to the surface from the depths of the earth. It would take more than a hundred million years before deposits of gold, silver, lead, iron, and uranium reached the surface. However, the process of dissolution and redepositing upward through the hydrothermal channels would continue nonstop until the riches of the deep were delivered to within reach of the yet to come humanity on the surface.

THE EXTINCTION

Sixty-six million years ago, a lone bistahieversor walked through the shadow of a great cliff and climbed the talus cone at its base to reach a shallow cavern in the cliff face. Early summer temperatures were unusually hot this season, and reptiles had to seek shade and sun to regulate their body temperatures. The carnivorous dinosaur was looking to relax in the shade and the coolness of the cavern. She stretched out her thirty-foot-long body to pass the rest of the day. The cavern was one of her favorite places to rest, and occasionally she could catch a large bird coming in to land on the ledge, an easy meal.

Looking out over the rocky plane below, she sees a wealth of wildlife, but very sparse vegetation and very little water. Hot desert temperatures and frequent wildfires reduced the vegetation in the area to a bare minimum. Shade was at a premium on the desert floor, and the smaller theropods spent the hot days in the shade of rocks or in the numerous gullies that crossed the landscape, trying to regulate their body temperatures. Some sonorasauruses were migrating to the east in search of better feeding grounds. A large swamp to the west was drying up, forcing the large herbivores to either compete with the remaining animals for food or find better forage elsewhere. The mature males, fifty feet long and weighing up to 15 tons, walked in front of and on the sides of the herd, their sheer size alone discouraging any predators in the area. Swinging around and whipping their tail could kill most small predators with one blow. Even the bistahieversor watching from above instinctively avoided the larger animals and always sought prey smaller than herself.

The bistahieversor was at the top of the local food chain and had no concern for being attacked while resting or asleep. From up on the ledge, the bistahieversor could see a veritable smorgasbord of smaller fauna, all candidates for easy prey before nightfall. Life and death were playing out on the desert floor with the occasional raptor swooping down to take a small rodent, unfortunate enough to show itself in the open. She was relaxed and content for the moment, even though reproductive instincts were urging her to find a mate for the breeding season. The last male she saw was north of the hot springs some twenty miles away, an easy walk for the large dinosaur. However, what she saw at that moment looking out from the cavern with a relaxed gaze was the last moments of the world as she knew it.

Out in space, a large asteroid was making its final excursion through the earth's orbit. Having made hundreds of trips on its elliptical orbit within the orbit of the earth, several of which were near misses, the large space rock was rounding the sun for the last time. The asteroid was a "wanderer" from deep space, captured by the gravitational pull of the sun some billion years or more before making this final journey. Heavy in lithium and measuring over six miles across, the massive rock was on a collision course with earth. As the asteroid neared the sun in its hyperbolic orbit, its speed increased to over forty-five thousand miles per hour. As it rounded the sun and neared the earth, its trajectory, which would have created a glancing blow, curved in pulled by the earth's gravity to score a near-perfect bulls-eye. The asteroid came screaming down through the atmosphere, friction with the air heats the surface beyond white-hot, to several times the brilliance of the sun. After billions of years of traveling through space, the asteroid ended its existence in a few seconds, vaporizing almost instantly upon impact with the crust of the earth.

The bistahieversor didn't see the asteroid itself, but she saw a brightening of the landscape from the light given off from the intense heat as it plowed through the atmosphere; seconds later, as the asteroid impacted sixteen-hundred miles to the southeast, a blinding light many times brighter than the sun blazed from behind the mountain. Several of the sonorasaurus saw the brilliant ball hurtling down from the heavens; then it disappeared behind the face of the cliff. In seconds an intensely hot fireball rose behind the cliff high enough that the sonorasauruses were no longer in the shade. Intense thermal radiation set fire to every exposed plant and animal. From the safety of the cavern, the bistahieversor saw hundreds of screaming burning animals, dinosaurs, and mammals alike, running afire and falling dead. The herd of sonorasaurus below was instantly nothing more than a smoldering mass of smoking flesh and bones.

The impact energy of the asteroid was more than a billion times greater than the two atomic bombs dropped in WWII. The huge fireball generated by the impact rose above the atmosphere of the earth, its infrared radiation scorching the earth for thousands of miles. Millions of tons of ejecta were thrown completely out of the atmosphere and within hours would circle the globe and rain down a global firestorm. Dust from the vaporized asteroid also circled the globe, and settling created a clay blanket rich in lithium, a lasting geological artifact of the event. Within hours the entire planet was involved in the firestorm. Eighty percent of all living things perished within one day. But the impact was only starting to change the earth forever. Dust circled the planet along with a sulfuric acid mist generated from the sulfur-bearing sediments at the impact site. Dark as night, the earth started to cool, and the *impact winter* that ensues results in ice that covers most of the sphere and lasts for millennia.

For the moment, the darkened landscape appears eerie, dotted by many fires. The bistahieversor ventures down from the cavern. The sky continues to darken, the air cools, but food for the large dinosaur is not a problem. A plethora of dead bodies from which to choose a meal covers the landscape. Instinctively, the last bistahieversor left alive crosses the devastated landscape, moving slowly to the hot springs on the desert floor to where for several years, she spent the winter months. The ground started to shake from the ripple earthquakes caused by the impact. Red hot pebbles and sand from the ejecta started to pelt her a few minutes later. Uncomfortable and burned, she arrives at the hot springs in the dark. The sun did not rise the next morning nor any other morning for several years. In a matter of hours, the earth's climate changed from a pleasant Pleistocene summer to a freezing-cold killing winter. Only the smallest dinosaurs and the fledgling mammal population were to survive the cosmic event.

As the temperature continued to drop, the Bistahieversor stayed closer and closer to the hot springs. Food soon became non-existent as the corpses of the massive killing slowly turned to uneatable rotten carrion and bones. As days passed, she grew weaker. Acid rain had all but blinded her and even her reptilian ability to sense heat and movement around her dims. She finally succumbs to starvation and fatigue and falls into a deep sleep at the edge of the hot springs. Her last reptilian thought is a feint passing urge to find a mate. She may have been the last large dinosaur to die on what was later to be called the North American Continent.

Her death would have been insignificant, just one in the billions of deaths during the extinction. However, she died on the hot spring that was still building the richest gold deposit in the future state of Arizona. Another 63.5 million years would pass before the first hominids would evolve. Harvest of the riches would wait another 2.5 million years after that humble beginning for humankind to find its treasure. In the meantime, with patient persistence and atom by atom, the gold deposit continued to grow. Silica and iron pyrite precipitated at the top of the springs and within a few hundred years, covered the remaining bones of the dinosaur. Fossilization is a peculiar process with silica replacing bones. Iron pyrite precipitated from the thermal waters, weathering to goethite and hematite, also played a role and preserved several of the animal's teeth. These would become the most prized artifacts in the competitive world of paleontology. Her death may have been insignificant in the larger theater of events, but her remains would be preserved and destined for much greater celebrity.

THE FIRST FIND

Along time ago, but not so long ago, a clan of humans as we know them today made their way across an ice bridge over the Bering Strait and down the west coast of North America. The relief they felt seeing the last of the ice and snowfields of the north was overwhelming.

Looking down to the south from a high mountain, the leader, Kaskae, could see the open, relatively flat land stretching miles to the south. Slowly and with great care, his small band made their way down the mountain to a small hill covered with large cottonwood trees at the top, surrounded by a mesquite forest on the slopes. Even from a distance, they could see that there would be good hunting around the hill and it would provide a resting place for his weary people. It would be the end of over a five-thousand-mile journey that started at the northern fringe of the temperate zone in Asia, over the ice bridge across the Bering Sea and along the coast of what would become Alaska, ever moving to the south to escape the ice and snow. His small band was composed mostly of family members, almost an equal number of men and women, which was a good balance and made for only rare social troubles.

There were over a hundred in the clan when they started on their long migration; many of the elders, including his father, who was their last chief, perished along the way from exposure, starvation, or animal attacks. Several of the stronger men perished at sea hunting small whales, seals, and walruses. No newborns survived on the trek; it was important to Kaskae to lead his people to a warmer clime because two of the young women were with child and would give birth soon.

While by the sea, they ate well with fish and occasionally one of the larger animals like seals or the occasional walrus. Inland they had to learn new hunting skills. While game was plentiful, the taking was not easy with spears and harpoons fashioned from straight tree limbs and animal bones for points. Approaching the hill, Kaskae halted the clan and signaled for Miki, a small woman and the best hunter in the band. Miki had the patience and cunning it took to walk right up and touch a deer before stabbing it in the heart with a spear. The only piece of whalebone left of her spear was the point. She replaced the shaft and the throwing grip with Northern Pacific coast yew and cured hide of the many deer she had killed since they had turned inland.

Miki didn't see any animals as she approached the base of the hill, but she could sense that they were there. As she neared the top, she noticed there was a warm spring flowing from under the grassy cover. A little further beyond, was a herd of deer bedded down in the grass and shade to pass the warm part of the day. Creeping ever so slowly, Miki silently moved toward the herd keeping trees and scrub bushes between herself and the unwary prey. When out in the open, she spent more than an hour moving the last fifty feet to within striking distance of a large buck. Again, with the slowness of a cold reptile, she raised her harpoon-like spear over her head and with one final swift move, drove it into the heart of the animal. Kaskae's band would eat well that night.

Out on the valley floor, the rest of the troop knew Miki had struck because over a hundred deer ran out of the miniature forest covering the hill. The hunters had spread out in every direction and surrounded the hill hiding along game trails in the mesquite; several more animals were taken down by the hunters from positions in the grass and bushes where they waited for Miki's first kill. Knowing they would eat well, as one, they all moved up through the mesquite forest and made their way up the gentle slope of the hill to the cottonwood trees at the top. Good mesquite firewood was plentiful, and the women soon started a fire using lumps of pyrite and quartz strikers. While the women prepared the animals for cooking on spits over the fires, the rest of the band unpacked their meager possession and made camp. They were accustomed to eating raw flesh and even though they were hungry, they waited patiently for the pleasure of eating cooked meat.

They had made it; they had survived. After a journey lasting five years, they rested, joked, and told stories and some tall tales of events along the trek. It was a way of remembering their culture and honoring their dead. Miki and the other successful hunters were spared the work of cooking and setting up the camp as the traditional reward for those that provided meat.

They sat in a small circle sharpening their spears and listening to Genen, the oldest woman of their tribe, relate tales of their glory days in Asia before the long migration began. Theirs was by far not the only group to cross the ice bridge. Driven from their homelands by fierce armies from the southwest, more than a hundred thousand people crossed over to North America. Kaskae led his people down along the coast. Many others fanned out from the ice bridge and became the Inuit people of the north, the tribes of the midwestern planes, the indigenous people of the northeastern forests, and the southeastern part of the continent. Kaskae's band was the first to move this far south and in the comfort of his new-found home and with everyone's stomach full, was thinking that they would stay on the little hill for many generations to come.

Night fell slowly, and as the tribe retired as couples or singles, lots were drawn to single out three members for fire duty. While they hadn't seen any mountain lions for several days, Kaskae was still wary of danger, and truth be told a little afraid of the dark. Despite his towering size and strong frame, the man didn't like being alone and particularly didn't like being alone in the dark. The three fire watchers took shifts, not unlike a modern military unit. Kaskae retired a little way away from the fire and signaled to Miki to join him. He noticed that for the first night in years, he wasn't reaching for extra animal skins to keep him warm. Drawing Miki close, he told her how valuable she was to the band and how pretty she was. The rest of the couples joined in sex in the soft light of the flames. The clan conceived several babies that night, but Miki, barren from birth, was not to be one of the future mothers, not that night nor any other night despite many efforts.

At sunrise, everyone stirred. The last fire watcher was a young man named Shesh; he was clever and made tools out of rocks. He spent his time by the fire fashioning a hide scraper from a large piece of jasper he found on the mountain. He presented it to a young woman he was fond of named Tanana. She set about scraping and stretching the hides from the previous day's kills. No part of the animal would go to waste. The men of the clan fashion the horns of the buck into points and other tools, the women prepare the meat and organs for their next meal; the bones and sinew for tools and tying are precious and carefully tended to. The hides join others for curing, destined for clothing, shelter, and adornments.

Some of the men moved off to hunt, and the rest of the women tended to the leftovers of the evening feast and the uncooked meat. Cutting the raw meat into thin strips with their crude knives of bones and rock chips, the raw meat was skewered and set high on the branches of scrub oak to dry. With that work done, the women sat near the drying meat to keep camp robber birds and other scavengers off the stash. Shesh took note of the crude knives and set off in search of more "good rock" to work into knives. Kaskae asked him if he could make a point and Shesh was intrigued by the challenge. He was in search of a glassy-black rock that was easy to work into a point. He didn't have to go far. A few miles to the south of the hill was a ledge of obsidian, perfect for his needs. He returned to the hill with all he could carry and immediately set to the process of trial and error to create a point.

That night one of the women went into labor. Genen thought, *not enough time had passed*, but with no way to mark a pregnancy other than the passing of the full moons, she gave little credence to the thought as using the light of the fire built up bright for the occasion, she helped the young mother deliver a perfect baby boy. Shtiga, one of the strong males and the father, held the newborn high, and with confidence, proclaimed in a loud voice for the spirit of creation to hear, "This one will survive."

Shesh, with numerous cuts on his hands from working the obsidian, secreted away Shtiga's spear and the next morning with the newborn at his mother's breast and Shtiga standing as a proud guard, Shesh presented the hunter with his spear tipped with a four-inch obsidian point. Shtiga took the spear and ran his hand over the point and cut his palm on the razor-sharp edge. Shtiga admired the point and in his primitive language, told Shesh that it was the best spear he ever made. Kaskae was looking on and smiled. He knew then that with a child born and the ability to make better spears, his people would not only survive but prosper. He also told Shesh that as chief, he deserved a bigger point and armed with his spear, and this time with a bag made from deer hide, Shesh set off for the obsidian ledge basking in the warm morning sun and the pride and praise of his clan bolstering his spirit.

One of the women named Pakak was intrigued by the hot water seeping out from under the top of the hill. The water was pleasantly warm on her skin, and she had the thought that she could lay down in the stream and feel the warmth over her whole body. Not content with the shallow water, she started to scoop out the bottom of the stream and piled the loose material to form a dam a little further down the hill. The digging was easy, with red soil and clay making up most of the hill. The mound about six-hundred-foot-high rose from the more arid floor of the valley. The mountain was more like a pile of loosely cemented red earth rather than a solid rock. It took days with her crude tools, but she finally had a pool deep enough to submerge herself in the warm water. Others noticed and after having been in the pool themselves, pitched in to deepen the pool and raise the dam. Before long, the pool was large enough for half the tribe to soak up the warmth at once.

Genen noticed that it was particularly good for sore muscles and was soon treating injured hunters and soreness and malaise of all kinds in the pool. Claiming the healing powers of the pool as her own, Genen soon had the honor of serving as a shaman to her people. The last shaman they had was drowned at sea on the long trek while trying to take a small whale. Genen was a natural for the position as the oldest of their people, wise with the stories of the past elders, and somewhat knowledgeable for using herbs for healing minor ailments and injuries. Strong in her belief that everything possessed a spirit, she catered to her people with herbal remedies and incantations to appease the spirits. Disease was understood to be the displeasure of a person's spirit for some violent or unkind act to other members of the tribe, a simple system of early religion, yet effective in keeping jealousy, covertness, and lust from ripping the delicate fabric of their society.

Miki rose in the middle of the night and walked to the pool in the light of a full moon. Sliding into the water, she marveled that the pool was deeper than ever, and in the middle, she couldn't reach the bottom with her feet. A familiar question came to mind while sitting in the warmth. Why, after being with Kaskae for over several years, wasn't she pregnant. She suspected that almost every woman in the band would bear a child now that they were safe and past the suffering, trials, and dangers of the last five years. She desperately wanted a child feeling her motherly instincts and also to solidify her relationship with Kaskae. The band didn't have any form of strict marriage rules, and couples often switched partners on a whim, but she knew that couples with children would probably stay together when she saw how proud Shtiga was and how he doted over the mother and the newborn. She desperately wanted that for Kaskae and herself. Though small in stature, she was the strongest of the women, and there shouldn't be any reason why she couldn't have a child. She kept slipping under the water to wash out her long hair and on a whim, held her breath and slid to the bottom of the pool. At the very bottom, her hand brushed over a rock, an unusually large rock compared to the pebbles and sand that made up the majority of the hill. Pushing back up to the surface, she held the rock up in the moonlight and was amazed that it had the shape and looked like a large tooth.

Walking naked to the firelight, much to the delight of the young man on watch, she held the four-inch-long tooth to the light to have a better look. She had never seen a tooth so big but knew of the bragging-right stories of some of the past elders, none of which survived the journey, about how big the teeth were in whales that they had taken. Surely it was a whale's tooth, but in the dim light, it didn't look like the white of ivory of a whale's tooth, but the dark brown or almost black of obsidian. Miki couldn't explain in her mind what she had found, and if it was a whale's tooth, how could it have gotten here from the ocean. She didn't return to Kaskae's bed but sat near the fire with her newly made obsidian knife and cut and sewed with sinew a leather cap for the top of the tooth. By sunrise, she had the tooth fashioned as an adornment and wore it around her neck. In her mind, she had concluded that the tooth was a powerful talisman and its spirit would somehow solve the problem of her childless condition.

Returning to Kaskae, she rolled him over in the dusky first light of dawn. Kaskae was erect; he was always erect in the morning. Clutching the talisman, she focused on the spirit and strength of the whale and lowered herself onto Kaskae's body. He awakened pleasantly surprised and was immediately an enthusiastic partner in the lovemaking. He wanted to pull Miki down on top of him but couldn't pry her hands apart and settled into the event with the bucking woman kneeling on top of him. He was quickly driven to release, and Miki pushed down hard until she couldn't feel him pumping inside of her any longer. Confident she was finally successful and believing she was finally with child, she got up and still clutching the talisman, walked to the edge of the camp where she could watch the sunrise. Filled with a sense of peace and happiness, she felt the warm rays of the sun bathe her in the morning light. The tribe was up to start the day, and she stood still naked in their midst and held the talisman up in front of her. Mystified, the men and women of the tribe gathered and just stared at the strange object she held with reverence in her hands. Genen proclaimed the talisman to contain the spirit of a great animal and would give Miki tremendous personal power. Miki looked at her and said, "I am finally with child." Genen said nothing, but in her mind, she thought to herself, *we shall see*.

Genen had been pressing Kaskae to father a child, preferably a son who could ascend to the position of chief. Kaskae was old in his middle thirties, and Genen knew that it would not be but a few more seasons before both of them were called away by the spirits. She saw in Kaskae the leadership and judgment that had brought them through the great trek to this warm paradise with ample food and resources for the people to enjoy a much better life. She hoped that Miki was right and used the sharp end of a burning ember to mark on a piece of rolled-up seal hide the beginning of Miki's pregnancy. She first made a symbol of a spear, and behind it put one dot representing the first moon of her pregnancy. There were nine other symbols for the other women in her midwifery care, but only one finished with nine dots followed by a symbol for a wolf; the newborn male child of Shtiga. Usually, she would not make an entry on her record until at least a moon cycle had passed, but with the confidence Miki displayed and with a sense of piety and homage for the mysterious talisman, she finished the marks. When she showed the sealskin to Miki, she pointed toward the end of the line where eight more marks would appear and said, "Here will be the symbol of the chief."

Miki was overwhelmed and started to weep. Her relationship with Kaskae was secure, along with the survival of their people. With a child designated to be chief, the band would stay together. A band without a leader would soon die off from mistakes or scatter in search of stronger groups to join. Several of the hunters had joined them on the trek under similar circumstances. She knew in her heart that would not happen to Kaskae's people. She looked forward to the future with great expectations, a future that nature and fate, however, were not to bring about.

As days and weeks passed, Genen kept a close eye on Miki. Miki wasn't suffering any of the symptoms of newfound motherhood, and Genen was starting to dread her serious mistake as she looked at the first mark behind Miki's spear. Comparing to her fingers, she once again checked on Shila, a woman whose symbol was flame. She had nine marks behind the symbol and soon would have ten if there was room in the line for more. Genen started to feel dread that the blessings of the spirits would not continue unless Shila gave birth soon. Her record-keeping wasn't flawed, Shila was now danger-ously late and every day that went by put her and the baby in more peril.

A few days later, Shila felt the first pangs of labor pains as she sat grinding mesquite beans between two rocks. While Genen was at first relieved, her relief progressed to fear as Shila's labor continued through to the darkness of night. This child wasn't Shila's first delivery; she had lost two babies along the great trek not being healthy enough to produce milk. From experience, Genen knew that the baby should have arrived hours ago. Something was wrong, and Genen had the men build two large fires for light through the moonless night to keep vigil. Several hours before dawn and after a full night of very hard labor Shila's pains became even more intense and more fre-quent. One way or another Genen knew this would be over soon.

By sunrise, Shila's pains were constant and more intense. While her screams had faded to a whimper, she finally passed out. Genen knew she had to do something or mother and child would soon be dead. Slipping her hand gently inside her vagina, Genen did not find a normal birth. With the end of her fingers, she did not feel the head of a baby. She felt only a foot with a little bit of leg above it. The baby was breech and two big for the young woman to push out on her own. Acting quickly, Genen fashioned a small noose at the end of a strip of deer hide and carefully pushed it up inside Shila and slipped the noose over the foot. Holding the noose above the baby's ankle, she drew the noose tight and drew back hoping that Shila had one more good push in her. When Shila moaned and her eyes fluttered open, Genen placed one hand at the top of her swollen belly and holding the tether nodded at Shila. The struggling mother knew what Genen wanted, and with the last of her strength pushed down in one final mighty effort, her scream echoed off the trunks of the cottonwoods and filled the woods surrounding the hill. Genen pulled on the tether, and she felt movement in the baby. One leg had started its journey out to daylight, but the other was still stubbornly lodged upwards in the womb. Pulling harder, Genen could feel the baby moving some more and with a deep breath, and a wish for forgiveness from the struggling mother pulled the baby into the world of the living.

It was a large child and arrived with a limp wail exhausted from the long ordeal. Genen tended to the umbilical cord and walked with the child around the fire to soothe and quiet him while the rest of the women starting cleaning up Shila. Genen was returning to place the baby to its mother's breast to nurse when the other women told her to look at Shila. She was bleeding profusely, and Genen knew that the worst had happened. She got up and quietly walked over to Shtiga's woman, who was sitting near with a look of dread on her face, her baby in her arms. Genen handed her the newborn and said, "Now it is for you to raise it as your own."

Genen went back and sat and raised Shila's head into her lap. Holding her hands, she comforted the young woman and told her she had done well, and the baby was healthy. Shila knew something was very wrong because the newborn was not at her breast. Shila was bleeding out rapidly, and in a few more minutes, she was completely unconscious. In another hour, the blood flow stopped. Shila was dead. A feeling of doom permeated through the tribe. Had the troubles of the great trek returned? Were the spirits unhappy with their easier life? With a multitude of unanswered questions, the men carried Shila down the hill and buried her in a shallow grave covered with heavy rocks to protect it from predators. Shtiga put his arm around Kaskae when they were done and said, "Our people are growing weak here; the spirits are not pleased with us." Kaskae hadn't looked at it that way, but now that he knew it was on the minds of his people, he would have to consider it. Kaskae wasn't the only one thinking about what the death meant to the future of his people. Genen was also thinking ahead and considering what she would have to do when the second dot appeared after Miki's spear on the sealskin.

In a few weeks, when the full moon started to wane, Genen reluctantly and with a great deal of unease made the second dot on Miki's line. She was going to have to confront Miki and tell her that she wasn't pregnant. She knew the young woman was going to resent that news and certainly wasn't going to accept what Genen knew must come next. A few days later, sitting with all the women in the warm morning sun, Genen looked seriously at Miki and told Miki that she wasn't pregnant. Miki controlled the anger Genen expected, but she was surprised when Miki clutched the talisman that hung between her breasts and vehemently told Genen, "You're wrong. I am pregnant, and I'm going to have Kaskae's baby". Picking up her spear Miki did what she always did when upset; she went hunting.

Genen and the rest of the women started the discussion of what to do about their childless chief. Some suggested that Kaskae take another woman to mother a child for him. Genen had a different and more expedient solution and presented her idea to the women. Sitting as a council of elders, one-by-one, the women all agreed that Shila's newborn son should be honored after the tragic death of the mother. The newborn would be proclaimed the son and progeny of Kaskae. Given the loose social structure of the tribe and the many nights the hunters camped away from the group on the long trek, it was at least plausible that Kaskae could have fathered the child. Shila didn't know who the father was, and none of the men stepped forward to claim her son as his own, which added credibility to the story. All that remained was to convince Miki. Convincing Miki, all agreed, was going to be a difficult task. Not so much for Kaskae's part because the women all knew that Kaskae made the rounds during the long trek. Several of them had been with him themselves and were ready to let Miki know that if need be. Their time would come, and sooner than they thought.

Over the next several days, Genen took Kaskae aside and told him her plan. Kaskae knew Miki wasn't going to step back for another woman. Kaskae said he couldn't claim to be the father of Shila's male child, but he couldn't deny it either. Genen was right; somewhere along the long trek, Kaskae had taken Shila to his shelter for sex and warmth through a long cold night. She lay in wait to confront Miki with the decision of the people and found that opportunity when Miki was relaxing in the pool after a long day of hunting. Bringing up Miki's lack of signs of any swelling or morning sickness and her continued strength, she emphasized once again that Miki wasn't pregnant, and something would have to be done soon to assure the band a new chieftain. Miki reacted strongly and clutched the talisman under the water for the moral high ground the strange tooth provided and accused Genen of being an old crone, past her prime, not a real shaman, and warned her to keep out of her affair with Kaskae. Threats among the people were rare, almost nonexistent, and Genen wondered if this was going to end in violence. She knew that with the heart of a hunter, Miki was certainly capable of it. Knowing that her seasons were limited to only a few more, she didn't fear death. She feared for the future of her people and vowed to push this issue to an end that would ensure their survival.

A few days later, Genen once again confronted Miki in front of the rest of the women. She knew Miki wouldn't step aside for another woman, so she told her what everyone now accepted as fact; Shila's baby was indeed Kaskae's and would be raised as the chief's son. Genen argued, "Just look at the size of that child, he is the biggest baby ever born to us, and he already looks like his father."

"No," Miki shouted and clutched the talisman while twisting her hands back and forth in opposite directions over the length of it with her eyes wide with anger creasing the lines of her face. She shouted again, "You're wrong, and all of you women are wrong. Just leave me alone." And like always, she picked up her spear and ran out of the camp.

"This is only the beginning," Genen told the rest of the women, "She is going to have to face up to it, and I am going to make her."

Through the week, Miki avoided contact with Genen and the rest of her tribe. She would be up before dawn, stay away all day and return late at night, usually with some game for the dinner. She would eat and retire to Kaskae's bed as soon as possible. Kaskae noticed the change in behavior, but he had seen this side of Miki before, giving it some time was the best remedy he could imagine. Miki would come around, but he was certain that Genen would not rest until Miki acknowledged the newborn child as Kaskae's and participate in the raising of the child as the next chief. Miki, on the other hand, was more obsessed than ever with her need to bear a child and the talisman that was going to help that become a reality. Genen wanted Miki to agree now, and Miki wanted more time to conceive a child. Inevitably this situation was going to come to a head. Kaskae hoped that it would resolve without lasting damage to his people. He didn't have to wait long for the conflict between the two strong-willed women to reach a breaking point. Internal conflicts among his people were rare and usually settled amicably, but an irreconcilable conflict could result in an aggrieved party leaving the band and striking out on their own. Life itself and survival were paramount, and any physical form of fighting among themselves, or a fight to the death was strictly taboo in the culture of his people.

A couple of weeks later, Miki left the camp several hours before dawn with the full moon in the crystal-clear sky lighting up the desert floor, brighter than the first light of dawn. She headed north following a ravine, carefully checking for deer bedded down in the grassy bottom. Near the mountains, the ravine was about twenty feet wide and not quite that deep. Rounding a bend, she saw a herd of deer in the bottom, and backtracking found a way down to the water. Heading upstream, she rounded the last bend and started her stealthy slow approach. It was still at least an hour before dawn with the moon setting in the west when she was just a few feet away from the unwary deer. As one, the deer bolted and ran out of sight further up the wash. She knew it wasn't her that startled the deer; she was instantly wary of another predator in the area. She would have been dead or at least badly mauled if a young mountain lion hadn't snarled on the rim above her before making his killing plunge at the young woman. As he leaped down to take her, Miki spun toward him and crouched down with the end of the spear anchored solidly on the sand. The lion impaled himself on the spear, instantly dead with the sharp point piercing his sternum and heart. But gravity and momentum kept him falling over the shaft of the spear. Miki pushed to the side, but the falling lion still hit her leg with his paw leaving a deep gash.

Binding the wound the best she could, Miki pulled the spear out of the lion and not wanting to leave the meat and pelt behind, started to limp back to the hill. Miki slung the young lion behind her neck and over both shoulders, its long tail in one hand, her spear in the other. The wound wasn't deep, but it was painful, and despite the binding, it never stopped oozing blood. Her spear was now a walking stick. She knew she would make it back and she was going to need Genen's help to close the wound. She wasn't looking forward to needing help from the woman who had become her nemesis and enemy, but she knew without it, she would be in a long battle to heal the wound and fight the fever that it would bring. It took her several hours to get back to the camp where the rest of the tribe was up cooking the breakfast and planning the day's hunt for the men and the work for the women. Miki walked in among them and silence fell as they looked at the cat around her neck and the wet blood that still ran down her leg. She threw the cat down and then collapsed unconscious from exhaustion and the loss of blood.

Genen went through her things and came back with her medical bag to tend to Miki. Setting her differences with the young woman aside, she set to the important work of stopping the bleeding and saving Miki's life. The men stretched Miki out on her back, so Genen had access to the wound and then marveled at the cat. They had seen mountain lions before, but never had they brought one of the wily creatures down. The women pushed the men aside and ribbed them over a woman being the first to bring in a cat. They dressed and skinned the animal and started to plan what to make out of the soft fur after it came off the drying racks.

It was good that Miki had passed out. Genen used strips of deer hide to bind the leg so that the two sides of the gash joined together. With an ember from the fire, Genen cauterized the top of the wound. The bleeding stanched, but she knew there would still be a fever. As Genen worked, she coughed mildly. And while her cough was not severe, it was also something she could not stop. When done with Miki, she had to sit back to rest and catch her breath. She knew about the coughing disease from the long trek; knew it was deadly and had seen it kill some people who fell ill with it in the cold climate to the north. What she didn't know was that growing in her lungs, was the fungus that many millennia later would become known as *valley fever*. She had drawn the spores that cause the disease deep into her lungs while smelling weeds and plants on the desert floor in search of new herbs and cures. Her condition was not yet severe but would become fatal within weeks as the fungus inflamed her lung tissues and turned them into useless scars.

It was several days before Miki broke the fever and was back on her feet. Too weak to leave the camp, she settled into the women's work, hoping that Genen would leave her alone. It was obvious that Genen was sick, but it seemed like something other than the coughing disease they knew up north.

Her cough was dry, and it was getting worse. While not vindictive, Miki was relieved because Genen was leaving her alone.

One morning Miki noticed the women making a carrying sack out of the lion skin she brought in. Asking what it was for, the women told her it was a carrying sack for the little chieftain. Slowly a rage that Miki had never experienced before overtook her body and soul. Rising onto her still shaky legs, she walked over as fast as she could to Genen and started yelling at her again about Shtiga's son. In the most hateful tone she could muster, she kept yelling, Genen answering in an infuriatingly calm voice, just like an elder was expected to do. Angrier, Miki was working the talisman again, wringing her hands back and forth over the long tooth. Finally, she crossed the last line and committed the most unforgivable dictate of the band's mores. Holding the talisman in front of her like a shield, Miki condemned the older woman saying, "You have no right to make Shtiga's son the chieftain. You aren't an elder; you are just an old woman with big ideas. My baby will be the chief." And then in a loud, hateful shout in front of all the people she screamed, "I wish you were dead. Why don't you cough yourself to death?"

Genen wanted to respond that her decision would stand, and Miki was three months with no signs of the child, but the words would not come. In her worked-up state despite her calm exterior, she started to cough. This time the cough was convulsive and the worst that the people had ever heard. Genen fell to her hands and knees expecting to bring up the phlegm of the coughing disease. Instead, after the worse convulsion yet, she started coughing up blood, only a little at first, and then more than a mouthful with every rasping cough. Genen was beyond hope, now having broken a large artery in her lung. In horror and fear, the band looked on as Genen hacked and drowned in the blood filling her lungs. After the last convulsion ended with the final death rattle, the band looked up to Miki with fear in their eyes. Even Kaskae looked at her in shock; Miki had done the unforgivable. Miki had wished death on another and made it happen with the talisman, a simple inanimate object now regarded as evil and feared by everyone.

Kaskae commanded Miki to stay in the camp as the band carried Genen's body down the hill for burial. Working as one, the women dug a deeper grave next to Shila's, and the men started gathering rocks for the protective cover.

Kaskae and his people spent the day finishing the grave and discussing the fate of Miki. Death or banishment were the only two options that the chief had, and by the end of the day, the consensus was that Miki would be banished, spared the death sentence because of her past service to the tribe. Kaskae also decided that they would leave the easy life on their hill and seek new hunting grounds. Everyone considered the hill an evil place now and doubted that the spirits would continue to bless them if they stayed there. Genen's horrible death instilled a deep fear in everyone. They didn't know that the disease Genen died of wasn't communicable; they didn't want to stay in the same spot where disease and evil would prey upon them until one-by-one, they would all be dead.

Returning to the hilltop, they found Miki sitting in almost a trance-like state. She knew the penalty for what she had done and expected to be executed by the clan at sunrise. After the meal was cooked and served, Kaskae had all his people sit around the fire as if in a council of elders. Standing inside the circle of his people with his back to the fire, he called Miki to stand in front of him. With a heavy heart and a strong solemn voice, he gave her the sentence as the full moon rose in the east, and a light breeze filled the trees. "Miki, with the sunrise, you are to be banished. If you ever return to our presence, we will kill you. There is no recourse to this decision; if you do not leave you will be killed here where you stand." Miki fell to her hands and knees and threw up. Everyone sat in silence until the retching woman quieted. An owl hooted, and out on the desert, a pack of coyotes started yipping and howling. The people's mood lightened, believing that the spirits were talking to them, affirming that their decision had been correct. In pairs, they retired to their beds. Kaskae was the last to leave, and Miki just lay down where she had fallen. Banishment was good as a death sentence. Without the protection of the tribe, she knew her days living alone on the desert would be limited.

Before sunrise, the tribe rose and packed up for their move. Miki still lay by the fire. None of the people would talk to the banished one. Silently they waited for dawn. As the first rays broke over the mountains to the east, Kaskae told Shtiga to take the people south. He would stay, and if Miki didn't leave, he would do his duty and kill her. Slowly the men and women picked up their packs and what few things they could carry in their hands and walked down the hill without looking back.

Kaskae picked up his pack and pulling Miki to her feet, said, "You will come with me." He started walking toward the north side of the hill. Miki fell into an awkward walk behind him. As they passed the pond, Kaskae turned and ripped the talisman from her neck. Jerked and surprised by the move, Miki looked at him with surprise and fear. Kaskae threw the talisman back into the pond from whence it came. Handing Miki her spear, he reinstated her as a hunter. He took her hand and together they walked down the hill to the north and up into the mountains, never to see their people again.

Shtiga grew impatient for Kaskae to join them and returned to the hilltop to find no trace of him. Shtiga expected to find him over the dead body of Miki, but there was no trace of her either. Looking in every direction from the hilltop, he finally gave up and walked south to the tribe. He told them that Kaskae must have joined Miki in banishment, and he would now be the chief. As one, the people accepted the announcement and turned south on another long trek that would take them much further south to settle new civilizations in the millenniums to come.

Kaskae and Miki looked down on the hill from the mountaintop. Each regretted leaving the safety of the hill and wondered if the talisman would curse that special spot on the desert floor forever. That night they ate well on a newly killed deer, cuddled by the fire, and after retiring to their bed, Miki, without the fear and anxiety of the previous months, finally conceived a child. The spirits were going to bless them after all. They were now the founders of a new civilization, the Yavapai, people of the earth that would stay in these mountains forever.

IMMIGRANTS

September 5th, 1841, Professor Aaden Callahan sat behind his desk in the history department of Columbia University and unfolded the copy of the New-York Daily Tribune. Callahan reached for his first coffee of the day. A headline jumped off the page with its four-inch type – **Congress Passes the Distributive Preemption Act.** As he read through details of the bill, a dream formed; one which he couldn't act on until his contract at the college expired in the spring. He was at the beginning of his fifth year of teaching, which he enjoyed, but didn't like teaching to the offspring of the privileged new wealthy families of New York. He was anxious to finish his contract and head west to start a new and very different life.

The young professor was born in 1816 and named Aaden Keller Callahan in Donaghadee, Ireland, into a wealthy family heavily involved in illegal whiskey brewing, thievery, and smuggling. Steadfast that the next generation of Callahans would be upstanding citizens, they sent their children to Trinity College in Dublin. Aaden was the oldest and the first to graduate. Proudly returning home to his family after graduation, he was devastated to learn that he was not to stay on his beloved coast and take over the family business.

After his homecoming party, his father presented him with a ticket for a cabin on a Baltimore Clipper, leaving Dublin in a week for New York. His father also gave him a letter of credit to the equivalent of ten thousand British Pounds that he had transferred to the Bank of New York, confident that his oldest son would prosper and grow his fortune in the promise of the vast new land. About a month later, spared the arduous and risky passage through Liverpool, the privileged traveler's fear of an uncertain future ebbed as he stood in the bow of the ship as the magnificent city slid by on the way to the docks on the Hudson River side of Manhattan. He disembarked and made his way to the customs and immigration office up the quay. After clearing customs with nothing more than a cursory look of a bored official at his steamer trunk, he went to the immigration office and immediately applied for citizenship.

With his steamer trunk in tow, he set out on foot to the Bank of New York in lower Manhattan to claim access to his funds. It was late August, and the air was hot and sticky and filled with the smells of the street. The usual street people and thieves that preyed on new arrivals left him alone because of his imposing size and the determination that his walk and demeanor portrayed of a man on a mission. Only a few prostitutes tried to snare him with their charms, almost having to run beside him to keep up with his long strides while pitching their wares. Street urchins ran along with him offering to pull the trunk or show him around. "You need anything, mister?" was the common mantra of the busy streets. Aaden knew where he was going from a map given to him by his father with the advice, "Watch yourself on the streets lad. Once you make it to the bank, you will be fine. And by the way, lad, good luck to you and go with God, and don't forget to write to us now."

Leaving the bank wealthy with two hundred dollars in his pocket, he took a carriage to Columbia University with a letter of introduction to the Dean of the History Department from the president of Trinity College. Having graduated Magna Cum Laude with a degree in European Modern History, he secured a position on the spot. His handsome appearance and comfortable style may have played a role, but more likely, his bilingual abilities founded in Gaelic and English since birth was perceived to be an asset to the department. Aaden settled in a boarding house south of the campus that was recommended by the Dean. The Dean's sister operated the boarding house and offered clean rooms, hot coffee with breakfast in the morning, and central heat for the winter months.

Within a few weeks, Aaden had his eye on a French woman who worked in the Language Department. Madeline Anne DuBois-Mercier was the same age as Aaden, but unlike Aaden was an only child when she immigrated to America some years previous with her parents. Her father was a banker who had worked in Paris but owned an estate near Tongeren in the northern part of France. Madeline spent most of her early years in Tongeren, where Dutch and German were as common as the French language. She was an accomplished linguist when her father chose to leave France, believing that the Napoleonic wars would eventually bring ruin to his homeland. Having sold the estate at Tongeren and several other houses on the edge of Paris, the

Merciers arrived in New York via first-class passage, and millions of times better off than the average immigrant.

Madeline had soon dropped the formality of her name and was known as Anna to her friends and coworkers. Her father enrolled her in the Wheaton Female Seminary in Norton, Massachusetts, shortly after their arrival in the states. She didn't like being away from her mother, so she pushed herself majoring in European languages and graduated in two years, successfully challenging all her upper-level coursework to finish early. She finished Magna Cum Laude and spoke as her class valedictorian to the issue of women's rights and suffrage and would retain the title *"Youngest Valedictorian"* in the Seminary's graduating classes for many years to come. Her mother, Denise Mercier, hugged her daughter with tears in her eyes after the ceremony and told her how proud she was of her. Mary Mason Lyon, the founder of Wheaton, came over to congratulate Anna and her family. Anna's father uttered a few pleasantries as if his duty to educate his daughter was complete and he was anxious to get back to New York.

After graduation, she returned to New York and again with her father's help and a substantial donation to the coffers of Columbia College; Anna hired on as a teacher's assistant; the all-male faculty and student policy at Columbia only hired women as assistants, secretaries, cooks and cleaning ladies. Anna was a better linguist than many of the "professors" in the language department, but she would never make full professor in the male structured school. She prepared lesson plans, tutored the slower students, and "joined" conversational sessions in French and German. In reality, she ran the conversational sessions; some of the professors were not even fluent in the languages they taught. Her strikingly beautiful appearance and easy to know manner assured almost perfect attendance in her French, Dutch and German sessions.

She lived with her family in an elegant brownstone several blocks south of the college on New York's upper west side. She met Aaden at faculty gatherings and was intrigued by his easy Irish manner and the lilt of his excellent but accented English. His physical stature, muscled body, and green eyes were a solid asset. Other women on the campus referred to him as an Irish god, but secretly wished he was more of a devil.

Aaden lived frugally and didn't socialize much off the campus. His life revolved around work and the boarding house that was populated mostly by other professors from the university; it made interesting conversations at night with a broad spectrum of subjects ranging from alchemy to zoology along with plenty of advice on how to navigate the politics of Columbia University. He took all of his meals in the faculty cafeteria, and Anna who saw him there, started moving closer to him each day, shyly hoping he would sooner or later notice her. Aaden noticed her early on and wondered about her intentions as she approached moving table by table closer to where he usually sat. Aaden was wondering what this was going to lead to, secretly hoping that it would lead to something. Anne was beautiful, and he wanted to get to know her but true to chivalry and the custom of the upper class of the day, he would try to finagle an invitation from someone close to her. It wasn't necessary; one day in early December, Aaden arrived late for lunch and found her sitting at his table. "And who might you be?" Aaden said as he took the seat next to her. From there, a mutual attraction and chemistry fermented a strong and lasting relationship.

Anne had asked around and found that Aaden was single, lived alone in a boarding house but was reasonably well off for a professor. Aaden had made several generous donations to causes at the university, most notably to the American Anti-Slavery Society that was growing stronger in New England. By year-end, they were close friends, and Anna invited him to the Mercier home for a Christmas Eve party. Aaden graciously accepted even though he had some reservations about fitting into the upper crust society her banker father enjoyed. He had also asked around and received a boatload of good advice from the evening sessions with the men in the boarding house as to how to win the young woman's heart and hand in marriage. Aaden had passed the brownstone on his way back from the downtown area and marveled at the exquisite façade with gas lights, white pillars, and a carriage house in the yard. The place was a mansion emanating power and money, for both of which he didn't have a care. He would have to find Anna an appropriate gift for Christmas Eve, and he only had a few days left.

He went shopping every evening for the perfect gift and was getting a little frustrated with his search. It was snowing with a cold wind when he turned into a brightly lit curio shop on Fifth Avenue. There he found a Belgian horse carved out of alabaster with a sterling silver knight straddling its broad width, fully clad in armor and holding a long battle lance. About eight inches long and about ten inches high with the knight on its back, the horse was in a full gallop with the knight leaning forward for an impact with an unseen enemy. Aaden loved the symbolism of wanting to be Anna's knight in shining armor and had the shopkeeper set it aside. He had to wait for the bank to open the next day to get enough cash to buy it. The silver knight and the alabaster horse cost several months of his professor's salary. He didn't care; as yet, he didn't have to draw on the nest egg that his father sent with him to America.

The next day, the last day of classes before Christmas Eve, Anna arrived in the cafeteria for lunch, carrying a plain-looking hat box hanging from her fore-arm from a golden string. She looked over at Aaden with the most beautiful smile, and Aaden wanted to give her the silver knight right then and there, but it was safely tucked away in a drawer in his office. Anna sat down with her food and set the box on the table between them. With eyebrows raised and a foolish look of surprise on his face, Aaden tried his best to look like he just noticed the box. Anna didn't wait for him to ask; she opened the string latches on the lid and drew out a black silk top hat. "For you to wear tomor-row night," she said softly, laughing as she put it on his head. Aaden drew her hand to his lips and kissed it, thanking the "luck-of-the-Irish" that he had found her the perfect gift. Anna didn't mind a bit with the public display of affection and felt emboldened by it.

"I rented a tuxedo for the party, but I didn't think of a hat. What can I bring a girl who has everything?"

Anna looked at him, coyly and said, "Why don't you consider a marriage license?" Aaden was shocked into silence, but his excitement broke through his quiet, stoic composure when he replied in his heaviest Irish lilt, "I'd be planning to make that happen, lassie." Little did either of them realize that it was a plan to prove much more difficult to bring to fruition than either of them expected.

The next night with the streets quiet and cold, Aaden arrived promptly at eight for the party only to discover that "fashionably late" was already the norm for the New York elite. Anna and her father met him with an impeccably dressed black butler, who said to call him Rufus and reminded Aaden of liveried servants in the grand homes in Ireland. He had on a striking blue topcoat lined with white stripes, brown buckskin shorts down to his knees, and long white socks that ended at the bottom cuffs of the shorts and silver-buckled shoes that shined a bright black adorned his feet. He took Aaden's hat and coat and the present and slid through one of the large double doors off the right side of the entryway. The gift box Aaden surrendered to Rufus was tastefully wrapped in gold paper tied with a red ribbon and a brass engraved nameplate that said "Anna" on both sides; a complimentary gift from the curio shop on Fifth Avenue.

It was obvious Anna dressed for the party, but she wore a long white linen smock and a light cloth over her hair that completely covered her hair and evening gown while helping in the kitchen. Anna's mother was still upstairs prepping for the party. Embarrassing as it was to be the first one there, Anna sensed Aaden's discomfort and smoothly introduced him to her father and handed him off for her father to entertain her *gentleman caller* while she went to the kitchen to check on the canapés. Mr. Mercier led Aaden to a library/office off of the entryway and from a sidebar poured two drinks of a fine whiskey, each several fingers deep. "To a fine Christmas," the older man toasted as he clicked his glass to Aaden's. "My best one yet in America," Aaden replied. As they drank, deep, resonant chimes sounded, and Mercier hurried back out to meet more arrivals.

A black maid short and round appeared with a tray of food. She wore the feminine version of the same style as the butler in a blue dress, white apron, and a white hair net. She looked at Aaden in a way that expressed happy approval, obviously sizing up Anna's choice of a partner for the evening. Aaden took a small dish and several of the offerings; lobster and scallops on a hard rye cracker. It was the best snack he had tasted since he left the shores of Ireland with its abundant supply of fresh seafood. While he could eat anywhere he wanted among the numerous restaurants of New York, Aaden was content with the cafeteria food at the college, but the seafood tray reminded him of home and similar parties at his father's grand house. He suddenly filled with a strong feeling of homesickness, deeply missing his own family.

Mercier returned with a portly gentleman wearing his black tie stretched tight around his neck like a hangman's noose. The man had put on consider-able weight since the last time his wife had stuffed him into what he called his *monkey suit*. Mercier introduced his friend as Sean O'Sullivan. Aaden re-laxed a little in the presence of a fellow Irishman who acted more out of place and felt more uncomfortable than he did.

Guests were frequently arriving now, and Anna looked in on him and gave him a reassuring smile. Mercier hurried back to the entryway, and O'Sullivan helped himself to a full glass of whiskey from the sidebar. After downing the first half like it was tea, he took a cigar out of his inside pocket and with a conspirator's smile, said in a low voice, "Don't tell my wife I'm smoking." He lit the cigar and took a long pull on it, blew the smoke into the fireplace, and gulped down the rest of the whiskey. O'Sullivan seemed eager to strike up a conversation. "Have you ever invested in a gold mine, son?"

Mercier returned from the entryway when he heard the words *gold mine* and joined in the conversation. He had a lot to say. Mercier was raising money to consolidate the gold mines in the Carolina Gold Belt and had al-ready purchased the John Reed Mine, site of the original discovery. "We are going to reopen the mines and go deeper. I hear you are a young man of some means. This stock offering would be an excellent chance for you to get in early. I intend to make a killing with better pumps and better processing techniques. Indeed, the John Reed is a chance of a lifetime."

O'Sullivan was quick to agree and told Aaden that he had made a substan-tial investment in the new venture, and was planning on buying more stock.

Aaden was cautious and politely responded that he favored investments with real assets. The gold mines in the Carolinas were host to the first gold rush in America, but they had been mined out years before. Aaden hadn't heard of any recent discoveries. Aaden had several questions. "What are the gold reserves? Who will manage the operations? Are any of these funda-mentals known as of yet?" Aaden could see that both men were uncomfort-able with the questions.

Mercier huffed and turned a little red but used the doorbell and more ar-riving guests to withdraw from the conversation.

O'Sullivan was put off by Aaden's questions and let Aaden know that the gold mining project was Mercier's brainchild, and he didn't like the hard questions to get in the way of his enthusiasm. "Let's go join the party, son," as he led Aaden to the great hall on the other side of the entryway.

Anna joined him at the doorway, took his arm, and once again reassuring him with even a more magnificent smile. "Hanna likes you," she said as they waited a moment to enter the great hall. Anna had shed the smock and head covering and was stunningly beautiful in a long royal blue gown that accented her full figure. The low-cut bodice had Aaden embarrassed that he was becoming sexually aroused. He focused on her face and hair hoping the manly urge would pass unnoticed. Anna wore her hair up in a stylish sweep and had lapis lazuli earrings trimmed with diamonds that added to her deep blue eyes. At that moment, Aaden was well beyond love, more determined than ever to cherish and make this woman his own.

The doors to the great hall stood closed when Aaden arrived, but now Rufas had swung them wide and the brilliant light from a huge-gas-light-crystal chandelier and what seemed like a thousand candles flooded into the hallway. There must have been at least a hundred people in the room by then, the men in tight groups discussing the markets, trade, and business. More black servants tended to every whim of the guests. But the women, the women stopped their idle chatter about the weather, children or their latest shopping sprees or affairs and stared fixated on the elegant couple in the doorway. Almost six-six and taller in his dress boots, Aaden was the most imposing figure to arrive in the great hall. His broad shoulders, filling the tuxedo as a perfect picture of strength, his vivid green eyes, and the sharp features of his face instilled a shockwave of lust among some of the looser women in the crowd. Anna put her other hand on Aaden's arm and leaned into him, staking and asserting her claim to ward off the envious, lascivious trance that overtook both the younger and older women alike.

The moment was awkward for Aaden, and he was ready to bolt and make a run for it when all eyes swept to the top of the stairway where Anna's mother was making her grand entrance. Anna's mother, Denise, was every bit as fetching as her daughter. Anna turned Aaden toward the bottom of the stairs as her mother neared the last step, another black maid holding the long train of the white evening gown until she was safely on the floor of the grand hall. Around her neck, on her wrists and in her hair, Denise wore what struck

Aaden as the entire bounty of a rich diamond mine. Anna introduced Aaden as Professor Aaden Kellan Callahan from Columbia University, he thought to impress the guests. The awkward moment passed as Denise kissed Aaden on the cheek and welcomed him to their home.

Aaden met dozens of people that night and learned that the round little man with the cigar was on the Board-of-Regents for Columbia; so much for remaining as inconspicuous as possible. Many women stopped to flirt, but with Anna glued to his arm, they withdrew to bide their time for a better opportunity. One attractive middle-aged woman also sporting her diamonds put her hand on Aaden's chest and said in a dreamy voice, "Aren't you the pretty one."

Anna stepped in and said, "Back off, Mary, you have so many young studs in your stable, you can't even keep their names straight anymore." The more self-righteous and moral women nodded their approval of Anna solidifying her claim on the young professor.

An orchestra composed of all black musicians started a waltz, and as Aaden and Anna danced, it was as if they were the only couple in the great hall. After about two hours of drinks and more delicious food and dancing, Rufus announced it was time to open gifts. There were about two dozen under the tall exquisitely decorated tree at the far end of the hall. It was obvious that only close friends brought gifts to exchange with their closest friends and of course, their gracious hosts. Rufus left Aaden's gift under the tree, standing guard over it until all the guests finished with their oohs and aahs. Aaden's discomfort returned when Rufus retrieved the gift with a sweep of his hand and with a loud, deep voice, announced that the gold box with the elegant name tag was from the "Professor" for Miss Anna. With a great flourish, he walked through the crowd and with a bow, handed the box to his young mistress.

Even Anna blushed with embarrassment and slapped Rufus playfully on the chest to lighten the moment. With the grand fanfare, the guests were silent watching to see what the "mere Professor" could afford for such a wealthy girl on his only passable salary at the university. With a little dread at what the crowd was going to think, she opened the present and with a look of awe, lifted the gift wrapped in a wad of tissue paper. She held the gift in front of her, and as she unwrapped it, immediately recognized the alabaster horse as a Belgian, and the symbology of the silver knight didn't escape her sharp mind for a moment. The guests gasped, many of the women had never received such an elegant gift even for their anniversaries. With tears running down her face, Anna pulled herself up with an arm around Aaden's neck and kissed him passionately full on the lips. "Thank you." She said, "It reminds me of Tongeren. I shouldn't be crying, but it is so beautiful," She kissed him again, longer than before.

Anna's father took note of the intimate exchange watching from the side of the Christmas tree while getting an earful from the fat little reagent about Aaden's anti-slavery viewpoint and his generous gifts to the Abolitionist Movement on the campus. Mercier could see this was going to be trouble. His daughter radiated the fervent love of a young woman ready to select a lifelong partner. Mercier would have been in his element, had he arrived previous to 1927, when New York abolished slavery within its borders. However, he regarded his servants as emancipated slaves, paid them meager wages, and still treated them as slaves.

Mercier determined that he would rid his daughter of this *too liberal* young man, even though his daughter's liberal views on slavery and the kindness she showed the blacks in the household would surely make her susceptible to the young man's political viewpoint in addition to his charms. Anna's mother, on the other hand, was filled with happiness for her daughter and thought only of the beautiful grandchildren they would produce. As Aaden left the mansion, Rufus handed him his hat and coat and said with a beaming smile, "You done good, Professor. Welcome to the family."

The day after Christmas, Aaden was horrified to read every detail about the party in the Tribune. The paper reported the alabaster horse and the silver knight in detail right down to the length of the silver lance. With a note from Mercier to the editor of the Tribune who owed him many favors, the article went on in a most negative way how the young upstart professor from Columbia was *worming* his way into one of the richest families in New York.

"Upstart indeed," Aaden muttered to himself as he read the article. He was wealthy in his own right. Aaden had invested wisely in companies that were still flying high after President Andrew Jackson paid off the national debt for the first time in 1835. Angry now knowing that Anna's father was against him, Aaden was more determined than ever to do all within his power to marry Anna and make her as happy as possible for the rest of her life. "I'm ready Mercier, this battle is joined," he muttered to himself. Any cost would be worth the price. From that moment on, Anna would be the only woman in his life. If he couldn't win her, he would probably remain single for the rest of his life.

THE DEPARTURE

Aaden didn't know how Mercier would attack him, but with instincts honed by millennia of constant strife and crisis in Ireland, he knew that the attack was imminent. He didn't have to wait long. In the middle of January, while the city was in the grips of brutal winter, Aaden found a summons to the President's office for a chat. There was also a letter from his father. Aaden had written to his family late last September to tell them about Anna and his plans to head west after his contract expired. He set the letter on his desk, donned his long wool coat, hat, and scarf and set out for the President's office. On his way past Renae, the secretary for the department, she looked up from her desk and said, "Be careful Professor Callahan." Aaden didn't know if she meant the icy sidewalks or his pending chat with the President, Dr. William Alexander Duer.

Dr. Duer was a prominent New York City attorney before he was elected President of the College. Aaden wondered if waiting an hour to see the President wasn't a simple lawyer's trick to unsettle him before their chat. Finally called in, he left his coat, hat, and scarf in the reception area and walked in with the Tribune pages from the financial section that he had been reading. Rather than unease, Aaden was feeling on top of the world. Investments he made now almost five years ago in the Bank of New York and several small but extremely successful shipping companies had more than doubled his savings. The dividends alone exceeded his annual salary from Columbia. He was pleased; he was going to need the money for his plans for the coming summer.

Dr. Duer welcomed him, sternly motioning him to one of the two chairs in front of his desk. No handshake, along with the stern welcome assured Aaden that the "chat" wasn't going to be easy. Dr. Duer got right to the point. "Aaden," he said, "it has come to my attention that your abolitionist politics have gotten out of hand. I have complaints from students and parents that your bias opinions are leading our young and impressionable down a road advocating slavery as an evil, which you teach has to be eliminated from our society. While Columbia is a liberal college, it is extremely necessary for our stance on this issue remain strictly middle-of-the-road, or we are going to lose considerable funding from one or the other of the factions."

Aaden did not doubt as to where the alleged "complaints" originated. No doubt, the regent O'Sullivan had been whispering in Dr. Duer's ear spurred on or threatened with financial ruin by Mercier. Strongly Aaden responded, "Sir, I have not ever stated my opinion about slavery in or out of the classroom. I teach history, and like it or not the history of slavery is an important part of Modern European History. Are you suggesting that I leave it out of the curriculum? Who exactly are making these complaints?"

Dr. Duer answered, "I don't want you to leave anything out of the normal curriculum, and I can't tell you who the complaints came from other than there are powerful people involved here, and they have asked me to put you on administrative probation. I am not going to do that without substantiation of these claims, but I am going to warn you, Professor Callahan, there are people out there in our college community who intend to bring you ill winds. It would do you well to take heed of their warning. You can go, you are dismissed."

The shift from his first name to his formal title told Aaden that Dr. Duer had made the transition from mentor to a bureaucratic administrator afloat in a troubled sea. He also worried because it was common knowledge that Dr. Duer's health was not good, and he would retire soon. It would be easy for the regents to replace him with someone more sympathetic to Mercier's influence. Walking back to his office, he was again thinking of moving west; he didn't want to quit and leave unless Anna would be going with him. He was looking forward to the letter from home as he walked back to his office, snow blowing in near blizzard conditions and the wind whipping at his face like an angry animal intent to have his nose for lunch.

Entering his office area, Renae asked, "How did it go?" Aaden answered, "Strange, hard to explain!" He didn't want to tell her that he had been wrongly threatened with administrative probation because it would be all over the college and their community. While very supportive and even defensive of the professors in her department, Renae was connected to the college grapevine as well as the ivy clinging to the outside of the walls waiting for spring.

Sitting at his desk, he opened the letter from his father. As expected, his parents were thrilled that he found a woman he wanted to marry. They teased him about how they thought he would be single forever, but the jocularity ended, and his father got on to more serious matters. He wrote that he feared a "black swan event" would soon come to America over the slavery issue. How timely, as Aaden seemed to be drawn unwittingly into this issue. A "black swan event" was an ancient saying originating in Roman times when black swans were not thought to exist anywhere in the world. After their discovery in Australia and New Zealand, the phrase endured meaning a completely unexpected happening driven by a catastrophic event in nature or a sudden change in the political climate. Aaden's father had been following the news on the growing strength of the abolitionists and the steadfast response from the southern states. He expected serious trouble for the young nation that Aaden was making his home.

On a lighter note, Conner, Aaden's next younger sibling, was coming to the Americas as captain of a fast schooner, designed specifically for the family trade. Conner was to learn the eastern coastline and ports, particularly the landing spots for smugglers that would become profitable ports-of-call if, in the event, the opportunity for smuggling presented itself in the troubled times to come. Conner's voyage was timed to reach New York in mid-June when Aaden would be able to leave his job in good standing. If Aaden was ready to leave, Conner was instructed to take him anywhere he wanted to go. Conner wasn't going to put into port, so there would be no record of him coming or of Aaden's leaving if he so wished. A bright smile spread across his face as he started to plan the exodus from New York.

The next weekend he bought a small skiff outfitted with a single lateen sail, two oars mounted on both sides of the boat, and a single ore on the back that could serve as a tiller or a rudder. The boat was housed in a warehouse down by the docks on the lower west side. He paid for several months on the storage and couldn't wait for warmer weather to put the little sailboat in the water. Aaden knew how to sail, a rite of passage for anyone with his family's background, but he wanted to be proficient and learn all the capabilities of the small craft. He was looking forward to taking Anna out on the river or even down to Lower Bay, weather permitting. In the meantime, Aaden started a study of small sailboats, what they could carry and how they would handle in rougher waters. There were plenty of Irish sailors along the docks and in the flops on the lower west side of Manhattan to assist in his education. Down in the slum, he blended in well with his command of Gaelic. He met some thugs that were all too willing to help with his Mercier problem of escaping New York for reasonable fees.

As the cold weeks of winter slowly plied forward, Aaden saw Anna every day either in the cafeteria or on long circuitous walks home to the grand mansion. Early in February, he received an invitation from Anna's mother to join them for dinner in a fine restaurant downtown. The note said to come to the house, and we will all go by carriage to the restaurant. Aaden walked Anna home and was surprised to see Rufus decked out again in his finest livery, tending to a carriage under the front portico of the mansion. The carriage even had a small cast iron wood stove on the rear to comfort the riders from the winter cold. In front was a matched pair of fine buckskin geldings. They had black manes and tails and four black feet. Their breath made clouds of fog with every exhale that floated away in the ice-cold breeze. Aaden greeted Rufus, who was glad to see him again, and Aaden, comfortable and able around horses walked up to stroke the snouts of both animals quietly cooing to them and admiring the fine work of the breastplates and collars and the rest of the rigging hitching the team to the carriage. Rufus produced a big carrot from the inside pocket of his coat and threw it to Aaden saying, "Half and half Mr. P." Aaden noticed his name had been reduced down to a typical black "familiar" for a family member.

"I thought you were the butler," Aaden said as he fed the horses their treat.

"Today I be the Whip," replied Rufus. "And I'm the best one in New York. Mr. M. doesn't trust anyone with this team of Morgans, but me." Pride beamed across the black man's face, and his wide smile showed teeth as white as the snow and ice.

Denise and Anna descended the stairs, and when the three of them were seated, said, "Marcell will meet us at the restaurant." Funny Aaden thought, it was the first time Denise or Anna ever referred to the man by his first name.

He was always Mercier to his friends, father, or Anna's father to Denise and Anna, or as Mr. M. When Mr. M. was around, Rufus always called him Sir. Rufus clicked his tongue two times, and the team trotted off. Rufus didn't have a whip despite how he referred to himself as he drove the team. Their passage down the city streets to the best part of Manhattan was fast. There were hardly any other carriages and only a handful of pedestrians out on the cold winter night. Aaden enjoyed the heat inside the carriage but wondered about the cold wind in the face of Rufus up in the driver's seat.

Pulling up in front of the restaurant, Rufus jumped down agile as a gazelle and opened the door for the ladies. On the sidewalk, Denise paused Aaden with a hand on his arm and said, "Anna's father is anxious to talk to you. Please be your congenial self regardless of what he may bring up. A bit confused, Aaden nodded a yes and reassured her with a smile. As they entered the restaurant a beautiful young woman, obviously a high-class harlot, looked them over and brushed past them out the door. Mercier was alone at a table toward the back, but a waiter was there pushing in a chair and picking up a small hors d'oeuvres plate from the table. Mercier looked a little guilty, and since the restaurant was nearly empty, the harlot had to have gotten up from the table when the banker and his harlot saw the carriage pull up to the door. *Interesting,* thought Aaden.

Dinner went reasonably well, but Mercier was getting drunk, and the waiter kept making the rounds every time Mercier's glass was empty, which was quite often. As Mercier grew louder and more aggressive, Denise and Anna carefully withdrew from the conversation and went to the lady's room in the back. Mercier took advantage of the opportunity without the women listening and launched into a diatribe about the abolitionist movement and ended with a statement, "No upstanding young man would ever go along with the nonsense. America has its roots anchored deep in slavery, and the fools that outlawed it in New York and the other slave-free states don't realize that they are breaking the back of America's economy.

Aaden didn't want to engage in an argument but felt compelled to answer. "There are two sides to every argument Mr. Mercier. The slave-free states haven't failed economically; I even have some very successful investments in factories in this northeast area that are operated entirely by free black men and women. I will not invest in any business that profits from slave labor or even one that treats blacks as indentured servants. That system of things and British oppression brought about the Irish Rebellion of 1798. A lot of my ancestors on the west side of Ireland died in that conflict. I won't be part of anything that perpetuates human misery and madness."

Mercier turned bright red and then almost purple. Aaden thought he was going to have a stroke or burst a blood vessel in his bright red nose. Mercier stood up, knocking his chair over backward. He pulled the napkin out of his vest and yelled, "You fool. You and your liberal friends think you know better how to run our world." And then even more vehemently and louder he shouted, "I'll never let you marry my daughter."

In a calm but commanding voice, Aaden replied, "Mr. Mercier, you can very respectfully go to hell. Anna can think for herself." Mercier turned, probably to come around the table to attempt a thrashing of the younger and stronger man but stopped short when he saw his wife and daughter standing horrified that the two men had clashed. Mercier threw down a hundred-dollar bill and a gold coin to cover the dinner and told his wife that he was going back to the office, and Rufus would return shortly to take them home. He stomped out still in his rage and didn't even stop to pick up his coat. In an attempt at levity, Aaden said in his heaviest Irish brogue, "Well me ladies, at least the bloke paid for the fair."

Both crying, the women gathered up their coats and waited in the foyer for Rufus to return. Aaden apologized to the restaurant owner and his staff, the few other patrons, and paid for all their dinners in a show of good faith. On the way home, Aaden sat with a still sobbing Anna and tried his best to comfort her. Denise assured Aaden that she wouldn't let Mercier follow through on his threat, but Aaden recognized Mercier's outrage as only a first salvo in a battle that the powerful man intended to win. Aaden fully expected the attack on him and his relationship with Anna to intensify.

When they reached the mansion, Rufus leaped down and opened the door. Denise put her hand on his chest and said, "Rufus tell me honestly, where did you take him?" "I dropped him at the Royal York madam; a young woman was waiting in the lobby. Mr. M. was madder than I had ever seen him before. He looked like he wanted to kill somebody."

"Thanks for your loyalty and your honesty, Rufus." Anna and Denise kissed Rufus on both his cheeks, both at the same time. Anna turned with a small goodnight wave and ran into the house. Denise turned to Aaden and said, "Things haven't been good between my husband and me for a long time. Don't worry; I won't let him hurt you and Anna. Aaden hoped she could handle the angry Mercier. Aaden knew deep in the darker areas of his Irish soul that this situation with Anna's father, could only end badly.

A month passed quietly on the Mercier front. Like the Christmas Party, the episode at the restaurant appeared in detail in the Tribune. No doubt, the restaurant owner or one of his staff sold the story to the newspaper. The Tribune was avid for new *dirt* to expose the wayward lives of the elite. Even the harlot that left in a rush was described right down to her age, dress, shoes, and hat. Aaden thought that should pull a scoop of dirt out of Mercier's moral high ground. He sat in his office early in April wondering what would happen next. Denise would send him an encouraging letter periodically, and he continued to see Anna daily at the college. She had agreed to marry him but couldn't see how it was going to happen. Aaden had told her to trust him; he was going to make it happen.

He was summoned to the President's office again the next day, and this time all the regents were present. O'Sullivan didn't wait for the niceties. He opened immediately with, "This trouble between you and Mercier has to stop. It's bad for the college. He is even threatening to challenge you to a duel for Christ's sake. If you keep this up, son, you're going to wind up dead."

Calmly Aaden replied in perfect New York English, "If it's a duel, I welcome it, and it is Mercier that will be dead." Then in his thickest Irish brogue, "But it be the coward in the man that I fear mates. The sorry blighter will probably just put some low life thugsie to knack me ballix in." He tipped his hat and finished back in perfect English, "Now O'Sullivan, you can join Mercier in hell." With a respectful bow to the president, Aaden turned and left the room.

O'Sullivan opened his mouth to speak, but Dr. Duer yelled, "Get out of my office." When the regents hesitated, he finished, "If you ever bring something this asinine before me again, you will be leaving with my resignation. The regents sulked out, knowing they made a serious error. Dr. Duer was immensely popular with students, parents, and, more importantly, with many wealthy alumni. He had the political support of the city, and they knew Duer's was not an idle threat.

Aaden was amazed as the next day, another detailed report of the meeting in Dr. Duer's office appeared in the Tribune. Anxious for more tabloid, the headline read, **"Banker Mercier to challenge Columbia Faculty Member to a duel."** "Oh-oh," Aaden thought, *how is Mercier going to get out of this one*. It had to be O'Sullivan again whispering to the editor, but this required a lot more thought.

That night Aaden sat in the great room of the boarding house and consulted the advisory committee. One of the other history professors had written a syllabus on dueling in Europe and America and gave a short dissertation on the etiquette of the gentleman's way of resolving disputes. He was sure that Mercier would have to challenge Aaden to a duel or face public humiliation for not rising to the challenge the newspaper put forth. He also related more of the rules. The challenger would usually arrive with a brace of pistols and several pairs of various swords from epees to even broadswords that were popular in medieval England. The challenged would be asked to choose his weapon, and the duel would proceed with whatever weapon he chose. The challenged even had the right to bring his own set of weapons, but usually, that was a brace of pistols since the flintlock pistols seemed to be the weapon of choice in the mid-nineteenth century. The challenger and challenged would have a second who tended to the weapons, loaded the pistols, or sharpened the swords. "Who will you choose for your second?" The professor asked as he ended the dissertation.

"I won't need one mate," Aaden answered as the bell on the front door rang to announce a visitor.

O'Sullivan was shown in and with an arrogant flare and a smirk on his face, handed Aaden the challenge. "May God have mercy on your soul," the fat man intoned." Then he spun around on one heel and walked out of the house.

The challenge was for the next day at 2:00 PM in Faculty Park, across the street from the front entrance of the Columbia College. Aaden got up and said, "Excuse me, gents, I have to walk down and catch the tram down to the lower west side."

Down on the west side, Aaden went to the warehouse, where he kept his boat. The warehouse owner went by *Dragoon* and lived in an apartment inside, which was raised on stilts to keep the warehouse floor clear. A guard at the door stepped out of the darkness and said, "You'll be needing something, Professor? I hear ye have a bit of trouble." News of the duel traveled like wildfire around town, no doubt spurred by some of Mercier's henchmen.

"I'll be needing some weapons come tomorrow," Aaden replied. "I think Dragoon can round up exactly what I need."

Dragoon came down the stairs. Despite the cold, the West Side boss wore his typical black leather vest, tattoos displayed up and down both arms. They had a short discussion, and Dragoon sent the guard to round up the requested items. The guard returned with the goods and two other burly men dressed like they spent their nights outside. Dragoon said, "These be two of my brothers. They are going to watch over you until this is over. I don't think Mercier is planning on you showing up for the duel. Good luck now and come back soon. It's almost time to put your boat in the water." Reluctantly, Aaden accepted the protection, and the three men walked uptown to catch the northbound tram. When they stopped at the end of the run, Aaden walked into a bar and bought two bottles of good Irish whiskey, knowing that his *guards* would leave them empty by morning.

The next morning the *protection* walked Aaden to the College. There was a gang of young toughs, *want-a-be-thugs*, the three men thought, waiting on the second corner. "Is this the best Mercier could do," Aaden challenged. One of the larger boys, obviously the leader, swung to hit Aaden with a roundhouse punch, but fast as a lightning bolt, Aaden knocked him out with a devastating slap to the face before he could land the punch. The rest of the boys scattered, and Aaden and the two burly men left the unconscious want-a-be lying in the street. The guards left him at the gates of Columbia, let Aaden know they would stay close, and walked across the street to case Faculty Park. Anna was waiting in his office when he got there.

As Aaden closed the door and was taking off his greatcoat, Anna sat behind her desk, wringing her hands with fear in her eyes. "Are you going to kill him?" she asked as he turned toward her.

"If he dies, it will be by accident. I don't intend to kill him, but I will win the duel. Aaden pulled her up out of his chair, and sitting down, pulled Anna onto his lap.

Holding her close to calm her, she put her forehead on his and said in a little girl's voice, "Thank you," then she kissed him. The time was right, and he told Anna about the skiff and his plans for their exodus. "What if your brother doesn't show up?" Anna asked.

"Not to worry, little lady, he is a Callahan and a man of the sea. Besides, he is sailing a brand-new schooner my father had built in the finest shipyard in Sweden. He'll be here. You should be ready to go near the middle of June." Still filled with trepidation Anna left his office.

She turned at the door and told him she would be watching from the top of the Administration Building. Then she added, "Please don't die, I love you, and I need you to live." She walked out past Renae's desk. Renae was quiet for once not knowing what to say. As Aaden watched her walk down the hall and don her hat and coat, Dr. Duer came into view accompanied by the Dean of the History College.

They walked Aaden into his office, Dr. Duer taking the seat behind his desk and the Dean the only other chair. Dr. Duer said, "Aaden, you can't do this; let's summon up the campus police and put a stop to this."

Aaden gathered his thoughts and replied in confidence, "The only way to stop this is to follow through with the duel. Don't worry; I'm not going to kill him. I promised Anna. And one more thing, I'm not going to let him kill me." Unconvinced, Aaden had to fill Dr. Duer and the Dean with more details of his plan. Opening his coat on the rack, Aaden showed them the weapons he would take to the duel. Reluctantly the older men agreed and bid him *good luck* as they opened the door and walked out past Renae.

Renae caught his eye and said, "Big doings going on," in hope Aaden would open up and tell her about the morning's visits.

Aaden just said, "Indeed," and turned and walked down the hall to his first lecture with the air of a man who intended to live forever.

Throughout the day, all his students wanted him to talk about the duel. Aaden responded with an assignment. Every student was to attend the event and write an accurate historical account of the duel, regardless of the outcome. Most of them moaned, but a few of the more astute wondered if the Professor would be around the next morning to collect the papers. That morning the Tribune ran a special addition heralding Mercier's skill with a pistol. It was all lies; Mercier only hunted occasionally and could hardly hit anything even with a shotgun. Aaden let the story run its course, and when he left the main gate of the College, he was amazed that there were well over two thousand people in the street but almost none in Faculty Park. Crossing the street, he could see the two burly guards at the gates holding the crowd at bay.

As Aaden entered the park, one of the guards asked, "Where's ye second, Professor?"

"I won't be a needin' one," he answered in his thickest Irish brogue. He walked to the center of the park. It lay rectangular along the street with a high stone wall on three sides, and a strong iron fence along the front on 118th street. The stone walls on the sides would be perfect for stopping lead balls, but there wouldn't be any lasting pockmarks in the stone that day.

Mercier arrived in the elegant carriage with Rufus, *the whip* dressed in ordinary carriage driver browns. Mercier got out of the carriage dressed in a modest suit with a gleaming black satin cape lined in red hanging down from his shoulders. A top hat donned his head, and he tilted it toward a group of reporters and posed for the artists madly sketching on their pads. After a few moments of Mercier basking in the limelight, his second got out of the carriage. He was a man Aaden didn't recognize, but he walked with the air of a military man with a pistol case in one hand and a black leather bag in the other. Six sword handles could be seen sticking out of the top of the bag, and the swords clattered when the second dropped the bag on the ground in the center of the park. Rufus was allowed in after he told the guards that he was driving mister M., but he was siding with Mr. P. Several reporters and artists were also let in after they agreed to stand beyond the firing line, not to block the view from the street.

"I'm surprised you're here," Mercier said with a sneer. "I expected you to be hiding in your office."

"No finer place to be on a fine spring day," Aaden replied. Then he added, "Lucky for me, you were stupid enough to send a gang of boys to do the work of men. Next time you want to dodge a duel, at least send someone who doesn't fall with a mere slap. I hope you didn't pay your *children* much because, as you can see, you didn't get much for your money." Mercier's anger flared, his teeth clenched tight, and the familiar red spread across his face, but he stayed in control for the moment, but his hands started shaking with the rage upon him. "That worked better than I thought," Aaden muttered to himself as he watched the reporters taking down every detail of the exchange.

The second took the swords out of the leather bag and stuck them in the brown grass. When the second opened the pistol case, Mercier sneered again and said, "Choose your weapon, Professor." Aaden looked at the fine weapons, polished walnut handles, brass adornments, and fine blued steel barrels. Aaden hesitated a moment, like he couldn't make up his mind and then walked about ten paces away.

Mercier was ready to shout coward for everyone to hear, but Aaden turned and said, "No need, I brought my own." He opened his coat and unclipped an Irish cudgel. Four feet long with a shaft of heavy black ebony and a heavy brass tip, the cudgel gleamed in the afternoon sun. Aaden flicked the cudgel across to Mercier, and the second reached out and grabbed it inches before it slammed into Mercier's face. Aaden seldom swore or used any form of foul language, but he unclipped his cudgel and in perfect French, said, "Temps écoulé, anus." The meaning was lost to most of the crowd but loosely translated, it meant, "On guard asshole."

Mercier instantly turned completely red in the face, then purple. Mercier looked completely insane and out of control. Knocking the cudgel out of the second's hand, he grabbed one of the pistols from the box and trying to hold his hand still; he fired at Aaden. The bullet passed so close to Aaden's left cheek he could feel the wind and heat from the lead ball as it whizzed by with a crack and then a thwack as it hit the stone wall behind him. There would be a scar on the wall, after all. Aaden walked toward Mercier, and terrified, Mercier grabbed for the second pistol. Not to be by the protocol and honor of dueling, Mercier's second closed the box before Mercier could reach the second pistol. Stepping forward a bit, the second opened the box offering the pistol to Aaden, and with a stern voice of authority, said, "Your shot

Professor."

Aaden took the pistol and counted off the mandatory twenty paces and turned and raised the gun dead steady, ready to fire. He waited a full minute to see if the trembling banker would run off rather than face his fire. Mercier knew that if he ran away his life in New York would be over. He didn't think the Professor could hit him anyway. With deadly calm, Aaden shot off Mercier's right earlobe. Mercier screamed, clapped his hand to the right side of his head, and withdrew it covered with blood. Mercier became animal-like. He picked up the cudgel and with the roar of the insane, ran forward to attack Aaden. Aaden waited until Mercier lifted the cudgel to deliver a crushing-killing downward blow, then just sidestepped and let Mercier stumble forward after not connecting with Aaden's head. As Mercier turned and readied for another attack, Aaden tapped him on the temple with a soft backhand stroke. He could have easily killed Mercier with a little more force behind the blow, but the tap with the heavy brass end of the cudgel was enough to put Mercier unconscious on the ground, still shaking from the adrenaline in his body.

Rufus walked up to Aaden, pulled the pistol out of his hand, and dropped it on top of Mercier. He then reached down and picked up his boss's cudgel, and with his arm around Aaden, walked him to the gate. Across the street, high up on the roof, Anna nearly fainted with relief as she watched Rufus and Aaden swarmed by the reporters and artists making quick sketches for the pen and ink drawings that would appear in the morning papers. In a few moments, Anna turned and slid down with her back to the parapet; her eyes closed tight. She didn't know that Renae had followed her up to the roof, but she opened her eyes when Renae's gloved hand touched the tears on her face. The older woman pulled her up into her arms and headed her to the stairs. Denise was waiting over in Anna's office, too filled with dread to watch the duel with her daughter.

Across the street, the reporters shouted their questions at Aaden. "Why didn't you kill him?" "Did you think you were dead when he shot at you?" On and on and never-ending.

Aaden's only comment was, "The man was a really poor shot and not worth a damn with a cudgel."

Rufus steered him to the ladder that led up to the driver's seat and said, "Come on, Mr. Aaden, let me take you home. He helped Aaden up into the driver's seat and saw the two burly bodyguards slip into the carriage but ignored them. With a double-click of his tongue, the pair of magnificent Morgans galloped down the street, hooves thundering on the granite stone pavement, manes and tails flared elegantly behind them. Thousands watched in awe as their hero left the field of battle.

Instead of going to the boarding house, Rufus went by a circuitous route to the mansion. Pulling out of sight behind the house and drawing the team to a halt, two stable hands rushed up to unhitch the carriage and care for the horses. The two bodyguards slipped out of the carriage, one taking up a position across the street and one walking to the south to catch the tram to downtown. Rufus lived above the carriage house with Hanna and Lily, their eight-year-old daughter. Hanna made coffee, sat Aaden down at the table and fed him a lunch of hearty chitlin soup and cornbread. Hanna said, "Eat now, I hear you had quite the afternoon." Aaden didn't know what he was eating, but it was completely obvious why Hanna was so round.

Three hours later, in pairs and individuals, more than a dozen men and women dressed as sweepers, ground-keepers, and even a man and a woman posing as missionaries took up stations around the neighborhood to watch and guard the carriage house. At dinner time, a vending wagon pulled up a block away and fed the contingent a hearty Irish stew topped off with rich dark ale. At midnight they were replaced by others walking into the neighborhood one-by-one and in pairs, just as stealthy as the first crew. Slipping into the darkness and hiding in the shrubs, they stayed out of sight until time to resume their assigned roles at sunrise.

A casual onlooker wouldn't see anything but a well-organized operation, efficient and under command by Dragoon, who had set up an operations center in a building down by the waterfront. By morning there were more than a hundred volunteers involved in the operation guarding the Professor. Dragoon's headquarters was equipped with a mess hall, cots for the rotating shifts, and some young boys employed as runners. The two burly men returned at dawn dressed in the casual attire of businessmen with a day off. They sat down on the steps of the mansion to enjoy coffee spiked with Irish whiskey that Hanna delivered from the main entrance of the mansion. When Hanna showed up with sandwiches for brunch, the two men smiled at each other. Guarding the Professor was going to be the best job they had all year.

The previous day Renae had taken Anna and Denise to the visitor's cottages on the campus. She feared that if the women went out on the street, they would be mobbed by reporters and what was left of the onlookers. Renae checked them into a comfortable bungalow and sent word to the cafeteria for food. The two women just sat at the dining room table in a silent daze with no idea as to what would come next. Around 11:00 AM, an open carriage drawn by a large black gelding showed up to take them down to the mansion. As it arrived at the portico, the two guards rushed forward to help the ladies down. One said, "Rufus hid the Professor up in the carriage house. We have around a dozen men and women around the neighborhood watching for trouble. Don't worry a bit; we got him covered." Denise went into the house welcomed home by Rufus and Hanna. Anna looked up and down the street to make sure they were alone, then walked to the carriage house and climbed the stairs. When Aaden stood up in the small sitting room, she didn't say a word but walked to him. He took her in his arms and swayed her back and forth for a long time. They finally sat down on the shabby sofa and started to discuss their future.

Mercier didn't have it so easy. When he had come to in the park, reporters surrounded him punching questions in his face. His second helped him to his feet and started weaving them through the crowd to the gate. The crowd parted, making a clear path to the gate, like a verbal gauntlet. Insults and booing filled the air and could be heard more than several blocks away and all over the twenty-seven acres of the College. Someone started a chant, and several people joined yelling coward, coward, coward. The chant was picked up in seconds and resounded with thousands of voices all the way down to quays on the waterfront. They tried to walk away to the east on 118th street, but the crowd followed them pushing in and jeering. The chant continued, the biggest *hatred* parade New York had ever seen. Mercier just stared at the ground and walked along with his second in a stoic daze. When the pair came to a corner several blocks up, they jumped on the tailgate of an empty cargo wagon pulled by two mules. The driver sensing that he had stumbled into trouble cracked his whip over the mules, and they went into their smooth trot and soon left the angry mob far to the rear.

Arriving at the Royal York in a cargo wagon raised quite a few eyebrows. The bellman rushed down to shoo the interloper off to the delivery dock at the rear of the hotel but stopped short when he saw Mercier and his second on the back of the wagon. Mercier slipped down to the street and without a word, walked into the hotel and sat down at his favorite table and indulging in fine scotch liquor, spent the rest of the day drinking himself into oblivion. Early in the evening, the bartender had him carried up to his suite. The second, Mercier's lifelong friend, left the tailgate, walked to his bank, and cleaned out all his accounts. Then he walked down to the docks and bought first-class passage to California. He was never seen in New York again.

The next morning all the papers in New York sported the story of the duel on the front page. The Tribune ran their full front-page account with the bold headline, **CALLAHAN SPARES THE COWARD**. A half-page illustration showed Mercier firing the pistol at the Professor armed only with a cudgel. An accurate account followed; it was obvious that Mercier was no longer the editors favored man. Mercier was portrayed not only as a coward but as an insane coward. Numerous eyewitness accounts followed the front page, and hundreds of historical essays appeared in a high pile on Renae's desk after the Professor's mailbox was full.

On Sunday evening, Aaden met with Dragoon in the garage. Sitting in the elegant carriage with Anna by his side and Dragoon in the opposing seat, Dragoon made his case for the Professor returning to his normal daily routine. He assured Anna that this time around, the burly bodyguards, who had become a permanent fixture at the mansion during the daylight hours, would accompany Aaden everywhere, even to class. "A little education will do the boys some good. Besides," Dragoon finished up, "It's time I made a decent sailor out of you. You have been a sorry landlubber too long."

The next morning Rufus had the carriage with the Morgan team in front of the carriage house ready to take Mr. P., whom he now called Sir and his two new unlikely looking students to the college. They could have walked the short distance, but Rufus wanted the Professor to appear in Mercier's finest carriage, the implication that Aaden would soon be a permanent resident at the mansion flouted as publicly as possible. When the threesome walked into the College of History building, teachers and students lined the halls and applauded Aaden's return. It was the same all day through, every lecture started with a standing ovation. That afternoon Rufus dropped the Professor and his bodyguards off at the boarding house. If Aaden's life was to return to normal, he needed to resume this part of the routine as well. Two other men arrived to relieve the bodyguards and stayed in the sitting room through the night.

As the other professors arrived in the early evening, they were thrilled with Aaden's return. Sitting down to dinner of roast turkey with all the trimmings, they all wanted his account of the duel. Everything seemed back to normal

Things weren't going so well for Mercier. After having repeated his performance of passing out at the bar several days in a row, the bar just sent up a bottle of the fine scotch every morning. Mercier wasn't eating, just drinking himself into a semi-conscious state every day, never leaving his rooms. After several weeks the daily bottle of scotch didn't arrive. Disheveled and unshaven, Mercier made his way to the manager's office to complain. The manager informed him that he had to post some money on his account. His bar bill was bigger than his room bill, and the manager noticed the almost nonexistent food bill. Mercier sat himself down rumpled and smelly in a large leather easy chair in the lobby and penned off a draft on his bank. When done, he had the concierge send a runner over to the New York Bank. Half an hour later, the runner returned not with funds, but with a letter from the bank president informing Mercier that his funds were frozen, pending several court actions filed by a team of his wife's lawyers. The letter was backed up with handwritten copies of all the filings including one for divorce based on abandonment and Mercier's long mental abuse of her and her daughter.

Mercier had some money stashed in his office, but he didn't walk there. He climbed the stairs to the roof of the five-story hotel and without hesitation, walked off the front of the building. With a sickening noise, his body hit the landing at the top of the stairs to the entrance of the hotel and bounced down the several steps to the sidewalk. His mangled body landed face up with his dead eyes staring at the sky; a large pool of blood started to form, oozing out of the back of his head.

News of his suicide spread echoing through the financial community, and investors rushed to withdraw or transfer their funds out of his investment company. Before the end of the day, many fortunes, too many to count, were lost when the stock of Mercier's company fell from hundreds of dollars down to pennies; the market handed Mercier his complete and total devastation. A robust and solid financial institution brought to ruin in a matter of hours.

With Mercier's last heartbeat, the court proceedings turned into a simple reading of the will just several days later. The judge cleared his docket to read the will in court. Short and to the point, the rest of Mercies' assets were divided equally between his wife and his only daughter. The judge rapped his gavel to end the proceedings. Denise and Anna set out to return to the mansion as two of the wealthiest women in New York, despite the ruin of Mercier Investments. With *The Whip* humming in a low voice, the Morgans pranced proudly through the streets and avenues lined with blooming white and pink dogwoods, cherry trees, and azaleas. The season was turning to spring, and the women's world had changed forever.

Leaving Columbia late that evening by the west gate, Aaden was pleased to see a three-masted schooner with beautiful lines and rigging built for speed plying up the waters of the Hudson. The schooner was painted a dull gray oddly enough rather than the enameled white of a fine ship that size, an old smugglers trick to make the ship invisible on the horizon while at sea. The schooner anchored on the Jersey side, where the water was shallow enough for a small ship to anchor away from the busy docks on the east side of the Hudson. Aaden smiled; Connor had arrived early. There was still one more week of the spring semester to go before contracts expired. Aaden walked down to Dragoon's field headquarters to finalize plans for their departure. When he got there, he was surprised to see Connor sitting in an easy chair in the warehouse. Aaden walked up casually, pulled his brother up into a warm, masculine hug and said, "What took you so long?"

In the dimming light of dusk, Conner slipped out of the warehouse, just another commoner on the streets. He sauntered down to the docks and joined his boatswain and six rowers who swiftly returned him to the schooner. Aaden returned to the mansion, and Denise sent a runner to summon her solicitors to draft the transfer of the Mercier fortune to the Bank of St. Louis. Aaden had them do the same for his funds even though the amount paled compared to Anna's. The mansion and other properties were going to be put up for sale, and the servants were given a substantial severance to start their lives as truly free people. The mansion personnel who wanted to stay on were to be given fair wages as long as they kept the great house and grounds spotless until the new owner arrived. The rest of the proceeds from the sales were to be held in trust in a prominent New York investment firm for later distribution to the grandchildren Denise hoped to have.

There was a problem. Denise and Anna would not leave Rufus and Hanna or Lily behind. Aaden would need to make at least two or maybe three trips in the tiny skiff to get them all aboard Connor's boat. He advanced the time of departure to 1:00 AM, allowing for the delays that were sure to occur and sent a runner to Dragoon to update him. The waning moon would rise around 3:30 AM. Aaden hoped he didn't run into anything in the dark out on the Hudson.

Rufus had the Morgans and the carriage ready to go promptly at 1:00 AM. He sat with Lily in the driver's seat. Hanna was in the cab with two duffel bags lashed to the roof. Denise had two trunks that were hoisted up by many hands, waiting to see them off. Anna carried a small wooden box with the figurine of the Belgian with the silver knight inside. That and the family Bible were the only items besides their clothes selected for the journey that the two women took from the house. With tearful hugs all around, the women boarded the carriage, and with the double click, the Morgans galloped off, heading west to the docks.

When they arrived at the quay, the problem of too many people and too much luggage was solved by Dragoon and another boatman bobbing in the gentle waves in two more skiffs identical to Aaden's. Lily, Denise, and Anna loaded into Aaden's boat; Rufus and half the luggage into the second and Hanna and half the luggage into the third. The three blacks were terrified, none of them knew how to swim, and they had never been out on the water before. Anna held Lily close as Dragoon hoisted the sail and looked over at Aaden and challenged, "I'll race you to the schooner, landlubber." With a gentle north wind, the little boats tacked easily over to the schooner.

As Aaden neared the back of the schooner guided in by three blue hurricane lamps on the stern, he saw the name of the boat was *Deannaithe af an Ghaoth*, *Blessed by the Wind*. He certainly hoped so. A ladder lowered from the railing, and one-by-one, the little boats disembarked their passengers and luggage onto the schooner. Dragoon reached out and shook Aaden's hand and wished the small party good luck and Godspeed. Aaden pulled Dragoon into a hug saying, "Besides my family, you're the best friend I've ever had." Aaden was last to board, and his little skiff was tied astern.

Aaden wanted to pay Dragoon more for his service, but Dragoon said, "Not to bother, you have paid my people fairly and well, and no one around here will ever forget you. Don't forget to write when you get where you're going." Dragoon left in his skiff; the other boat already was gone. The crew doused the lanterns, lifted the anchor as quietly as possible, and hoisted the sails. Sailing large with the wind to his back, Connor skillfully conned the schooner down the Hudson using the lights from New York on his port side and a few lights and fires on the Jersey shore to keep him in the middle of the channel. As he rounded the tip of Manhattan and headed east out to sea through Lower Bay, the waning moon rose on the horizon. By sunrise, they were well to sea, and Aaden had a very strange thought as he stood by the helm with his brother, with the sea breeze in his face listening to the Irish lilt of the sailors. *What if Connor is in league with their crafty and cunning father to kidnap me back to Ireland.* He admonished himself for not trusting his brother but still felt a sense of relief when Connor spun the wheel and turned south, destination New Orleans.

New York woke up with no sleek grey schooner anchored in the Hudson and a soon to be discovered empty mansion. Aaden and his small entourage had vanished in the night. With the morning sun warming them as the schooner rose and fell with the swells, Aaden took Anna's hand and walked her to Captain Connor Callahan behind the helm and asked him to marry them. Aaden produced a single gold band from his pocket thinking he was going to surprise Anna with it. Anna cocked her head a little, twitched her right eyebrow up and down, and with a comical imitation of the Irish lilt said, "Me man here is a little thick about these things. He's not the only one here with a ring. He probably be thikin' he'll just walk around with a naked finger and let some harlot take him off me arm." She opened her hand and sitting on her palm was a simple gold band for Aaden. Aaden knew then he would never be one step ahead of this woman.

Captain Connor knew he had the authority but said he never married anyone and didn't know how to recite the vows or even conduct the ceremony. Denise stepped forward, and imitating the Irish lilt said, "Not to worry, lad, I have me Bible, and I'll lead you through the hard part." Everyone was laughing at the antics, and Rufus stepped up insisting he was the Best Man; Hanna did the same claiming the Maid-of-Honor slot. Lily stepped up holding a bouquet of yes – lilies. *Where in the hell did she get those*, Aaden wondered but kept his amazement to himself.

With the sails full and the first-mate at the wheel, the wedding party stood on the main deck with the rest of the crew watching, and Denise led Connor through the ceremony. Vows were repeated, read off a page in the back of the Bible, the rings exchanged, and Aaden kissed his bride with a hip-hip-hurray from the crew. Denise went down to the mess, sat in the captain's chair, and with a beautiful hand, wrote in Aaden and Anna's full names into the family tree. Beneath that she wrote in Rufus and Hanna Sawyer – Witnesses – freeman and woman of the United States of America. Below that, she wrote – Captain Conner Callahan officiating. Conner recorded the marriage at sea in the ship's log, and closing the book said, "It's official."

Happily, the sleek schooner plied south. Connor had Lily up on a whiskey keg steering the boat. Connor had moved his brother and his new wife into the captain's cabin for space and the privacy it offered, but the newlyweds stood on the bow of the boat with the spray from the swell wetting them. The crew looked on admiring them and collectively wondered when the groom would get to it. Connor put Denise in the first mate's cabin and Rufus and Hanna in the second mate's, Rufus, on the floor with a sleeping mat, and Hanna on the bunk. Lily was put up with the cook, the only other woman on the ship. She was fixing a feast and baking the best she could manage in the cramped ship's galley, a wedding cake. Conner and his mates were happy to sleep with the crew in the forecastle. Conner knew his crew well, and every man trusted the others with their lives. Sleeping side by side in hammocks swaying back and forth with the rocking of the ship was no uncomfortable matter at all.

Rufus and Hanna were deep in the grips off seasickness within the first hour of getting into the swells of the open ocean. Connor was wise to put Lily up on top of a whiskey keg behind the helm steering the schooner so that she would keep her eyes on the horizon. Lily was having the time of her life watching the compass and getting the feel of the helm, amazed at how just a little turn of the great wheel would instantly make the agile ship slew left or right to her every whim. Connor built on her enthusiasm and with wider swings had her calling out **"BOOM"** every time the fore and aft mainsails swung deadly and fast over the deck, with the sails snapping tight to take the wind on the new tack. Lily was on her way to becoming an able *sea-woman* while her mother and father stayed on the rails, heaving violently and turning a little strange looking with a green hue coloring their deep brown skin.

Sailing large, the schooner was twenty-five leagues to the south by night-fall. The crew and passengers retired in the early evening after the wedding feast. Aaden and Anna retired to the elegant captain's cabin over the stern of the ship to consummate their marriage, a marriage that would last the rest of their lives. Everyone but Rufus and Hanna dreamed of seeing New Orleans for the first time. Little did they know there would be a lot more danger and adventure before they arrived at the mouth of the Mississippi.

DELAWARE BAY

When the sun rose to a beautiful pink sky, *Blessed by the Wind* turned into the mouth of Delaware Bay. Connor was concerned that Rufus and Hanna lay comatose on the main deck with Lily sitting cross-legged nearby. They were in no hurry, having left New York far behind. With a swift decisiveness characteristic of the young captain, he put the ship hard to starboard to spill the wind from the sails and lay adrift in Delaware Bay. The crew had not been ashore since they left Ireland, some time in Dover would do them good.

Sheltered inland, the steady north wind that drove them with record speed down the coast was just a whisper across a calm bay. After the morning mess, Lily walked aft to the poop deck. As she walked to the con, she wanted to check out more of the instruments, Connor slipped a lanyard with a loop over her and pulled it tight around her waist. Lily screamed as he swung her over the stern. Laughing, Connor lowered her into Aaden's skiff. Laughing again as he threw her the bitter end of the lanyard, a crewman pulled the line through the eyelet in the bow of the skiff and released Lily to the whims of the wind and tide of the bay. "Good sailing mate, come back when you're hungry, the mess is at eight bells," the seaman yelled waving his hat in a broad arc over his head in the fashion of a final farewell.

Set adrift, Lily sat on the thwart with fear in her eyes as she drifted further and further to the south in the light wind. Connor watched approvingly when about a hundred yards astern Lily got the mast of the little boat into the pocket and was hoisting the lateen. Another hundred yards and she had figured out the rigging and was sitting in the stern with her hand on the tiller. By the time she turned into the wind, she was a quarter of a mile away. The little skiff was not blessed at all, and would only hold about a thirty-degree tact sailing against the wind. She knew it was possible because Connor demonstrated the seaworthiness of *Blessed by the Wind* the previous day.

After floundering several times, she was skillfully tacking back and forth, working her way up the bay. By four bells, she was well north of the ship.

Turning south with the wind at her back, she slid smoothly toward the port side of the ship and hoisted a black pirate's flag with the skull and crossbones. The seaman who cast her off had thrown the flag into the skiff. Lily yelled, "Heave to lubbers, or I'll blow your sorry arses out of the water."

Connor just smiled, but the four seamen and the boatswain who stood by with one of the tenders in case Lily got into trouble whooped back as one, "Take ye to hell pirate, we be the *Blessed* and we ain't no easy mark." The girl was a natural-born sailor, and Connor and crew were amazed at how much of the seamen's slang she had picked up in just one day. With a great deal of parental pride, they all thought, "The hell with the parents, this girl belongs to us."

By eight bells, Lily had circled the ship three times, spewing pirate threats. Already with a sense of time at sea, she put in just at eight bells. Tying off on the port side, she scrambled up the ladder and over the bulwarks the happiest kid in the world. Her parents were up, still sick, but recovering quickly without the rolling seas. Getting over the dread of the morning when they heard Lily's scream and saw her set adrift, their feeling turned to jealousy when Lily skipped across the deck and grabbed Conner in the best bear hug an eight-year-old could muster.

Connor released the crew that was holding back and lowered the second tender off the starboard side. Aaden noticed that the tenders were bigger with higher gunwales than usual, and in minutes he could see why. The thwarts were released and laid on the flat floor. In less than a minute, the tender converted into a cargo boat. From behind him, he heard a strange thumping sound, and a whiskey keg shot up out of a hatch just behind and to the side of the mainmast. There was a similar hatch on the other side of the mainmast. Four seamen swung the keg past the end of a beam that had been swung down from the mainmast that had a pulley at the end. They draped the rope holding the keg over the pulley and swung the beam, so the keg was over the tender. Connor signaled the purser at the bulwark who was working a brass lever, and the keg lowered into a saddle at the bottom of the cargo boat. Five more kegs finished the load, the mast and sail raised, and the last seaman swung down on a lanyard and landed straddling a keg. Riding low in the water with the boatswain at the rudder and the purser next to him making notes in a leather-bound notebook, the whiskey boat headed for the docks of Dover. The whole operation took less than five minutes.

Aaden looked down the hatch and saw a steam-driven hoist. Connor walked up behind him and asked, "Would you like a tour of the rest of the ship now?" They headed down the small hatch where Connor explained the workings of the steam hoist. There was a high-pressure boiler amidships and two steam-driven winches on either side of the mainmast. Under each hatch and below the winch deck were two sets of double wooden rails where a single whiskey drum lay waiting to be hoisted up through the hatch above. Conner explained with pride that the boiler was a closed system with a seawater-cooled condenser below the waterline under the floor. "She doesn't make a bit of telltale steam even on the coldest day. If the steam isn't going through the engines, it is blown off down into the bottom of the condenser. The boiler burns coal, and there is only a wee bit of smoke when we first start the fire. The smoke is exhausted up through the port ventilator on the deck."

"This is amazing!" Aaden exclaimed, "What's behind the bulkhead behind the boiler?" Conner walked over and worked a lever behind the coal bin and pushed it forward on its hidden coasters to reveal a low door in the wall.

In a room about twenty feet long and as wide as the beam sat two complicated cannons of a type Aaden had never seen before; the forward cannon faced starboard, and the aft one faced to port. Now Conner got excited and wanted to get on with his dissertation on what was the pride of the ship but paused to introduce a middle-aged man who stood up between the guns a wrench held in his greasy hand. "This is Max McGregor of Aberdeen, and this is my brother Aaden," Connor said. "Max is the inventor of these guns." In the dim light of four whale oil lamps hanging in the compartment, the two men shook hands.

Aaden hadn't seen Max on the ship yet and wasn't around the seamen's mess the night before or at breakfast that morning. "Max lives with his guns," Conner explained. "I'm going to let him explain the workings here to you while I look to a few matters topside."

Aaden learned that his father commissioned Max some years before to build a better naval gun, one that would be much more powerful than the common front-loading cannon of the day. While it took two months to build one gun, it had taken several years to build the machine tools that could rifle the barrels and make the complicated interrupted-screw breechblock that allowed the gunners to load a shell from the back instead of the front of the piece. Max rotated a heavy lever at the back of the port gun about a quarter turn and pulled back the center of the breach and easily rotated the apparatus to the side on a hinge mounted on the side of the barrel.

"These are the first of their kind lad, state-of-the-art, ahead of their time and will change naval warfare forever when your dad can mass produce them." Max went on to explain the breech-loader and rifling gave a muzzle velocity at least twice as fast as a smooth bore front loader. He went to the front of the gun and held the lantern in front of the bore so Aaden could sight down the barrel. "What does it shoot," Aaden asked. Max reached over to the wall and slid back a metal door, and what looked like a very large bullet about six inches in diameter rolled into a tray in front of the door.

"It took longer to get this shell right than it took to develop the gun," Max explained as he lifted the shell into the breach and closed it. "We first tested them, dropping them down an abandoned mine shaft on an iron mine, but the testing led to some bad decisions because we couldn't match the velocity that we got with these guns.

"You're not going to shoot it here!" Aaden said as he looked on in horror. "There isn't even a gun port!"

"Not to worry lad, these shells are difficult to make and cost a small fortune to produce. We only have twenty for each gun. There's no powder behind the shell nor a primer in the firing mechanism." As for the gun port, he set the lantern on a shelf on the wall revealing a square hole in the hull a little taller than the lamp. "The holes are covered on the outside with several layers of tarred canvas and sealed watertight with rosin. There is no need to uncover the gun ports before firing. The muzzle blast blows the cover completely away."

Aaden said, "Tell me about the shells."

"Ahhh!" Max said. "Now there is a wonder of science and engineering in itself. We had to keep the shell strong enough to penetrate the side of a man-of-war ship, but we wanted a shell that would explode inside the target. It took years to get the impact fuse right, and we didn't get it right until we had a real gun to shoot it in. We make the fuse out of the coarsest powder we could find. Your cousin James Drewry, our ship's purser, invented a way to grind gunpowder finer than flour, and that is what fills the rest of the shell. When it works right, the shell explodes about four to ten feet inside the hull of the target. For a wee bit of extra fun, a mate in the machine shop learned how to machine a magnesium ribbon off a plate made in an electrolytic cell; he burned down two machine shops before he slowed the cutting machine down far enough not to ignite the ribbon. The shell is lined with the magnesium ribbon, and the ribbon burns white-hot as it spreads out with the shrapnel. The copper rings are annealed and slid onto the casings before the shell is assembled. The back of the shell is screwed on after the loading is complete."

"Oh, by the way," Max went on. "Never come down here when we are at battle. The vacuum created by the blast through the gun hole will suck your eardrums out unless you have one of these on." Max held up a spring clip, and ear covers fitted to a helmet. Also, when the guns fire, they slide back in the ways at their sides, and air pistons absorb the shock. You want to be well clear, and they slam back forward as fast as they recoil."

Aaden noted the heavy mechanisms were solidly bolted down to the deck. It looked like the ship must have been built around them. "How do you aim them?"

"Now that lad is the captain's doing. I am sure he will want to tell you all about the system he invented." As Aaden started to duck through the access hole, Max reached up with a hammer and rang a brass bell anchored to the ceiling. "Make sure the captain tells you about the bell," Max called as Aaden pushed the coal bin back in place and turned toward the ladder.

Topside Aaden walked to the back of the main deck. It was clear that the main hatch was set back to accommodate the gunroom. He walked down the stairs to the mess, past the galley to the cabin and checked on Anna. She was asleep on the bed facing the row of windows on the stern. He went back out and found Connor on the poop deck behind the con. "Now I've seen why you have more men aboard than it takes to operate a schooner this size," Aaden said.

Conner was excited to explain. "It takes two men to operate the big guns along with Max overseeing and watching for problems. We can fire four shells each from each gun in about ninety seconds, but then they are too hot to operate safely and have to cool for about half an hour before they can fire again. That cooling-off time might be longer when we get to the heat of the Caribbean. There are two battle stations on each side of the ship, and one on the bow and one on the stern. These battlements are mounted with swivel guns when needed, and the bow and stern gun set in a binnacle like a compass so they can swing one hundred eighty degrees. It takes eight extra men plus Max to man all the battle stations. The two men on the main deck will switch from side to side as needed. Along with the five able-bodied seamen it takes to handle the ship, the purser, the cook the two mates and myself, we are a nineteen-man crew, the deadliest crew at sea right now."

"How do you aim the guns?" Aaden asked.

"Give me a hand here, brother," Connor said as he stepped over to the starboard rail. Bending down, he pulled a handle up out of the deck. With a grunt, Connor raised a steel plate out of a recess in the deck. The two men lifted it to the vertical position, and it latched to the side of the *pulpit*, the stand that held the helm. Walking around the horseshoe-shaped rear counsel of the cockpit, Connor pulled up a similar handle from the port side deck. Taking a rope from the bulwark, he slipped a hook into the handle. Stepping behind the wheel, he motioned Aaden to come in beside him and un-battened a rope from the side of the helm. The two of them heaved on the rope, and the port side panel rose up and locked in place. Connor opened two doors in the rear console to reveal a pull handle and a small armory, including long rifles and handguns. Connor slid back a cover in the top of the console that revealed a curved glass tube filled with a green liquid similar to a level. The tube was marked every five degrees in both directions from the zero mark at the top dead center to twenty degrees in both directions. A bubble about an inch long sat dead center on the zero marks. For the final touch on what was now an armored cockpit, Connor fastened two brass aiming rails into notches on top of the side plates.

"At battle stations, the purser would be in here with me to con the boat. Sailing plumb, the big guns would hit a target at the water line at five hundred yards. Heeled over at fifteen degrees, the guns can fire up to three miles, but a hit at anything over a mile would be a damned lucky shot. When we went out to train the first time with dad aboard, I hit a rock prominence the size of a British man-of-war amidships from two miles away with the first shot. Probably a bit of luck-of-the-Irish there, but the guns are quite precise. The only problem with aiming is the guns sit seventy feet in front of the aiming rails. It's a judgment call to aim the gun that distance afore or aft of the target to compensate for the offset of the aiming rail. Max's engineers back at Aberdeen are working on a gun that will elevate and swivel along with an aiming mechanism to eliminate the guesswork needed to operate this system."

"This is a mechanical marvel," Aaden said with admiration in his voice.

"The industrial revolution is one hundred fifty years old now," Connor replied. "We haven't seen anything yet. Dad is a visionary far more than you would expect from a simple smuggler. He is going to change the world."

With that, Connor reached down and pulled the handle three times. "That is the signal for battle stations. There is a bell in the mess, one in the main hold, and one in the forecastle." He waited for about ten seconds and pulled the handle once. There was a muted pop from the forward part of the boat. "That was a percussion cap in the starboard gun; we wouldn't waste ammunition in a demonstration." He waited about five seconds and pulled the handle twice, and the muted pop sounded again. "That was the port gun. Any questions?"

"One hell of a whiskey boat," Aaden replied. "Tell me how much she will carry."

"With cutting out the space for the gunroom and having two aisles in the main hold for the rail tracks under the gun room, we are cut down to about five hundred kegs. But here is another state-of-the-art feature. For accurate handling and the gunnery, the ship must handle the same when loaded or empty. As we offload whiskey, there are tanks below the deck of the main hold one on each side of the keel; these are flooded to keep the weight of the boat the same. The centerline of gravity on the cargo changes but by-and-large that affects the handling very little."

"Next question; Is the ship profitable with nineteen men and only five hundred kegs?"

"Running whiskey won't be our only trade," Connor replied with a sly smile. "With the help of the Irish ambassador to England and the British Sea Lord himself, we will be secreting envoys to colonies or British friends or enemies all over the Globe for premium fees. Your dad expects that to be more profitable than the whiskey trade. The crew is paid a wage for every day they are away from home, and they each have a half share in the profits, paid when we return home. None of us intend to go home with empty pockets."

"One last thing; I saw your compilation of warships with all the powder magazines circled down on your desk in your cabin. I was also impressed by your complete charts of seas all over the globe. It didn't make sense for a smuggler who was going to operate between Ireland and America."

"Now you have the whole picture," Connor said as he released the portside shield. "Let's go hit up the cook for some dinner and a round of grog. I told the crew to be back by dawn and in shape to sail on the noontide. There isn't a hard drinker among them, but you can never tell what will come about with the ladies onshore."

Over dinner, Connor filled Aaden and the other travelers on the plan for the rest of the voyage. "We are stopping in Savannah, Charleston, and St. Augustine to offload the rest of the whiskey and are to then head to Jamaica to replace it with the finest rum we can buy – all white rum and no screech. Then we sail up to Havana for a port-of-call and a mail drop to the British Ambassador, then northwest and up to New Orleans. We might spend another month at sea pending no serious storms or trouble."

The next morning the crew returned with the two tenders rigged back to seats and oars. All were smiling when the captain looked them over, but there wasn't a hungover one in the lot. At eight bells, they weighed anchor and set sail for Savanna. Captain Conner figured the trip would take about five days, but after they rounded Diamond Shoals and turned southwest, the strong north wind of winter changed to the southwestern trade wind blowing up the coast. While the schooner was able to negotiate the warm but ill wind, they would soon be in the trade routes from South America to Europe; the trades would shift blowing from the east in the Caribbean, making it easy sailing to Jamaica.

The biggest threat to a whiskey ship was other bootleggers, avid to steal the cargo, or police or warships of the nations denied their lucrative liquor taxes. The *Blessed* was built to outrun most threats, but it is also deadly with a good captain and seasoned crew trained to fight any threat at a moment's notice.

PAMLICO SOUND

Rufus and Hannah were a lot better, and Connor had them standing in the bow with their eyes on the horizon when he left the bay and turned south down the coast. He let the ship run *large* with the wind at their back for about an hour, then called Aaden up to the con and said, "Help me roll this empty keg over the stern, and I'm going to show you what this wee little boat can do. We won't be firing the big guns, but I'm going to put the crew through my *rig for battle drill*. Opening the rear console, he pulled the lever for the signal bells four quick times.

Immediately every hand on the ship was running to his battle station. James and two seamen ran out of the companionway from the forecastle and up onto the poop deck. The purser took the con, and the seamen raised the shields into place and then raced back to the main deck. By the time they got there, four swivel guns were mounted in sockets in the bulwarks, two on each side of the main deck. The second mate set a swivel gun into a binnacle at the bow, and the first mate had one set up similarly on the stern. Connor shouted in a booming voice, "Rig for *by*."

The hands on the main deck ran to the davits and worked the rigging to loosen the topsails. The mainsail and mizzen were lowered a bit with the crew on the capstan working the rigging for the mainsail and then the aft main. The second mate worked the rigging for the three foresails himself. When all hands were back to the guns, the Purser spun the wheel to port, and the *Blessed* swung around like a racing yacht directly into the wind. "Steady as she goes," Connor commanded.

Aaden was amazed and thought the ship was going just to be blown backward in the sea once the forward momentum bled off, but that didn't happen. The purser had the ship about fifteen degrees off the wind, and the rudder almost hard to port. The boat slowed and then made slow progress directly into the wind. Looking up Aaden could see that the sails were now lifting instead of pulling. Connor explained, "The aerodynamics and hydrodynamics of making a boat sail into the wind like this are difficult to explain, but the concept has been at work in the Mediterranean for thousands of years. It took a lot of research and several prototypes that were good, but couldn't quite make it dead into the wind. The *Blessed* is the first boat of its size that accomplished it. It will make about two knots against the wind, three if we have time to trim the sails to work better with the wind," Connor explained.

Aaden asked about the how fast the ship had spun about. Connor went on to explain that the keel was short and made of cast iron the same shape as a racing skiff. The rudder is also steel and extends down below the stern six feet to make the bottom of the rudder even with the bottom of the keel. Sailing into the wind, the two of them together hold the boat steady, so the wind coming over the sails creates the lift just like a bird's wing. When the lift on the sails overcomes the drag on the hull, the boat moves forward.

It took nearly ten minutes to sail upwind, but when they were abreast of the keg on the port side, Connor boomed out the command, "Repel boarders." The port guns on the main deck and the ones on the bow and stern boomed simultaneously, shredding the keg. "The swivel guns have two-inch bores,and have opening breaches. They can shoot a single lead ball or a charge of quarter-inch lead shot. One gun can shred a longboat and kill most of the occupants. The guns can fire six rounds a minute. No one will ever get close to the ship. "Secure battle stations and rig for *large*," Connor boomed out.

As fast as the battle stations had gone up, they came down. When the seamen lowered the shields, Connor told Aaden to gather up the passengers and meet him in the mess. When assembled, Connor explained that he didn't expect a sea battle on this voyage, but you need to understand what to do when we are at battle stations. Leading them down the companionway to the cabins under the poop deck, he opened a hatch in the floor. Stairs were leading down about ten feet to a square compartment at the bottom. "When we go to battle stations, you all need to come down here. It's below the waterline, so you will have a degree of protection given a direct hit from a cannonball."

Lily protested, "I won't come down here. I want to be on deck."

"Little lady," Connor answered calmly, "Up on deck, it will be life and death for the crew. Rufus, you're in charge of getting her down here. I can't have a non-combatant loose on the decks if we have to fight the ship." Rufus nodded his understanding. "One more thing, two sets of five bells mean abandon ship, three bells signal battle stations; four is a drill. Two sets of five bells, no matter what the cause, means to abandon ship. Rufus, you and your family go to the starboard tender. Aaden, you and the ladies, go to port. The crew will be there to take care of you, and they won't leave the ship until you're safe aboard the tenders. So, step lively, so their lives are not at risk any more than necessary."

The somber passengers made their way up the stairs and back out onto the main deck. Hanna wasn't feeling so good down in the confines of the safehold and made her way back up to the bow to watch the horizon. Anna and Denise retired to the captain's cabin, and Aaden headed to the galley. Rufus was lecturing Lily, who was standing steadfast with her hands on her hips and her jaw set in a hard line; the teenage years appeared to be arriving early. Aaden came out of the galley with a sandwich and said, "Lily, how would you ever expect to be a good mate on a ship if you can't follow the captain's orders." Lily looked to soften her stance a bit but didn't show even a trace of acceptance.

In three days, they were around the knob of Diamond Shoals. Max wanted to put in somewhere as soon as possible because, during the drill, one of the gunners stumbled in the dark and falling, broke the handle off the air pump used to keep the recoil system up to pressure. It could wait until their next port of call, but Conner turned west and entered the Pamlico Sound through the barrier islands that separated the Sound from the Atlantic. He knew Hanna could use another break on calmer waters, and he knew Lily would revel in the pirate history of Bath, seventy-five miles inland. He had read in an account of the pirate era, that the house where Blackbeard lived and the tavern where he drank, was still standing.

It took the rest of the day to sail across Pamlico Sound. Connor had a man on the bow with a sounding line, and he had trimmed the ship down so they could maneuver quickly if the waters turned shallow. It was nearly dark when they got to the little village. There was a small eight-gun brig that had seen better days tied off on the end of the dock and some small sloops tied along the pilings. None of the boats looked well-kept, and the seamen made numerous jokes about the sad repair of the ragtag fleet. Connor let the wind take them several hundred yards back down the inlet and anchored on the far side of the channel.

With four seamen at the oars and one barrel of whiskey, they put the tender into the dock and tied off. The crew stayed with the boat, armed with Ferguson rifles and revolvers. As the men stepped ashore, they primed the flintlock rifles and stood at the ready. Connor, Aaden, and Max went looking for the blacksmith, Lily staying close to the three men. Rufus and Hannah wouldn't come ashore in such a remote area of a slave state. Anna and her mother would go ashore in the morning if they went ashore at all.

They found the blacksmith shop closed. A young boy, a black slave, was watching the shop and told them that the blacksmith was in the tavern a few doors up the street. There were about a dozen rough-looking men in the tavern, most of them already drunk. The room was dim with several lamps burning behind the bar and one out by a collection of mismatched tables and chairs. The air was heavy with tobacco smoke and feculent with the smell of the unwashed. The men around the tables looked as bad as the room smelled. Silence fell as the new arrivals stood by the door. Faces from all the continents stared, some with curiosity, some with wicked smiles and some with outright malice.

The blacksmith was obvious with his callused hands, massive forearms, and bulging biceps standing at the bar. He, too, was drunk, but not as far gone as the rest of the motley patrons, all who eyed the well-dressed new-comers. Aaden and Max walked over to the blacksmith to see if he would open the shop, and Connor started to negotiate with the tavern owner to sell him the barrel of whiskey on the tender. That deal made after some intense haggling; Connor left with about half a dozen staggering patrons to get the barrel off the tender. Aaden and Max gave up on the blacksmith, but he at least agreed to do their work first thing in the morning.

As the three turned to the door, one of the drunks rose and got in Aaden's way. Pointing at Lily, he said, "I'll give you a Spanish gold doubloon for the *niglet* there hiding behind yah." Aaden stared the man down, and Max slipped his hands into his pockets. When Aaden said nothing, the drunk pulled two doubloons from his pocket and held them up to sweeten the offer,

"Solid gold with the king of Spain on um, look for yourself." Aaden didn't take the coins nor did he say anything; he just shifted his feet a bit ready for a fight.

The drunk in front of him wasn't a small man, and he looked like he had been in more than one barroom fight, some of which he came off worse for the wear. Aaden said calmly, "You don't want a piece of our trouble mate, make way." Aaden brushed by the drunk as Lily ran around him and out the door. Looking back for Max to follow, a bowie knife thrown from the back of the room hit the door jamb with a deadly thwack and split it a few inches in front of Aaden's face.

"I said I want to buy the *niglet*," said the drunk as the remainder of the men were standing, acting ready for some action. Aaden stepped back toward the drunk and decked him with a massive uppercut. Max drew two Colt-Patterson 0.36 caliber revolvers out of his jacket pockets and leveled the guns at the rest of the drunks. Most of the derelicts had never seen a revolver before, but it didn't take many smarts to recognize the guns as deadly weapons. Those that could count to five realized the guns held enough bullets to kill all of them twice. Slowly all the drunks sat down, and the atmosphere turned heavier with frowns and hatred. The man with the two doubloons was still standing and said, "We'll settle this in the morning."

The blacksmith edged over with his palms up in a sign of peace and gently ushered Max and Aaden out of the tavern and down the street to his shop. Aaden pulled the bowie knife out of the jam as he walked by the door. He slipped it into his belt, careful not to cut the belt or himself with the razor-sharp blade.

"That's a bad un to mess with," the blacksmith said. "His name is William Knapp." As he readied the forge and set his "boy" to building up the fire, he said, "I'll have your handle fixed up by morning, but you better get out of here for tonight. The swilled arse you decked over there is the captain of the old brig out by the dock. He won't let this pass. There are about a hundred men around here who will come to his beck-and-call to steal, smuggle or plunder. Most of the boats out there on the dock belong to them. You should lay off in the bay, maybe a little off to the west. I'll row out with the handle at first light; you can meet me there then be on your way." After a pause, "Tell me, is the girl a slave?"

Lily stepped out from behind Aaden, assumed her most defiant stance, and with her fists doubled up on her hips, said, "I am a free woman of the United States of America." She remembered the words Anna had written in the Bible and spoke them well with a loud commanding voice.

Taken aback, the blacksmith said, "And right you are, little lady. I think that I will free my boy here when he's big enough to take care of himself." Turning to Aaden, he asked, "Tell me if I were to free him right now would you take him with you? He's already a good blacksmith, he needs to fill out a bit of muscle, and he'll be good as me."

Conner was back with the men from the tavern and two crewmen from the tender, armed with Ferguson rifles, standing guard over the whiskey. The drunks from the bar were badly in need of a break. Some were sitting on the keg, and the others stood around, breathing hard. Hard work was not their forte.

Connor overheard the blacksmith and walked over to the young negro and asked, "What's your name, son?"

"Benjamin Franklin," said the boy proudly, "I can read and write too. Mr. Higgins, there has had me since I was a baby, and he taught me well. If he turns me free, I will probably be beaten to death right here in the street by the goons of the slavers. I'll work hard for you, and I hate leaving Mr. Higgins, but I need to get out of here before they kidnap me off to a farm or kill me."

Connor looked to Aaden, who gave him a wink and said, "You can join the crew, and you will be put off a free man in New Orleans. Wait here; I have to deliver some whiskey, and then we'll go back to the ship."

While Higgins started packing up some things for Ben to take with him, Aaden took Connor aside and said, "Let the drunks take the whiskey. We need to get back aboard *Blessed* and lay up for the night further up the bay. There's going to be some trouble. Higgins is going to row out with the handle in the morning."

Higgins gave Ben a long fatherly hug and said, "Take care, son, and don't forget me. Slavery won't last forever. Come back when you can, and I'll stand you a drink over at the tavern, and you can tell me about your adventure." With tears running down his cheeks, he turned to Connor and said, "Take care Captain, Knapp believes he's a reincarnated pirate, and he is sure to come after you. Unless you're sailing a warship, I would fear for your life."

Lily walked up to Higgins and hugged him, then the shore party turned and led the boy down to the docks with Ben chattering away about William Knapp and his exploits, crimes, and the smuggling business that Knapp and his men ran in the open out of the old pirate's lair of Bath. The smuggling included blacks, most of them free Negroes kidnapped from free-states up north. Connor took it all in walking with his arm around Ben's shoulders. He knew from experience that Ben was nervous about leaving and was putting up a brave front, trying not to break down, having left the only father he had known. Higgins raised the boy well, but it was his greatest and kindness act as a parent and mentor to set the young man free. "That couldn't have been easy," Aaden commented as the shore party loaded back into the tender.

Connor took Higgins' advice, and when they reached the ship, he put the other tender in the water. With the wind and the tide against them, the two strong boat crews turned the schooner and towed her out of the inlet. Connor wanted to raise some sail to move west in the bay, but the men in the boats argued they needed the exercise and to just let them pull the *Blessed* up the bay about a mile. Again, at anchor, Connor doubled the watch and had the swivel guns mounted, manned and ready.

In the first light of dawn, Higgins was in his rowboat off the mouth of the Bath inlet. Already rigged for light sailing, Connor raised anchor and made for the blacksmith. Laying by, Connor took Higgins on board. The handle for the air pump was brand new, made of fine steel, unlike the cast iron original. Max pulled a ten-dollar gold piece out of his pocket to pay Higgins. "You have paid me enough," Higgins said as he pulled Ben to him with his strong arm around the boy's shoulders, "I won't take your money. But be careful, Knapp will be blocking the ship channel down by Indian Island. That's his favorite place to ambush unarmed merchants."

Higgins eyed the swivel guns and said, "Those are no match a broadside from four-pound cannons. He probably can't sink you with his hung-over gunners, but he can hurt you badly if you try to sail past him. I wish you were a warship. It would be good to get rid of him and his lot for good."

"Not to worry," said Connor, "We won't be the ones going to the bottom."

Higgins gave Ben his last farewell hug kissing him on the cheek like the good father he was. "Go with God, son, and don't forget to write."

Higgins spun on his heel and was over the bulwark and casting off in the rowboat when Connor offered, "Why don't you come with us. Life isn't going to be easy for you around here after helping us." Ben's heart leaped as Higgins turned the rowboat and tied off again on the bulwark; Ben was giddy and crying with joy as he helped Higgins back onto the main deck. Connor said, "You'll be a passenger, Mr. Higgins, but you will earn your keep while you're on my ship."

"What about my tools?" Higgins asked, holding on to Ben again. "And by the way, please call me Irwin."

"Irwin, forget the tools. We will set you up when we get to the next port-of-call." "Lily, show Mr. ----- Irwin and Ben the safe hold. I expect you will be in need of it soon." With that, Connor went up to the con and quickly had the ship turned to take the wind with the crew raising the rest of the sails. One of the crew climbed the mainmast and perched straddling the spar at the top, a makeshift crow's nest for the ship's lookout, a spyglass raised to his eye.

True to form, Knapp was laid to in the ship channel about fifteen miles down the sound. The lookout reported that Knapp was *double anchored* – tied off fore and aft – to hold the brig broadside in the wind, four cannons facing the channel. "No sloops in site," the lookout called down. Connor smiled as he opened the console behind the helm and pulled three bells.

Rufus tried to usher Higgins into the mess, but Higgins stopped abruptly and yelled up to the captain, "I can fight as good as any man. I'm not hiding with the women."

"Okay," was the response. "Stay with my brother on the main deck and man a gun if we lose one of the mates." The shields were up around the con, and this time, steel plates were swung up to either side of all six swivel guns.

As the purser sailed them past Indian Island, five sloops set sail and came out to tail them down the Sound. If the *Blessed* were a slower ship, the sloops could have easily caught them, but Connor ferruled all the foresails and top-sails so he could let the sloops close to about two hundred yards by the time he was almost in range of Knapp's guns. The sloops carried ragtag men of every color and numerous nationalities. Their weapons were as varied as the men themselves. One even brandished an ancient blunderbuss over his head.

At one thousand yards, Knapp fired his first shot that fell woefully short of a traditional shot across the bow. Connor was lowering the sails to convince Knapp that he was going to stop but drifted to within five hundred yards of the brig, and turned into the wind to halt their progress. The sloops closed to a hundred yards, and the drunk that threw the knife shouted across the water, "We'll be taking the *niglet* and the blacksmith's *nigger*, or we'll put you on the bottom. I'll be wanting my knife back too."

Connor kept his eye on the port aiming rail as the *Blessed* kept turning slowly to the south. When he pulled two bells, the port gun fired, the shell taking the brig amidships about a foot above the waterline. The shell exploded under the main deck, and instantly the *Blessed* turned the brig into the ship of the *Damned*. The main deck of the brig heaved up, and the little ship broke cleanly in two halves. The magnesium shrapnel looked like a fourth of July star shell as everything left afloat was burning, and the two halves sank into the sound. "Holy Mother of God," Higgins intoned, watching the carnage. He wasn't the only one impressed. Lily had snuck back up the stairs in the dark and was watching from a porthole in Denise's cabin. She didn't care that she would catch hell when Rufus discovered she was gone.

Connor turned toward the sloops and gave the command, "Repel boarders." As one, two swivel guns barked and shredded the boat the knife thrower was on. They took the second boat before the stunned crews could turn around and catch the wind to flee. The few thugs that knew how to swim were diving off the boats as the third boat was raked broadside. The swivel guns raked the last two boats from the rear, killing everyone left aboard.

Connor ordered the first mate to cut loose Higgins's rowboat for the survivors among the wreckage. Calling, "Secure from battle stations," the purser turned the unscathed schooner to take the wind and turned the con back over to the Captain. As they slid past the remainder of the burning wreckage, Connor uttered a grim eulogy for Knapp and his mates, "Burn in hell asshole. I'll keep me *niggers* a bit longer if you please." Aaden heard the eulogy and drew the bowie knife out of his belt and was going to throw it into the middle of the burning wreckage then thought better of it. He would give it to Lily later, less she never forget her visit to Bath.

Late in the day when they made the open sea outside the shoals, Connor wrote in the ship's log that he was pronouncing Benjamin Franklin Higgins of Bath, North Carolina, a free man of the United States, June 15th year of our Lord 1841. Anna had written an *Affidavit of Freedom* to that effect in her beautiful hand, and all the passengers and crew signed it, congratulating Ben, the men shaking his hand and the women affectionately hugging the young man. Hanna noticed that Lily held the embrace a bit too long.

As the ship made its way tacking against the trades, the cook served a meal of fried chicken, mashed potatoes, and gravy. Connor wondered where she could have gotten chickens while at anchor off of Bath, and Aaden thought here is another woman he would never underestimate again.

Back at sea, the passengers and crew settled back into the routine of the ship: mess three times a day with watches changing every four hours, and the antics of Ben and Lily. A mate hanging over the side of the bulwark in a boatswain's chair replaced the cover on the port gun.

All-in-all, during the week it took to sail to Savannah, Georgia, the passengers became seasoned sailors. Hanna was over the seasickness and joined the cook preparing magnificent meals. Higgins spent his time with Max, learning every part of the boiler and steam winch. When the boatswain was free, he was teaching Ben and Lily every knot he knew. When they were proficiently tying the knots in the daylight on the deck, he got them tying them in the dark of the safehold.

Anna spent most of her day with Denise in the captain's cabin. Anna was writing a detailed account of her life in France and New York. Denise was teaching Ben and Lily math, English, and basic French with which they would benefit by in Louisiana. It was hard to get the youngsters away from the lure of the ship, but Rufus and Higgins would round them up every afternoon for at least two hours of class. Every evening the passengers retired to a chorus of sea shanties played rather expertly by crew members on several harmonicas and a fiddle. Every night finished with a seaman's prayer and Amazing Grace as the passengers retired to their quarters.

Life was good aboard the *Blessed* with the encounter in Pamlico Sound well behind them. Connor, ever wary of passing ships, the weather, and every detail of the ship and crew, intended to keep it that way. He knew that many a happy, complacent ship fell prey to the awesome power of the sea while sailing with the illusion of safety rather than constant vigilance.

PORTS OF CALL

It took six days of sailing to cover the three hundred fifty miles to the first port of call, Savannah, Georgia. The *Blessed* was contracted before it left Ireland to deliver to Savannah, Jacksonville, and St. Augustine on its way south to Jamaica. Selling whiskey was the legitimate side of the business with shipments paid for and insured by Lloyds of London for delivery.

As Conner turned the *Blessed* into the mouth of the Savannah River, he trimmed sails to slow and carefully make way up the river to the docks. Traffic on the river was heavy, with cotton and rice being shipped down the river and goods and materials moving up the river, arriving from the industrial north and ports all over the world. Arriving at the docks of the Georgia Inland Freight Company, they had to stand off for a day before there was a berth free. Connor and James went ashore to conclude the business with the freight company and the bank. Ben and Lily took the skiff for a day of sailing up and down the river and did some fishing. While Georgia was still a slave state, Savannah was a free city. Rufus and Hannah, along with Irwin Higgins, had little concern for the youngsters to be away from the safety of the ship as long as they stayed in sight. Bigger ships filled the river waiting to unload at the docks. The little skiff could go up and down to the docks, a couple of miles away from the ship, and still be within sight.

Ben and Lily found a good place to fish on the north shore across from the *Blessed* and had enough fresh fish for dinner by the early afternoon. Largemouth bass seemed to be voraciously hungry, and large schools of bream could be seen from time to time in the clear water of the Savannah. Lily asked, "I wonder what it would be like to swim in a school of fish."

Ben replied, "Mr. Higgins taught me how to swim."

"You can swim! How did he teach you?"

With that, Ben grabbed Lily, and with a wicked smile, threw her into the river. She went completely under but surfaced with a frantic dog paddle trying to stay afloat and make it back to the boat. As she pulled up on the side of the skiff, Ben pushed her back in. After several rounds of this Ben just jumped in with her. Grabbing Lily around the waist to hold her up, he said, "Relax now, you're not going to drown. Grab onto the stern there, stretch out and kick your feet up and down." After about five minutes, Ben said, "Now watch me." With a smooth arm-over-arm stroke, Ben swam around the skiff several times. "Now you," was his next instruction, "I'll be right with you, so please give it a try."

Trusting Ben, Lily pushed off and flailing away with her arms sank below the water. Ben pulled her up and said, "You forgot to kick." On the second try, Lily made some headway, and by the time she made it three times around the skiff, she was doing reasonably well. Ben let her rest holding on again and said, "Now one last thing, and it's the hardest part. You have to put your face down in the water and lift your head to breath with every stroke." Lily gave it her best try and came up spitting water and coughing. "You have to work on the timing. Don't open your mouth to breathe in until you are sure it's above the water." Again, and again Lily pushed off, and after about an hour, she finally got it and swam a long victory lap about fifty feet away from the skiff. Her strokes were still a little clumsy, but like everything else Lily set out to do, she knew how to swim by the time they headed back to the ship.

Sending the catch up took four to five full buckets hoisted up by the cook. Hannah helping with the fish, said, "I see you have been playing in the water." Ben assured her they were only cooling off in the shallows, but Hanna eyed Lily with the skeptical eye only a mother could manage.

By the time Connor and the purser were back in the late afternoon, Hannah and Ben were completely dry. As Connor climbed over the bulwark, Lily said, "Watch this." Turning, she jumped into the water. She went under for what seemed like a long time and came up screaming, "Help! Help!" reverting to her frantic dog paddle to finish up the ruse by spitting out a mouthful of the water, yelling, "I'm drowning!"

Connor was up on the bulwark and with a graceful dive dove in to save the hapless girl. When he came back up to the surface, Lily was about ten feet away, swimming toward the bow. Connor set out to catch the little charlatan but found that she was doing fine and not that easy to catch. He let Lily swim all the way around the boat and then with a few strong strokes caught up with her and gave her a good dunking. Hanna came out on deck about then and screamed, "Stop him. He's drowning her." But then Connor was pulled under the surface. Both of the swimmers bobbed up laughing and made their way to the ladder and climbed aboard.

"How did you learn to swim"? Connor asked.

"It was the Higgins' method," Lilly explained without further elaboration and went to her cabin for some dry clothes. Ben just smiled broadly, and Connor gave him two thumbs up. Later that night, the passengers and crew feasted on fresh river fish; Lily excitedly telling everyone how she learned to swim that day.

The next morning a slip was vacated, and the *Blessed* was pulled in under a steam-driven crane. Two hundred drums unloaded in about three hours with the dockside crane working directly through the two hatches on the deck. The contracted delivery completed and paid for with letters of transfer between the bank for Inland Georgia Freight and accounts in London. Connor noted the transaction in the ship's log, and the purser as well noted the delivery on the manifest for the cargo and calculated the profits and noted each crew member's share in his ledger.

Higgins and Max had gone ashore at first light to find a forge. They were on the dock waiting for the crane to finish unloading the kegs. They stood by a cargo wagon filled with the makings of a well-equipped ship's forge along with pipes, flanges, valves, and billets of steel of all shapes. Max had the team unhitched, and the driver returned with them to the city. The drawbar was detached and lashed to the side of the wagon. It was a maximum load for the crane, but the entire wagon was lifted down onto the deck and maneuvered to the front of the cargo hold. The crew set to lashing the wagon securely to the bulwarks on each side of the deck. Connor was uneasy if Max and Higgins were planning to fire up the blacksmith's shop up at sea. Fire aboard ship was confined safely to the galley stove and the whale oil hurricane lamps used at night or below decks when needed. Max's intent became clear when six or seven crew lifted a steam-driven bilge pump out of the wagon.

Done with Savannah, the ship was backed out into the river by a small steam paddleboat and raising light sail, slowly started the trip down the river to the open sea. The *Blessed* set course for the next port-of-call, Jacksonville,

Florida. Jacksonville was only one hundred twenty miles down the coast, but Connor tacked southeast about fifty miles and then tacked to the southwest and expertly came to the mouth of the St. Johns River, the access to the Jacksonville port about fifteen miles inland. The wind was directly from the south, which made navigating the north-flowing river more difficult. Connor anchored in the calm waters in the mouth of the river and loaded both tenders with six barrels of whiskey each. They set sail up the lazy river to the dock of the St. Johns International Freight Company, Connor in one tender and James in the other. It was a wise decision not to take the schooner into the river. Traffic was heavy, with some large merchantmen making their way down the river on the favorable wind. The small, agile tenders could easily manage the tacking back and forth it took to work their way up to the docks, darting back and forth between the merchantmen and other vessels. It would take five more trips with both boats to complete the delivery, but that was the decision made by all after reaching the docks. With the south wind and the traffic, the river was no place for the schooner.

When the tenders returned to the schooner in the late afternoon, Max and Higgins had the forge loaded on a tender, and they put into the beach to set it up where there was ample driftwood for fuel and no danger of fire to the ship. The first step in installing the bilge pump was to make the steel mounts that would bridge two ribs in the rudder compartment, beneath and to the rear of the safe hold. Higgins and Ben worked into the night under the watchful eye of Max, constantly measuring and checking as the heavy mounts emerged out of solid billets of steel. Lily made frequent trips back and forth, taking food and water to the team onshore and occasionally bringing Max back to the ship for more measurements and checking. By midnight the two mounts were finished, and by first light, the crew secured the mounts to the ribs in the rudder hold.

After the first mess, the tenders were reloaded and set sail to the port. Max and Ben disassembled the bilge pump, and piece by piece, it was passed down the small hatch into the rudder compartment and reassembled on the mounts. The forward bilge in the rudder compartment was the deepest part of the hull and the ideal place for the pump suction. The pump itself was a converted walking beam double cylinder pump. One of the cylinders had been removed and replaced with a reciprocating steam piston. The pump just fit into the tight confines of the compartment.

Higgins was down below the main hold. Several planks had been removed, exposing the keel and the ribs of the ship. He was joining lengths of pipe to run live steam to the pump and return the spent steam to the condensate sump by the boiler. The steam pipe was one-inch in diameter, and the condensate return was two inches. The pipes came in oddball lengths from four to ten feet long. Each pipe had grooves cut into both ends. Two pipes joined with a coupling that covered their grooved ends. A coupling was applied red hot, and as it shrunk upon cooling, it seized both pipes making a watertight seal. To ensure that the joint could never blow apart, the ends of the collar were hammered down in a crimp to close over the grooves in the pipes.

The procedure was hot, demanding work. Ben was up on deck with the forge heating the collars to a yellow heat. When Irwin was ready down below, Ben would take a collar out of the fire and toss it down to a seaman who caught it in a metal bucket. Higgins would remove it with a pair of tongs, slip it over the end of the last pipe on the run, and two seamen would drive the new pipe in shoving or pounding it home if necessary, with a block of wood and a sledgehammer. Pounding the malleable collar down over the first groove went easily as the seamen rotated the pipe. If they worked fast, the collar was still a dull red by the time Irwin finished with the first groove. The second one took much longer because the metal cooled and was much harder to work. It would take two to three minutes to the hammer collar on the second groove, then the pipe would be pushed aft through the bilges, and the process would start over again. There was a seaman under the deck to lift the flanged end of the pipe over the ribs of the hull as pipe by pipe the run made its way to the rudder compartment. When the pipeline was complete, flanges on both ends remained, and the connections to the pump and boiler were plumbed with fittings. The only difficult task after that would be fashioning the pump suction and discharge. Max was counting on getting those parts made at an on-shore blacksmith shop in St. Augustine.

The tenders made three trips into Jacksonville harbor the first day. By six bells the second day, the delivery was complete. With the tenders raised on their davits, Connor gave the order to raise sails, and the *Blessed* was bound for St. Augustine. The wind had shifted to the west, so it wasn't necessary to tack out to sea and back to sail south down the coast. While it made for smooth sailing, Connor was concerned about the weather. A shift in a strong system like the trades meant there was a storm in the area to cause it. By evening though, they were safely into the St. Augustine inlet and anchored under the guns of Castillo de San Marcos. The whiskey trade would wait a day, and the crew drew lots to see who would be staying on the watch for the night. Captain, crew, and passengers went ashore to spend the night in the oldest city in the United States.

Aaden, back to his role as History Professor, acted as a tour guide through the streets of the city that the Spanish founded in 1565. Connor booked rooms for everyone in the Matanzas Hotel, but Aaden and Anna rented a carriage and took Rufus, Hannah, Ben, and Lily to Fort Mosé, known in colonial times as Gracia Real de Santa Teresa de Mosé, two miles north of the city. Under Spanish rule from 1738 till 1763, Fort Mosé was a gathering place for slaves escaping the British Colonies. Slaves were given freedom upon reaching the fort; the able-bodied males were pressed into the Spanish military, and the women were settled in the area around the fort. Aaden checked his *free blacks* into the Joy of Teresa, a *black hotel*. It was a nice enough establishment with a good dining room but lacked the amenities of the Matanzas. Aaden told Lily and Ben that while at Fort Mosé, he wanted them to learn the important role the fort played in black freedom in early America. He kidded that there would be a test when they got back to the ship. Everyone laughed, but Lily, in particular, resented the separation from the rest of the crew and passengers, whom she now thought of as her family.

Over dinner at the *white hotel,* Aaden ran through the entire history of St. Augustine. He railed against the government in Washington, D.C., changing the name of the Castillo de San Marcos to Fort Marion. After all, history was history; if you didn't respect it, you had to relive it, but it wasn't likely that Florida would ever again fall under the Spanish or British flags. Several army officers sitting close by obviously took exception to Aaden's viewpoint but chose not to challenge what looked like a well-led superior force. The officers spent their time ogling Anna and Denise. Caitlín, the cook aboard the *Blessed,* who wasn't a bad looking woman herself, was the only one in the party that noticed the unwanted attention. She leaned over and elbowed Aaden in the side and said in a low playful voice, "You better keep an eye on your ladies, son." Aaden, who had assimilated the good looks of his wife and mother-in-law, was oblivious to the meaning of her whispered warning. He looked around the dining hall and finally spotted the Army men after Caitlín was quite amused to point them out while shaking her head with her best exasperated sad look, an obvious comment on the stupidity of men.

Happy and sated with a fine meal of lobsters, shrimp, and the-catch-of-the-day, the *Blessed* contingent retired to their rooms for the night. Some of the mates excused themselves politely and went in search of more grog and the pleasures of the night the city had to offer.

The next day the remainder of the whiskey was offloaded at the docks of the Matanzas Bay Freight Company. Old-timers and the manager of the freight company advised Connor to lie to in the harbor for several days. It was a tropical storm or a hurricane that was blowing off the Gulf of Mexico onto the western shore of Florida that caused the shift in the trade wind. Connor heeded the advice and anchored in the south end of the bay well away from other ships. The passengers were put safely ashore, and the crew went about battening down the ship for a heavy blow. Max was down in the rudder compartment, installing the suction on the bilge pump and routing the discharge line out the side of the ship above the waterline. Max and Higgins had the four-inch cast iron pipes fabricated in a small shipyard in St. Augustine. The pipes and fittings were well beyond what they could accomplish in the small ship's forge. The second day they were at anchor, the pipes arrived, and the mate that operated the small steam-driven cargo boat from the shipyard again warned, "We're in for a bad one." Aaden, fearing this storm warning would come true, went ashore in the skiff and gathered up all the passengers and took them to the Episcopal Trinity Church and stayed there with them to weather the storm.

That night the storm swept in from the west and lived up to the foretelling of the old-timers. Gale force winds quickly kicked up, and four-foot waves raked across the bay. Damage to the docks and smaller crafts was extensive. Massive trees that lined the bay were blowing down, and flying debris damaged the schooner. First, the storm blew from the north, then the east, swinging the ship around on its anchor. After about six hours, the wind shifted to the south and died. Connor figured they had been south of the eye of the storm and was relieved when the sun rose again on a tranquil bay. The only benefit he could think of from the passing storm was that Max got to test the bilge pump for real.

The first mate put a tender in the water and sailed up the bay looking for the passengers. He found them standing on the quay in front of the Plaza de la Constitución with the spires of their refuge from the storm still standing behind them. Happily, the shore party boarded the small boat. As they turned out into the bay to make their way back to the south, Lily looked back at the marketplace building on the north end of the Plaza. She couldn't explain the bad feelings she had when they had walked through the ancient market building on the way from the church to the quay. Some years later, she would learn that the building was named – *The Slave Market*.

Back on the *Blessed*, life quickly returned to the normal routine of shipboard life. Repairs were completed, and by eight bells, the sails were raised, and they set to sea. Once safely offshore and with Lily at the con, Connor called a meeting of the mates, Max and Higgins. Sitting around the table in the mess, the cook served strong coffee, and the meeting turned to a discussion of what they would do if they met such a storm at sea. Connor could see that although they didn't mean to, the lull of the now quiet seas soothed their anxieties of the stormy past. Aaden piped up, "The Greeks used sea anchors as early as the seventh century to stabilize ships at sea during heavy storms in the Mediterranean." The bit of history set everyone to thinking about what they had on the ship that they could fabricate into a sea anchor.

Higgins provided an easy solution, "We could use the cargo wagon." The next day's work was organized to accomplish that, and everyone retired for the night excited about the adventures of the next port, the angst of meeting a hurricane at sea arrested for the moment.

TRIAL BY STORM

While the bay was calm after the storm, the open ocean was still rough. Lily was struggling to keep the ship on a course of 120°; a mate would pitch in and help if the helm got unwieldy. Connor's crew meeting went on for several hours, and the *Blessed* was well out of sight of land by the time the captain came up to ask Lily a strange question. "Where are we?"

Not wanting to be caught short without an answer, Lily replied, "Three hours and twenty minutes out of St. Augustine on a course of 120° south by east, captain."

"That's an excellent answer, but where **exactly** are we?"

Finally, not knowing what he was driving at, Lily answered, "I have no idea."

It's time to fix that," and opening the top of the rear console, Connor showed Lily three ornate oak boxes clad with brass corners, a heavy latch, and a brass plate with the full name of the ship engraved on them in Gaelic. There was also a chart and a *Readings Log* in the compartment, which he pointed out and said, "We'll use these in a bit. Opening the first box he carefully withdrew a complicated instrument with mirrors and a telescope and a lot of knobs for adjustments. "This is a sextant; it is how we find ourselves at sea when there are no landmarks to guide us. The second box contained a clock set to approximately the ship's clock on the pulpit, and the third box contained a clock that to Lily seemed to be set wrong. "These are chronometers, two of the most accurate made. The first clock marks the ship's time, and the second one shows us Greenwich Mean Time. Let the mate take the helm; you're going to be in navigation school for a while."

Painstakingly Connor pointed out every part of the sextant. He would then have Lily repeat the names of the parts as he pointed at each in turn. If Lily got one wrong or couldn't answer, he would tell her the correct name and start over again. At seven bells, he ended the drill and showed Lily how to use the instrument to take a sun shot. He would use the sextant to measure the angle between the sun and the horizon, set the instrument back to zero degrees and then have Lily repeat the measurement. Over and over again, Lily would measure, lock the slide on the protractor and make the fine adjustment with a micrometer till the angle was perfect. She would read the angle; Connor would check it, and they would write down the measurement and the time from the shipboard chronometer in the readings log. As she got more and more into it, rather than just rocking the sextant back and forth to set the angle precisely, Lily would sway back and forth like a Hawaiian dancer or a trumpet player reciting a slow tune. Working with the sextant was a hell of a lot better than washing dishes down in the galley.

With a reading every three minutes, Connor pointed out that the reading was increasing a bit with every measurement. Then ten minutes after eight bells, the readings started to decrease. Connor took a brass key from his pocket and set the shipboard clock to 12:00 and told the mate at the helm to mark noon, and the mate set the clock next to the compass at 12:00. Ten more readings and Connor said, "That's enough, stow the sextant and bring the chart and the chalkboard down to the mess." By the time Lily got below, Connor had the globe from his cabin, a large tome entitled *Nautical Almanac*, and a variety of rulers and calipers laid on the table. Connor unrolled the chart and was weighing down the corners when Caitrín set a cup of coffee on Connor's corner and a cup of hot cocoa on Lily's. Giving Lily an affectionate pat on the head and a conspiratorial wink to Connor she said, "Pay attention, little one. Being able to navigate well can save your life one day."

The school was in session. Lily learned about parallels and meridians, Greenwich Mean Time, arcs, and minutes. "Let's plot our position from your bearing and sailing time. Going up to the helm, Connor ordered, "Heave the log." Connor explained that the command was an old seafarer's expression when a log tethered with a rope knotted at intervals was thrown off the back of the ship, and a thirty-second *hourglass* was used to determine how many *knots* were trailed out behind the ship in thirty seconds.

"We have a more sophisticated log these days," and as Connor took the helm as the first mate opened a chest on the port rail and removed a glass ball about a foot in diameter secured with rope netting around it and a light steel plate hanging about three feet from the bottom of the netting. The first mate explained, "The steel plate acts as a sea anchor so that the float doesn't move very far in the wind. This rope the float is attached to is one hundred meters long, and we are going to time exactly how many seconds it takes for the *log* to stretch out the rope." The mate yelled, "Mark," and swung the float in a wide arc and heaved the float over the side. As the ship moved on, Jack trailed the tether rope out on the water, and when the float pulled it tight, the mate yelled, "Mark," again. Connor wrote down the time in the Readings Log, and when the float was reeled in and stowed back in its chest, Connor and Lily went down to the mess.

For the rest of the day, as the ship sailed on-and-on, Connor taught Lili how to find her position from the sailing time, the speed they measured, and the bearing they sailed. They marked that on the chart, a point fifty-seven miles on a bearing of 120°. Then they extended that to the time it took to reach noon, as per the measurement with the sextant, and marked the position of the ship as determined by *dead reckoning* – 65.5 miles down the bearing from St. Augustine. Lily asked, "Why do they call it *dead reckoning*?"

"It's an old seafarer's term. Maybe they meant you were dead if you got it wrong." Connor went on writing down step by step the complicated math used to convert the sextant readings into the true position of the ship. For accuracy, the calculations were done by hand or by using logarithm tables for multiplication and division. To hasten the lesson, Connor borrowed Max's slide rule and taught Lily how to use it. They worked through the afternoon, and Lily was surprised when Caitrín told them to clear the table for the evening meal. Lily rolled up the chart, noting that the dead reckoning and true position of the ship was off by about five nautical miles. Not a huge error but deadly if you were sailing up to a shoreline in the middle of a starless night.

Caitrín and Hanna served a remarkable meal rich with Florida cuisine. The first course was conch chowder, followed by alligator boudin and a black bean and rice salad. After everyone ate their fill, they brought out guava pie for dessert. Everyone grabbed their stomachs and moaned, but everyone also put away a generous portion of the pie. The crew and passengers retired for the night complaining about how much they ate, except for Connor and Lily, who went up with the second dog-watch to wait for sunset.

Lily retrieved the sextant case from the rear console and joined Connor sitting on some sailcloth chairs on the forecastle. As the first stars appeared, Connor was teaching about the constellations in the northern sky and in particular, the Big Dipper and the North Star. As it darkened, the North Star appeared, and Lily used the sextant to measure its angle to the rapidly disappearing horizon. Stowing the sextant, Lily went back down to the mess, and in the dim light of a whale oil lamp, she rolled out the chart and determined their latitude from the degree scales marked on the edges of the map. She was amazed that the noon reading and the north-star shot only varied by one second, a distance of only one hundred feet and some change. She worked late into the night working the math over and over again. At midnight Caitrín gently woke her and blew out the lamp. "Time for bed, Navigator," said Caitrín and led Lily back to her cabin in the dark for a well-earned good night's sleep.

Connor took in some sail to slow the ship a bit. He wanted to arrive in the area off Grand Turk Island, where the trades would be starting to shift to the west. He would take the ship down the deep channel to the west of Cockburn Town and then southwest to Jamaica. Lily was constantly at the charts, practicing sun shots and working the difficult math of navigation. Rufus looked on with pride wondering how he could ever have wound up with such a smart girl. Hanna even excused her from dish duty in the galley and encouraged her to learn everything she could.

Before dawn on the third day out, about one hundred eighty miles north of Grand Turk Island, Connor noticed a change in the seas. Ground swells built from the southeast, and at sunrise, the skies darkened to the deep gray of an oncoming storm. When the ground swells reached six feet, he turned the *Blessed* northeast, hoping to outrun the oncoming storm. The maneuver didn't work.

Two hours later and running hard, a squall line from horizon to horizon was bearing down on the ship. Connor ordered the boiler lit, and the crew went about unloading the forge wagon and rigging it with a harness to hang it by the axles behind all four wheels. The crew tied the harness to a two-inch hawser; the bitter end was passed around the outside of the boat, under the bowsprit and through the hawse holes for the anchor chain and tied off to itself on the outside of the hull to form a noose securing the wagon to the front of the ship. Connor made a mental note that the next ship his father designed to send south would be fitted with proper bitts fore and aft for fastening a sea anchor. He also had in mind the design for a sea anchor worthy of a large ship. For this storm, the makeshift drogue they fashioned out of the wagon would have to do.

When the crew was finished tying off the wagon, they lowered it into the sea with the steam winch. Connor ordered all the sails struck, and the *Blessed* turned into the wind and waves, dragging the anchor through the sea. The ship rolled wickedly from side to side as it was broadside to the ground swells. Aaden and the rest of the passengers huddled in the cabins holding on or sitting on the deck, fearing the boat would capsize and drown all aboard. But faithfully, the stalwart ship righted itself and turned straight into the wind and waves. Of all aboard, Hanna, holding Lily tight, was the most pleased she had found her sea legs and wasn't a bit ill. The crew was pleased with their captain deciding to rig for heavy seas as the ground swells built to twenty feet, and the winds went above gale force.

Connor and the first mate were the only crew topside decked out with oiled slickers and tethered to cleats on the sides of the rear transom with short lanyards. They would note the bearing every hour and hope that the storm would pass as quickly as the one in St. Augustine. James and the second spelled them every two hours, making their way to the helm on lifelines strung up and down the decks. Waves would break over the bow and run like a river down the deck. Before the storm hit, the crew reinforced the main hatchway, and all prayed it would hold if the rivers of seawater got high enough to flow over the hatch cover. After rotating through four shifts, captain and crew knew they were in for a long haul, caught in the cyclonic winds of a large hurricane.

At the mercy of the wind and waves, the ship endured for two days, every minute a terrifying experience. Two times they were pulled around the great circle of the hurricane. Whenever possible, the crew nudged the ship to starboard, hoping to make it out of the edge of the storm. Crew and passengers alike feared for their lives with every rise and fall of the ship. If the wagon broke free or fell apart, they could turn broadside to a big wave and be rolled over in an instant. While the experienced sailors knew there were reports of ships surviving that particular disaster, it would be unlikely that the ship would stay afloat long if the cargo shifted and broke through the hatch cover. Every time the ship sunk into the trough of the next wave, everyone held their breath until it started to rise again. Over and over again for two days and three nights the harrowing experience seemed like it never would end. Anna knew they were still alive, but she thought, *this must be what seamen's hell must be like.* With the howling wind and the wild pitching of the boat, no one was able to sleep. Caitrín led the small party in prayer from time to time, but mostly everyone just cuddled in the dark vowing never to sail on the ocean again.

On the morning of the third day, with everyone nearly dead from exhaustion, the ship finally cleared the south edge of the storm. With the ship adrift in a calming sea, Caitrín fed everyone a hearty meal of salt pork over noodles, and then the crew got busy assessing the damage and readying the ship for sail. There were only two serious injuries. A crewman had broken his arm, falling from the top of a whiskey rack in the main hold, and the top of the mainmast was missing. In all, the damage was not crippling, and necessary repairs were completed reasonably fast, considering that all aboard were ready to drop from fatigue.

As the crew labored to bring the hawser around from the bow to raise it with the steam winch, Max told the crew that they were out of coal and that the fire in the boiler was going out. The decision made, a crewman appeared with an ax and cut the waterlogged wagon loose. Caitrín straightened and set the broken arm in a splint, and with hoisting the sails, Connor handed the sextant to Lily and said, "Navigator, find out where we are." The pride Lily felt radiated from her in every way possible. She knew that if Connor approved of her finding the position of the ship in this difficult situation, she indeed was the ship's Navigator. Rufus helped man the manual rocking beam bilge pump, and the last of the water shipped during the storm was pumped out. By the time they finished with the water, the four men crew on the pump knew they would have never survived if it wasn't for Max and Higgins installing the steam-driven pump.

With the sails raised and Connor sailing with caution until Lily marked their position, Aaden and Anna stood in the bow. Anna had been a little ill during the storm, and Aaden kidded her about being seasick. Anna put her arms around her female-ignorant husband and said, "I don't think it was seasickness; I think I might be pregnant." With tears of joy in his eyes, Aaden kissed her deeply and fondly, then ran back to the helm to tell his brother. Denise gave Anna a "thumbs up" from the companionway of the mess and turned to write a detailed account of the storm in her journal. She already had made a small line under Anna and Aaden in the family Bible and wondered what name would appear there in nine months. With a great feeling of peace and well-being, she wrote in *"Blessed Survivor"* – leaving room for the full name of the child that would come later.

REVELATIONS AND REPAIRS

As Lily started taking readings with the sextant to find the high noon sun, Connor, Max, Higgins, and the two mates sat at the mess table discussing ways they could repair the mainmast. The ship would sail fine, but the main topsails were essential to laying the ship over to achieve maximum range for the guns. They did not expect trouble until they reached the Caribbean, but Connor wanted the topsail replaced as soon as possible. Connor discussed several ideas with James and Max, but the one that seemed most practical would be to attach a spar to the top of the mainmast. They had two spare spars lashed to the sides of the main hatch, so wood wasn't the problem. Hoisting a spar to the top of the mainmast was the challenge because the pulley for the steam winch left with the top of the mainmast during the storm. Also, a means of fastening the spar to the top of the mainmast would be best if it was a permanent fix. Rope lashings were expedient but would weather and become undependable. Connor didn't want to find out how undependable during some event where he would be relying heavily on the topsail.

At three bells, Lily came into the mess, looking perplexed. From the look on her face, Connor had to ask, "What's wrong?"

"I've worked the math several times and even had James check it. Our position is 27°18' N by 73°37' W. We are way off course and almost halfway back to St. Augustine. The storm moved us almost three hundred miles."

"Hum! Let's roll out the chart and see where we can go from here." With the chart spread on the table, everyone leaned in interested as to how they would get to Jamaica. "If we sail on a bearing of 230°, with these winds and currents, we should make landfall on the north end of Russell Island. From there, it's not far to Nassau. Nassau is considerably bigger than Cockburn Town, and we should be able to find everything we need to build a proper topgallant."

Max agreed. He had the ship's plans out and pointed out that the spars they had on board would fall short of the lost topgallant and the replacement wouldn't be as strong. "Also, we will have to be in fairly calm waters to work safely up top. One more thing, a fully equipped blacksmith's shop would be a great help to forge the U-bolts and plates it's going to take to fasten the topgallant mast to the stub of the topmast. I vote we pull into Nassau."

Everyone nodded approval, and Connor turning to Lily said, "Take us there." Lily bounded off with the chart in hand and a wide smile. When she got to the con, she told the seaman at the helm that they were going to Nassau and gave him the bearing. As he spun the great wheel, he started to hum *Londonderry Aare*. With the seas back to a low chop and a southeasterly wind, the schooner made good progress, but it would still take more than three days to reach Russell Island. Lily vowed to be extra diligent when the ship neared the shore.

Dissent among the crew was rare, but while Lily was up on deck, the second mate questioned whether or not everyone on board should trust the young girl with their lives. "Do you trust her?" he asked Connor.

"With my life," was the reply, "and don't forget it will take more than three days to get there. We'll have many more positions in the logbook before we near the shores. I don't want to insult her, but just to set your mind to rest, we will be taking two shots when we approach Russell Island. I'll tell her its standard procedure, especially if we expect to make landfall in the dark." The second mate was satisfied, with reassurance, the concern forgot, the committee got back to planning the details of fixing the ship.

It took five days instead of three to reach Nassau and the *Blessed* anchored safely in the calm waters behind Paradise Island. Nassau was a safe-haven under British rule, a heavily armed seaport with four forts defending the inlets to the bay. All but the duty watch went ashore on the tenders, anxious to explore the town, walk the beaches and enjoy the warm air and exquisite food. The men went looking for what they needed to repair the ship, and the women strolled casually along Bay Street and Esplanade Beach. Ben and Lily disappeared into the town with a little money in their pockets, looking for exotic souvenirs among the shops and the vendors who plied the streets.

Toward the west end of the beach near Arawak Cay, the four women stopped to watch a beautiful black woman walking slowly toward them, followed by an entourage of about twenty strong-looking men and ten women. All the women were dressed colorfully in purple, yellow and red dresses adorned with seashell jewelry. One woman who walked casually in front of the rest wore a long white silk dress and a single pearl necklace. She was dark-skinned, but her long hair flowed in graceful waves down her back typical of an East Indian. Denise admired the way she carried herself, a beautiful and noble lady, and she felt drawn to her. As the seafarers neared, the woman in white beckoned with her hand for them to come to her. Turning down the beach to approach the entourage, the men formed a protective ring in front of the woman in white, and one of them pointed at Denise. It was obvious Denise was the only one of their party that would be allowed to talk to the woman in white. Drawn by the silent mystique, or just wanting to find out who she was, Denise stepped through the ring of men as they parted for her. The woman smelled of jasmine and looked solemnly at Denise and said, "I've been waiting for you."

Somewhat amused, Denise asked, "Really, how long?"

Waiting for a few laps of the waves from the bay, she answered, "At least for days or even longer; maybe since your husband died."

Denise was stunned. News of her husband's death could have reached Nassau, but who in this remote place would even care. "Who are you," Denise asked, "and why the bodyguards?"

"I am mantic, the profit of Nassau. Many here fear me as a witch, and others don't like what they hear, or they feel they can change the future if they bring me harm or even death. I live away from town up in the hills. I came here today to meet with you. Our God paths crossed before our births. You were given a mission, and now it is fulfilled."

Uneasy now, Denise stepped back a pace, and Anna sensed her mother's distress. She took a step forward, but the large man in front of her pursed his lips, shrugged his shoulders and shook his head *no* as he held up his hand palm out in the universal sign for stop. His whole being was sending the message -- don't worry – Anna accepted it and stepped back. Caitlín and Hanna stepped near her and put their hands on Anna's shoulders, not to restrain her but to reassure her.

Inside the ring, Denise asked, "What is your name?"

In perfect French, the woman answered, "Celeste Doucette, but that is not important. My father was Yoruba, and my mother came from French Guiana, but she was born and raised in India amid a village of mystics. *Seeing* runs deep in my heritage, but let's talk about you. You are also an immigrant, born in Northern France, and came to the Americas already a wealthy and privileged woman. My preference would be to tell you your troubles are behind you, but that is not yet to be. A stranger will join your party soon, and he will cause you great trouble, particularly for your man. Be careful, this stranger is evil and dangerous and will attempt to cause you great harm."

Now skeptical, Denise replied, "I don't have a man, and why should I believe you?"

"Belief is a personal thing. I can't help you with that – Denise Monique."

Now shocked and somewhat afraid, Denise backed off wide-eyed. She didn't like or use her middle name, and no one on this side of the Atlantic even knew it, but Anna and her late husband. She asked, "What is this mission you say I have completed?" The ring of men parted, and Anna rushed to her mother as the woman in white looked knowingly at mother and daughter, then turned and walked down the beach to the soft waves lapping at her bare feet as she walked on the wet sand.

Anna turned her mother up the beach and said, "Don't listen to her. She can't possibly know these things about you. It's some kind of trickery. I don't know how she found out about us, but she can't be real."

Hanna, who understood some French, chimed in, "It's voodoo magic. It's evil and should be left alone."

Caitlín could only ask, "What did she say?" On the way back to Bay Street, Anna related the whole event for Hanna and Caitlín's benefit. Denise was either deep in thought or still too stunned to talk; she just walked in silence while Anna and the other two women kept throwing out theories as to how the woman in white could have gotten so much information so quickly about them.

As they got back onto Bay Street, Denise said, "Let's go back to the ship, I'm not comfortable here." The street was busy, and the temperature and humidity were soaring. Men, women, and children of all ages thronged up and down the street, going about their business unaffected by the heat. Vendors of all sorts plied their goods, and at times it was difficult for the four women to stay together, making their way through the crowd. Unnoticed to them, several men from the entourage on the beach were following them back to the docks.

As they approached the dock, they saw a cargo wagon with a team of burly men carrying bags of coal up the gangplank and onto the ship. The foreman was a medium-sized man with a strong build and an elaborate scrimshaw pendant hanging on his neck. Anna asked him, "Do you know of Celeste Doucette?"

"I know of her. Everyone knows of her, and most white folks fear her. She is our priestess and healer. Without her, we would be alone here. We would not know the future. She is our Iyalawo, our Mother of Secrets, our pathway to Olódùmarè, our God. All black folks on the island protect her. She is the most powerful person on the island. It would be good for you to stay away from her. She is well guarded. Many of the white leaders in town wish her dead, but they don't have the juju or fear of what would happen if they killed her. Celeste is our leader, and we are ten to one against the whites here. The woman walks where she wants. Talks to whomever she wants. Sees whatever she sees. She is Orish, and no harm can come to her. If she has talked with you, you have received a great honor. Celeste bears no one harm but is watchful; she will have you followed everywhere until you leave here."

Unsettled and wondering why this strange woman would have them followed, Anna turned and walked up the gangplank. She remained at the bulwark for a long time trying to spot watchers in the sea of black faces on the docks and streets lining the bay. On the deck, the coal delivery was complete, and the crew was filling the coal locker in the winch room and stowing extra bags below decks. None of the shore party was allowed below decks or to roam free on the ship. Finished with the delivery, the foreman turned the coal wagon up the dock with his men riding in the bed of the wagon, chattering away about the strangeness of the *Blessed*. The foreman made his way slowly off the dock. Connor, Aaden, Max, and Higgins were waiting for the collier to clear the wharf. They had returned with a long spar and two wagons loaded with supplies of all kinds. James went down to meet them and started adding the inventory to his logbook while Higgins and Max were discussing how to get the spar up to the top of the mainmast. Anna looked hard at the crowds for a long time but didn't see a single black face showing anything but a passing interest in the ship.

Over the evening meal of fresh fish and steamed Calico Scallops with sweet grapefruit, Anna related the strange story of the woman on the beach. All speculated on whom the stranger could be and which of Denise's men would be troubled? Denise sat in silence with the feeling of unease and foreboding returning; she changed the topic to Lily and Ben and the treasures they found in the town. Excited to participate Lily pulled some shells from her pocket and her proudest purchase – seven pearls. James took a jeweler's loop from a vest pocket and inspected each of the pearls. One was real, and the rest were fake, nothing but pearl colored glass. Lily was outraged, but James softened her anger by teaching her how to tell the real ones from the fake ones. At the end of the lesson, Lily was determined to get a jeweler's loop of her own. "You can have this one," James said, "And tomorrow I will go back to the shop where you purchased this one and teach you how to get your money's worth."

Then the conversation turned to the repair of the mainmast, and one-by-one, the women turned in for the night. Connor and the rest of the men talked long into the night planning the repair and who would be responsible for each part of the job. Satisfied with the plan for the next day's work, Connor headed to the forecastle for a good night's sleep; but before he retired, he doubled the watch and armed them with Colt Patterson revolvers from the small arms locker. He didn't feel the same unease as Denise, but heading the words of the coal foreman that Celeste would be watching, he opted for the extra caution any sea captain would want in an unfamiliar port in a foreign land. He didn't believe in the *luck-of-the-Irish*. He believed in planning and preparation before *bad luck* could turn a situation into a disaster.

The next day, the work started at sunrise and went smoothly. First, the top of the splintered topmast had to be sawed off. A seaman scaled the topmast, and tying off, started sawing through the foot-thick timber. Taking a break now and then, he could look out from his perch a hundred feet above the deck and see the entire island of Nassau at one time. Next came bolting an iron hoop with an eye forged on it to the top of the mast. Max retrieved a pulley from his spares, and it was hoisted up and attached to the eye. With that complete, the steam winch would serve to raise the spar that would become the new topgallant. The back saddle and U-bolts that would secure the spar were sent up next using the steam winch. With those secured, the work crew broke at eight bells for the noon meal.

The next job was raising the spar itself. Already outfitted with the top pulley, the spar was hung from above its center of gravity so that it hung vertically on the winch rope. With several men now tethered off on the top main, the spar was hoisted up with the chug of the steam winch, threaded through the U-bolts, and secured to the top main mast. The winch rope was untied and run through a pulley on the bottom of the spar, up the other side and tied off in the eye bolt in the top of the mast. Working the clutch on the winch as gently as he could, Max raised the spar through the U-bolts, and the mates up top started tightening down the bolts. It took about thirty minutes, but the spar was now ready for a new topgallant. A mate shimmied up and threaded the two leads for the topsails and a lead for their flag of Ireland through the pulleys at the very top of the mast, one hundred and thirty feet above the deck. Everyone held their breath until the seaman was safely down then cheered when they ran up the Irish flag. They would sail the next morning at six bells when the tide would turn to the west, flowing through the shoals into the Caribbean.

By the evening mess, James returned with Ben and Lily. Lily had a pocket full of real pearls and a wide grin on her face. With James's expert help and a threat from the police station on Parliament Street, the woman who ran the shop was repentant, claiming she didn't know the pearls were cheap imitations, and she was more than willing to sell the rest of her real stock at bargain prices. Gemology was one of Lily's new loves. Ben had an ornate pocket watch; no doubt looted from one of the many wrecked ships on the shoals. Salvage was the second biggest industry on Nassau, and it is common knowledge among experienced seamen that troops of salvage companies set out lights to lure unwary ships to a watery grave on the Nassau shoals. The British governor tolerated the practice because it wasn't exactly piracy, but it wasn't exactly legal either, and most of the wrecked ships were Spanish.

The following day everyone was up before dawn. The night before, Anna was the last to bed, still looking for watchers from the beach. Around midnight she caught a glimpse of three men in the light cast by an opening saloon door about a block up the street from the dock. It was just a few seconds, but she was sure one of them was the man that seemed to control the bodyguards around Celeste two days before. She stood at the shoreward bulwark even before first light and saw the three men closer to the ship, spread out along Bay Street. As the sun rose above the horizon with the promise of another hot day, the three men were lost to the throngs of people out on the street for the day's business. A second-rate British man-of-war on its maiden voyage – *The Collingwood* -- had anchored in the bay, sailing in on the tide with the help of a clear night and a full moon.

Through the morning, four hundred sailors and one hundred marines came ashore after nearly two months at sea. The dock filled with vendors, whores, and pickpockets profiting from the inflow of sailors fresh off the long Atlantic cruise. At four bells, the dock was still crowded with townsfolk, but the men allowed shore duty were all ashore, and the traffic from the warship changed to small boats from Nassau rowing out and back to ply their wares. By five bells, though, the dock was clear of people; not a single person remained. Anna was watching again, wondering what had happened to all the people, and then she saw Celeste emerge from her entourage on Bay Street and walk alone down the dock to the foot of the gangplank. She stood perfectly still, and again; Anna noticed how regal she looked as her long wavy hair swayed back and forth in the eastern breeze. Denise leaned on the bulwark, and Celeste held up a gold pendant on a gold chain, a clear motion of offering. "This is for you," she said fixing her gaze on Denise.

"No," Anna shouted, "leave my mother alone!" The crew was sliding the gangplank back down to the dock, and the mooring lines from the dock were cast off. Connor gave the command to raise the foresails; the topsails filled with the breeze, and the schooner started to move slowly away from the dock. Celeste looked sadly at Denise and her daughter and dropped the pendant into the bay. She was turning to walk back to Bay Street but stopped at the sound of a splash. Lily had dived off the bulwark and caught the pendant before it was even halfway to the bottom. She surfaced and was up the side of the ship in seconds. Clutching the pendant to her bosom in a clear move that said "mine," she looked first at Denise and then down to Celeste.

Celeste smiled knowingly at Lily and said in a way only Lily could hear or understand, "I'll see you again soon, little one."

JAMAICA

As the *Blessed* made its way to round the west end of Nassau Island, Hanna chided Lily and tried to get her to throw the amulet back into the sea. "It has to be evil," Hanna cajoled, "keeping it will only bring you ill." True to the form of her teenage years, the more Hanna and Rufus pleaded, the more steadfast Lily became. She hid the trinket under a flour sack in the food storage hold, and Hanna and Rufus started leaving Lily alone, assuming the girl had come to her senses and the *gift* from Celeste lay on the bottom of the sea.

It would be four hundred miles to Punta de Maisi, where they would round the eastern tip of Cuba and then another three hundred miles to the southern shore of Jamaica and into the port of Kingston. Back in the open sea and with relatively easy sailing, Connor expected to be in the harbor behind Port Royal in about ten days. The crew and passengers slipped seamlessly back into the routine of shipboard life. Several of the seamen had stocked up with whale's teeth in Nassau and were busy on deck trying to learn the art of scrimshaw and cursed quietly among themselves every time a sailor jabbed his finger with an awl or cut his hand with a knife. Ben went back to knot tying, and Lily reported to Connor every morning for more navigation school.

At first, Lily was resistant, thinking she was already a navigator, but Connor soon had her learning how to adjust every mirror on the sextant, given that if it were bumped or somehow thrown out of kilter, she would know how to make it right. After a couple of days when she was expert on readjusting the sextant every time Connor purposely misaligned a mirror or the protractor scale, Connor would fiddle with all four adjustments at once, and time Lily as she set the sextant back into perfect adjustment. After Lily could handle anything he threw at her in less than two minutes, he repeated the exercise time-and-time again, while asking Lily questions or coming up with some other foolish antics to distract her. The object of these sessions was to train the student to perform under pressure and in all circumstances. Lily was a fast study and was onto his tactics almost immediately. Connor considered her completely trained when she started her own campaign to put him off balance.

Denise spent most of their day in the Captain's Cabin; Denise working on her journal, and Anna was teaching Ben more math, literature, and languages. Ben, too, was resistant, especially on the difficult pronunciation of French, but Anna kept it up until he could passably rattle off about twenty useful sentences. If Irwin and Ben remained in Louisiana, Anna wanted Ben to be able to say he was a free black man of the United States. Other useful phrases like, "Where is the bathroom?" And, "Irwin Higgins is my father," were drilled into him by rote until he could banter back and forth with Anna and Denise at a comfortable pace. He was still miles away from fluency, but by the time they rounded the tip of Cuba, Anna was sure he would be able to hold his own by the time they reached New Orleans.

Every night before falling asleep with Aaden, and even at the evening mess, Anna would bring up the mantic woman and her ominous prophecy. Few new theories were put forth for how Celeste could have gotten the information from New York so quickly. Hanna, however, noticed that every time the subject came up, Lily would withdraw from the conversation or even excuse herself from the table. Hanna started to suspect Lily still had the pendant but didn't want to further alienate her daughter with another round of accusations and lectures on the evils of voodoo. Lily was changing fast, growing into a young woman and Hannah knew it wouldn't be long as a responsible mother, she would have to turn her loose to find her way in the world.

Eight days into this leg of the voyage, *Blessed* rounded Punta de Maisi, and Connor had Lily plot and set the course for the eastern tip of Jamaica. While close to shore, Connor taught Lily how to use the sextant to measure angles between landmarks. With a little practice, Lily was soon able to find their exact position by triangulation and even calculate the speed of the ship and the displacements from their bearing by the fickle currents of the Caribbean. With the eastern trade winds now filling the sails, the ship was making near seventeen knots, a yar ship indeed, right at the maximum speed possible governed by the length of the hull. In two days, Lily turned west with Jamaica on her starboard beam and several hours later turned the ship due north past Port Royal into the bay below Kingston. She no longer stood on a whiskey keg but stood to the side of the pulpit, working the great wheel with one hand. Striking the sails abreast of the docks of the Appleton Estate Rum Company and dropping anchor, Connor turned to her and said, "Good job. I couldn't have done it better myself."

A whaleboat with six strong rowers set out from the Appleton Docks. There was a man with a logbook clutched to his chest standing in the bow, a shore-bound equivalent of James. Coming aboard, he asked for the Captain, and when shown over to Connor said, "You're late."

"Nice to meet you, too," Connor replied. "We had an unscheduled training session with a hurricane north of the Bahamas, and the seminar went on for a couple of days. We lay into Nassau for repairs; however, we made record time once we turned west with the wind to our backs. Sorry for the inconvenience."

"Not a problem," was the reply. "My name is Jack Brennan, and I am the shipping master for Appleton. I am glad you're here. Two inbound ships from South Africa are now a week overdue. We fear they are lost at sea. There will be a birth on the dock free in the morning, and we can load you then and have you on your way. Our master scheduling board says you're on your way to New Orleans via Havana to deliver a diplomatic pouch. You should have clear sailing up through the Gulf but be wary; the seas are full of English, French, and Argentine warships. Something is going on with the Uruguayan Revolt. We haven't learned what that might be, but two major sea power nations, along with the dismal Argentine fleet, are here in the Caribbean trying to stop something."

Connor and Aaden listened intently to everything Brennan had to relate. The man was more than a shipping master; he was a local news institution unto himself. Appleton had a master schedule that tracked production in many locations and ships and the transport of their products all over the world. Connor was up to date on the Uruguayan Revolt. Conflicts had been going on for control of Argentina and Uruguay for more than a decade. It was confusing to know which side the superpowers were on at any given moment. Currently, France, Britain, and Argentina were allied to stop shipping up the Rio de Plata. With that blockade, the superpowers could control shipping to Buenos Aires and Montevideo, thus influencing the outcome of the war. The loyalties of the superpowers would change with the sway to-and-fro of land battles and different leaders coming and going from the various fields of battle. France and Britain made for strange bedfellows, but they always could be counted on to act in their best interest at any moment in any given situation.

With the rum shipment prearranged with letters of credit in place in London and the rum in inventory in Appleton's dock warehouse, Brennan made his way back to the docks. Connor granted half the crew shore leave, and the passengers joined in for a walk around Kingston to stretch their legs. Aaden remained with Connor on the ship and was glad to see Rufus join in the shore party to watch over the women. As Rufus was helping the women onto a tender, Lily came bounding out of the companionway from the mess. Her hands were white, like from flour, and she was wearing one of Caitlín's high collar shirts. When she swung down to the tender on a rope, she noticed her hands were white and in a slow but self-conscious move, hid them behind her back. Hanna, the ever-watchful mother, knew that Lily had led her on to believe the pendant was on the bottom of the ocean. Resolved to another conflict with her daughter, Hannah sat quietly in thought as the crew rowed to shore.

As usual, Max and Higgins went their way to search for anything that would look useful to their onboard forge. This time Ben and Lily stayed with the rest of the party. As they roamed the streets and shops of Kingston, more wares and treasures had been offered them than they had yet seen on their journey south. They roamed until they were hungry and stopped for an evening meal in a seafood restaurant specializing in Jamaican recipes. Hanna knew there were dark forces at play here beyond her control; she feared for her daughter but knew that whatever lay in the future between Lily and the mysterious woman from Nassau, Lily would have to work that future out for herself.

It was approaching evening when Rufus and the others stopped at a small park on a prominence to watch what promised to be a spectacular Jamaican sunset. Leaving the park in time to return to the ship before total darkness, Rufus and the happy travelers were about three blocks from the quay when four rough-looking men stepped out of an ally in front of them. The street they were on was empty, and the small crew of robbers must have been lying in wait for some easy prey. One who acted as the leader brandished an ancient flintlock pistol, the only white man of the gang. He put the gun up to Rufus's face and said, "Your ladies look like finery, and I'm sure they would like to contribute to the drinking fund of my boys and me. We have a long night ahead of us, and we don't want to go it dry."

Time stopped, all stopped; robbers and victims alike. All but Lily; in a flash, she broke off from the party and ran down the alley with Ben at her heels. They ran down an alley opposite the one the robbers had used for their ambush. Two of the gang chased after Lily and Ben. While the leader was distracted, watching the two men break for the alley, Rufus swung his left hand up and batted the pistol away from his face. The leader pulled the trigger, but the flintlock merely clicked. It wouldn't have mattered; Rufus broke the man's neck with a powerful jab that hit the man square in the face with a fist the size of Rhode Island. Caitlín stepped in front of the remaining thief and stabbed him through the heart with a knife she pulled from a sheath on her belt. Denise and Anna were still frozen, horrified by the dead men at their feet. Rufus and Hannah, though, ran to follow Lily and Ben down the alley.

The alley turned ninety degrees after the first fifty feet and dead-ended in another fifty at a locked door that displayed an ornate sign that read *Bernice's Brothel*. Lily turned to face her attackers, and one of the men reached for the gold chain around her neck and pulled the pendant out of her shirt. His eyes went wide in fear, and dropping the pendant turned to run. He and his partner only got about ten feet. Rufus felled the closest with a massive blow to the stomach. The man would probably die from internal bleeding later. Ben shot forward, lunged and grabbed the ankle of the other man and the robber fell flat on his face with a sickening splat. Hanna fell on his back with both knees hearing a satisfying crunch of ribs or spine. Lily stood wide-eyed and amazed at her loving, and gentle parents suddenly turned protectively vicious. She knew her father was a bodyguard to the late Mercier, but she just reached a new level of respect for her mother. Hanna put her arm around Lily and pulled her into a heartfelt hug.

Rufus left and then returned, dragging the dead men from the street, one in each hand. "Let's go; it's time to get out of here and back to the ship." Anna and her mother stood arm-in-arm out on the street, still in shock. Rufus turned them, and they all went down to the quay. James was there with a tender and a crew. As they rowed out to the ship, James knew something had happened because everyone was too quiet for a return from an outing in a strange and exciting city.

When Rufus and the ladies were alone at the table in the mess, he said, "We will tell no one about this but Connor and Aaden. They need to know if the authorities come looking for us in the morning. I'll take care of that now; you ladies head for bed."

As total darkness fell over the harbor, Rufus and Caitlín sat over mugs of hot cocoa with Connor and Aaden at the table. As they discussed the incident ashore, the concern that the two brothers felt could not be masked, despite the calm looks on their faces. Connor called James into the conversation, and James, experienced with travel in the Caribbean, imparted some reassuring insight. "Killings on the quays of these port cities and towns are as common as seagulls. It's unlikely that anyone saw you kill these men because it seems they picked out their spot for an ambush favoring empty back streets rather than the main thoroughfares. In that, they rendered you a great service. Also, they were lowlifes, to begin with, and no one will mourn them. No one is going to be surprised they are mysteriously dead, and it is unlikely anyone will even miss them. I don't think we will hear from the authorities, but if we do, we will gather up Jack Brennan from the warehouse and tell our story to the magistrate. While we are at the docks tomorrow, all of you that were ashore should stay in the cabins. We'll load up and be out of here as fast as possible. Now, I suggest we get some sleep."

Rufus and Caitlín made to get up, but Aaden took both their hands, and turning from one to the other said, "You done well. I'm proud of you both; you can be my bodyguards anytime. I'm going to commend Lily and Hannah in the morning, but for now, let's return things to normal." Lily didn't need praise in the morning; she was listening from the shadows behind Caitlín's cabin door. She held onto the amulet, wondering about the power it held that caused the men in the alley to turn and run. Caitlín caught her behind the door but didn't admonish her for eavesdropping. She just turned Lily into the cabin for a good night's sleep.

Soon after the first watch came on duty and by the last light of the moon, a single man in a rowboat bumped the side of the ship and called up, "Hola la nave. Quiero hablar con el Capitán."

"Sí, venid a bordo," the seaman on watch replied, and he sent for Connor and Santiago from the forecastle. Santiago was the only Spaniard aboard and the best Spanish translator in the crew. As they sat around the table in the mess with coffee mugs all around, Connor was apprehensive that they were going hear a blackmail demand from a witness to the killings the night before. Instead, as Santiago translated sentence by sentence, the man related a far different tale.

His name was Mauricio Bustamante, and he was the representative of Fructoso Rivera, the leader of the Colorado Liberals in Uruguay. They had been at war now for almost a decade trying to establish Uruguay as a slave-free state. The Portuguese from Brazil, the Spaniards from Chile, and the conservative government in Buenos Aires were against them. The slave-free nations of France and England favored their cause. He was trying to arrange passage for another man, Bagnor Muños, to a country where he could buy weapons and ammunition for their beleaguered forces back home. Muños was traveling with two hundred pounds of gold and was hiding out with sympathizers at Port Morant toward the southeast end of the island. They were put ashore there after their ship took damage in a sea battle with an Argentine frigate. Muños offered to pay dearly for safe transport to the United States, particularly to a slave-free liberal-state with a good weapons industry. New York would be perfect.

Connor was interested. The rum they were going to take on in the morning was consigned half to New York and a half to Portland, Maine. The offer looked like easy money, but warship's Brennan mentioned the previous day still weighed heavy on Connor's mind.

Bustamante went on. If the captain was interested, he would lay-to offshore in Morant Bay and send for a doctor to come to the ship to treat five malaria victims. Exactly five, he stressed is the code that Muños would recognize to come out to the ship with the gold. Connor thought this man could make a good smuggler if he set his mind to it. Instead of accepting the deal, Connor said he would consider the offer in the morning with his officers and his brother. Until then, Connor had Santiago take Bustamante down to the safehold until the decision could be made unanimous among the crew.

At first light, a steam tender from the docks took the *Blessed* into one of the three Appleton piers. As expected, it took about three hours to load the ship. James and Jack Brennan signed a duplicate manifest for the five hundred barrels of rum, and James climbed aboard as Brennan signaled the tender to pull the ship back out into the harbor. Connor was talking to Aaden and his two officers as James sat down with them in the mess. It was time for a decision, but Connor left it to Aaden, who had a much higher stake in the safety of the passengers. After Aaden was confident that Connor and the crew could outsail any warship in the Caribbean, he finally nodded his approval. His sympathies for the anti-slavery movement probably played a big part in his decision. He hoped they wouldn't regret their becoming Uruguayan sympathizers. Aaden knew if he said no, Connor and the mates would respect his decision. That alone now made him responsible for their fate.

Once free of the tender, Connor raised the sails and left the safety of the bay. He told Lily to get them into Morant Bay, and Lily set to unrolling the chart and plotting the new course. With the wind from the east, she was going to take the ship out to the southeast and then tack back in to make Morant Bay. Connor gave his approval and left her at the con to tell the other passengers of the new plans. Anna was distressed that there was now a *stranger* on board, but Denise told her not to worry, nothing was going to happen to them with Connor in command and under the watchful eye of the crew.

Two hours to the southeast and two hours to the northeast and Lily had the *Blessed* anchored in Morant Bay. It was approaching three bells, and the sun hung hot and high in the humid air. The crew had been outfitting Busta-mante's rowboat into a replacement skiff for Lily, so James had the crew put the small boat into the water, and he sailed in alone to request the doc-tor. Returning to the ship, he didn't have to wait long when a tender left the quay below the town and set sail out to the ship. One of the men in the tender was his next passenger, and Connor welcomed Muños aboard. Max lifted the heavy crate of gold out of the tender with the steam winch. He lowered it down the port hatch and had the crew hide it in the hold under the forecastle among the extra bags of coal. Muñoz saw the crew of the tender off and handed the leader of the small crew a kilogram bar of gold in thanks for their service. They had hidden Muños and the gold for weeks waiting for safe transport to arrive.

Connor knew that everyone in Kingston anticipated that they would sail around the eastern tip of Jamaica and north to clear the eastern tip of Cuba. From there, they would make their way west off the north coast of Cuba to Havana. Connor had been watching a small sloop off to the south. Through his spyglass, he could see that it was flying the Argentine flag; if he could see them well enough to make their flag, they certainly witnessed the transfer of Muños and the gold. So instead of turning east into the wind, he turned west. Taking the long way around Jamaica to Havana didn't bother him a bit, so as he turned west, the trades filled the sails, and the *Blessed* surged forward. Connor was elated that he was back in the smuggling busi-ness with additional profits for the journey almost in hand. The sloop tried to follow out to the south, but the *Blessed* was leaving it behind as they passed Port Royal doing fifteen knots.

Connor's elation didn't last long as the lookout called down from his perch on the stub of the top main that there were three French frigates fifteen miles out to the west. The frigates were laid-to drifting in the wind on a north-south line, spaced about five miles apart in typical blockade fashion. Connor closed another five miles, and when the frigates unfurled their sails as if to engage, Connor had Lily put the ship to the southeast. The huge frigates could only make about five knots sailing by the wind. Connor was making eight and was turned into the wind at least twenty more degrees. He calculated that in less than two hours, they would be well out of sight. He planned to turn back up to the northeast as soon as he lost his unwelcome French company.

Lily smiled and waved a farewell as they passed the sloop that followed them out of Port Morant. It had turned into the wind and was trying to beat its way back up the coast. She was enjoying this adventure and admired Connor's cunning at outwitting the French. Her fun would only last until they reached Morant Point on the eastern tip of Jamaica. There they found three small sloops armed with two eight-pound cannons, each bearing down on them from the east. Connor turned north up the coast knowing that he could keep the sloops and their eight-pound guns well out of range. When the sloops knew they were well out-sailed, they turned as one and fired a three-gun salvo at the *Blessed*. Connor wondered why, as all the shots fell short, but as he rounded Morant Point, he could see that the salvo was nothing more than an alert to a larger vessel lying about eight miles to the northeast.

With his spyglass, Connor could see that the larger vessel was a French-made sloop-of-war flying the Argentine flag. The bigger ship was rigged with three masts and carried up to eighteen 36-pound guns on a single gun deck. The effective range of the guns was about two and a quarter mile, but a good captain and well-trained gunners could do damage with a lucky shot at three miles. If they carried exploding shells, a single hit would be fatal to a ship the size of the *Blessed*. Connor had a decision to make, and he had to make it quickly. It would be close, but working his slide rule, he told Lily to get everyone into the safehold and pulled three bells to bring the ship to battle stations.

He ordered every square inch of sail raised and told James to sail as close to the shoals north of Morant Point as he dared and then turn northwest to catch more wind as soon as possible. The sloop-of-war had unfurled its sails and was already sailing large with the wind dead astern on an intercept course to force the *Blessed* to heave to and await boarding. Agonizing minutes ticked by slowly as Connor willed his ship forward. When the distance closed to about three miles, the Argentine captain put a shot across the bow of the *Blessed* with an eight-inch-long gun mounted on his bow just for that purpose. Connor would have complied if he wasn't guilty of smuggling the Uruguayans, but he sailed on carefully, estimating the distance to the warship every few seconds.

Still, out of range, the Argentine captain was now anxious for a kill. He brought his ship around to the south and ordered his gunners to fire at will. The smoke from the salvo raised a tremendous cloud and completely obscured the larger ship from Connor's view. The salvo arrived before the boom of the canons. Connor hadn't noticed, but Muños had come up on deck to watch the action. All of the shots from the salvo missed falling short or wide, but one cannonball splintered the bulwark about six feet from where Muños was standing. The shot had passed over the main hatch but bounced back off on the port bulwark and rolled around on the deck. As Connor looked forward, assessing the damage, he saw Muños stagger across the deck, gushing blood from a large splinter in his neck. Muños fell dead in front of the companionway to the mess. Connor could care less about the careless man's death but was relieved that the cannonball was not an exploding shell. The Argentine captain was probably saving his live rounds for a more significant target if he had any exploding shells at all.

Like of one mind with Connor, James turned into the wind to slow the ship and waited until the smoke from the salvo started to clear. He then veered back as soon as they could see the Argentinean clearly, and Connor ordered ten more degrees to port. As the *Blessed* responded to the helm, the enemy was busy readying his guns for another salvo. *That was the trouble with muzzleloaders*, Connor thought as he waited for his single gun to bear on the warship. Satisfied with the aim, he pulled one bell, and the starboard gun roared. It took several seconds for the shell to travel the distance to the warship, just enough time for the captain of the more superior vessel to realize he was just fired upon by an unarmed sloop. "God damn Irish," he yelled as the shell hit the mainmast about twenty feet above the gun deck. The shell exploded and sheared the mast off clean. The concussion and shrapnel killed more than half the men on the gun deck. Burning magnesium ignited the falling canvas, and total pandemonium among the men left alive on the deck ensued.

Angry now that he had taken a hit, the captain turned to bring his port guns to bear on the sloop. James was faster though spinning the agile little sloop around in the water. As the port gun came to bear, Connor put a round into the stern of the warship just above the waterline. The round traveled through the stern and exploded in the powder magazine just forward of the mizzenmast. In a split second, the big ship disappeared in a white-hot fireball. All that remained of the Argentinean was a mushroom cloud and burning wreckage falling back down to the sea. The shock wave from the enormous explosion leaned the *Blessed* so far to starboard the sea poured into the gun port. James quickly righted the ship and turned north to set the course for the east end of Cuba. He felt no remorse for the Argentinean, the Captain of the warship let his Latin temper get the best of him. He would have survived if he just lay by and fought the fires on the gun deck with the remaining crew. Connor knew when he fired the second shot that the *Blessed* would not survive another salvo. The distance between the two ships had closed to less than a mile and a half, and he had to put the warship down to survive. Even the poorest of gunners could hit them at that range; the situation had left him with no choice. Connor didn't ring four bells until the crew had Muños's body removed from the companionway.

As they sailed for Havana, Muños's body was wrapped and stitched in sailcloth in preparation for burial at sea. Connor presided over a simple ceremony. Bustamante said a few words in Spanish that Santiago translated, and then the body was slid off a plank and committed the Uruguayan to the depths. The crew had weighed down Muños with the cannonball that killed him.

All through the ceremony and at the evening mess, Connor and Aaden both noticed how Bustamante couldn't take his eyes off Denise. Anna was relieved that there was now only one *stranger* to watch, but she also noticed the attention that the Uruguayan focused on her mother. Catching Aaden's attention, she nodded her head toward Denise, but Aaden simply nodded his head *yes*; he already noticed the potential for trouble here with the Uruguayan fixated on his mother-in-law.

CUBA

After the evening meal, Denise was walking on deck to take in the evening air. Bustamante walked up behind her and put his hand on her shoulder. Denise shrugged it off and turned around and said, "De nada."

Bustamante pursed his lips and motioned with both hands for her to come to him for a kiss, "Dame un beso, por favor." Without answering, Denise turned and walked back to her cabin shaking her head *no*. It wasn't that she wasn't attracted to the handsome fellow; Celeste's revelation was ever-present on her mind now that it was slowly turning to reality. She wasn't inclined to take an interest in a foreigner nor do anything at all until she knew who "her man" was.

Santiago overheard the exchange, and walking up to Bustamante said, "The woman is recently widowed, and I don't think she is looking for another man. It would be wise for you to leave her alone." Bustamante wasn't pleased with the advice, but he would bide his time and wait for another opportunity. His Latino lust for the beautiful woman was driving him a bit mad. He had plans to take Muños' place and would announce them soon. That would make her see that he was destined to be a wealthy and important man. In his mind, it would be impossible for her to reject him then. As he opened the hatch to the safehold, he noticed Denise leaving the Captain's Cabin and stepping into the first door on the right. Closing the hatch and making his way down the stairs in the dark, he could think of nothing else but how sweet it would be to seduce the widow.

Two days later, the *Blessed* rounded Punta de Maisí and turned to follow the coast to Havana. Connor left Aaden, Anna, and Denise in his cabin when he felt a change in the rhythm of the ship. Lily was at the helm and was trimming the schooner back to only the foresails. James had a large fishing pole with a complicated bunch of shiny metal on the end of the line. Ben held up the line and said, "I made this; it's called a lure." He attached a small fish to a large fish hook on one of the several shiny plates of the lure, and James cast the line off the back of the ship.

"Marlin fishing," James said as the baited lure trailed off astern. About two hundred feet out, the line drew taught, and the lure could be seen just under the surface with an occasional flash from the shiny metal catching the sun.

Connor never ceased to be amazed at James' resourcefulness. James was the most trusted man in his father's company, *Callahan's Seas, LTD*. When his father first assigned James to the *Blessed*, Connor felt some resentment thinking that his father was assigning his Chief of Purser's to the *Blessed* to oversee the youngest captain in the fleet. As they trained together at gunnery, though, Connor came to realize that James had a lot more to teach besides how to hit a ship at three miles. In return, James came to respect Connor's judgment and iron will. Together they were a formidable team as the events of the last few days proved. Connor wasn't in a hurry to reach Havana. He sent a seaman to round up the passengers to watch James catch a big fish for dinner.

As everyone gathered around the stern, Ben went below and fetched chairs for everyone. When Denise went to sit down, Mauricio sprang forward to hold her chair. Denise and Anna starred him down, and Mauricio backed off chagrined. Lily was at the helm and yelled, "Look." A large school of tuna was breaking the surface off the starboard bow. Conner said to steer right through it, not knowing what to expect.

As they passed over the school of fish, no one could believe the size of the tuna roiling the water. James said, "I hope we don't hook one big enough to pull me off the ship. To his relief, the lure went through the school of tuna with only some minor tugs on the line, and James reeled it in. The bait was gone, but everyone clapped and cheered anyway, having a grand time lending moral support.

James just about had all the line trailed out again when an Atlantic blue marlin flew up completely out of the sea, taking the baited hook in its mouth. The spectators jumped to their feet with a resounding cheer and James engaged in the long fight to land the fish. Caitlín looked at James and said, "I hope this tastes good."

Ben ran to the main deck to fetch a long-boat hook that was in storage with the extra spars. Lily put the wind on her beam to stop the boat. Santiago came aft with Ben to help pull the fish aboard. James was tiring quickly with one foot up on the stern railing pulling up the pole and reeling in about a foot of line at a time. The spectators cheered him on yelling, "Pull," each time he let the pole drop. Finally, getting the fish under the stern, Ben hooked it through the gills with the boat hook, and Santiago helped him lift it onto the stern. Everyone was up gawking at the beautiful fish, and James sat down in one of the empty chairs with his arms and legs akimbo and said, "God, that was good. Why don't these monsters grow in the Irish Channel?"

As marlins went, this one was mid-sized about eighty inches long, weighing one-hundred-fifty pounds. Caitlín pulled out her knife, but Santiago stopped her and said, "I'll take care of this. If you let me, I'll help you cook it up for dinner."

That night they dined on a variety of dishes from fish chowder to ceviche. Santiago had to kid most of the northerners to get them to eat it, but one-by-one as they tasted it, the resistance to eating raw fish dwindled. The only holdout was Lily, but finally, she tried it and wide-eyed and delighted by the taste, she ate all the rest. Caitlín and Hanna arrived with the Marlin steaks, and Santiago brought out a salsa for the topping. All through the meal, Mauricio ogled Denise. Anna would catch him and glare him down, but she knew there was going to be trouble. It was five hundred miles to Havana and then six hundred more to New Orleans. It was obvious the Latino wasn't going to put his obsession behind him anytime soon. For at least two more weeks, her mother would have to suffer unwanted attention.

Everyone helped clear the table then quieted down with Santiago tapping on a glass with a spoon to draw everyone's attention. "Señor Bustamante has something important to say and has asked me to translate."

Standing up, Mauricio addressed the Captain, Santiago, translated sentence by sentence. "Señor Bustamante says he has a letter from Fructoso Rivera signed by him and Badnor Muños. It says that if anything untoward happens to Señor Muños, I am to take over his position and carry on with the mission to New York." With that, he pulled a letter out from his pocket and presented it to Santiago to read. Santiago read the letter but then said in English, "This looks like a piece of James' stationary and the top is cut away where the Callahan's Seas letterhead should be." Connor took the letter and pretended to read it; that done, he motioned for Santiago to go on.

Mauricio became more animated and continued, "I intend to put the gold in a bank in New Orleans and arrange separate transport up the Mississippi and then on overland stage to New York. That will be safer than going back out to sea, regardless of your excellent seamanship and fine boat." As Santiago translated, eyebrows rose, and skeptical glances flittered back and forth across the table. "I also intend to stay close to Mrs. Mercier in New Orleans. I intend to convince her to marry me."

Denise didn't need a translation to understand Mauricio's intent. She stood up, abruptly knocking back her chair and shouted, "You fool. I will never marry you. Again, **leave me alone**!" That said, she flung a hot cup of coffee across the table into her want-a-be suitor's face.

Bustamante was infuriated. His face turned red and not just from the hot coffee. Anna immediately thought of her father and his abuse. She pushed back and followed Denise back to her cabin. Bustamante stomped out to the main deck and stood, hands on the bulwark, still shaking with rage. "She's going to get what she deserves," he muttered to himself. It was dark when he made his way aft to go down to the safehold. He thought about going to Denise's cabin, but the light from the Captain's cabin lit the companionway. Aaden sat at the desk, watching him through the opened door. As he closed the hatch above him, Mauricio muttered to himself, "My chance will come."

The next morning Connor told Lily to report to Santiago for some training. She was turning to go, but Connor stopped her and presented her with the late Knapp's bowie knife. "If you are going ashore in Cuba, you are going to know how to use this. Santiago is an artist with a knife. He's going to train you."

Lily took the knife with great reverence and went down to the main deck to find Santiago adjusting a scabbard on a shoulder harness. "You can wear these several different ways, but for now, we are going to train with it on your back." Santiago slipped Lily's arms through the harness and adjusted the straps snugly around her shoulders. The large knife hung in the middle of her back, the hilt even with the nape of her neck. Lily looked like a medieval fighter in breeches and a linen shirt with a long sword hanging on her back. "Be careful, Señorita Lily; the knife is very sharp. You're going to learn how to use it without cutting yourself to pieces."

"Where did you get this scabbard," Lily asked. Santiago told her how Aaden wanted to give her the knife on the way down from North Carolina. He had told Aaden to wait until he could teach her how to use it, and they had to get somewhere he could buy some suitable leather for the scabbard. He had found the leather in Nassau and made the scabbard in the forecastle at night, so he could keep it a secret.

Santiago drilled her through about a dozen moves from drawing and slashing to thrusts and sidestepping thrusts. Slow at first but then repeated until the moves were second nature. Offensive moves mostly, but also how to recover if someone drew the knife out of the scabbard from behind. It was four more days before they reached Havana, and Lily was murderously sore each morning when she started the drills. When they sailed down the *Canal de Entrada* to the Port of Havana, Lily was skilled in all the moves and could even stick the knife in a wooden target on the mainmast from ten feet away.

Santiago was pleased when Lily went ashore with Connor and Max, ostensibly assigned to guard the diplomatic pouch Connor was delivering to the British Embassy. Denise was pleased that Bustamante went ashore with Connor; she was less pleased when he returned later in the afternoon with two bottles of rum and a bottle of Irish whiskey. The only good she could see in that was the whiskey bore the Callahan family seal. She already didn't like the Uruguayan; she thought if he were drunk, she would like him even less if that was possible. She knew Lily had found more treasures, and she wondered what the young woman would come up with now. More puzzling, however, was Max. He had waited for Mauricio to disappear off the deck, and then the tender crew started throwing eight-pound cannonballs up from the tender. She counted twenty-five as they flew up from the tender, across the deck and down into the port hatch. The whole transfer only took about two minutes with the deft hands of the sailors. When the cannonballs were all below, Max looked around to see if anyone was watching. Seeing only Denise up by the con, he smiled and held one finger vertical to his lips. Denise gave him thumbs up, agreeing to keep the secret no matter what Max was doing.

The *Blessed* put out to sea on the afternoon tide. After the evening mess, Lily took several gems from her pocket and showed them proudly around the table. Connor smiled when Lily explained how, with the Bowie knife on her back, no shopkeeper this time around dared to swindle her. Mauricio was late for the evening meal, and he was staggering drunk. He ate little, and each time he looked up from the table, he only looked at Denise. His plate was still full when the dishes cleared, and he looked almost comatose during the after-dinner discussions. Denise was relieved when he went out to the head and then down to the safehold early.

For two days, life at sea plodded on with the ever-present rolling with the waves and the nonstop routine of the bell ringing time, changing of the watch, and three meals a day. Mauricio appeared only for the occasional meal and was quiet and then left the table as soon as possible. He was still drinking but not as heavily as before. *Two or three more days*, everyone thought, *then we will be rid of him*. But Mauricio was determined as ever to teach Denise a lesson before they reached New Orleans.

On the third night out from Cuba, Mauricio lay awake, waiting for three bells on the middle watch to be sure everyone in the cabins was asleep. He came up the stairs and quietly opened the hatch and left it open as he made his way back to Denise's cabin door. He waited for several minutes listening for any sound of movement, then opened her door and stepped in. Denise lay on top of the covers in a white nightdress. Mauricio could see that she had fallen asleep while writing her journal, pencil still in hand. As was her custom, Denise would only put about a tablespoon of oil in the lamp above her bed not wanting it to burn on through the night, the lamp was out, and the light from the lamps in the companionway spilled through the doorway in a meager effort to lighten the cabin.

Mauricio forgot to close the cabin door in his haste to attack. Standing over the bed, he clamped a hand down hard over Denise's mouth and with the other, pulled up her nightgown. He grabbed her roughly between her legs and pushed several fingers up inside her as far as he could and squeezed hard. Only half-awake Denise knew she was being raped and striking upward with the pencil, drove it into her attacker's left bicep. Had Mauricio been sober, he probably could have stifled the involuntary scream that escaped his throat and pressed on with the rape. He recoiled some and let out an anguished scream but didn't let go. Denise got a foot on his chest, though, and pushed him back towards the door. Rufus burst in, grabbed Mauricio by the back of the neck, and spun him into the door. Mauricio hit the edge of the door face on and hard enough to put him down, but Rufus held him up and threw him at the companionway. Mauricio fell halfway into the open hatch and then went all the way in falling upside down on the stairs. He struggled to catch himself but only succeeded to tumble all the way to the bottom.

Aaden and Anna rushed out of the captain's cabin. Anna rushed to her mother, who was rolled up in a fetal position on the bed with both hands clamped between her legs. Half moaning and half choking out a guttural sob, she was bleeding and in a lot of pain. Aaden made his way past Rufus and when he saw the open hatch knew Bustamante was the attacker. He started down the stairs to the safehold, and Rufus handed him one of the lamps from the companionway as Aaden went down.

Mauricio was crumpled at the bottom, unconscious but alive. Aaden put the lamp in a holder on the wall and searched Mauricio's pockets and the rest of his belongings looking for a weapon. Finding none, he took the oil lamp from the wall and climbed the stairs. At the top, he told Rufus to close the hatch. Hannah and Caitlín were already with Denise, and Lily was standing wide-eyed at the door of her cabin. "Get Connor and Max," Aaden told Lily, and to Rufus, "Don't let him out, we're going to lock him in till we put his sorry ass off in New Orleans."

Aaden tried to look in on Denise, but Hannah wouldn't let him through the door. She said, "Caitlín went to fetch her medical kit and boil some water. Just stay out of the way for now. Aaden, this is woman's work."

Connor and Max met Aaden and Rufus in the mess. Lily went into the galley, and she and Caitlín came out with four cups of coffee. Aaden asked about Denise, but Caitlín just shook her head *no* and turned and walked back to her stove. Coming out of the galley with her medical bag, Caitlín told Lily to watch the water and bring it back as soon as it boiled with as many clean towels as she could find. She looked briefly at all the men in turn and then walked back to tend to Denise.

Lily returned to the mess table after she delivered the water. The men were deep in discussion as she sat down to listen. Max had gone forward to find a hasp, and Rufus and Connor were arguing with Aaden. Rufus wanted to feed him to the sharks and Connor agreed with him. Aaden argued, "The Argentines and French know we have him. If we kill him, this will follow you all around the world, the inquiries and accusations will never end. Don't forget the gold. The Colorados were counting on these men to bring back weapons. They will want to know what happened to their treasure. I tell you again; this will never end." Max returned with a hasp for the hatch along with James who sat down and joined the discussion.

After a while, James put in his opinion. "Aaden is right; we can't just kill him even though he deserves it. When we get to New Orleans, I'm going to hold him back a couple of hours to let you find a magistrate and explain what happened. Then I'll put him ashore with his gold and let him find his way to a bank. He is bound to produce his forged "letter-of-marque" and claim diplomatic immunity as an ambassador from Uruguay. As such, the authorities will listen to him. I suggest we spend as little time in New Orleans as possible. Aaden, you will have to arrange transport up to St. Louis. Several small steam-driven sternwheelers ferry cargo and passengers for a modest fee. I have US Double Eagles to pay all our expenses ashore."

Max chimed in, "That's a good plan, but I want to suggest one change. James, you have to take Denise either to a doctor or a hospital when we reach New Orleans. You are the only one who can pay the bill with a bank draft if she's in the hospital for several days. I'll stay back and release Mauricio. Once everything is settled, and Aaden and his family are safely away up the river, you should be ready to sail at a moment's notice."

Caitlín overheard Max's input on her way back from Denise's cabin. She sat at the table and said, "I was able to stop the bleeding for now, but Max is right. She may have to stay in the hospital for a while, especially if she gets an infection. If she starts bleeding again, she may even need a surgeon and a longer stay in the hospital. Let's not make any plans until she is stable and out of danger. Her condition is fragile and could still turn worse."

For the next several days, Caitlín would take Bustamante two meals a day. Lily would accompany her with the knife on her back and a lamp. Caitlín cleaned the wound on his arm, but there was bound to be an infection. In the evening, Rufus would bring him up to empty his chamber pot and use the head. Other than that brief freedom, Bustamante spent the rest of the voyage in the dark, in the safe hold. Alone with his thoughts and only the creaking of the ship for company, he formed a plan for New Orleans. He wouldn't put this aside. He had to act on the offense, or he was going to face the consequences of the attack on the widow. He had to keep his freedom. He had to get the gold into a bank where he could use it to fund the rest of his life. He wasn't going to New York. He wasn't going back to Uruguay. He had to figure it out before they put him ashore.

NEW ORLEANS

The *Blessed* arrived off the mouth of the Mississippi at six bells in the middle watch. Connor instructed the watch to lay to until first light. As the sky lightened in the east to murky overcast dawn, Connor entered the river at South Pass in the Mississippi Delta. Sailing the river was tricky with currents, eddies, and many larger ships. At every turn of the river, another ship would be coming downstream, and the captains of both ships would immediately start planning how to pass each other safely. While the current was with the larger ships, the wind was not. Steam tugs did a good business guiding the big ships down the river. One had to expect that the river would be unforgiving for the simplest of misjudgments. The agile schooner handled the passage easily, but it still took all day to sail the one-hundred-fifteen miles to New Orleans. They arrived off the French Quarter just before nightfall and seeing an empty pier Connor expertly steered the *Blessed* in as the crew struck the sails.

James disembarked immediately and met the outraged owner of the pier halfway to the door of the warehouse. The man was shouting at James, who just waited until he calmed a bit and then told the owner he needed a coach to take a sick woman to the Charity Hospital. Connor had to agree on a price for the dockage, which included both money and a dozen barrels of rum before the owner would help him. The owner sent a *boy* for a coach, and Aaden and Anna readied Denise for the trip. She was improving with the pain, but as Caitlín warned, an infection had set in. The hospital was about a mile away, and it was all Denise could do to get herself up the ladder on the bulwark, down the gangplank, and into the coach. James told Connor to find the St. Pierre hotel, and he would meet them there when he could.

Following their plan, Max went down to the safehold and released Bustamante and took him into the kitchen. Caitlín cleaned him up some, changed the dressing on his arm, and gave him a clean change of clothes. As Santiago translated, she told the rapist, "I suggest you wash up before you put them on. Right now, you smell worse than you look, and you look pretty bad." Bustamante's bruised face and his right eye looked like he was in the ring for a bare-knuckle round with a champion. Bustamante railed on about the inhuman treatment he was subject to locked in the safe hold, but Lily stood at the door, sharpening her knife on the galley whetstone. He went out on the deck, stripped down and washed in a bucket of cold river water; the soap and cold water had a restoring quality to it. He dressed, then Connor had Santiago tell him he could leave any time, but the banks wouldn't be open until about mid-morning. Santiago translated, "I want to leave at four bells. I will take some gold out of the crate for the bank to open an account, and I'll take the crate with me and have it stored in their vault." With that, he turned and went over to a deck chair. He would spend the night there sleeping in the warm, humid air; he wasn't going back down in the safehold ever again.

In the morning, Max took Bustamante down into the boiler room and had the crew bring the gold crate out of the hold under the forecastle. The lid of the crate was pried off, and Mauricio knelt and removed some packing. It was the first time he had seen the gold; his brow wrinkled with worry as he saw that the gold was in the form of ingots from the Sabara refinery in Brazil. The crate was larger than need be, constructed as such to mask the density or the gold it contained. In the center, blocked in a neat cube, was a stack of small gold bars. There must have been more than a thousand of them, each one bearing the seal of the mint, a serial number, and 999 stamped into them. The identification markings were not good; this gold was traceable, which didn't fit into his plans. He removed about a kilo of the small bars and slipped them into his jacket pockets. "Seal it up," he said, "I'm taking it to a bank." Max noted that Bustamante conveniently forgot that he owed Callahan's Seas, Ltd. for his passage to the United States, but he let it pass.

Max had a cargo wagon waiting on the dock. Bustamante was impatiently waiting for the crate to be lifted out and swung over to the wagon. "What's taking so long?" he railed at Santiago.

"We're building steam; it will just be a few minutes more. I instructed the wagon driver to take you to the *Banque de la Louisiana*. You will be out of here and on your way soon. Do you want some hands to see you safely there? That's a lot of gold to move through the city streets alone."

"I'm done with you, Irish-sons-of-whores." And with that, he turned and went down the gangplank as the steam winch swung the crate to shore. *Good riddance*, thought Santiago as he turned to help Rufus and his family out of the companionway with their luggage. Connor was sending the passengers to the St. Pierre Hotel to await the outcome of Denise's visit to the hospital. Sadly, he had Aaden, Anna, and Denise's luggage packed and sent it on to the St. Pierre along with Rufus and Hannah. It wouldn't be long, and he would be saying his goodbyes to Aaden and his family. He had some business to conduct with the owner of the dock and then he would join them later at the hotel.

Max and Higgins stayed behind. They wanted to comb the machine shops and merchants for a steam-driven capstan. Connor noticed Ben went with the Sawyers staying close to Lily. Connor needed a way out of the dock if he wanted to leave suddenly or in the darkness of night. His smuggler instincts never let him alone even though he was in a safe harbor with a legitimate cargo; he still wanted all his options open. The owner of the dock was an elderly Armenian named Barsamian with good connections in New England. Barsamian had a brother who ran an import/export business with the prestigious address of Number 4 Wall Street in New York City. Another brother was a lobbyist in Washington, D.C. The old Armenian had Connor pegged for a smuggler as soon as he saw the grey schooner. He only feigned anger at their arrival to open the negotiation for the dockage fee. With a sly smile, he reassured Connor that he could slip away any time he wanted and wouldn't have to summon a harbor tug nor turn the ship around at the dock; a sure give away if you wanted to leave unnoticed. Old smuggler/young smuggler, a lasting friendship was formed over several glasses of Armenian ohgi. Was it the luck-of-the-Irish, or were smugglers just naturally attracted to each other? This dock wasn't the only empty one when the *Blessed* arrived the previous evening.

It was midday when Connor, Max, and Higgins arrived in the lobby of the St. Pierre. Aaden, sleeping in one of the large leather chairs, snored like a foghorn down at the river. Rufus sat across from him and was waiving off the hotel staff that would rather have a sleeping patron up in a room. Anna had spent the night at the hospital and was still there. Hannah and Lily were out treasure hunting with Ben tagging along to carry their bags. Aaden rose from his nap and settled the rest of the party with their room numbers and keys. He went into the hotel bar with the rest of the men for a libation and a more private discussion.

Aaden reported, "After a brief exam in the emergency room, the hospital summoned the surgeons, and they took Denise into surgery. They had given her a heavy dose of laudanum to put her out and cauterized the wound and treated the infection with silver nitrate. The surgeon said that Caitlín's emergency care aboard ship was excellent and probably had saved her life. He said he would testify if Denise wanted to press charges against her attacker. This morning she was still groggy from the laudanum, but most of the fever broke overnight. They will keep her one more day, but her condition is good. Anna won't leave her side, and Caitlín is upstairs, asleep. She said to give this to you." Aaden took an envelope out of his pocket and handed it to Max. Max took it and met Aaden's knowing gaze as it was obvious the envelope contained a room key.

Connor related the events of his meeting with Barsamian. Also, he had Bustamante followed, sending Santiago and a couple of hands to keep an eye on him. The man went to the bank and deposited the gold. Santiago said he passed some of the gold to the bank manager to open an account and had the crate put in the vault for safekeeping. After that, he went to City Hall and was waiting to talk to one of the judges of the *First Judicial Court of New Orleans.* Connor was pleased that he had anticipated trouble and had formed a friendship with the Armenian. Max was more than relieved that Bustamante had not opened the gold crate at the bank.

Suddenly there was a commotion in the lobby. Through the ornate glass windows separating the bar and the lobby, they could see a city constable and several armed policemen talking to the clerk behind the front desk of the hotel. The clerk pointed at Connor, and the constable came into the bar. Aaden and the rest of the men stood to meet him but Constable Parker, as his name tag read, pulled a warrant from his pocket and said, "Rufus Sawyer – you're under arrest for the assault and battery of Mauricio Bustamante – the Uruguayan Ambassador to these United States of America. I suggest you come peacefully, or you will be restrained and marched out of here like a criminal rather than an accused."

Rufus looked at Aaden, who gave him a quiet nod. As they turned to the swinging doors to leave, Bustamante slithered into the bar behind the policemen from the lobby with a look of victory on his battered face. From the safety of the armed police around him, he shouted some outrage in Spanish. The constable turned him toward the door and said, "You better quit while you're ahead," and with that led Rufus out of the bar. City Hall was close by, so they were on foot, there was no paddy wagon in sight. Rufus turned and looked at Aaden as the police escorted him up the street to the jail.

"Amigos," the bartender called from the top of the hotel steps. "The man with the black eye said you all belong in jail, and you would be there with the *nigger* if it weren't for the weak-ass magistrate at City Hall." Aaden thought, *"Where in the hell is James?"*

Aaden shouldn't have worried. When Santiago saw Bustamante go into City Hall, he went to the *Charity Hospital* and gathered up James. Together they walked to City Hall and asked the Chief of Court Clerks to name the most prominent law firm in New Orleans. It was just across the street, and James and Santiago walked over to *Nichols, Harrison & Gregory*. James was pleased to see on a list of qualifications posted in the lobby – Black Representation – and he hoped they were good at it. They had to wait an hour to meet with the founder and his partners who were skeptical at first because James didn't, as yet, have a specific case for them to address. James wrote a bank draft for a hefty retainer. The partners called in the secretary from the lobby and told her to go across the street and find out what was going on. She was gone only a few minutes, and she ran back across to report that they were bringing in a Rufus Sawyer for an assault on the Uruguayan Ambassador.

James and Santiago both moaned then went on to relate the details of the attempted rape aboard the *Blessed*. When they finished, the lawyers said they would have taken the case pro bono had they known the details beforehand. James assured them they were going to earn their keep. Callahan's Seas, Ltd. was going to have a presence in New Orleans for a long time. James told the lawyers he had made an offer on a derelict warehouse and pier near the inland shipping terminals on the west side of the city early that morning. He tasked the lawyers to close the deal and let them know he could be reached at the St. Pierre or the river dock on the *Blessed* any time day or night when news about Rufus broke. With that, James and Santiago walked to the St. Pierre. Along the way, Santiago offered to kill Bustamante, but James told him, "Hold off. Let's play the system for a while, as I am sure that the court will dismiss the charges against Rufus when it finds out about the attack on Denise. Don't worry; we'll take care of Bustamante in due time."

As they neared the St. Pierre, Aaden was in the street, rushing toward them with anger boiling over like lava from the Kilauea caldera. He started yelling from forty feet away, "They arrested Rufus, they took him to the Pol-----."

James cut him off. "I've already covered it; I retained the best law firm in New Orleans. I expect we'll have him out as soon as the judge looks at the charges." Aaden started to see James in the same light as his brother. "Go to the Charity and try to get Anna to come back with you and rest." Aaden didn't know how to tell Denise that Rufus was under arrested for rescuing her that night on the *Blessed*. The anger he had been carrying turned into weary fatigue, and he ambled off like a defeated young bull that just lost a fight over a potential mate. Connor turned to Santiago, "Go with him to the hospital and stay with him. I'm going back to City Hall to see if I can post bail."

The senior lawyer of the firm, Nichols, was already there arguing with the bailiff. "He isn't a slave; he is a free man of the United States and has the same rights as you and me. I need to see Judge Davis --- Now."

"He's in chambers with the ambassador from Uruguay." With a sneer full of racial overtones, the bailiff then said, "And after that, he has a full day ahead of him with *white people* on the docket. You're not going to get in front of the Judge till at least Monday morning."

"You fool," that *ambassador*" is an imposter, and he tried to rape Denise Mercier, one of the richest women in New York. Mr. Sawyer is her *employee*, not her *slave*. New Orleans will be lucky to even own a City Hall by the time she gets through with you." The bailiff just shrugged as if it wasn't his problem and turned away. Nichols went up and pushed his way into the courtroom, made his way up to the front, and sat down at the defendant's table to wait for Judge Davis.

Later with the courtroom filling with spectators, plaintiffs, and defendants, Judge Davis walked out of his chambers with Bustamante in tow. Seeing Nichols standing to address him, he told the bailiff to put the lawyer out of his courtroom. On the way out, Nichols said to the Judge, "This one is going to bite you in the ass, Frank, and I'm going to make that happen." Bustamante looked concerned; he wasn't expecting opposition in his move against Rufus. He saw through the looks on the people behind the rail, who were shaking their fists and nodding their heads with smug looks on their faces, a very determined solicitor. Bustamante thought the expression of public opinion was about him, but Judge Frank Davis was not respected by most around town and openly hated by many others. James was going to learn a lot about the *Honorable Frankland S. Davis* by Monday morning.

The weekend passed too quickly for the passengers and crew from the *Blessed*. All three lawyers with their secretary and two other court recorders took depositions starting with Connor, James, the mates, and all the seamen down to the youngest member of the crew. They also collected a lengthy deposition from Denise, starting with Mauricio's first unwanted attention to her release from the hospital. Caitlín and the attending doctor were deposed and put into evidence the nature of the injury and the treatments. The law-yers cautioned Hannah and Lily before they swore then in that they were un-der oath and not to say anything that they didn't want to hear again in court. It was obvious that they wanted to kill Bustamante. The depositions finished by Sunday evening. Working with a crew overnight, the law firm had three handwritten copies ready to present to the court on Monday morning.

James had learned from Barsamian that Davis was a crooked judge and had rendered many judgments based on the highest bribe paid. He often took money from both sides in a case and was hated by all who went before him. A winner one time could be the loser the next if he didn't pay the high-est bribe the second time around. Plaintiffs and defendants alike were abused, and Davis kept the money from both sides of the aisle to maintain his mansion in the *Garden District*, and the several beautiful women who lived with him. He was under the watchful eye of a platoon of bodyguards ever since an unsuccessful attempt on his life. The judge owned slaves and was unsympathetic to women who brought cases before him, especially al-leged rape cases. He was up for reelection, but the ballot box would surely be bought off, and he was expected to remain in office. Barsamian recom-mended that James pay the highest bribe and have the case against Rufus dismissed. James, not committing to any course of action, said, "I'll think about it." It was time to plan for some contingencies.

Monday morning, the passengers and quite a few of the crew from the *Blessed* were waiting in the dark on the steps of City Hall. Their mood was as lugubrious as the fog that wafted up the streets from the river and surround-ing swamps. They not only wanted front row seats for the arraignment but also wanted to fill the courtroom with a solid block of formidable men wear-ing the gray uniforms of *Callahan's Seas, Ltd*. As they finally entered the courtroom, James made sure that the few empty seats left said *Reserved for Reporters*. A black couple was admitted to the standing room only area by the windows, and as they passed Lily, the woman lifted the pendant off the young girl's blouse and looked at her with the kindest smile she had seen in days. The woman pulled a golden chain up and out of the front of the dress and showed Lily that she had the same-exact pendant. The man patted his chest and just nodded his head in a *me to* gesture.

As time labored on to the start time for the hearing, Bustamante and a Mr. Mel A. Parker, his lawyer, made their way through the crowd in the hall-way and entered the courtroom. Walking to the front amid a sea of grey emanating silent hatred and loathing, Bustamante was relieved to be able to turn his back on the crew from the *Blessed* and sat down at the plaintiff's table. His sleazy looking lawyer did notice that Connor had to restrain Lily as Bustamante walked past her. The black couple from the side aisle was watching the incident intently; their eyes fixed on Lily as Connor held her soothingly in his arms.

It was already hot, and the large open windows offered little breeze to ease the tension. All three partners from the law firm arrived with the secretary and took up positions at the defendant's table, stacking up the depositions in the order that they would enter them into evidence. Rufus was led in through a door on the right, looking rumpled and worried, still dressed in the clothes he wore at his arrest. He looked appreciatively at his family and the impressive presence of the seamen. Hannah and Lily leaned over the railing and kissed him reassuringly before he sat down. The standing-room-only space filled with spectators and the only empty seats left were the twelve in the jury box, the one behind the bench, and the chair reserved for witnesses. The court recorder sat down, and the bailiff opened the same door he had brought Rufus through on the right and led twelve armed policemen into the jury box. The bailiff was no fool; he recognized a well-organized and motivated force when he first looked out on the crew from the *Blessed,* and above all else, he was going to maintain order.

Minutes drug on with only an occasional cough or the shuffling of papers to accompany the loud tick-tock of the large clock mounted above the door on the back wall of the courtroom. Nichols was more and more annoyed at the ploy. He had given Davis a copy of the depositions early that morning and could only see this delay as making the courtroom uncomfortable in the heat and eager for a quick end to the proceedings. Finally, the bailiff called, "All stand," and Davis entered and took his seat behind the bench. Davis started to talk before the courtroom was even seated. He was trying to hold a stern composure, but his nervousness was as clear as the sweat forming on his brow.

Davis spoke, "Rufus Sawyer, you are accused of assault and battery by the Ambassador from Uraguay. Despite evidence that you acted in her defense during the alleged attempted rape of your employer, you acted with excessive force, far and above what was necessary to control the incident. This court is going to respect the diplomatic immunity of Ambassador Bustamante. The charges filed against him will not be dropped but will be forwarded to the New Orleans Federal Court to consider the evidence against him." There was a considerable stir in the courtroom, and the reporters were writing furiously to record Davis' words verbatim. "On the other hand, you Rufus Sawyer will be remanded to the custody of the Federal Prison until this matter is taken up by that higher authority." Davis slammed his gavel down to end the proceedings, and Rufus lowered his head, and his shoulders slumped back in bondage again.

Anna jumped up and screamed, "That savage bastard raped my mother and you – YOU, YOU SORRY EXCUSE FOR JUSTICE --- **ARE SETTING HIM FREE**!" The courtroom erupted in chaos. Davis was banging his gavel shouting for Anna's removal from the courtroom. The policemen in the jury box were on their feet, and the grey-force of the *Blessed* moved in tight around Rufus, the lawyers, and the family in the front row. Lily was straining against Conner, who was keeping her from leaping the rail and attacking Bustamante. Busta-mante was sitting with a smug look on his face until he saw Santiago draw his finger across his throat and then point at him. Aaden diffused the situation with a wink and a nod to Rufus, indicating that he should leave with the policemen.

Despite the tension in the air, not a single gun appeared. The crew parted to let Rufus through to exit the bailiff's door and return to jail. Seeing that the left leaving with their prisoner, Davis nearly tripped over his robes exiting through the door to his chambers. For the first time, he could see that his plan to delay action in the case to extract more money from both sides may have been not only a mistake but a very bad idea. Outside his open window, there were thousands of people, both black and white, moving quickly from bystanders to an angry mob. A rock sailed through the upper panes of glass and showered him with shards. Police wagons outside and behind City Hall were turned over and set afire.

As news of Davis's decision spread throughout the city, so did the riot. By nightfall, all of New Orleans rioted, and Davis's mansion in the Garden District burnt to the ground. Davis himself spent the night in the courthouse, but slept on a cot in the jail, fearing a firebomb would fly through his busted-out chamber windows. Bustamante waited until dark then slipped off the loading dock behind City Hall. The lawyer put him up in his balconied townhouse in the French Quarter and was late into the night reviewing what happened with his client. Before they retired for the night, the lawyer was demanding a large sum of money in advance for continuing the case. Bustamante reassured him that he had plenty, and they would go to the bank when it was safe.

Walking surrounded by the crew of the *Blessed,* Aaden and his party walked up the street to the St. Pierre. When the crowd recognized Denise and Anna, they reverently parted and took up the quiet chant, "Take the bastard down. Take the bastard down." When they reached the lobby of the St. Pierre, an army of reporters was waiting for them. Denise made a short statement stating that she had traveled a long way but finally found a cause she would take up and support to her death. She was going to fight corruption in the criminal justice system starting in New Orleans but taking in the whole country. Cheers went up all around, and the reporters were rushing back to their newspapers. Denise was news, and her's was going to be a hell of a story.

Conner had stayed back and learned from the bailiff that they would move Rufus the next night after things quieted in the streets. *Perfect,* he thought, *more than enough time to prepare.* What he was planning, he considered fun. He made his way carefully back to the docks.

The next morning, the city was quiet, its streets full of trash but empty of people. Still tense, New Orleans was ready to break its mainspring again at the slightest provocation. The newspapers hit the streets, and angry gangs formed and roamed the streets looking for Parker. They surrounded the lawyer's house in the French Quarter but left it standing. Burning down a brownstone in the Garden District was one thing. Setting a fire in the French Quarter with its many wood structures and warehouses could take down the entire city. They were content with just holding the lawyer and Bustamante at bay. City police and some federal marshals arrived to make sure the crowd remained peaceful.

Early evening, James had two carriages waiting to take the Merciers and Sawyers to an inland shipping dock on the west side of the city. Connor and Aaden were not with the families, but everyone was casual and quiet concerning their absence. James and the rest of the crew rode in several carriages back down to the *Blessed.* James smiled as he walked into Barsamian's office. Conner said, "All is at the ready." Barsamian was pouring two generous glasses of ohgi with a smile on his face, and admiration for the younger man.

"To your health and success," Barsamian toasted. "This is the most fun I've had in years. My granddaughter teaches law at the University of

Louisiana. She sweetly talked me out of a large donation to found the *Black Freedom League.* She spent too much time with Lady Mercier and her daughter this morning. But it is all good; she will take Davis, Parker, and his cronies down, and if they live through the riot, she will hound them to the ends of the earth and right into hell. Davis and Parker are finished; they will never work in the US again. Oh, by the way, all is ready for your departure. Again, to your success."

The City Hall stables were two blocks west of the courthouse where a team was hitched to a paddy wagon. The paddy wagon was painted black and ornate with brass lanterns like a hearse. The *New Orleans City Jail* adorned both sides in bright gold script. Two policemen were up on the driver's seat. With the team in place, a stable hand passed the policemen the reins, and with a gentle snap of the reins and a clicking of tongues, the team moved to the door. A Federal Marshall stepped out of the shadows and stopped the team. He walked up to the driver and handed him an envelope for the jailer at City Hall. As he held up the paddy wagon, another man lit a fuse beneath the back of the wagon and disappeared back into the shadows. As the team pulled out of the stable, the first of many strings of firecrackers started to fall from the bottom of the wagon and explode. The stable sat opposite a tee in the intersection of a road that hooked up with the highway headed north. The team bolted, and when the driver pulled back on the reins to take control, they fell loose from the bridles and trailed down under the wagon. This particular police detail was on its way to Baton Rouge. Every time the horses slowed, another round of explosions would send them running wide-eyed and full-out up the highway. Dogs, chickens, people, and other wagons made way for the *Paddy Wagon Stampede.*

Down the street, a little farther to the west, an identical paddy wagon pulled out of the dark of a Barsamian warehouse. It passed the City Hall stable and went up the street, the driver tipping his hat as he passed. Connor was a little worried that someone at City Hall would notice that the paint was not quite dry. As they came in sight of the loading dock, a policeman rushed inside to announce their arrival. They only had to wait a moment, and the bailiff, along with half a dozen armed police led Rufus out from the jail. Rufus was startled to see Connor and Aaden up in the driver's seat, but he just raised his eyebrows in recognition as they loaded him into the back of the paddy wagon. Connor clicked, and the team walked out of the other end of the alley with Rufus watching in amazement through the bars on the back window. Connor turned as if to make for the federal prison and passed the front of City Hall on his way south. Passing City Hall was the dangerous part of the caper. If the mob was still in the streets looking to free Rufus from the police, things could go wrong quickly. While the street was full of people, no one tried to stop the paddy wagon.

They traveled a few blocks without incident, then turned back to the west and made their way to the back door of the Barsamian warehouse. In a heartbeat, Rufus and Aaden boarded a different carriage. Connor changed into the plain clothes of a *whip* and set out for the inland shipping docks. Barsamian tossed Connor a farewell salute and closed the warehouse door behind him. On the west side of the city, a small sternwheeler was full of steam and waiting for the last of the passengers to arrive. Connor pulled up and opened the carriage door for Aaden and Rufus. With a tearful hug, Connor pushed his brother away and said, "I'll see you again troublemaker."

Higgins and Ben, along with Lily, waited on the floating pier next to their little steamboat, and Rufus rushed up to hug his daughter. Lily pushed back and announced, "I'm going with Connor." Rufus looked back and forth between Connor and his daughter. Hannah ran off the boat and pulled her daughter to her and held her tightly. Lily looked up at her and said, "I'm going back to Nassau. If you try to stop me now, I'll just run away later. I will be safe with Connor; besides, he has offered me a job as navigator of the *Blessed*." Connor nodded, and it took several moments for Hannah and Rufus to accept Lily's decision. Finally, they kissed their daughter goodbye with tears in their eyes. Connor put his arm around Lily and walked her to the carriage.

Ben took a step toward the carriage, then stopped and looked back at his father. Higgins said, "It's time to follow your heart, son. Higgins handed Ben his gold watch, shook his hand, and with a last massive bear, hug turned him loose and walked onto the boat. Rufus and Hannah followed him over the gangplank, and they all watched as the crew cast off and the steam engine started to turn the paddle. It was a full moon, and the river was nearly empty of nighttime traffic. Aaden and Anna stood hand in hand under the running light in the bow of the boat watching their future unfold as their past slipped behind them in the brown current of the Mississippi. Denise sat at a small table in the captain's tiny quarters and penned a letter to her lawyers in New York, instructing them to open offices in all the major cities for the *Black Freedom League* and to hire managers and recruiters to staff them.

Connor arrived at the dock with Ben and Lily. Barsamian saw the three of them onto the schooner. A stevedore mounted the carriage and turned it to deliver it back to the warehouse downtown. From across the street, a large black man dressed like Rufus walked by two members of the night watch and onto the pier. With the night watch observing every detail, the black man walked past Barsamian and boarded the ship. The mooring lines were cast off, and the *Blessed* backed itself into the river winding a hawser with the capstan. The hawser was attached to an anchor about a hundred yards off the end of the pier. The *Blessed* drifted with the current, and a buoy was attached to the end of the hawser and cast off to be picked up later. With a final wave, Connor noticed that a green Irish flag was flying under the Barsamian banner in the light that illuminated the end of the dock.

Several miles down the river, a fast paddle wheeler was overtaking the *Blessed*. Coming alongside Connor could see it was a police boat, and an officer on deck ordered them with a bullhorn to heave to and anchor. They were coming aboard to seize the fugitive and return him to jail. Connor did as instructed, welcoming the police Captain and several officers aboard. He indicated that the man they wanted was in the mess, and led them to the companionway. The black man they wanted was sitting at the head of the table playing pinochle with Max and Caitlín. But it wasn't Rufus Sawyer; it was the janitor from City Hall. Caitlín turned and said, "Can I offer you men some coffee cake and a hot cup of cocoa? It's some of my best." Connor, Max, and Caitlín were trying their best to stifle laughter as the police took the janitor off the boat, threatening to put him in jail for impersonating a fugitive. The janitor said, "No way, the Captain here was just kind enough to give me a ride down to Lake Grande Ecaille to see my mother."

The next morning when the *Blessed* reached the deep waters of the gulf, Connor turned the con over to Lily and said, "Take us to Nassau, Navigator." He went downstairs to breakfast. Caitlín had told everyone that she would be a little late because Max was cooking, and he was serving up something special. Connor and his crew sat down around the table, but Max wasn't in the kitchen. He was sitting with Caitlín in the middle of the table. Max called for silence then said, "With everything being a little tense the last couple of days, I cooked up something I know you will enjoy." With that, Caitlín lifted the lid of a large-silver serving dish to reveal nearly one-thousand three-ounce gold ingots neatly stacked in the shape of the schooner. There was dead silence for a moment; then, everyone started laughing. They laughed until tears rolled freely down their cheeks.

At that same time, Bustamante and his lawyer entered the bank vault in New Orleans. A teller entered with a crowbar and was instructed to pry off the lid. As the lid was pulled up to the creaking of nails, the bank president and the two other men looked down on twenty-five eight-pound cannonballs that neatly just filled the space inside the box. Bustamante clutched his fists in rage and screamed in Spanish that no one could understand, "Those God damned Irish."

The bank president had the enraged Latino physically thrown out of the front door of the bank. On the front stairs, the banker turned to Parker and said, "You're going to have a hell of a time collecting the rest of your fee counselor."

Bustamante walked along the streets and alleyways of New Orleans. He was without hope without the gold, a foreigner in a foreign country. Unable to speak the language and not knowing what he would do or where he would go, he wandered without direction. In the last light of day, he stumbled into the Ruelle d' Orleans Sud, later to become known to the locals as Pirate Alley. He was never seen again, but the next morning he was on his way back to Uruguay, face down in the Mississippi River. The fishermen who pulled him out of the water could only wonder about the strange symbol carved into his chest. It was the same symbol they had seen on the gold pendants worn by black men and women who worked on the docks up in the city.

VICKSBURG

The sternwheeler James had arranged for the first leg of the trip to St. Louis had seen better days. The paint was peeling, but the name on the wheelhouse was readable and indicated the riverboat was christened the *Bijou Belle,* an unknown number of years ago. It was small for a river steamer at only ninety feet long. Originally built for passenger service, it was soon made obsolete by the bigger boats sporting a hundred cabins, gambling, women, and fine dining. The Belle stayed alive and useful by being converted into a floating post office. The Belle only had four cabins, which were more like closets than sleeping berths. The mailroom was almost as big as the boiler room, and most of the deck space was taken up with cords of firewood. The *Bijou Belle* was aptly named stopping at every bay, dock, and hamlet along the Mississippi.

Aaden was pleased that James had gotten them safely away from New Orleans and pleased that he had the wisdom to hide them in plain sight. Rufus worked in the boiler room as a stoker, and Hanna filled in as a galley slave during the daylight hours. By late afternoon on the first day, they were docked at Donalsonville. Mailbags came and went into the town as a police boat from New Orleans steamed by without giving the Belle a second glance. As sternwheelers went, the mail boat was only a couple of steps up from a garbage scow in the eyes of the elite travelers of the time. It was only about two hundred fifty river miles to Vicksburg, Mississippi; however, with the mail stops, it would take the Belle six days to get there. Aaden didn't mind, he was living his dream, and Anna was happy because her husband was happy. Denise was busy with her writing, and Rufus was glad to be out of jail. Hannah treated the happy little ship with meals far and above what was the usual fare on the mail run. However, all the meals but one with chicken were basically catfish.

In Donaldsonville, everyone stayed aboard except Irwin, who was drawn by the noise and activity of a sawmill not far from the dock. He walked over and was taken in by the complexity of the machinery. He talked to the owner some and then just stood and watched the complicated machine turning pine logs into the wood for boxes and window sashes. All the labors except the white man operating the saw deck were slaves. They lived in wood hovels, only a step up from a tent. Sanitary conditions were horrible, and the women and children around the hovels looked unhealthily thin. The owner invited Irwin over for a drink and dinner at his home and pointed at an elegant Victorian home up on the corner of the sawmill lot. Irwin declined and walked back to the mail boat. There would be a full moon up tonight, and the captain would continue up the river after dark. He was intimately familiar with the currents and sandbars, and while there were stretches of the river he would only do in daylight, this leg of the journey was safe under a full moon.

As they moved further north up the winding river, the heavy, humid air of the delta gave way to cooler nights and clearer days. The mangrove trees, seabirds, and alligators surrendered the river to egrets, ducks, and geese. Pairs of otter played in the shallows and beaver were busy up the shores gnawing down trees for dams and dens. Herds of deer were common on the river banks, and the forests turned to hardwood trees and pine. By the fourth day, the languid river pervaded the mood of the travelers. Denise was the first to ask Aaden to find a faster way to St. Louis when they reached the end of the mail run in Vicksburg. They could stay on the river and find a faster transport or they could go inland by stagecoach. Rufus wasn't against traveling inland, but he warned the women that riding on country roads was nowhere near their comfortable rides in the carriage on the streets of New York. Aaden and Higgins were cautious and only committed to a, "Let's see when we get there."

Two days later, they docked at Vicksburg. Aaden and Higgins went ashore and roamed the docks, listening to the hubbub and making their way to the Riverboat Ticket Office. There was a lad selling papers on the front stairs of the ticket office. The headline on the *Vicksburg Sentinel* read, **RIOTS IN NEW ORLEANS**. Aaden bought two copies, and they sat down on a bench across the street under a magnolia tree laden with sweet-smelling blossoms. They were appalled to read about their New Orleans adventure in more detail than they even witnessed firsthand. City Hall police and Judge Parker were portrayed as buffoons. The escapade with the firecrackers and the paddywagon was portrayed as the work of a genius. The Judge was derided as an outstanding example of the worst kind of corruption – an obvious product of the *City of Sin*. The only good that came out of the taking down of *The*

Dishonorable Melvin R. Parker was the founding of the *Black Freedom League.*

Aaden moaned when he got to the end of the story where Rufus Sawyer was portrayed as a *folk hero, and* still at large and believed to be traveling upriver with the wealthy widow Mercier of New York City and her daughter Anna, wife of Aaden Callahan. All this information was readily available from the guest register at the St. Pierre. The headline story finished with a description of Rufus and Hanna, Denise, Anna, and Aaden. Higgins, reading much slower than the professor, asked, "What's wrong?"

"Read the last paragraph," Aaden replied, "We need a better plan." Under the magnolia, both men agreed that they had to split the party up. Denise and Anna couldn't travel together as beautiful, wealthy blond women from New York. Their appearance and northern accents would stand out like a beacon to Rufus and Hanna. Fortunately, the artist's rendition of Rufus was so poor that there were at least a million black men in the south that would fit the description. The only person who remained anonymous in their group was Irwin Higgins. The newspapers hadn't bothered with the blacksmith. His name was on the register at the St. Pierre, but he wasn't rich and famous, just a mysterious southerner who slipped by as anonymous as a seaman on the *Blessed.*

They walked a couple of doors up the street to a good-looking hotel and booked a two-room suite for Mr. and Mrs. Higgins. Aaden hoped Denise wouldn't balk at her new identity or the arrangement. They walked several more doors to a hotel that advertised **Black accommodations in the back** and booked a room for Mr. and Mrs. Aaron Miller and an accommodation for their slave/maid "Henrietta" and her husband. Rufus was going to stay on the mail boat for the night as it was on its two-day layover on the north end of its run.

With that done, Aaden asked Higgins to go back to the boat and break the news to the rest of the party. He went to the ticket office and bought two tickets on the River Queen, captained by Vernon J. McGrew, to take Mr. and Mrs. Higgins to St. Louis – due to leave the next day. He bought four tickets to ride the newly constructed railroad to Clinton and then stagecoach from there to Memphis. Lastly, he walked into a lawyer's office and had him draw up an affidavit declaring Dixon R. Callahan, a free man of the United States. Vicksburg didn't have a formal courthouse yet, but the lawyer directed Aaden to the Warren County Recorder's Office, where he could make the affidavit official. The hardest part of putting together the new identities was finding clothes that would fit *Dixon*; Rufus was still wearing the same clothes he was arrested in and looked the part of a fireman on a packet boat. He hoped that was the hardest task; he didn't know how Denise was going to take to being married again.

It didn't take as much convincing as he thought as the women finished reading the newspaper article. Anna and *Henrietta* walked to their hotel. A little while later, Mr. and *Mrs. Higgins* left for their hotel, walking casually hand-in-hand, looking in the shop windows along Washington Street, a perfect couple just enjoying their trip up the Mississippi. After a few minutes, Aaden paid the captain of the mailboat handsomely over and above the generous fee James had paid him in New Orleans. The captain smiled with a copy of the *Vicksburg Sentinel* under his arm; he was proud to be a part of the **New Orleans Caper**. Aaden and Rufus walked down Levee Road and took a ferry across to Delta Point. Lost in the industrial maze, they found an aggregate yard with a *black* dry-room, where Rufus could clean up and emerge as Dixon R. Callahan. Aaden chatted with the owner until *Dixon* emerged from the dry. Pleased with the appearance of his new *man*, Aaden handed Rufus his new affidavit. Dixon R. Callahan smiled broadly as he read the document and said in his newly adopted southern accent, "Why thank you, Mr. Callahan, I feel twice as free now as I did before."

As the pair of best friends walked to a workman's restaurant close to the ferry dock, Aaden put his arm up and around the big man's shoulders and told him he should call him Dr. Miller until they reached St. Louis. After that, if he ever heard Rufus call him Mr. or Dr. again, he was going to tear up his Affidavit of Freedom, hire a team of white thugs to hold him down and give him the whipping a belligerent slave deserved. Laughing, they entered the restaurant that advertised Real Meat Dinners. That sounded attractive since neither of them was going to eat catfish again for a good long time and ordered two steak dinners. "We only got beef stew tonight," a young black woman intoned looking wistfully at the clean good-looking black man. Most of the clientele was a mix of black and white workers, and all of them were dirty and didn't smell very good either. Aaden and Rufus ate heartedly, but Aaden was sure the meat was horse, and not a very young one at that.

After dark and sated with stew and a hit of cheap corn liquor, they returned on the ferry and walked toward the hotel. The street was alive with passengers, hucksters, and gamblers boarding a huge sternwheeler at the riverboat dock. Vendors lined the gangways looking for a last-minute sale and some women-of-the-night kissing their last customers goodbye. Several approached Aaden and Rufus but were warded off, some with just a nod of the head and others of the more persistent with a stronger *no* reiterated several times over. Aaden was pleased that Rufus got more offers than he did. His new persona for *Dixon*, dressed in a casual suit of clothes with an ornate cane topped by a brass cobra, was working just fine.

When they entered the hotel lobby, Hannah was sitting alone in a comfortable looking chair in the middle of an array of well-done wicker furniture. She indicated that Anna was in the dining room and shooed Aaden along with an upside-down wave of her fingers. Aaden looked into the dining room, but there was no Anna. There were only a few couples at the tables. Most patrons were gone, either already on the riverboat or waiting in line to hand over their tickets to board. One single woman with raven black hair, wearing a royal blue silk dress, sat at the far side of the room, her back to the door. Aaden looked back at Hannah and shrugged, but she was admiring her man and just gave him another annoyed upside-down wave to get him into the restaurant. Aaden walked back to the single woman and was shocked deeply into lust and then love when she turned her deep blue eyes on him. Aaden stroked her hair with the back of his fingers and touched a lapis lazuli brooch that pinned back her hair to the left side of her face. "I see you have been rock hunting," he said.

They both laughed deeply, and as Aaden sat down to admire his wife and her new look, she said, "Wait until you see my mother." Aaden gave her hair a little tug to see it was real and sat back and ordered a couple of brandies. He couldn't wait to get her upstairs.

The next morning Aaden and Anna sat on the bench beneath the magnolia tree and watched the smokestacks of the *Delta Queen* work its way up around the river bends below Vicksburg. When it rounded the last turn and came into view of the docks, the captain rocked the town with a horn worthy of a Trans-Atlantic steamer. People streamed down the streets and out of the hotels to line up at the riverboat dock. *Dixon* and Hannah walked by hand in hand. Rufus swung Hannah along in his right hand and had the biggest Saint Bernard dog in Mississippi on a leash in the other. *What a clever addition to the disguise,* Aaden thought. He noticed too that Hannah wasn't as round anymore, starting to show the emerging figure of an elegant black woman. She wore a bright yellow dress decked out with red polka dots and carried a matching bag about the same size as the Saint Bernard. They certainly weren't servants and many quantum levels above slaves as they walked confidently up the street. Rufus winked at Aaden and nodded up the street to the hotel where they had booked Higgins and Denise.

Irwin was stepping off the porch of the hotel with a striking redhead on his arm. Aaden had to look twice to see that the woman was Denise. He shook his head, thinking, *everyone is enjoying this too much.* Anna poked him in the side and told him not to worry; it was only a wig. Almost no one disembarked from the elegant riverboat, and less than forty people were waiting to get on. The *Delta Queen* was a luxury liner compared to the riverboats that plied the river and quite expensive for the average traveler. Mr. and Mrs. Higgins were riding to Saint Louis in style. They walked casually to the gangplank and kissed as several policemen stood aside to let them up the ramp. Captain V. J. McGrew met them at the top of the ramp and welcomed them aboard. As soon as they stepped to the side railing, a steam winch raised the gangplanks, and the big boat backed into the river and turned upstream. With another massive blast of the foghorn, the stern wheel stopped and then rotated forward, and the big boat started the long river trip to Saint Louis. Higgins waved a farewell, and Denise blew a kiss to shore. Anna was crying; she hoped seeing them together was real and that it would last. It was the happiest she had ever seen her mother, and she clung tighter to Aaden's arm as she laid her head on his shoulder. They both sat and watched until the stacks of the *River Queen* were out of sight.

As they walked into the lobby of the hotel to pack their few belongings for the train ride to Clinton, a note was waiting for Aaden with the key to their room. It simply read, "The Bank – August 10th." Obviously, the happy couple on the boat didn't want to rush the reunion. As they walked up to the train depot with just one suitcase each, the porters were trying to coax the Saint Bernard into the baggage car. Finally, one proter came from the diner car with some raw meat. The Saint Bernard was going to take his hand off along with the meat after he was given a smell, but the porter deftly threw it into the baggage car, and the big dog lunged in after it. Aaden could see clearly that the dog had a smile on his face, and Aaden was thankful that Rufus showed up with only a dog the size of a horse rather than a real horse.

There were only a few cars on the train, a compartmented car for the elite, a regular passenger car with open seating, and a diner car with the baggage/mail car and a caboose trailing behind. The engine was about half the size of the locomotives that were lined up to pull empty flatbed timber cars and boxcars back to Clinton to load more cargo. The train only made ten miles an hour, but it was state of the art. As Aaden and Anna sat down in the passenger car, the conductor walked up to them and said, "Sir, Mr. Dixon Callahan, and his wife, have invited you to join them in their compartment up forward. We'll be serving lunch in an hour. I hope you have a pleasant ride to Clinton."

As the train pulled out of the station, Aaden and Anna entered the compartment. Hannah jumped up and hugged Anna, and they both started to cry. "Miss Anna, I don't know how to thank you. And did you see your mother?"

Aaden touched Hannah fondly on the shoulder and said, "It's just Anna and Aaden now." When she looked doubtful, he added, "Ask Ruf – Dixon about it."

Rufus just smiled and nodded his huge head. He opened the window and said, "I'm going to miss this," but before flinging the cane out the window, he twisted off the brass cobra and put it into Hannah's bag. They walked back to the dining car and ate a lunch of smoked turkey, cranberry sauce, and steamed brussels sprouts. They drank a bottle of fine wine and only hoped the stage company to Memphis could match half the quality. When they got back to the compartment, Hannah took her bag to the lady's room and came back dressed in a simple blue shift. Rufus did the same and came back from the men's room dressed in a pair of buckskin pants and a simple brown shirt. They watched the lush Mississippi countryside pass by. Endless fields of rice and cotton, black slaves singing and sweating with their backs bent in the hot sun to their day's work. Anna noted the stark contrast between the slaves in the fields and the Greek architecture mansions lying in the background. She rode along quietly, thinking, *the Black Freedom League is going to have a lot of work ahead of it*.

In Clinton, several stages were waiting to take the passengers heading north up through the town and up the road to the north. The road was relatively straight and amazingly smooth for a country road. Aaden learned at the first stop to water the horses that the roadbed was what would become the rest of the railroad to Memphis. The stage would make sixty miles a day, and inns along the way would provide meals and rest for the travel-weary at night. It was a lot better than they expected after Rufus's warning about travel on country roads. The driver assured them that the ride would be a lot faster in the winter months when the horses could work harder and longer without the heat and humidity. Then he said to wait until they completed the rail line. The trains would run at over forty miles an hour and make the trip in one day.

As they boarded their coach, a little man who appeared to be an East Indian got into the coach at the last minute carrying a leather briefcase. Aaden was annoyed since he had paid for all six seats, but the little man said he would get off at the next watering stop. The little man was dressed reasonably well, given the hot weather, in a light brown suit with a white shirt and string tie. He tipped his hat to Anna and just looked askance at Hannah. Rufus and Hannah took up the entire front seat of the coach, so the little man moved over and made to wedge into the back seat next to Anna. Anna moved closer to Aaden to let him in, annoyed at the imposition. The little man seemed eager to sit by the most beautiful woman he had seen since he started working up and down the stage line. He was pleasant enough with chit-chat about the train ride and the amenities of Vicksburg and then cleverly brought the conversation around to what everyone did for a living. Aaden introduced himself as Dr. Miller, a history teacher from New York and Anna, as his wife. Mr. Dixon Callahan was a brewery owner in upstate New York and a strong supporter of Columbia College, where Dr. Miller taught -- half-truth, half-lies – easy to remember. With some strained politeness, Anna asked what he did for a living.

"My name is Randal Chopra; you can call me Randy. I am a broker for the railroad company, and I am selling their stock to finance the completion of the railroad up the Natchez Trace to Memphis. I am authorized to sell twenty share certificates for one hundred dollars each. This railroad is soon to become one of the most important in the south. You rode up from Vicksburg, imagine being able to go all the way to Jackson or Memphis in the same comfort." With that, he opened his case and handed a stock certificate to Aaden and another to Rufus. Aaden, a stickler for details, noticed that the name of the railroad was *The Vicksburg to Clinton Railroad*, and the stock was an offering by the *Commerce Railroad Bank of Vicksburg*. The real name of the railroad was *The Clinton & Vicksburg Railroad,* and he had read the name of the bank on the way to the train station. It was the *Commercial & Railroad Bank of Vicksburg.* The little man should have spent more time at the printers proofreading his offering.

Aaden had seen fake stock certificates sold by charlatan brokers in New York during his due diligence research for his investments. As a certificate,

Chopra's were impressive work printed on fine parchment and embossed with the company seal in gold leaf. Below the seal and to the right side, a Baldwin locomotive was portrayed, pulling a long train of flatbed cars loaded with cotton bales trailing back to the horizon. A small map of the railroad route appeared on the left. The seal and the artwork were beautiful, and the customary clause, "This is to certify -- etc." appeared in elaborate script. The certificates were numbered No. <u>783</u>, Rufus had No. <u>785</u>. Oops, another foible, where was No. 784? Numbered stocks were usually sold in order.

Aaden politely declined, claiming that the Mississippi issued stock would be hard to sell in New York. The little man grew more animated and started talking faster. The faster he talked, the more pronounced his East Indian accent became. "You're missing the opportunity of a lifetime" – and on and on. Aaden finally turned to look him in the eye and said, "You, my man, are a fraud, and you didn't even get the name of the railroad or the bank right on your certificates."

Rufus reached over and took the little man by his shirt front and twisted it in his massive hand and started to choke him. In his cantering accent, the little man came clean. He had a family. He had to make a living. He didn't steal from poor people. Surely a hundred dollars isn't going to hurt you – and on and on, he prattled. Rufus pulled him up and made like he was going to throw the Indian out the window. Aaden stood up and stopped him. Chopra was relieved for a moment, but then Aaden unlatched the door and threw him out the door by the nape of his neck and the seat of his pants. He shot out of the coach like a torpedo and landed in a shallow ditch. He stood up wet and muddy, shaking his fist, cursing in a foreign language. Rufus said, "Why didn't you let me do that?"

"I'm in the education business, and that man was in bad need of a lesson. Besides, I was getting to feel left out with you being the only one here accused of assault."

Anna picked up the case and threw it out the window. The stock certificates scattered in the wind with a good deal of it landing in the ditch with the angry little man. "With a laugh, she said, "I think Chopra's stock just underwent an unexpected distribution, and Mississippi frogs just became his major shareholders."

The driver and his hand didn't see Chopra sneak into the stagecoach at the watering stop. They cheered, however, when they saw him flung into the ditch. Evidently, the con man was well known up and down the line.

The foursome lumbered happily on. In Memphis, they would switch back to river travel for the easy trip up to St. Louis. They had plenty of time to get to the bank and wondered what the rendezvous with Mr. and Mrs. Higgins would bring next.

SAINT LOUIS

The foursome reached Memphis without further incident, and the stage put them off near the riverboat docks. Aaden immediately bought a paper and was relieved that the reporters had moved on to other issues leaving the New Orleans riots for better-selling news. They walked on the bluff overlooking the river and were amazed at the scores of boats of all kinds below them on the docks. Anna commented that they should invest in a good riverboat company, but Aaden wasn't enthusiastic about the idea. Riverboats were doomed to the advancing railroads, he thought. Look at the freight they were moving from Clinton to Vicksburg. No sandbars, no boiler explosions, no floods or low water – if you could start a fire in the boiler of a locomotive, you can go day or night or any time of the year. Rufus pointed out that the trains could only go where the rails took them. There would always be freight companies to move cargo to and from the rails. The men debated, which would be the better investment, and the women gazed at room models set up in an elaborate display across the street from the construction site of the Gayoso Hotel. The builders spared no expense with lavish furnishings, bathtubs with hot water in every room, and a dining room that was to be the best in Tennessee.

Anna told Aaden that he had to bring her back here when the hotel opened for business. Maybe we should be in the hotel business she added. They checked into a hotel for the night, where they could bathe and eat a hearty meal before setting out in the morning for a riverboat ride to St. Louis. Hannah and Rufus had to stay in the black section and eat in a separate dining room. Anna told Aaden that when she owned a hotel, everyone would stay together and eat together. They talked more over dinner. Emancipation for all the slaves was a growing movement in the country, and it couldn't be long before the south came around to more humane treatment of the blacks. Overheard from the tables around them, many slave owners listened intently to what the northerners were discussing. One man sitting alone nearby stood up, obviously a little drunk. He walked over and told Aaden and Anna bluntly that they could go back north with their liberal ideas. When Aaden stood up to address him, the man turned and stomped out of the restaurant. He probably thought better than to pick a fight with a man Aaden's size, but he also saw Anna slip a hand into her purse, so maybe he thought she was armed.

Retiring early, Anna went on with only Aaden to listen. "The North didn't fail when they freed the slaves, and I would bet that all those rich plantations we passed on the way up here could afford to pay wages and treat the blacks like humans."

Aaden was deep in thought through the evening, and when he and Anna snuggled into a great soft bed for a good night's sleep, he told her what they could accomplish with a farm-based industry that would feed into the rapidly growing economy of the south. "I wanted to come out here because we can settle land under the Preemption Act in Missouri and Kansas. There has to be a better way to run a farm than by exploiting slaves. Look at my family back in Ireland. They have built an empire with something as simple as the whiskey trade. There has to be something out there that will offer the same opportunity. We have to go out there and find it."

The next morning the two couples rejoined in front of the hotel and walked down to the riverboat ticket office. Aaden still couldn't get over how good his wife looked with raven black hair blowing in a gentle breeze. They had their choice of accommodations, so Aaden purchased first-class tickets for himself and Anna, and the best accommodations afforded free blacks on one of the new riverboats. They booked passage to St. Louis on a boat named *River Demon*. It was equipped with four high-pressure boilers and guaranteed a one-day trip to St. Louis. It was a far cry from the luxury boat that Irwin and Denise rode on, but compared to the mail packet from New Orleans, the boat was several levels up in riverboat heaven while the packet never made it out of *catfish hell*.

Onboard and underway by 9:00 AM, Anna waved her racist privilege, and ignoring many looks of disapproval from the white passengers and crew, sat with Hannah and Rufus in deck chairs in the black section of the boat. "Why the long faces?" Anna asked.

"Today is our baby's birthday, and we don't even know where she is," Hannah said on the brink of tears.

"She is in good hands," Anna replied. "Connor and James got us here, didn't they? Who would you trust more? I'm sure she is just fine." Despite her efforts to cheer them up, it would be a year or more before Rufus and Hannah would see their daughter again; the parents were going to brood about their daughter all the way to St. Louis, and there was nothing she could do about it.

Anna walked back forward, looking for her husband. She found him looking over a poker table in the Grand Saloon. There was a gambler there dealing Blackjack. Aaden was watching the game but wasn't playing. Anna looked over the gambler. She had heard of *dandies* plying their trade on the Mississippi, and this man was a good example of one. He had on a snow-white ruffled shirt and a green and gold brocade vest with black armbands holding back his long flowing sleeves. His black pants were sharply creased, and there was a matching coat hanging over the chair behind him. He stood up when Anna approached the table and with an Irish lilt in his voice, introduced himself as Donald E. McCarthy from Dublin. Aaden answered him in Gaelic and introduced himself and Anna as his wife. Aaden was reluctant to gamble, but Anna sat down, opened her purse, and took out a handful of double eagles. She pushed them over to McCarthy and got a pile of poker chips in return. Anna looked at the chips and asked, "Why don't we just play with the gold coins?" McCarthy assessed the beautiful woman with obvious wealth; it was more than apparent that he was taken in with her good looks and her charm, but he was also looking forward to taking her money.

McCarthy shuffled and started to deal. Anna picked up the first card and said, "These cards are greasy. Surely if we are going to play for gold, the house can afford to break out a new deck." Anna flicked the card back to him across the table and just sat there looking innocent. Aaden thought that maybe his wife knew more about this game than she was letting on. McCarthy signaled the pit boss for a new deck. He broke open the paper package and took out the two jokers and shuffled the deck. He started to deal again, but Anna held up her hand and said, "From the shoe, Mr. McCarthy, isn't that how the game is played?"

"Yes, of course." McCarthy loaded the shoe and burned the first card. It was a queen of hearts. *How appropriate,* the gambler thought, staring at Anna's ample bosom a little too long.

McCarthy dealt the round, and Anna received a jack and a king. She split the two *tens* and put a hundred more dollars on each. Two of the other three men at the table folded and left the table. Anna figured that the one who remained was the house-shill. McCarthy thought this was going to be easy, but the next card out of the shoe was an ace. He moaned and acknowledged the blackjack and tried to pay the two hundred and forty dollars owed with paper money.

Anna just smiled at him, raised her eyebrows, and said, "Mr. McCarthy! I thought we were playing for gold?" He signaled the pit boss again, and a poker chip caddy was brought over to the table loaded with ten stacks of double eagles, ten to a stack, two thousand dollars. McCarthy dealt the next card from the shoe. It was another jack. Anna stood on a count of twenty. McCarthy was in trouble. He had a ten and a five. He had to draw, and he had to make twenty-one to beat Anna's hand. He drew a four; he had nineteen. Anna reached over to the shoe and said, "Allow me." She drew out the card and turned it over. It was a tray. McCarthy owed her another one hundred twenty dollars. Anna got playful and asked, "Did you know this game came from France? It was first known as *Vingt et Un*, or twenty-and-one. Tell me, Mr. McCarthy, could you tell I was born there?"

McCarthy was off balance. Anna had unbuttoned the top of her blouse when he wasn't looking, and now he was staring at the swell of her breasts and her cleavage that was all the more alluring with a wave of her long raven black hair covering the right side of her chest. His attention wasn't exactly on the game anymore. Anna's attention focused on counting the tens and aces played, and she smiled when she knew she was in control of McCarthy's game. She bet only twenty dollars on the next two hands and lost both of them. Then she was dealt a two and a five. She called for another card, and it was a four. She already had a hundred dollars on the bet and doubled down, meaning she would get one more card. It was a king; she had twenty-one. The best McCarthy could do, would be to match her to win a *push*, where the dealer and the player both got their money back. McCarthy had fourteen, and the deck was heavy with tens. Anna kept count. There were twelve face cards in the deck and four tens. Only three face cards and one ten had been played, and more than half the cards in the shoe were already gone. McCarthy drew a ten and paid off another four hundred. They had only played four hands, and he was already down seven hundred twenty dollars. Even the pit boss was edgy.

The afternoon wore on. Anna had all the gold from the first caddy and was well on her way to winning the second when the Captain stepped in and invited Anna and Aaden to dinner up in his cabin on the Texas deck. Anna was glad the game was going to come to an end. She didn't want to own a riverboat, and she didn't want to draw any more attention to herself than she already had. By the time the Captain interceded, everyone in the Grand Salon had stopped gambling and were watching the card-slinging duel between Anna and McCarthy. When the captain broke up the game, Anna piped up with a last-minute proposal. McCarthy had an emerald stickpin centered in his black bow tie. "I'll cut the cards for your stickpin. They call those a *head-light*, right?" She pushed her pile of gold across the table as her stake in the game and called for a new deck of cards. She shuffled the cards several times. The crowd fell silent as she spread them out in front of her. McCarthy drew a card; it was the king of clubs. Anna smiled and pretended to close her eyes and drew out the ace of spades. The crowd gasped. McCarthy had met his match in the petite woman with the raven black hair.

For a moment, McCarthy was worried about being broke and even worried about his job, but then he laughed. It was worth every penny, and he would do it again if the Captain let him before they reached St. Louis. Anna asked the pit boss for a black armband. She slipped it over her head and pulled her hair through it and fastened the emerald at the side of her head forward of her right ear. She smiled and took her husband's arm as the Captain led them up to the Texas, the top deck of the riverboat. At dinner, the Captain asked her how she did what she did. "I cheat, of course." And she pushed the bag of gold over to the Captain. "I don't want to take this from you; I just wanted to teach your dealer a lesson. I won what I wanted," and she touched the emerald lovingly as only women could do when fondling fine jewelry. The Captain didn't quite believe her, so after a sumptuous dinner of shrimp and catfish fillets baked in a wine sauce, he got out a new deck of cards and said, "I don't believe you cheat. Prove it."

Anna shuffled the cards several times and then spread them out on the table. Again, she pretended to close her eyes and drew out the ace of spades. She shuffled several times again and spread out the cards. "You realize the odds of me drawing the ace of spades two times in a row are twenty-seven hundred and four to one against me." She pretended again to close her eyes, but she was squinting. In the dim light of the dining room, it wasn't noticeable. She drew out the ace of spades again.

After a third time, the Captain asked, amazed, "How do you do it?"

"Surely, you don't expect a lady to reveal her secrets, do you, Captain?" Later in the privacy of their cabin Aaden also asked how she did it. Again, she wouldn't give up her secret of the card trick but got playful and said, "I might show you depending on how you perform in bed." Aaden didn't care if he ever knew how she did it. He was making love to the smartest and most beautiful woman on the Mississippi, and there was little else that mattered.

The *River Demon* lived up to its claims and delivered them to St. Louis in twenty-six hours. Because they were early, they had to lay off the riverboat dock for several hours for the *Demon's* sister ship, the *River Angel,* to leave for her run downstream to Vicksburg. Passenger and cargo boats lined the banks of the Mississippi side by side for a mile up and down the river bank. Cargo and people swarmed back and forth from the city streets. Passengers from the *Demon* who were anxious to get ashore had to find a place to land in a rowboat, and then slog through the mud up to the streets to escape the chaos on the river bank.

When the *Demon* finally docked at St. Louis, gangplanks on the bow lowered to the boardwalks on the bank; the passengers started to line up to disembark. Rufus went back to the cargo area on the back of the boat and retrieved the big St. Bernard. Aaden and Rufus, women, bags, and the big St. Bernard were about in the middle of the two lines leaving the boat. They were almost to the gangplanks when a packet boat exploded about a hundred yards upstream. Scalding steam killed everyone on the packet instantly, and burning embers and wreckage ignited several boats to either side. Panic was instantaneous. Boats that had steam up backed out into the river. Men used polls and pushed boats with their boilers cold out into the river. Others were being pulled offshore strung together by a side wheeler tug. On the *Demon,* the passengers stampeded and clogged the gangplanks. Terrified people trampled ones that fell in a rush, and screams matched those from the burning boats upstream. The boardwalks were no better. Aaden could see that more people were swarming to the boardwalks from the north rather than slipping and sliding on the muddy banks.

The crew of the *Demon* was breaking out the fire hoses, and soon the bilge pumps were spraying hundreds of gallons of water on the nearby boats. The Captain had to make a decision; he blew a deafening blast on the shrill boat whistle and started backing the *Demon* out into the river with the gangplanks still down. Disaster ensued as the big boat backed right over a fishing boat the Captain couldn't see from the bridge. The massive paddle wheel on the stern turned into the wreckage, and the big boat was adrift in the river. Rufus had the women pressed up against the cabin wall to protect them from the stampeding passengers. Out in the river, the panic eased off, and Aaden led the foursome through the salon and onto the rowboat that had ferried the anxious to shore earlier in the day. As they pushed off, the big dog leaped into the river behind the rowboat. Anna was relieved he didn't land in the boat to capsize them. As he swam up to her, she reached down and caught him by the collar to keep him close.

Rufus rowed them downstream about a mile to a small fishing dock. They tied the little boat off and crossed over the decks of two fishing boats to reach the pier. Rufus carried Anna down a steep set of poor looking stairs and up a muddy walk to reach a dirt road. Hannah followed behind him, holding onto his belt for support, and Aaden trailed up with their bags. They had all laughed when the St. Bernard shook off a couple of gallons of water, most of which landed on Aaden. They had landed in the middle of the black ghetto south of the city. Women and children lined the riverside on the road, watching with frightened faces at the fire and chaos spreading on the city shores. Most of the men were at work in factories in the city or had run up from the ghetto to the city to help battle the fires. Their livelihood was at stake, and if the fire on the river made it into the city streets, St. Louis could end up as smoke and ashes.

It was August 5th, and Aaden was thinking about where they would stay until the rendezvous with Irwin Higgins at the bank. All thought of that disappeared in an instant when he saw a painter on a ladder painting *Black Freedom League* on an old wood structure hotel a couple of blocks into the city. The hotel occupied a quarter block on the west side of River Road with an unobstructed view of the Mississippi. They walked into the lobby and saw Denise sitting at a desk with plans laid out in front of her, quibbling with a contractor. The red hair was gone, and she had to do a double-take of her raven-black-haired daughter, but she lit up like a million gas lamps when Aaden said in his best Irish lilt, "We'll be a needing some rooms for five nights ma'am. We're goin-a-be-a meetin with some friends up at the bank in five days, and we heard this was a good place to stay."

Denise began to cry as she jumped up and pulled Anna into a bear hug, swaying her back and forth as if she was still a child. Denise turned to the contractor and said, "You're fired! collect up your slaves and get the hell out of here and don't come back."

"What are you doing here?" Anna asked incredulously as Denise pulled Hannah into the hug.

"Let's go sit down out in the kitchen, and I'll explain the whole thing to you."

"Where is Irwin?" Aaden asked.

"Down those stairs in the basement, fixing the freshwater pump to the tank on the roof," Denise answered pointing to the stairs. She went on to explain that the bank owned the rundown hotel; she bought it out of bankruptcy, sight unseen the day she arrived. The fourth floor was being gutted and divided into classrooms. The next two floors were being remodeled with running water and flush toilet bathrooms. The first floor would still be a kitchen and dining room, but the lobby and bar opposite the dining room were being divided into offices for the headquarters of the Missouri Chapter of the *Black Freedom League*. She was going to use her inexhaustible wealth to buy men, women, and children out of slavery, feed and house them in the hotel and teach them how to read and write.

Anna commented that she was going to need a lot more space, considering what she saw in the Mississippi countryside. "Not to worry. Our banker is negotiating to buy the warehouse on the back half of the block, and the man who owns the riverfront is already in love with me and thinking of offering the property cheap to get me into bed."

Anna's head was spinning. "What about Irwin?" Anna asked.

"I already asked him to marry me, but he said no. He says he has to make his fortune before he could marry the richest woman in Missouri. We're going to stay friends and see each other from time to time when our needs overtake our common sense. Don't worry about that; we are both comfortable with the arrangement."

Anna thought, *who is this woman, where is my mother?*

Denise changed the subject with a simple statement, "You are beginning to show." She touched her daughter's stomach, and from there, the three women slipped seamlessly into women's talk about Anna's pregnancy, childbirth, and names for the unborn. Anna claimed it was too early to be showing and blamed her slightly larger stomach to the rich food along the river.

Irwin Higgins was up to his elbows in grease and pump parts when Aaden and Rufus walked down the stairs. The freshwater pump needed the seats for the check valves turned, and Irwin had them out and on their way to a machine shop in the city. He jumped up, and shaking hands told the two new arrivals how glad he was to see they escaped the fire. Aaden and Rufus brought Irwin up to date, relating their travels up through Mississippi and the river trip up from Memphis. Irwin said they were all worried that you might be in the fire on the river. He had gone up to the top floor and saw that it was all packet boats involved and then reassured Denise that you couldn't possibly be involved. That was a close call, none of them ever wanted to ride on a riverboat again. Even on the *Delta Queen*, Irwin was not happy with the workmanship on the boilers. "When I fire this old girl up, we are going to evacuate the hotel just in case."

The three men updated each other and started making plans for traveling to Independence. Riverboats were out of the question, so stagecoach or cargo wagons were the only choices, other than walking. Rufus suggested that they buy wagons because whatever they wound up doing out in Independence, they were bound to have to move things around. Higgins pointed out that it was only about one-hundred-fifty miles west, and the roads out there were well established. There were water stations and inns along the way, so they didn't have to camp out along the trail unless they wanted to. All in all, it would take less than a week to get there even if they traveled at an easy pace. Denise broke up the planning session calling for them to come up for some dinner.

There weren't any guests in the hotel, but the kitchen was functional and stocked to cook breakfast and lunch for the contractors working on the renovations. A young Mexican served them, and when she went to feed the big dog a slab of half-cooked horse meat, she asked, "What's his name?" Everyone looked at each other dumbfounded. In their haste to leave Vicksburg, no one had thought to give the dog a name. The young woman laughed and said, "I'll just call him *Sin Nombre*." With that, she patted the newly named giant on the head. He was well mannered and took the slab of horse meat out of her hand, as gently and carefully as a lamb, then devoured it in just a few bites.

Over dinner, Denise rambled on about the huge untapped human resource of the slave states – namely the ability to free slaves, educate them, and turn them to productive enterprises. Aaden left the conversation for the rest of the meal. He was deep in thought about the millions of people in the slave states, both black and white, that were working inefficiently at hand labor. They were in the age of machines, and there had to be something that could be mechanized, some industries that could turn free land and free people into a productive enterprise. He was determined to find it and more excited than ever for going overland to Independence. He needed to see this land first hand for himself.

After dinner and a few libations in the bar, everyone but Rufus and Hannah walked up River Street to the Planters Hotel. Rufus and Hannah bedded down in a suite that Denise was saving for her residence. Rufus, in particular, was more than tired of the segregation imposed on free black people in the south. Like Aaden, he was looking for something new -- something without the taint of discrimination and slavery. That night Rufus told Hannah that he wanted to stay with Aaden and Anna and go west to find a new way of life, one with real freedom. Hannah had long recognized the need for self-determination in her husband. It was the main reason she let Lily go with Connor at the dock in New Orleans. Lily had that particular need even stronger than Rufus. Hannah said, "Rufus, you know I will follow you wherever." With that, she started to play, her long-standing invitation with her husband for sex. Sated, they both fell asleep thinking of Lily; her need to go back to Nassau and their future adventures. *Sin Nombre* slept lightly down by the opened front door of the hotel.

The next morning the men went searching for wagons and horses. They found that draft horses were in short supply, but mules were plentiful. They found an outfitter that was manufacturing cargo wagons that were called *Conestogas*. He had a large field full of mules, and there was a large round pen just behind the small factory with a black man working two teams of four mules each. He had a long whip that he would crack in the air, but never hit the mules with the whip. He was young, maybe only twenty and sweat made his muscular body gleam in the morning sun. "Who is that?" Aaden asked.

"That's Jackson," the outfitter replied, "He's nothing but trouble. He is good with the mules – horses too. I've had him since he was born. His father and mother were my domestic slaves. He is always heckling me for his emancipation, and I can't keep him away from the young women in town. He'll be alright as soon as he outgrows his teenaged urges and ideas."

Rufus laughed, "I haven't outgrown mine, and I am older than you."

"How much do you want for him?" Aaden asked.

The outfitter reflected in deep thought. He could probably get more than a thousand dollars for Jackson down in New Orleans, but they were far up the river, and he already made the mistake of telling these men that Jackson was trouble. That always drove down the price. "I'd take six-fifty for him, but you can't hold me accountable if he runs off."

Aaden put his hands in his pockets and turned to his partners and whispered, "What do you think? Give us a moment," he told the outfitter.

Irwin said, "He reminds me of Ben; I'd give him a chance."

"I guarantee he won't run off," Rufus said with a wicked smile.

Aaden walked over to the outfitter, who had a foot up on the bottom rail of the pen. The outfitter motioned Jackson over, and with a loud command of *Halt*, Jackson brought the teams to a stop and had them standing perfectly still.

Jackson vaulted over the wall with a flare of athletic grace, and Aaden asked him, "Do you like it here, Jackson?"

Jackson gave the outfitter a sharp look, and seeing an opportunity to lodge a complaint in front of an audience, said in a strong and steady voice, "Fuck no. Bossman here works me hard. Feed the mules, train the mules, feed the broodmares, muck out the birthing stable – day after day it never stops. Bossman, he thinks I'm *Super Nigger,* and he won't even let me have a woman. He thinks slaves come from the auctions. Tells me I can't afford a woman. If he gave me a woman, I would make him all the slaves he would ever want."

The outfitter moaned. He knew that this sort of outburst would drive down the price. Higgins caught the mood and gave Aaden a down sign pointing at the ground several times. "He does look and sound like trouble; I'll give you four hundred."

"No, that's not enough; I can't replace him for less than five-fifty."

"Five hundred," Aaden said.

"Five twenty-five."

"Sold!" Aaden couldn't believe that he just became a slave owner. Jackson just stood there, wide-eyed. Without a single document, with no legal proceedings of any kind, Jackson became the property of another man standing next to a corral on the outskirts of St. Louis, traded as easily as a mule. Jackson had no idea that this was the luckiest day of his life.

Aaden asked Jackson if he could read and, Not a word, was the reply. And to the question of what his last name was, "I don't got a last name. I'm just Jackson."

Rufus wrote out the name *Black Freedom League* on a page of the little pocket book he was using to keep account of their expenditures and told Jackson to bring two Conestoga wagons to the old hotel on South River Street the next day. Rufus also told Jackson that he wanted him to pick out the best teams, and don't worry about the price. Aaden was going to pay the *Boss Man* well for his services.

The threesome spent the rest of the day filling out the rest of their requirements. They bought a spring buckboard and a two-horse team to pull it. Much to Rufus's disgust, there weren't any Morgans in St. Louis. They bought two sturdy tents, a cookstove, two double beds, and things they thought a kitchen should have. Irwin bought a forge and a good set of blacksmith tools. Saws, shovels, axes, and anything else that looked like it belonged on a homestead. All was to be delivered to the *Black Freedom League* the next day.

Anna and Hannah had been out shopping as well. They had a sturdy set of dishes, cloth, and a foot-operated sewing machine coming. They had bought sturdy clothes, buckskins, and boots for the men and the same for themselves. They settled down for an evening meal with Denise in the hotel dining room, and after hearing about the day's outings, she asked, "Did you buy any guns?" She looked around to a table full of dumbfounded looks and said, "Stupid easterners, you are not ready for the trail."

Denise went over to a large locked cabinet by the door of the dining room and unlocked it. Inside were a dozen Hawken rifles and as many Colt Paterson 0.36 caliber revolvers. The bottom of the cabinet was full of ammunition for the weapons. "Irwin knows how to shoot. He taught me already. You will each have a rifle and a revolver and keep them loaded at all times." With that, she took a Hawken rifle out of the cabinet, raised it to her shoulder, and shot a mounted buffalo head on the opposite wall between the eyes. The massive .54 caliber ball split the mounting board, and the buffalo head fell to the floor with a dusty thud. Lowering the rifle, Denise blew the smoke from the barrel and said, "Got him." Everyone sat stunned to silence, with their ears ringing and the acrid air, heavy with gunsmoke, burning their eyes and throats.

All but Irwin, who smiled and said, "God, I love that woman."

The next morning Jackson was in front of the *Black Freedom League* with the two Conestoga wagons and another driver. The buckboard was clopping along, coming up the street as Hannah came down the stairs. She gathered up the drivers and took them in for breakfast. The teams were left tethered to the hitching posts on the other side of the street. Jackson was uncomfortable going into the hotel, but he patted *Sin Nombre* on the head and relaxed. The white teamsters gave the big dog a wide berth and made their way to the dining-room door.

Over the breakfast table, Rufus told the teamsters of their plans to head west and find land to homestead. Rufus offered to hire them to drive to Independence, but both men declined. They were forming a chapter of the Teamsters Union here in St. Louis. Both had families, and they were building a union hall in their free time. Neither would leave St. Louis, so Rufus hired them on for the day to help load the Conestoga wagons when all their purchases arrived. Hannah promised a hearty lunch, and based on the breakfast they just ate, that sweetened the deal considerably.

When Anna arrived from the Planters Hotel, Rufus asked, "Where's Aaden?"

"He had some business in town. He'll be around in a while," Anna replied. "Who are these guys?"

Rufus introduced the teamsters along with Jackson, and Denise said, "Good morning, gents. If you are done eating, for your first job, you can make that dead buffalo disappear." All laughed, Jackson and the teamsters headed out with the buffalo head, and the rest settled into breakfast. *Sin Nombre* followed Jackson out the door.

Anna turned her attention to an old newspaper laid out as part of the tablecloth; the headline read – **TORNADO LEVELS NATCHEZ**. The paper was dated May 8, 1840. Anna read with a growing sense of dread. They had passed through Natchez on the mail packet. Anna remembered that the pilot had pointed out leveled timber on the bluff below the town. She had asked at the time, how do you know if a tornado is coming. The pilot told her that she would know; there is nothing in the world like it. Her sense of dread grew as she read on. Over two hundred fifty were estimated dead, one hundred of the boatmen drowned in the river. She knew they were heading into the heart of tornado country; she could only reflect in prayer that they would never meet one of the deadly storms.

All through the day, the goods purchased the day before arrived, and Jackson and the teamsters packed each Conestoga full. They lashed down the high loads so that shifting cargo wouldn't tear the canvas tops and put the mattresses from the bed frames on the top of the loads. Aaden showed up mid-morning, and Irwin took the travelers down south of town where they could learn how to shoot the guns. All the work and training finished up by late afternoon. A solicitor had arrived after lunch and gave Denise the deed and keys to the warehouse behind the hotel. Jackson moved the wagons to the warehouse and put the mules in the old stable. Irwin sent for some fresh straw, and Jackson readied the stalls for the night. Irwin put his arm around Jackson and said, "Let's go get some dinner and some sleep. We'll be on the road early tomorrow morning." Jackson accepted dinner but declined the accommodation for the night. He would rather stay with the mules and guard his *Master's* possessions. The big dog now stayed with Jackson like an afternoon shadow.

Everyone was up well before dawn the next morning. They ate their last breakfast in the comfort of the dining room, and by the time they finished, Irwin and Jackson had the teams and wagons waiting in the street. Jackson ran back to the warehouse and got the buckboard. They loaded two dilapidated easy chairs in the back of the buckboard for the women. Denise unlocked the gun cabinet, and with the farewell hugs and kisses finished, the travelers walked out of the hotel, stowed their guns on their transports, and climbed aboard.

Aaden got up in the driver's seat of the lead wagon with Jackson. He took a paper out of the inside pocket of his jacket and told the boy, "This is your *Affidavit of Freedom.* You're free to go now anywhere you want, but I hope you will at least drive us to Independence. Maybe I'll buy you a woman when we get there."

Jackson could hardly believe what his *Master* just said; he finally, with tears welling in his eyes, choked out a "Thank ya, *Sir.*"

Aaden climbed down, but before walking back to take up the reins of the buckboard said, "You will call me Aaden from now on, or Mr. Callahan if you must. Rufus will fill you in on what happens to belligerent blacks who don't honor that simple request."

With Jackson in the lead and Rufus and Irwin on the second wagon, the Callahan Wagon Train set out for Independence. Jackson had never been to Independence, but he knew it was out the west side of the city. Now and then, he would open a book that he had on the seat beside him. It was a book on breeding horses and mules he found in the stable the night before. The book was his only possession in the entire world besides the rags on his back, and he slipped the affidavit into the middle of the book. He slipped the book behind the headboard of the wagon, still not believing what just happened. *Who was this man,* he wondered as he fell into line on the highway heading west. The sun was full up, now lighting the way to a new future for everyone.

INDEPENDENCE

Jackson didn't know how to get to Independence, but since it was a long word, he figured the longest name on the road signs would get them there. Traffic was heavy in both directions, and while the mules could have gone faster, many wagons on the road pulled by oxen held the pace down. The first night they pulled off the road and made a camp in a small meadow surrounded by huge oak and hickory trees. Many of the trees were well over one hundred feet tall, and Aaden was amazed at the many settlers he saw along the road, trying to cut down the trees and burn them to clear land for crops. Most of the settlements had less than one acre cleared even though the weathered cabins told a story of many years of hard labor. In some areas where the people had given up and walked away, the forest was rapidly reclaiming the cleared ground as its own. *Sin Nombre* walked beside the lead wagon for the first five miles and then was content to fall back and jump up onto the tailgate of the buckboard.

As the day pushed into the afternoon, Anna broke out the sandwiches and cold tea Denise had the kitchen prepare for them. They had a barrel of salt pork and one of corned beef that would easily see them through the trip, but Aaden bought a small deer from two hunters along the road, thinking they would dine on venison and have plenty of fresh meat to feed *Sin Nombre*. Aaden estimated that the dog weighed more than two hundred pounds and stood a full three feet at the shoulders. Rufus said the man who gave him the dog in Vicksburg said he was still a puppy, only around one year old. He wasn't done growing. When they pulled into a well-trodden campsite with a ready-made fire ring, Jackson unhitched the mules, fed and watered them, and shackled them for the night. Irwin set to making a fire and putting up a spit to roast the deer. *Sin Nombre* sat, mesmerized by the deer slowly turning on the spit, salivating profusely each time the aroma of cooked meat wafted through the air. The travelers ate tenderloin, and *Sin Nombre* ate a whole front quarter of the deer by himself. He was contentedly crunching the bones and devouring the last of it as the camp made ready for a good night's sleep.

The women slept on the mattresses in the Conestoga wagons, and the four men slept in hammocks strung between the two wagons. The sky was dark with no moon, and a light overcast turned the thin clouds above to a dull illuminated canopy. But the forest was not dark. Millions of fireflies streaked through the trees, each lighting its pathway through the limbs of the tall trees for about a second and then blinking out. The forest wasn't quiet either. First, the crickets started then the cicadas. Everyone but Jackson was fascinated by the forest's nighttime display but soon fell into the deep sleep of the weary traveler. Jackson lay awake, reciting the first six letters of the alphabet that Anna had taught him while Hannah cooked dinner. Anna also taught him the letter I for Independence when he confessed how he *read* the highway signs leaving St. Louis. He was determined to learn how to read and write. A was for Affidavit, and with the horse and mule book clutched to his chest, he finally fell asleep cradled in the arms of his new life. The big dog stretched out on the ground under his hammock, Jackson's hand hanging down resting on his head.

The night passed without incident, and dawn slowly crept in. Dawn didn't *break* in the forest; the darkness just gave way to a lighter and lighter ambiance. One-by-one, the participants in the night time calliope quieted to wait through the long hot day before starting another concert with its accompanying light show at nightfall. Aaden awoke to the smell of bacon frying and a pan full of pulled venison, eggs, and potatoes sizzling on the fire. Jackson was tending to the mules, *Sin Nombre* close on his heels. Soon everyone was up, and as they sat around the fire ring, Jackson asked what the name *Sin Nombre* meant in Spanish. Anna told him, *Without Name,* and Ben shook his head and said, "That's not right. He is an animal deserving of a king." All agreed that Jackson should give the dog a better name, and the young man fell deep in thought. Finally, not knowing the names of any kings, knights, or other regal characters, Jackson announced, "We'll call him Goliath."

Rufus and Hannah were particularly pleased that the young man picked a biblical name and doubted that Jackson knew that Goliath was slain by a single stone from the sling of David, a courageous young man facing the giant Goliath in single combat in the valley of Elah. Before they finished with breakfast, the same mix of Conestoga wagons, smaller cargo wagons, and coaches started to fill the road. They broke camp as the dust from the road started to get heavy. As Jackson was hitching up the mules, Anna complained about the dust. Jackson assured her the dust was better than the mud after a rainstorm. They only had to wait until the afternoon to find out that was true.

About twenty miles from Jefferson City, it started to rain. Just a slow-moving front at first, but then with more and more wind. In an hour, the wind was howling through the tops of the trees, and the rain turned torrential. All traffic stopped on the road, and word spread like wildfire down the crowded highway that there was a tornado ahead. Aaden and Anna only knew of tornados from accounts in the newspapers back east and the story of Natchez. They knew the storms were deadly, so, slogging through the mud, they got everyone sheltered in a deep ditch at the side of the road.

The tornado didn't pass over them but came close enough that the lightning and roar of the wind was terrifying. Along with the flash of lightning and the boom of thunder came the frequent sickening crash of great trees hitting the ground. Deer, badger, birds, and squirrels were fleeing from the path of the tornado. A huge black bear ran to the edge of the ditch but veered off and continued down the road when Goliath stood and produced a tremendous woof that drowned out the noise of the storm and left their ears ringing. As the roaring drew closer, Aaden had everyone join hands. Rufus sheltered Anna between himself and Hannah and clamped onto Jackson's ankle with his free hand. Jackson had both arms around Goliath, and his eyes shut in prayer.

The tornado swept over the road about a quarter-mile in front of the terrified travelers. It was suddenly almost quiet. Light rain still fell, and the strong wind soon subsided to a quiet breeze. The men walked up the road and saw that at least a hundred trees lay across the highway, felled by the tornado. They could see the wreckage of wagons and some people moaning and trying to get up off the ground. Only the pines still stood, the mighty oak trees and the older hickory were all laying down, their root balls tipped up and dripping mud. When the men got back, Jackson said he could get the wagons into a field on the side of the road only a hundred or so feet away. He skillfully guided the lead Conestoga through the traffic ahead of him and turned into the field. Higgins and Aaden followed, and as soon as they were off the road and set up in the side-by-side layout for their camp, Jackson started unhitching the teams from the wagons.

Jackson hitched the two teams together, and when asked what he was doing said that he was going to go help clear the road. Aaden and Irwin set up one of their tents, and Hanna got the chest of medical supplies and set up a makeshift field hospital. Rufus had gone with Jackson and Goliath and returned with a man and a woman, his arm around the man, and a child of three in his arms. The man had a broken arm, and the woman was in shock. The child seemed alright but just stood in a daze as Hannah set the broken arm and tied it onto a wooden splint. Soon other injured people came straggling in, mostly men whose wagons stood untouched among the fallen trees or lay crushed beneath the heavy limbs. Anna was working as an emergency nurse and had some men building a fire to heat water. Others were setting up the spit and then went up the road to butcher some of the dead horses for dinner.

Rufus and Jackson were already hitching up fallen trees and pulling them here and there, mostly sideways to clear the road. Goliath suddenly went crazy and was standing on top of the crown of a fallen oak, barking. A young black woman lay pinned under the branches. Jackson brought the teams up and hitched on high to a limb that stood vertically about halfway up the trunk. As Rufus urged the mules forward and rolled the tree off the woman, Jackson freed her and carried her back to the safety of some open ground on the edge of the highway. More than a hundred men were going through the wreckage and carrying more injured people back to the open field. Several others were digging roadside graves for the dead. Jackson asked the young woman who she was and learned that she was Jessica, slave to the Jones family. She could see the back of the Jones' Conestoga up ahead, two children sitting under it at the back and crying. She ran to comfort the children and saw arms and legs sticking out from under a huge tree trunk that had fallen across the driver's seat. The oxen were uninjured, and Jackson unhitched them and turned them around to go back to the field. He told Jessica to take the children and the ox team and lead them back to the field.

With saws and axes, mules, and oxen, it still took two days to clear the road. There were a dozen graves in the impromptu graveyard. Mrs. Jones was the only woman noted on the crude crosses hammered together from the wreckage of the wagons and crates that perished in the storm. Most of the injured helped with the camp gathering what they could salvage from the wreckage, and made plans to continue onto Jefferson City when the road cleared. Several men tried to claim Jessica as their own slave woman, but Rufus only had to put his massive hand on the young girl's shoulder and shake his head no, to have them back off. The two Jones children, a boy of five and a girl of three, stayed clutched to Jessica and only would let go after falling asleep in her arms. Jessica laid them on a pallet under the buckboard and slept on the ground next to them, wondering what would happen to them now that the children's parents and her owners were dead.

The morning of the third day after the storm found the wagon train ready to move again. As they packed the temporary settlement into the wagons, Aaden answered Jessica's question and told her that she and the children were going to Independence with them. Aaden took her hand, raised her from the ground and, slipped her hand into Jackson's. "This man needs a wife. If you'll have him, he's yours. When we get to Jefferson City, I will give you an *Affidavit of Freedom,* and you can stay with us or go your own way. Anna and I are going to adopt the children, and I think it would be better all-around if you just stayed with us."

Jessica looked up with tears running down her cheeks and turned to Jackson and asked, "Are you a good man?"

"I'm a damn good man – one of the best, and I would be honored to be your husband."

The children clutched tighter to Jessica's legs, and as she gave Jackson a light kiss, she said, "You better be, or these kids will tear you apart."

They discarded the old chairs from the buckboard and loaded some valuables from the Jones' Conestoga onto it. Other items like the saws and axes piled on top of the loads in their wagons. Aaden found the Jones family Bible and saw that the only living relatives the children had were two sets of grandparents in England. He kept the Bible and, when reaching Jefferson City, offered it up to a *Justice of the Peace,* named Frank Bixler, as proof that the children were orphaned. He had the clerk for the tiny courtroom, who was Bixler's wife, draw up the *Affidavit of Freedom* for Jessica, and the Justice of the Peace joined Jackson and Jessica in a simple civil ceremony. Rufus and Hannah signed the marriage certificate as *Free Men and Women of the United States.* The issue of the children came up, and Jackson asked, "Could Jessica and I be the parents?"

Bixler was an abolitionist but looked skeptical about creating a mixed-race family. Aaden sensed his concern and said, "I'll adopt Jackson if that would set your mind a little easier." Mrs. Bixler looked at the children clinging to Jessica and told her husband to go ahead with the adoption. They never did that before, but with a simple document and the names of the grandparents recorded as *too far away to confirm,* the Jones children on the heels of the death that the tornado wrought, became the first mixed-race family in

Missouri. When Bixler asked the children their names, the children wouldn't speak.

"Isaac and Elizabeth," Jessica contributed. When Bixler looked up for the last name, Aaden didn't wait for the question, "Jones," was his preemptive answer. He would write the grandparents and assure them that the children would be raised by good God-fearing people, and there would still be a Jones family presence in the American West. With the formalities finished, Aaden booked Anna and Hannah into the last available room in Jefferson City. The tornado had displaced many from homes and businesses for more than forty miles up to the north. The men slept in the stable, and the stable master gave up his simple room for Jessica and the children. Jackson just lay down in the water trough to rid himself of the dust and mud from the highway. The other three men settled for a cold-water bucket shower and found some clean clothes from the trunks in their wagons.

They sat around a fire behind the stable as the sun went down and had a drink from a bottle of bad corn liquor they passed around. Aaden joked, "I know two things we can do to make a living in this place -- cut wood and make some decent whiskey." All the men laughed, but they might have been more serious if they only knew how the future would unfold.

The next morning Aaden took Jessica and the children to a cobbler and had them in sturdy boots for the trail by noon. As they were hitching up and loading up, Rufus said, "Damn those women look good in buckskins. Anna had on a long leather skirt and a red blouse. Hannah had on buckskin britches and a yellow polka dot blouse with a blue bandana tied around her neck. Jackson proudly led them out of the west side of Jefferson City with his wife beside him and the children sitting up on the load behind them. Jessica started singing a song the children loved, and soon the new family sat content, relaxing into their new circumstances. The road was more open, and it was easy to pass the few oxen pulled wagons they encountered. The forest was still thick, and the first night they camped in a clearing along the road. The second day they pulled into Independence full of hope and high expectations.

As they pulled into town, Irwin pointed out a wagon works that built Conestoga wagons and a smaller cargo wagon with a heavier carriage and wheels. The ring of hammers and the smoke from the forges were as familiar to him as his small shop back in Bath. As Aaden was arranging rooms for the women and locating the land office, Irwin made the acquaintance of Hiram Young, an

African American blacksmith who owned the wagon works. Hiram bought slaves and gave them their independence after four years of work in the wagon factory. They made a wagon every two days, starting with oak logs and billets of iron. The factory had a backlog of over forty orders, Conestoga wagons, and the heavy cargo wagons. "What's your biggest problem?" Irwin asked.

"Iron is no problem; there is more than enough coming up the river that winds up as scrap, or I can order it from the mill below St. Louis. Wood is the problem. The trees in this area are too damn big. Most of the lumber coming to town is hand sawed by settlers out in the forest. They are more interested in clearing land than making lumber. The supply is meager, and the quality is poor. If I had a reliable source, I could build a Conestoga in one day."

"Have you ever considered a sawmill?" Irwin asked.

"I own a sawmill; it's over there in those crates. It's all the metal parts and a boiler that has to be assembled along with a steam engine to run it. The problem is I don't have anybody to put it together and operate it. Also, the most desirable wood is oak and hickory. The logs are too heavy to handle in the forest; that is, if you can get them down in the first place. I can only run one business at a time, and all the partnerships I have tried around here have failed but one."

"Which one is that?" Irwin asked.

"It's Dan Jacobs over there in the saloon. He and I came here together from Tennessee."

Irwin told Young that he would introduce him to Aaden Callahan. Irwin would find him, and maybe they could sit down in Jacob's saloon and talk some business over a drink. Hiram said, "Dan's got a *boy* for a runner, have him sent to get me when you get settled down."

Irwin found Aaden in the middle of maps and conversation with the government land man several blocks up the street. He sat down and listened to the conversation. Most of the open land to the north and west was taken up in the opening land rush. There were over two hundred thousand acres of heavily forested land to the south and east of town. He drew a circle around an area about twelve miles south of town and said there was only one homesteader down there. A man named Jonathan Green had shown up with his wife the first day the land office was opened and said he would take a homestead wherever the road to the south ended. He also added, "If you were a man of means, I am authorized to sell twenty thousand acres down there that include the swamps and the lakes. That is pretty undesirable land, and I would accept any reasonable offer."

"We will look at it tomorrow," Aaden said, and they left the land office. The landman thought to himself; *I hope this city slicker is fool enough to buy the whole farm on this.* He had a quota to meet, and it was getting harder all the time with most of the good land already taken.

Aaden and Irwin sat down in the saloon and sent the runner over for Hiram Young. Dan Jacobs came over with a bottle of his best whiskey and a couple of glasses and poured the newcomers a drink. "It takes a real man to drink this stuff. The first one is on me."

With that, Aaden and Irwin quaffed their drinks and nearly spat out the foul liquor. Irwin stood up coughing, and Aaden said, "Jesus Christ buddy, doesn't anyone out here know how to make a decent whiskey? This rot is the worst I have ever tasted."

"Out here, friend, you have to take what you can get, and you have to be tougher than the rest to enjoy it. I have beer, but it isn't cold, I'll get you a couple of those." The two men drank the beer; it wasn't much better than the whiskey, but at least their vision cleared, and they quit sweating.

Hiram Young came in and just shook his head and laughed when he saw the whiskey bottle on the table. "Welcome to Independence, the land of plenty with hardly anything worth drinking." He opted for a beer, and Jacobs sat down with a couple more bottles.

Aaden laid out what he wanted to do. They learned how to move logs on their way to Independence, and they already knew how to make whiskey. Aaden liked the business model that Hiram used to operate his wagon works. He related his theory that the slave states were full of untapped labor with unskilled and uneducated blacks working inefficiently at back-breaking labor that makes the economy work. He went on, "Slave owners don't have any interest to improve the lot of the slaves, and they lack the imagination and foresight to put the machinery of the industrial revolution to work. I want to raise the welfare of the blacks, and improve the overall productivity of everything from farming to manufacturing."

Hiram liked what he was hearing, and when Aaden told him about the land for sale down south, he put forth a proposal. "If you decide to buy into that track, I'll let you take the sawmill down there and set it up. You will have to cut all the wood pieces that go into it by hand, and I'll send down a workforce of my trainees to help with that. The only condition is that if you decide to quit, you return the mill in working order. For my share, I want first right of refusal on all the lumber you produce. I'll broker what I don't need in my factory down to St. Louis, where it will bring top dollar. I want a twenty percent share of the proceeds from the lumber sales, and I don't want you stealing my laborers. I'll help you get all the manpower you will need. With the offer of freedom, you'll have more than you'll need standing in line to go to work for you. If you agree, let's shake on the deal and drink to our new partnership. Dan, I know you have a bottle of whiskey back there that won't give a man stomach cancer. Break it out partner; we are opening up a new frontier here."

The next day Aaden, Rufus, and Jackson took the buckboard and found the road to the south. Jonathan Green met them standing in a door of an outbuilding of his meager farm with a double-barrel shotgun cocked and leveled at them. All the men in the buckboard raised their hands halfway, palms out in the universal sign of supplication. Aaden said, "We mean you no harm, Mr. Green, we are here to talk to you." Green lowered the shotgun but didn't put it down. He just asked if the big dog was a biter.

Aaden got down and introduced himself and the other men. Green invited them over to the house where they sat at a picnic table, and Mrs. Green brought out a pitcher of cold tea and glasses. A couple of children watched from the cabin door. Visitors were not very common, and they stood half-hidden behind the door of the cabin, barefooted and dirty listening to the men talk to their father. Green agreed to show them down around the lakes and knew all the high ground in the swamp suitable for buildings and fields. It was the only reasonable land for farming down here. He had been living on his homestead since the land was first opened to homesteading, and still had around five months to go before he would own the land outright.

As they spent the day walking around the twenty thousand acres, Aaden saw millions of board feet of lumber on the stump, a swamp that needed draining, and lakes teeming with bass. Green told him that the land was just about worthless. One man couldn't clear enough land to farm before he starved to death. The forest was full of deer, and that is what he fed his family. Green pointed out copperheads and rattlesnakes and said that everything out here wanted to stab you, bite you, or suck your blood. It was hardly a fitting place for a man to bring his family, and if Aaden was going to buy the large tract from the landsman, he should only pay fifteen cents an acre or less.

Aaden offered Green a deal. "I'll buy your land for twice what you paid for it if you agree to finish out your fourteen months, so you have a clear title. We will relieve you of the need to constantly hunt to feed you and your family until you get your title. After that you can choose to stay on or leave, it will be up to you. In return, you will help us locate the best spot and help us build a sawmill. I will pay you fifty dollars a month for your work. Green had been working from dawn to dusk trying to clear land for farming, and in nearly a year's work, had only cleared enough for a passable garden and a couple of outbuildings. His was a hard life, and he accepted the deal without even discussing it with his wife. Both were tired and welcomed salvation from the hard life they had naively chosen for themselves.

The next morning Aaden went to the land office and bought the twenty thousand acres for three thousand dollars. He also filed four homesteads across the northern border of the track for himself and the other three men. If green sold him his land, they would control 20,640 acres of forest lakes and swamp, from which they would carve out their future. Aaden walked to Young's wagon works and was surprised to see the sawmill loaded on three cargo wagons waiting to head south. Jackson had the teams out of the stable and hitched to their own Conestoga wagons, and the three women were sitting in the buckboard ready to go. Hiram said, "You don't have to show me the deed; I knew you would buy the land when you left here yesterday." With that, he extended his hand and said, "Best of luck, I don't want you to let me down."

With that, the pioneers left town with the sawmill and Hiram's work crew following. As the sun shined down on their new adventure, Jessica sang, and the children joined in. She was surprised when the work crew joined in, and they all headed south to a new life. Anna was pleased; she could feel the baby stirring in her womb and wondered how their child would grow up, carving a life out on the frontier. The three women rocked back and forth on the seat of the buckboard, and Goliath looked up at them now and then like they were all from a different planet. When they got to the Green homestead, Aaden told Mr. Green about the land purchase and the homesteads. They selected a site on a high spot along the road, and Hiram's crew set to unloading the sawmill and carefully unpacking all the parts.

By nightfall, the two tents were set up in Green's bit of cleared land. Hannah had unpacked the kitchen and Mrs. Green; her first name was Mary, marveled at the cookstove and accessories that Anna laid out when it was time to serve dinner. Hiram's crew headed back to town as the workday ended with the sun setting in the west. The men had started cutting out the wood pieces they would need from pines that they fell near the road. After dinner, Irwin sat by the light of an oil lamp reading the assembly manual for the sawmill and learned the names of all the parts. Great care would be taken not to lose any of the nuts and bolts. The iron parts he could make, but a nut and bolt were well beyond the art of the simple forge. The mill was a complex machine with a double set of circular saws, each more than three feet in diameter. Everything was provided right down to the files needed to keep the blades sharp, along with a spare for each blade. He worked long into the night on the instructions and, at first light, was up, building a fire in the forge to heat the rivets that would join the plates of the boiler together.

Anna had unpacked her school books and had tutored Jackson and Jessica on the alphabet and taught them how to sign their names. The Green children finally lost some of their fear when Anna started reading a story about a girl and a boy and their dog. They sat at her feet, listening until they fell asleep using Goliath for a pillow. John and Mary carried their children back to the cabin and put them to bed. Their names were John Junior and Donna. It took them a while to speak up, but before they fell asleep, they told Anna that they wanted to learn to read.

Rufus had divided their sleeping tent with canvas, and the two couples retired for the night. Before she fell asleep, Anna told Aaden that he was a good man and everything was going to work better than he expected. He had to lead with confidence and keep the start of his commune motivated and heading in the right direction. Aaden fell asleep with his hand on her belly trying to feel the stirrings of their child.

Jackson and Jessica retired to the hammocks strung between the empty Conestoga wagons and wrapped Isaac and Elizabeth in blankets for the night. Elizabeth asked Jessica when her mommy would come to see them, and it broke Jessica's heart to tell the girl that her mother was with God, and she would have to stay there for a long time. There were four hammocks, but only three were used that night as Jackson and Jessica worked at adding to their ready-made family.

All slept the sleep of the exhausted pioneer. The next day would come soon enough, all full of work, just like many more to follow. They were landholders; all they had to do was carve their home out of the pristine forest, drain the swamps, and clear the land for crops. Dawn came all too soon, and all awoke with empty stomachs and sore muscles. No one complained, they were living their destiny; this is what all the miles traveled had meant. Here was their dream, and with hard work and determination, it would become their future.

THE FIRSTBORN

For two days, the pioneers were up before dawn, and by the time they were halfway through breakfast, Hiram's crew from town was arriving. The crew always ate before leaving town, but they would come to the camp for coffee and a piece of toast slathered with butter and jam. Breakfast was like an operations meeting, and by the time the men were ready to start a day's work, Irwin had everyone lined out on their job for the day. Irwin finished the meeting with a summary, "We'll have the boiler together by the end of today, and Hiram's crew will have the last of the sawmill set up. I believe that we will be able to saw logs tomorrow."

Irwin was right. Around five in the afternoon, Hiram pulled in with a freight wagon with kegs of nails and spikes, more carpenter tools, and the remnants of a small boiler and steam engine he had salvaged from a wrecked packet boat. He had two more men with him and told Aaden, "These men have earned their freedom as of next week, and they would like to stay with you. One is a carpenter, and one is a mason. I don't think you would regret taking them on. When are you going to fire up the mill?"

"In the morning," Aaden replied as Irwin was looking over the items in the wagon.

"I need some rigging," Irwin said as he walked over to shake Hiram's hand. The two men walked off with Irwin explaining his ideas with Hiram listening and making an occasional suggestion. Hiram's smile grew wider and wider as he toured the mill and admired the work, especially the riveting on the boiler. He was pleased and praised Irwin as only a fellow master blacksmith could do.

Hiram had one last suggestion, "When you fire this up in the morning, start the fire with only enough wood to bring up the steam. Get everyone well away from the mill and wait till the pop-off valve blows off the pressure. Assume nothing, a lot of good men are dead because they expected the pop-off valve to work as per its specs.

"What if it blows?" Irwin asked.

"That's why the boiler is over here, and the mill is over there." With that, Hiram got up into the freight wagon and left for town.

That night they dined on wild boar. It was a feral pig that had gotten away from a farm down in Independence. The pigs had no natural predators in the forest and were a nuisance to any unprotected garden. The pig was as tough as the pine they would saw the next morning, but it tasted good and filled their stomachs after a hard day's work. With the table cleared, Anna set up for A-B-C's. She was pleased when the two new men said they knew their letters, and they would help with the lessons. Jackson ran and got his book and took out his *Affidavit of Freedom* and asked, "Can you read this?"

Reverently and with perfect diction, the carpenter read the document like it was a prophecy from the Bible. In a week, he would be reading his own. "Teach me," Jackson pleaded, and a lifelong friendship was in the making as the carpenter, and the mason sat with Jackson around the fire outside the tent.

The next morning everyone was alive with the excitement of firing up the mill. Irwin and Hiram's crew set the firebox under the boiler ablaze. They watched as the temperature rose, and Irwin stayed with the boiler until the pressure gauge started to climb then he let go a blast on the steam whistle and walked up the road to join the rest of the spectators. It took about fifteen minutes with no one knowing what to expect, and then with a resounding hiss that filled the forest with the sound of its pending doom, a steam cloud filled the air above the boiler. A cheer went up, and Irwin and the crew walked back and started the steam engine that was the heart and soul of the mill. He moved the carriage back and forth and engaged all the saw blades. Each of the main saw blades was five feet in diameter and set one over the other so the mill could saw a five-foot log between them. That, however, would have to wait until they had the means to turn a log that large on the carriage. That would come when they got a structure over the mill that could handle a crane.

Everyone moved in as the first log rolled onto the carriage. Irwin set the dogs that held the log and adjusted the depth of cut with the ratchet. He pulled the carriage control back, and the log advanced through the saws. A slab of slash fell from the log, and the air filled with the scent of fresh-cut pine. Everyone cheered again as the slab glided out of the mill, and men pulled it off the back end of the flat rack. The next board slid down the flat rack, and the carpenter set the gang saws that trimmed it into a neat board.

It fell onto a table, and two men pushed the board through cut off saws that took off the crooked ends and turned the slab into a perfect board, ten feet long. Aaden took the board and carried it over to Anna and said, "Here is the first board of your new house."

Anna reached for the board, her mouth opened with a gasp and a look of surprise, and she reached out to Aaden's shoulder to steady herself. Alarmed, Aaden asked, "What's the matter?"

"It's the baby, it moved!" Anna moved into her husband's embrace and was content to sway back and forth with sunshine and the noise of industry filling the forest. "Don't be late for dinner, darling." She picked up the board and walked back to the camp. *A simple board,* she thought, *a symbol of a dream coming true.* She was going to make it into something special.

By the time Hiram pulled around midafternoon, Irwin was sawing the last of the pine logs, and an appreciable pile of one-inch boards waited for shipment to Independence on the load-out deck behind the mill. Stickers were between the layers to keep the boards flat as they dried. Hiram couldn't be more pleased. He tried to talk but just jiggled like a child every time he opened his mouth. The wagons he had with him carried a long heavy chain, block and tackle, pulleys, and two spools of heavy rope.

Anna invited Hiram to stay for the evening meal; they were preparing fresh fish from the lake. Jackson and the men were unloading the gear Hiram had brought in the meadow below the mill. After dinner, Irwin was going to show everyone how to deal with an oak tree.

They broke for the evening meal. Green had spent the day with the children at the lake teaching the newcomers how to fish. Jessica and Goliath stood guard watching for snakes that Mr. Green had warned them about as the four children caught *a mess* of smallmouth bass and perch. Every time they pulled one in, they squealed with glee and jumped up and down, clapping their hands. Jessica was pleased that the children could enjoy themselves and move a little further away from the loss of their parents. By afternoon, they had two buckets of fish, and the children carried them proudly between them as they made their way back to camp.

The fish dinner was much appreciated, but Goliath was happier eating leftover pig. There were still two hours of light when they finished dinner, and Irwin took everyone down to the mill. Jackson hitched up the mules. One of Hiram's men put on a set of climbing spurs and went up an oak on the side of the meadow like a monkey. He had a short rope and a pulley on his climbing belt and pulled a rope up the tree as he climbed. He got to the first branch and then climbed as high as he could up through the branches and tied the pulley he had carried up with the short rope. He threaded the rope he had pulled up with him through the pulley, and holding a loop under his arms, the men on the ground lowered him.

Irwin was across the meadow rigging the block and tackle and tying it to the base of another great oak. Jackson brought the mule teams into the meadow. The heavy chain was still in a cargo wagon parked at the bottom of the oak tree, and the line from the pulley was tied on the chain about eight feet from the end. The men tied the other end of the line to the drawbar on the trailing team of mules, and with a click of his tongue Jackson pulled the heavy chain up into the tree. This time the *monkey* rode up in style with his foot through a loop on the end of the chain. Up at the top, the monkey looped the free end of the chain around the tree and secured it back to the chain with a double-ended hook made specifically for that purpose. He untied the rope, yelled, "Clear," and let it drop to the ground. He untied the pulley and let it and the short rope fall to the ground, and then he climbed down.

The rest of the men pulled the rest of the chain to the block and tackle and tied it off as tight as they could. Jackson moved the cargo wagon out of the way, and Jackson tied the rope from the block and tackle to the drawbar. He moved the team off perpendicular to the block and tackle and with another click of his tongue, pulled the chain taut with the mules moving down the meadow. Moving now to the rump of the lead mule, he said, "Come on now Jorge; it's time to pull this monster down." The mules dug in, and the rope made a popping noise as it wound through the block and tackle with ever more tension. The oak tree leaned, but it didn't come down — yet. Irwin and the men pulled the slack end of the chain around the base of the anchor tree and hooked it back on itself. Jackson backed the mules up. The men unhooked the lead block from the chain, and the men stretched out the block and tackle as Jackson backed the mules. The men took another bite, hooking the lead block back to the chain. Jackson clicked his tongue, and again, the mules dug in straining against the pull of the already taught chain. The great oak tree leaned further, and then with a thump of a root breaking beneath the soil, it came crashing down into the meadow. Everybody stood quiet, amazed at what they just witnessed, and then the children started clapping, and soon, the meadow echoed with the cheers of the spectators.

Hiram looked at Aaden and said, "You know, I may not be the smartest man in Independence anymore." The block and tackle with its mechanical advantage had increased the pulling power of the mules from eight to thirty-two. Hiram said he would send for more men, and they would work through the night sawing the trunk into eight-foot-long saw logs for the mill. As darkness fell, Hiram was in the meadow with fires built high. He had five teams with two-man saws cutting the massive trunk into four perfectly cut eight-foot long saw logs. By dawn, his men had the first log onto the ways of the sawmill. He desperately needed oak beams for the wagon factory, and if he didn't get them soon, the factory would be idle, and there would be a lot fewer wagons rolling west.

They weren't the only ones who worked through the night. The women were up before dawn, making pulled pork out of the left-over pig and frying potatoes to feed the army working in the meadow. Goliath watched in dismay as he saw the last of the meat go into the big frying pan but jumped up and barked a command as Hannah picked up the large bone from the hindquarter she had been stripping. She threw Goliath the bone, and he caught it in the air and settled down next to the table to devour it. Anna was making gravy, and Jessica was baking bread. As the sun rose, Jessica called the men up from the meadow to eat. They didn't have enough plates for everyone, and Hannah commented that they were going to need a bigger kitchen and a real mess hall. The men who weren't eating were in serious discussion with Irwin about an idea they had for sawing up the big tree trunks. They had the parts out of wrecked packet boats, all they needed was bigger slash saws, and they thought they could make those down in Hiram's wagon works. In short order, a plan to build an automated slash saw on the back of a wagon took shape. In a week, the labor-intensive job of cutting the tree trunks into saw logs was only going to require one man, freeing up the other labors to turn the top of the trees into cordwood. The small branches were stacked and would be used for compost, bird habitats, or burnt next summer after they were dry.

By that evening, all the saw logs were turned into 4x4 timbers, loaded on cargo wagons, and headed into town. The day's activities set a pattern for a routine, and by the time fall and winter overtook the camp, Aaden had constructed warm, weatherproof cabins for all the married couples. They constructed a big kitchen and mess hall, a large bunkhouse for the unmarried men, and started on a smaller one planned for single women who would come to work at the camp. Their numbers were growing. Most of Hiram's emancipated slaves came up to stay on, taking up homesteads adjoining the original acreage. That first season, the lumber camp grew to over twenty workers. A sturdy frame supported a roof over the sawmill, and the big logs were no longer moved by hand but by a steam winch. The camp made dimension lumber out of pine and oak and shipped countless bundles of hickory to factories all over the country for handles for axes, shovels, and every kind of tool that could had a wood handle. They burned slash for heat, and the stumps were broken up and sent down to the docks in independence for fuel for the steamboats.

The small meadow where it all started was now more than thirty acres of reasonably good farmland. It was time for Aaden to make good on his promise to come up with some good whiskey. He sent away for corn and rye seed and a large still. The still was advertised as state of the art, made of copper, and had fancy brass fittings and valves. Blackberries were plentiful in the forest, and he was sending for peach and apricot seedlings to plant in the spring. He also sent for several thousand feet of cast iron pipe. He was determined to start new houses for Rufus, Higgins, and Anna come spring, and he was determined to have hot running water and flush toilets for Anna and the new baby.

Aaden was a regular at the slave auctions down in town, and he was always looking for men and women who showed promise at being assets to the homesteads. Anna constantly reminded him that he didn't just need strong young bucks and women with *child-hips*. Aaden was becoming known in the west end of the state as a man of considerable means and influence. The camp celebrated Christmas and the New Year with generous parties thrown in the mess hall. Many prominent men and women from Independence thought highly of an invitation to one of the affairs. Anna waddled around in her eighth month of pregnancy, and every woman who came up to the parties had advice for the mother-to-be. She just assured them that she had Hannah and that Hannah is an accomplished midwife. Hannah was there when Anna was born and was all that she would ever need in the way of assistance with the birth. The roads froze, and Anna received a lot of advice from the townsfolk that when the roads thawed, it would be impossible for her to get to town if she had trouble. Anna was strong and healthy and listened to the advice but was confident she could deliver the baby up here at the camp. She had seen Hannah work miracles with the sick and wounded. She trusted her

Nana more than any sophisticated doctor back east, let alone a frontier practitioner in town.

January passed by incredibly slow. The snows and cold winter nights seemed endless, and the short days slowed down the work at the mill. Every hour of the day, though, the hammers rang, the sawmill buzzed and sang the songs of the complicated machinery, and occasionally the sound of another giant tree crashing to the ground would echo through the forest. Aaden spent his time overseeing the operation, making sure that the steady stream of cattle and food supplies never fell short of the voracious appetites of the workers. At the same time, he kept an eagle eye on Anna. He was waiting for the first signs of labor with all the joy and trepidation of the first-time father.

On the first of February, Isaac came running into the mess hall with the news that there was a carriage down at the mill trying to get past the cargo wagons waiting to load out with the day's production. Aaden stepped to the door just in time to see Denise step down into a foot of mud in the road. Denise wasn't expecting paving stones, but she also wasn't expecting so much mud. As mud flowed into the top of her fashionable traveling boot, her driver shook his head and laughed to himself. Aaden ran down and rescued her before she could put her other foot down, and when he picked her up, the mud sucked the boot right off her foot. As Aaden carried her into the mess hall, he kissed her on the cheek and asked, "Why are you here?"

With her best New York nose in the air, she sniffed, "I'm here to become a grandmother." She arched her brow, and everything about her glance conveyed *you moron*. Back to the indignity of losing her boot in the mud, she asked, "Where is your city engineer? I want to complain about the mud in your streets." Aaden laughed and put her down and sent Isaac out to fetch the boot. Hannah came out of the kitchen, and the two women embraced, renewing their lifelong friendship with one long hug. "Where's Anna?" Denise asked again.

"She's over in her cabin resting. Her time is close, and I don't want her falling on the snow and ice or – getting stuck in the mud," Aaden replied. I'll take you over there as soon as we get you some suitable footwear. Welcome to the frontier, by the way."

Isaac came in with the muddy boot, but Hannah took it and went into the kitchen. She came in with a pair of real boots and dry socks and soon had Denise shod for the trip across to the cabin. Aaden took her across and kept her on the boardwalks so he wouldn't have to hear her rant on again about the mud. When he opened the door, Anna saw her mother and tried to jump up, but the best she could manage was to roll off the bed and struggle to her feet. Mother and daughter hugged and cried and finally sat down at the table. Aaden threw another log into the woodstove and made Denise a cup of tea. The chatter was all about the baby. Anna thought her mother was the embodiment of all the women from Independence rolled into one and then some. Anna finally got a word in and said, "Everything will be fine. I've got Hannah."

Irwin burst in through the door, and as Denise went to get up, he swept her off her feet and spun her around a couple of times and said, "My God, it's been a long time. I haven't seen you since last year." They all laughed, and after some more talk, Irwin took Denise out to show her around the camp. "Everything you see here but Green's old cabin was built in the last few months. We are pushing roads through to the adjoining homesteads. In the spring, we will start a water system to bring water down from a spring up in the hills. The men are clearing an acre of land every two days and can make more lumber than the freight wagons can carry away. The meadow is going to become a fenced field for corn and rye, and the rest of the land we clear this summer will be planted in apples, peaches, and apricots. When we get the trees cleared down to the south, we're going to build a great house at the top of the meadow for Aaden and Anna." Irwin finished up with, "Aaden is an organizational genius. We have only been making lumber for a few months, and already the camp is running at a profit. All the blacks who work here are free men and women and all eligible for homesteads. Aaden has filed for them on the surrounding properties. There will be cabins on all the homesteads by the end of next summer. We'll probably be raising cows or pigs or maybe both for our table. Each of the homesteaders will have a specific job or be raising a specific crop for the mess hall."

"Where did Aaden get all the people?" Denise asked.

"They are everywhere. We have a waiting list of blacks wanting to come in. Anna does all the interviews and screenings every week on Sunday afternoons. Aaden keeps his eye on the slave auction down in Independence along with Hiram Young, his partner in the sawmill."

"What will happen when you run out of trees?"

Irwin laughed, "Denise, there is enough wood and limestone here to build a city the size of New York. We aren't going to run out, and we are turning the cleared land into useful farmland as we go. The worst that can happen here is that we all wind up behind a plow -- but not to worry; Aaden has help coming from Ireland. We are going to make some really good whiskeys. The trails west will never run dry once we get started. I have ordered the saws and jigs that are needed to make barrel staves. I expect that in a few years, you will be able to order a glass of Missouri brandy at a bar on Fifth Avenue in New York City."

Denise put her arms around Irwin and with her head lying on his shoulder, said, "You have found yourself here, haven't you." Irwin had never thought about that, but he finally nodded his head, *yes*, wondering what that would mean for the two of them. Denise was busy with the *Black Freedom League* and working to turn Missouri into a slave-free state. She had recruited other people sympathetic to her cause and was opening offices in Chicago, Philadelphia and Washington, D.C. With that northern base established, she was going to start in the capital cities of the southern states. She had a lot of work ahead of her. She was also wondering what that would mean for the two of them.

Heavy snow started to fall as Irwin toured Denise through the camp. They spent a long time in the sawmill, Denise was mesmerized by all the moving components of the mill driven by one stationary steam engine chugging away under the watchful eye of the boiler man. It was warm near the boiler, and as they were warming up, Isaac ran up to them out of breath and excited and yelled, "Come quick, Mrs. Callahan is having her baby."

Denise smiled and said, "No, hurry, it's her first." She couldn't have been righter.

When they entered Anna's cabin, Hannah and Jessica were cleaning up the bed and getting the cabin ready for the delivery. The women shooed Aaden and Irwin out. Anna had broken her water while resting on the bed and had to stagger to the door to get Isaac's attention. The children had been playing nearby, enjoying a snowball fight in the newly fallen snow. Aaden didn't like abandoning Anna to the pain of childbirth, but Irwin put his arm around him and led him down the boardwalk to the mess hall. "Let's go cut some wood or figure out some other way to take over the world. The first child is going to take a while."

All the predictions were correct. Anna labored through the night and into the next day. When night fell on the second day, Aaden was a nervous wreck listening to Anna's gasps and screams. On the morning of the third day, Anna delivered a healthy baby boy. Aaden was asleep at a table in the mess hall, Denise had to wake him to tell him he was a new father. Aaden jumped up and ran for the door. Goliath was in his way, massive tail thumping on the floor. Aaden leaped over the dog but landed with his thigh bone on the corner of a table. He spun around in the air and fell flat on his back thinking he must have broken his leg. Denise shook her head as Goliath got up and licked Aaden's face with his huge tongue as if to apologize. "It's just a baby, Aaden, no need to kill yourself over a piece of good news."

Aaden got up and limped up to the cabin. His didn't break his leg, and the happiness and relief of the moment dulled his pain. Anna was sitting in an armchair, wrapped in a blanket near the woodstove. The newborn suckled at her breast, eyes drooping, almost asleep; both mother and child were worn down from the long ordeal. Aaden and Anna had agreed that if a boy arrived, he would be named Eli, and if it were a girl, she would be named Suzette. No carrying on of the French tradition where children wound up with four names. The first name would be French, and Callahan needed no explanation. "Eli Callahan," Anna said proudly, looking up at her husband and then nodded off asleep. Hannah shooed him out again, assuring Aaden that everything was fine. She would call him back after Anna and Eli got some much-needed rest.

Over in the mess hall, Irwin had broken out two bottles of the Missouri moonshine and was ready to toast the new father when he limped in the door. "Time to hoist one," Irwin said. Aaden accepted a glass and hoisting it high with the mill crew toasted, "Here's to Eli Callahan." The men cheered, and all drank the white, fiery liquor. The more experienced drinkers didn't cough, but the horrible liquor brought tears to their eyes and made them catch their breath.

Irwin demanded, "When does the still arrive?" Soon, was the reply after Aaden's breathing returned to normal. The party went on through dinner and into the night. The men needed a break, and wet snow was falling, a foot of snow had already accumulated by the time the men headed to the bunkhouse to await the inevitable hangover that would arrive at dawn. Aaden told Irwin that he was glad that it was over, and Irwin chuckled, "Well, unless you figured out how you got this one, it's not over."

Aaden almost blushed but simply raised his glass in a toast, "To the future." Irwin repeated the toast, lifting his glass as he tapped it to Aaden's. They quaffed the last of the whiskey, ignoring the hangover that would greet them at sunrise

THE ASSASSIN

The winter slowly gave way to spring, and with the change of the seasons came rain instead of snow. The rain made the big trees easier to pull down, but working in the mud was no one's idea of a good time. The work crew was growing and started calling the project *Callahan's Meadows*. Aaden liked the name and thought it would look good on labels of fine brandies. It was time to formalize the structure of his communal farm, and sitting at his desk in the newly built sawmill office, he drew up the *Articles of Incorporation* for *Callahan Meadows, Inc*. The company was already deeply engaged in the lumber business, but following his vision, he added farming, ranching, and distilling to the charter. Anna, Irwin, and Aaden would hold sixty percent of the stock. The rest would be held in reserve and proportioned out to the homesteaders that settled land around the original twenty thousand acres. There were already fourteen homesteads on the north and east side of the original block.

Aaden and Anna traveled to Jefferson City to file the document with the state government and also filed *Callahan Meadows* as a trademark. On their way through Independence, Aaden had opened bank accounts for each of the shareholders of the corporation and the homesteaders. Profits would be split and deposited to the accounts by the banker, but twenty percent of all the proceeds would accumulate as a cash reserve for capital investments. On the riverboat downstream from Independence, Anna wrote an article about *Callahan Meadows* and how the enterprise operated with free blacks. She gave it to the editor of the *Jefferson City News*. Anna was proud of what they had accomplished, and she felt that some notoriety in the press would only serve to grow their business. The editor, however, who was a staunch pro-slavery advocate, rewrote the article and portrayed *Callahan Meadows* as a threat to the very fabric of the slave-based Missouri economy.

Anna felt outraged and decided to continue to St. Louis to enlist the help of her mother and the *Black Freedom League,* to right the wrong. Aaden had to return to Independence. Irwin was building the brewery, and people were arriving from his father's business in Ireland to train the workforce and ensure that the blends and formulas for good whiskeys and brandies went into the first liquors produced. As Aaden put his wife on the riverboat to St. Louis, they both felt a bit lost. This separation would be the first the couple spent apart since they left New York.

Anna's trip to the *Black Freedom League* was not in vain. When she walked from the riverboat landing down to the old hotel, she could see that her mother had worked her magic on the building. Anna walked into what used to be the lobby of the hotel only to find a foyer with a reception desk worthy of any New York successful business. There was a polite secretary behind the desk who radiated confidence and two guards, one white and one black. Both the guards were armed and searched her travel bag before they turned her over to the receptionist. It only took telling her name, and the receptionist pushed the first button on a console that held many, and within thirty seconds, the sounds of locks and deadbolts being thrown open on the great oaken door to the side of the foyer announced Denise's arrival. Denise was surprised and thrilled to see her daughter, but immediately demanded with her hands on her hips, "Where is my grandson?"

As they walked back to Denise's office, Anna explained that Eli was with Jessica and that she hadn't planned to come to St. Louis when she and Aaden went to Jefferson City. "Why all the security?" Anna asked.

"There have been problems. There are several court cases here in St. Louis and others in Jefferson City that have the pro-slavery advocates stirred up to violence. The school out back was a target at first, but now there is a waiting list of kids for first through eight. The high school will start next semester. I made it fashionable for domestic slaves to be able to read and write, so the night school for adults is full and has a waiting list."

"This must have cost you a lot of money."

"No. Just at first. Now all the operating costs and then some are covered with donations from our old rich friends in New York. I'm putting the extra funds into law school for smart black men and women. We already have eight lawyers on staff; some black some white and some East Indian. But tell me, what is it that brings you here?"

Anna took out the article she wrote and a copy of the newspaper article for comparison. Denise sipped coffee as she read both, starting with Anna's. She sent for a young lawyer and gave him the task of researching the owner-ship of all the newspapers in Missouri. She asked him to get the file on the *Jefferson City News.* The young man left for some time, and when he came back in, he had two women paralegals with him. The file was thick. The summary by the lawyer told an interesting story. The editor of the paper was Rexford Halverson, a forty percent shareholder in *Missouri Publishers, Inc.* He was originally a sole proprietor but incorporated and sold stock to keep the paper afloat during hard times of his own making. His political views weren't popular, and his other shareholders came and went depending on their sympathies with the paper's current point of view. The editor's problem was that his viewpoint frequently changed, with whichever way the political wind was blowing. Denise noted that *Missouri Publishers* also owned a tabloid in St. Louis and was planning to start one up in Independence.

Denise stood up abruptly and said, "Enough study, let's walk up to the bank." She thanked her crew for the excellent report and led Anna back out to the foyer. As they left the building, the two guards fell in behind them as they walked up River Street. Anna found the guards a little spooky but didn't question her mother's judgment. The banker, who was also Denise's broker, was glad to see them and welcomed them warmly into his office. Denise and Anna sat in the big leather chairs, and the first words spoken by Denise were, "I'm going to buy *Missouri Publishers, Inc.*"

The banker was impressed. To date, all of Mrs. Mercier's investments were in solid producing companies. He didn't know why she wanted a newspaper, but he was more than ready to help the wealthy widow obtain it. It would be a hostile takeover. The first offer for the stock would be a couple of dollars over the current market price. The first offer would take in all the opportunists that mistakenly thought the paper was a good investment and let them realize a profit. Then the offer would be lowered to several dollars below the going price, and that would work the fear angle with many investors thinking that the stock would be worthless soon. After that, they would have to work with individual shareholders in private offerings to get fifty-one percent of the company. They would publish the offers in all the papers in St. Louis, and they would send notices of the offers to Jefferson City and Independence. A seller could mail their stock certificate into the bank, where it would be held in escrow until payment was delivered in full. The process would take two months at the minimum, but the banker assured Denise she was going to control *Missouri Publishers* by the end of the exercise. Anna turned to her mother and said, "I'm impressed with your actions. It is much more than I expected."

As they walked back from the bank, Anna asked about the security at the hotel. "What about the woman behind the reception desk? If someone came in to cause harm, what would happen to her if the two guards were dead?"

"I'll show you," was all she got out of Denise.

When they walked into the foyer, Anna noted that two other guards had replaced the ones that had walked them to the bank. Denise walked up to the reception desk; it was a high counter – probably the old front desk from the hotel looking new with a fine finish. Denise said. "Edna, it's time for you to disappear." The girl smiled and brought her fist down on what looked like a black tile insert on the desktop. A trapdoor released under her feet, and she slid down a chute into the basement. Anna was speechless. "Now, let's get you up to a room. I hope you will stay for a while." Anna declined, she told her mother that she had a school of her own to run and felt strange being away from Aaden and Eli. Denise put her arm around Anna, and as they walked to the heavy oak door, she said, "Stay a newlywed all your life, but stay here tonight." She wasn't a bit taken in by the comment about the school.

The next morning Anna set out by riverboat to return to Independence. By late afternoon she was standing by the railing on the Texas as the riverboat docked in Jefferson City. Passengers were walking down the gangplank, and the crew carried bundles of newspapers for delivery in the city. She could see the *Jefferson City News* building from the second deck of the riverboat. She wondered how Halverson would react to the hostile takeover. She saw as copies of the newspaper came aboard, that the editor was still on a rant about Callahan Meadows, the evils of blacks forming collective farms, and the destruction of the Missouri economy. She had no way of knowing that numerous shareholders had seen the banker in St. Louis the previous day and already signed over their stock. Anna did know that if Halverson was a competent journalist, he could easily find that the Black Freedom League was behind the takeover and make the connection from Denise to Callahan Meadows. She didn't want to make trouble for Aaden, but it was very satisfying for her vehement dislike of the editor to know he was doomed. After she read all the articles the *Jefferson City News* published over the last few days, Anna was glad that she would beat the news home so that she could raise the alert that trouble was coming.

As the riverboat was pulling away from the dock, Halverson was reading through the St. Louis papers that came to him regularly on the riverboats. On the front page of the Saint Louis Gazette, was the Callahan woman's story. Underneath was his article followed by an exposé of how he had wronged Anna Callahan, the author. Halverson clenched his fists together, and his face turned red as he scanned the stories. He turned to his window overlooking the river and saw Anna at the upper railing of the riverboat. She must have been watching his building because she picked up one of the fliers about the stock sale and dropped it into the river. Halverson didn't know what the paper was, but the symbolism of it was obvious and strong. He didn't have to wait long. One of the newsboys came running up to his office and handed him a copy of the flyer. Rage turned to vindictive hatred. Misogyny was to weak a word to describe what he was feeling.

When Anna got home, she hugged her husband and baby and then gave all the papers to Aaden and Irwin. They sat at a table in the dining hall, and after the men read all the stories, Anna apologized for the trouble she had stirred up. She was worried about one of Halverson's articles that portrayed all the blacks on the farm as runaways. The article showed a crude map of Independence with the location noted to the south with the headline in bold print that read, **RUNAWAY NIGGER HAVEN**. Irwin was the first to speak up. "Don't worry, Anna; this was bound to come up sooner or later. We will prepare for the *slave catchers* this article is sure to bring.

Catching runaway slaves was big business in the south. There was a lot of tension between Missouri and the Kansas Territory north of the river over the issue. There were abuses, even killings, perpetrated by the stronger advocates on each side of the debate. Starting that day, Irwin organized the Teamsters into convoys. The convoys included the Callahan freight wagons and also Hiram's. This way, they could be armed and guarded as they made the trek to town. The first convoy left later that day with Irwin and Jackson in the lead wagon. The daily production from the mill now filled eight wagons. About two miles south of Independence, two rough-looking men stopped the mules and rode up to the driver's seat. One of them said, "We'll be taking your nigger."

Irwin raised his Hawken Rifle from behind the footboard and said, "I only have one shot. Which one of you assholes want to die today?"

Jackson pulled a Colt out of his vest pocket and said, "That's okay, Mr. Higgins. I have enough bullets to kill the other one five times." With that, he shot the hat off the slave catcher closest to him then lowered his aim to put the next round right between the man's eyes, but he didn't pull the trigger.

The Assassin · 195

The slave catchers turned tail and rode back towards town as fast as they could. "That won't be the end of it," Jackson said as he loaded the empty cylinder of the revolver. He picked up the reins and with the customary click of his tongue, led the convoy into town.

The next day Aaden staged an ambush about a hundred yards south of the north property line. He wasn't exactly sure where the property line was, but that would be solved soon with a surveying company from Jefferson City. They didn't have to wait long. The next morning, four riders came up the road riding wary and looking all around. As they got up close to a small bank beside a rise in the road, a tree came crashing down on the road just ahead of them. In less time than it took for the tree to fall, twenty men and women stepped out leveling rifles and revolvers at the slave catchers. Aaden walked out into the road unarmed, told the men they were trespassing on private property, and to drop their guns to the ground. One man looked like he was going to attempt a shot, and Jessica caught his attention with a menacing swing of her rifle and a look on her face that told the man he was about to die. Aaden's people collected up all the guns and knives and then had the men dismount.

Aaden issued a command. "Turn around fellows; you're walking back to town."

Three other men, including Jackson, mounted up and in a slow march, headed the slave catchers back to town. One of the slave catchers said, "If you keep those horses, you will hang as horse thieves."

Aaden answered, "On *Callahan Meadows*, kidnapping a free black will get you hung just as fast."

When they got to town, Aaden marched the four men to the constable's office and put them behind bars. One of the men turned as the cell door closed behind him and said, "You won't get away with this Callahan."

Aaden reached through the bars and jerked the man forward by the shirt, and his head made a dull crack as his face tried to slide between the bars. "I just did, you idiot. You won't believe what's coming next."

That afternoon the men were arraigned in the district court and charged with illegal trespass with the intent to commit the crime of kidnapping free men and women of the United States. The judge said they would be held over for a formal trial but didn't set a date. By the end of the week, the constable had twenty men in jail, and the judge had to either try the men or come up with something that would clear out the jail. On Friday afternoon, the judge had all twenty men standing before him. His dictate was simple. "Boy's, you can plead your innocence and wait for a trial. I think that might be available on my docket sometime in the fall. Or, you can plead guilty, in which case you will walk free. Your horses, saddles, and weapons are going to be sold at public auction, and the proceeds will go to Anna Callahan's school for blacks here in town. How do you plead?"

One-by-one, all the men pleaded guilty – the meager diet and hot, cramped conditions in the cell probably had a lot to do with that being the favorite option. "One last thing before I release you. If you are ever caught in Jackson County taking a free-black out of here, I will hang you. If you are caught down on Callahan's farm, I won't have that problem. You will never get out of there alive. There are no slaves down there, and if I have anything to do with it, all of Jackson County will be a slave-free area before long. Do I make myself clear?"

All the accused shook their heads yes, but on their way out of the court-room, the man with the bruised face turned to Aaden and said, "You're a dead man."

Stoically and without a trace of concern, Aaden answered, "Everyone dies. The only question here is if you are smart enough to die of natural causes or surrender up your old age the next time I see you." As the men filed out, Irwin offered them free tickets on a riverboat ready to leave for St. Louis. Most men took the ticket, but some opted to hire out as guards on the wagon trains heading west on the Santa Fe and California trails. Aaden posted an account of the hearing in the local rag and made sure the account got posted at every saloon in town and the lobby of every hotel. He also paid a newsboy five dollars to meet every riverboat docking in Independence for the next month. He made sure the lad wouldn't run out of flyers that carried the ac-count of the hearing.

Slave catchers weren't the only ones reading fliers. In Jefferson City, fliers soliciting for the stock of Missouri Publishers were everywhere. The price was now at six dollars a share. Worse than the low price, editorials were being published in the St. Louis newspapers recapping all the issues over the years that Halverson had received negative backlash. All in all, it was a strong case that his company was in trouble. It was obvious that someone was vying for control of the stock. He was waiting for his investigative reporter to return from St. Louis to see if there was any information as to who his attacker was. A raider couldn't accomplish move like this in total anonymity. Someone had to know who was making the bid for his company. Whoever the attacker, they were smart. The investors that were holding the stock for profit had already sent their certificates to the bank in St. Louis to cash in. He was receiving requests daily to verify the certificates by number and by owner. He was refusing to answer the requests, but he knew that was futile and that a court order demanding the information would arrive when the attacker got close to a majority interest in the company.

Several days later, when Halverson came to work, the reporter he sent to St. Louis was waiting for him in his office. Halverson closed his door; he alone wanted to control whatever information the man had. The reporter was anxious to relate how clever he was getting to the bottom of the attack. He had represented himself as a large shareholder. He did own some legitimate stock in the company; it was only ten shares, but he had altered the number on the certificate to read 1,000 instead of 10. When he showed the certificate to the banker, he kept the written-out amount concealed in a folder. He only pulled the certificate up far enough so that the 1,000 was showing. He said he wanted to sell, but he wanted to know who the buyer was. The banker said he would talk to the buyer, but he wouldn't reveal the name.

The reporter watched the bank, and, in an hour, an elegant woman walked up the street with two guards. He knew she was the buyer, but he didn't know her name. She left the bank after meeting with the manager and walked down River Road to the old hotel. The reporter said, "The hotel is rebuilt, and it is a fortress. It is the headquarters of the *Black Freedom League*." He slid an article from the St. Louis Gazette across the desk. It was a write up on the founding of the *League* and had a little background information on Denise Mercier, the wealthy widow from New York City. He slid another article across the desk that was from the New York Tribune. There was a picture of the millionaire Mercier with his wife on his left arm, and his right arm was around none other than -- Anna Callahan!

Halverson was pleased. Two and two now made four. He took five double eagles out of his pocket and slid them across to the reporter. "Only you and I will know about this." The reporter swore his silence and picked up the coins, wondering where he would spend his good fortune. Halverson had a more serious thought, though. He was planning his revenge. After the reporter left, Halverson called in his secretary and told her to send for Haden Pierce. Pierce was a noted slave catcher and had a reputation as a gunman and a killer. Halverson didn't just want revenge anymore; he wanted Anna Callahan dead.

Another month went by, and the situation settled down at *The Meadows.* Slave catchers were nonexistent these days, and the work on houses and production facilities was going well. The mason had started on the limestone block foundations for a large home for Aaden and Anna. It was a casual afternoon, and Anna and Hannah had walked up to the home site to look over the progress on the foundation. Looking down the meadow, which had now grown into a field more than a mile long and half a mile wide, they saw Rufus and Jackson leading a Belgian horse from the seat of an elegant carriage. When he pulled up to the foundations, he dismounted the driver's seat and with a great flourish, opened the door and said, "Look what else I found in town."

Lily stepped down first followed by Ben and James. Hannah almost passed out with relief, and Lily rushed up to catch her mother in a supportive embrace. Lily looked great; she had grown a little more and had a healthy radiance about her. Ben had also matured, and now both were wearing the gold pendant of Nassau. The women broke into active chatter with Lily who asked about the baby. Rufus and Jackson showed Ben around the basement of the great house explaining where this, and that would be when the house was completed. Anna wanted to show Lily and Ben the orchards they had planted down in the meadow. Rufus got up in the driver's seat and left to return the carriage to the stables. The Belgian was a great replacement for the Morgans he cared for in New York. The pride he took in having the only Belgian in Missouri showed every time he talked about the great animal.

Aaden joined them from the orchards as they walked down to the meadow. Aaden hugged Lily tightly and asked her to tell them everything she and Ben had done since they parted in New Orleans. Lily told of their experience on Nassau:

> *"Celeste was walking out to the end of the pier as Connor docked the schooner. She waited until the gangplank was raised to the bulwark then walked aboard, Connor took her hand to help her down from the railing. "I have come for the girl," she announced when Connor gave her his best why-are-you-here skeptical look with his head cocked and eyebrows raised. An argument started but ended as Ben, and I stepped*

out of the companionway with sailcloth bags holding all of our possessions. I was wearing the gold pendant and had my knife in its scabbard on my back. Connor and Celeste agreed. James was going to stay on the island and buy land. I was going to be educated in the ways of my people. Ben would stay with me and report to James from time to time. James concluded the negotiation with, 'By the way, we need ten kegs of good white rum to replace some stock we had to barter away in New Orleans.'" Connor would make the rum delivery to New York and then return to Nassau before sailing back to Ireland."

"Celeste told me I had tremendous potential for becoming a priestess of the Yoruba religion. Her tutoring would dispel all the myths about voodoo and teach Ben and I the values of our traditional West African beliefs. She taught me about seeing. It's a gift she explained, not a sham. We played a simple game with a partition with shelves on each side. On each shelf were six colored stones. Celeste would remove one of the stones, and Lily would have to guess which one it was. I was really bad at first but then got better with the meditation and cleansing diet shared by all in her community. By the time Connor returned from New York, I was master of the game and right more than ninety percent of the time. James was busy too; he had bought up all the swampland on the island and most of the good farmland for pennies an acre and established Nassau Sugar & Rice, Ltd. The elite of British Nassau thought he was crazy but changed their minds watching the farm industry grow."

Everyone was pleased to hear that Lily's time was well spent. They all laughed at the news that James was taking over Nassau.

Lily stopped the group about halfway down the orchard, suddenly urgent to tell them why she was there. "You are in grave danger, Anna. You have to believe me, and you have to take precautions."

Anna asked, "How do you know this?"

"I talked to your mother in St. Louis, but beyond that, I just know. I can't explain how it works, but I am going to stay with you until this danger passes."

Anna could see Lily was determined and decided to let it rest for the moment. She would discuss it with Aaden that night. The group walked on, heading for the original camp. There were seedlings planted in neat rows with exact spacing between trees. Orchards of apples, peaches, and apricots were flourishing, the young trees protected by tall wooden fences. The deer fences would stay in place until the trees were tall enough that the leaves would be out of reach of the deer. Then the fences would come down and be moved to protect more new seedlings. They got to the end of the orchards and were passing through two twenty-acre vegetable gardens surrounded by an eight-foot deer fence. When they got to the end of the aisle between the two gardens, they would turn toward the original camp. Lily was excited to see Eli and Jessica's new baby. The women were always talking about babies.

Haden Pierce concealed himself behind a rotten log on the north end of the meadow, close to the area that was first cleared when the sawmill started operations. He couldn't believe his good fortune. He had intended to sneak into the camp after nightfall and kill the Callahan woman in her cabin. He had a horse hobbled on a game trail two hundred yards into the woods and figured he could easily escape even if he shot the woman in broad daylight. Anna's killing would be quick, and, in his mind, he thought – *less risky than going into the camp with a knife in the dark.* He was about three-hundred-fifty yards from Anna, which was starting to push the effective range of the Hawken rifle, a weapon with which he took pride as a marksman.

He rose to a kneeling position and resting the rifle on top of the rotten log he took careful aim at the Callahan woman. The small party stopped in the road at the end of the aisle between the two gardens, and the women were chatting about something that caught their interest along the way. He could have missed because of the gnat worrying the edge of his eyelid; he could have missed because he misjudged the drop of the bullet; he could have missed because of the distraction of the money he would get for killing Halverson's nemeses. He set the back trigger that armed the front trigger as a "hair trigger" that would fire the deadly shot. His aim was true, and he should have killed the woman, but he missed because as he pulled the trigger, the black girl tackled his target in a burr of motion and knocked her to the ground. The bullet cracked as it ripped by and hit the hair bundled on the back of the black girl's head. The group didn't run away, and Pierce figured he could reload and take one more shot. That was the last bad decision he made in his sorry life.

Aaden and Jackson had everyone down. Aaden had a Hawken of his own and aimed it at the smoke cloud from the black powder that was lingering in front of the rotten log. Aaden was talking Jackson through where the assassin was as Jackson spread two legs from the front of the barrel of his Harper's Ferry Model 1849 rifle. Jackson was an excellent shot and had recently won the rifle in a shooting contest up at Fort Leavenworth. He knew that he had at least twenty seconds before the shooter could reload and try again. Running wasn't an option; they were too far away from the camp, and running in the open would surely get one of them killed. Jackson took sight on the top of the log through the V-notch on the back of the gun. The V-notch showed calibrations for distance, and he locked the rear blade of the sight on 400 yards and concentrated on the top of the log. "Deep breath, let out half of it and stop. Don't hold your breath," Aaden intoned. "Take your time; I've got another shot and can hold him down with the revolver if you miss. If he is smart, he will crawl away and disappear."

The shooter wasn't smart; he lifted the barrel up and over the log. Jackson took the shot, and the bullet pierced the shooter dead-center below his chin, severing his brain stem and killing him instantly. "Stay down," Aaden commanded. "Jackson, reload, but don't stand up." Men were running down from the sawmill, guns in hand. They got within fifty yards of the log and formed a scrimmage line. They advanced in one-line converging on the log while two other three-man groups flanked the log from both sides. There was a simple, brutal beauty to the movement but it was unnecessary. Pierce lay on his back, surprised eyes staring emptily at nothing. The bullet hole under his chin was obvious. The lack of blood indicated the man had died instantly. The men signaled Aaden over, and Aaden was surprised to see that it was the man who had threatened him in the courtroom more than a month ago.

They went through the shooter's pockets and found him to be the licensed slave catcher Haden Pierce. The man had twenty double eagles in a pouch tied to his belt. More importantly, in his shirt pocket was a bank draft to be paid upon the approval of Rexford Halverson. The amount on the draft was for eight hundred more dollars. Aaden commended Jackson on his good shooting and asked him to get his fastest horse ready. He was taking the money and the bank draft to Denise in St. Louis. Halverson wasn't just losing his newspaper; he was going to lose his freedom for a good long time.

After getting the *all-clear* from the rotten log, Lily helped Anna up to her feet. Lily asked, "Do you know you are pregnant?

Anna was surprised but answered, "I thought I was, but I wasn't going to tell Aaden until I was sure. Anyway, how do you know?"

Lily told her that as she held Anna down, she sensed that she was protecting three spirits. Hannah cocked an eyebrow and said, "For a young girl, you seem to know a lot about pregnancy. And what do you mean? Three spirits?"

"Don't worry mother, in my training with Celeste, Ben and I have both taken the vow of celibacy. Celeste says it's important if I am to reach my full potential as a seer. I will be in my twenties before Ben and I marry. Until then, James is our chaperone; he is not very comfortable with my being able to tell what he is thinking all the time. Three spirits; Anna is pregnant with twins."

Aaden left as soon as his horse was ready. He rode through the night and the next day. Resting a few hours, he continued through the next night, waking proprietors in the way stations every twenty miles to trade out for a new mount. He arrived in St. Louis the next morning and went into the *Black Freedom League* headquarters and handed the evidence over to Denise. She was relieved to hear that the assassination attempt failed, but she smiled, now knowing that the situation was going to come to an end soon. She got Aaden settled in a room for a good rest and then went down and bought a ticket on the fastest packet boat for Jefferson City. She was going to have a very interesting chat with the owner of Missouri Publishers.

When Denise walked into Halverson's office the next day, she had the Constable with her. She sat down in one of the chairs in front of the publisher's desk, and the Constable remained standing at her side. "Mr. Halverson, may I call you Rex?" Denise nodded with the grace and full expectation that she deserved that he would say yes. She paused until he acquiesced. Halverson finally nodded, and she continued tilting her head to the side for emphasis. "Rex, it has come to my attention that your paper is in trouble. I am here to make my final offer. I'm offering ten cents on the dollar for the par value of your shares in Missouri Publishers."

Rexford clenched his fists and turned purple, and Denise thought he was going to foam at the mouth before he blurted out, "Get out of here." Denise didn't respond; she just reached into her purse and slid the ten double eagles onto the desk.

When Halverson still didn't respond, she handed the bank draft to the Constable along with a lithograph of the assassin that had covered the top of the front page of the Independence rag. The accompanying article explained in full the attempt on Anna's life and recapped Anna's write up on *Callahan Meadows*. It also included Halverson's corrupted version. The Constable shook his head sadly at the paling newsman and said, "Come with me, Halverson. You are under arrest for the attempted murder of Anna Callahan." He stood Rexford up and cuffed his hands behind his back and led the broken man from his office.

Within a day, Denise bought the remaining stock for pennies on the dollar. Even Halverson sold her his shares to pay for his legal defense. Denise happily took a stage to Independence for a much-awaited family reunion.

MARRIAGE AND CELEBRATION

As evening fell on the night of the attack and the day's work, and excitement settled into uncomfortable memories, Irwin called a meeting of all the shareholders. All gathered in the newly completed church as the forest woke to its evening symphony of insects and frogs with fireflies dancing in the trees to the music. The night was warm, summer was coming on fast, and soon the work of expanding the orchards and gardens would be joined in earnest. Anna settled everyone down and introduced Lily, Ben, and James, holding Lily affectionately at her side, as sisters would after a long separation, and told the story of how Lily had saved her life that day. She told some humorous stories of Lily's antics as a young girl in New York, and how Ben came into their lives and how he left them in New Orleans to stay with Lily on Nassau. Lily was training to be a priestess of the West African religions, and the young couple was planning to marry when Lily's training was complete.

Rufus and Hannah held hands and looked on with great pride as Anna finished letting the group know that Lily was *mantic*, able to read the thoughts of those close to her, and very handy with the knife she carried on her back. She joked that everyone should be careful of what they were thinking around the young woman. She finished up with letting everyone know that the visitors were going to stay for three weeks. Lily was going to teach West African religion here in the church for anyone interested, and James and Ben would spend their time in the brewery. The gathering cheered, like good Christians everywhere, they deplored drunkenness but savored fine liquor.

James took the floor. He modestly related his history of growing up with the founders of Callahan Seas. He downplayed his role in the company as the Chief Operating Officer and gave a summary of the ports-of-call and the trade that the conglomerate conducted. When he got to the subject of Nassau, he became more animated and told how they came by the gold and how it was used to take up a significant land position for sugar cane production on the island. Soon fine cane sugar and molasses would be arriving to feed the fermenters at the brewery. James had taken the liberty to quadruple Aaden's order for the stills, and the brewery would have to be expanded by the fall to accommodate the new equipment. Someone asked if they were going to make beer. James smiled and replied, "Anyone can make beer; you are going to make some of the finest whiskeys and brandies your American west has ever seen."

With that, Irwin took the floor. He put up a map of the landholdings and beamed with pride as he told James what each homestead was specializing in producing. They were already raising pigs and cattle, making forty-gallon barrels for the brewery and furniture for the homes. Roads were complete to half of the now twenty-four homesteads, and the remainder would be complete by the end of summer. The sawmill was producing over twenty wagon loads of lumber a day, most went into Independence, but the priority was house construction at *The Meadows*. A lime kiln was under construction – a large beehive furnace – and soon, *The Meadows* would have all the lime needed for mortar with excess to sell in Independence. James was impressed; he joked that he wanted to buy stock in the corporation, but Irwin sadly told him that he would have to take up a homestead and stay here fourteen months to get a title for the land. James said, "It's tempting, but the sea is my mother and my sister-wife. If I stay on land, I have to be where a fog horn wakes me in the morning. But don't worry, I'll visit often, and I will always be working in the background on your behalf." The meeting wound down, the women stayed in the church to talk, and the men walked over to the dining hall for a manlier closeout to the session.

Irwin produced two bottles of the first corn whiskey from the brewery. There was to be a toast. All had a glass, and some of the men who had very bad experiences with the *white lightning* down in town looked a little skeptical, but none refused the drink. Ben was the only one to beg off. James hoisted his glass, "To Aaden Callahan and *The Meadows*."

"To Aaden Callahan and *The Meadows*," the men replied loudly and quaffed their drinks. None coughed or spat it out; this was indeed a different brand of the white liquor.

James looked at his glass and said, "That is a great step toward *uisge baugh,* the water-of-life to the Irish. It isn't half bad."

Irwin perked up anxious to explain, "It is only two days old, wait till we age it a bit and add some flavor, and you're going to like it even better." Irwin explained further, "Anna translated a copy of the Francois Andre Michaux account of his trip down the Mississippi in 1804. He was following the whiskey from Kentucky down the river and found that the whiskey tasted better the further downstream he went. On flat rafts adrift on the river currents, the whiskey took nine months to reach New Orleans. The whiskey shipped in a variety of recycled oak barrels that the brewers charred on the inside for purification. We brew up the typical white lightning, adjust the alcohol down to fifty percent, and drip it through a charcoal filter. We also char the inside of our new barrels. Want another drink?"

When it was time to bring the day to a close, the men shook hands with James and Ben and walked across to the church to collect their women and return to their camps and cabins. The single men retired to the barracks, and Anna, Hannah, and Lily came over and settled in the kitchen. Jessica held the baby, and Lily smiled as she ran her hand over Eli's head. "This one will be great," she said as she looked into the eyes of everyone in the room. Hannah was serving coffee and apple pie made from preserves put up last fall.

Lily was holding the infant and murmuring to him as she held Eli to her cheek. Irwin asked Lily, "How do you *see* things about to happen, and how do you do what you do?"

"Every living thing has a spirit, Mr. Higgins. It is the spirit that I can see, and it is timeless."

"What can you see for me? And by the way, please call me Irwin. We are old friends."

Lily took Irwin's hand, and after a careful inspection of the strong, calloused hand of the blacksmith said, "You are a happy but a very, very lonely man. But the loneliness is going to change soon. You have much on your mind to work out, and then everything will be okay."

"You can tell all this from looking at my hand! It's hard for me to believe that what is in my mind is connected to my hand."

"Look down your arm," was all Lily said with a serene and serious look as she turned his hand loose.

Everyone sat silent for a few moments, and then Anna started to laugh. Even Irwin joined in, and all laughed until they had tears in their eyes, a very fitting close to a very trying day. Anna walked back to her cabin, let Eli suckle until he was content for the night. She shed her clothes and pulled on her nightdress, and as she lay on the bed, she cuddled Eli and murmured, "You're going to be great, my little man." She went to sleep missing Aaden and wondering when he would be back and how he would be with the prediction of twins. She would have to ask Lily in the morning if they were to be girls or boys or one of each. She fell asleep as four armed men emerged from the barracks and silently took up positions at the four corners of Anna's cabin. Until all threat to her life was settled and final forever, she would never be left unguarded at night or any other time when she was away in town.

It took more than a week for Aaden to return. He arrived in an open buckboard with Denise sitting next to him dressed in buckskins and a large straw hat held down with a hurricane strap. Anna noted that the ensemble was a far cry from the elegant clothes her mother wore for steamboat travel. To Anna's amazement, she also had a gun belt strapped to her waist and carried a Colt Patterson Revolver low on her hip like a gunfighter rather than a woman of fashion.

Aaden had caught up with Denise in Halverson's office writing articles for the paper. She was making an offer to any interested past shareholders on the abolitionist side of the slave issue to buy back their shares at a fair price. She had already received several death threats from the pro-slavery side of the issue and had an artist generate a drawing of her in her gunslinger's outfit to publish on the front page of the paper to rebuke the threats. Her intent was clearly to shift the hatred from Anna to herself. Aaden didn't approve of the tactic because he didn't want either woman in danger, but he couldn't argue with the inspiration of the strategy. When Anna asked about the *new look* her mother was sporting, Aaden just shook his head and handed her the *Jefferson City News* with Denise's picture on the front page.

James and Irwin came down from the lumber mill office, and Irwin noted the gun on his woman's hip and asked as he took Denise in his arms, "Are you here to join the security team? They work at night, which might interfere with my plans for you."

Denise kissed him and murmured seductively in his ear, "Later, baby, you can disarm me later."

They took the reunion down to a picnic area next to the church. Aaden was eager to show James the plans for the brewery. While in St. Louis, he had ordered a new invention for a still called fractional distillation. He used a drawing to help explain how the new still worked. "Like all stills, this one has a condenser. This condenser, though, is different. The condenser is built in stages and extracts three separate *cuts* of the vapor coming from the still. The *middle-cut* advances to aging barrels as the final product. The *bottom-cut* returns to the still. The *top-cut,* the strongest alcohol, is filtered through limestone and charcoal and used for brandy production or diluted to join the whiskey stock. The *fractionator,* the name for the whole condenser, makes the process continuous. The still will no longer be connected to just one condenser. The brewing pots themselves will be a heated-continuous operation, and the spent mash from the last tank in the line is fed to the pigs. In the heat of summer, the brewing pots will be cooled with the spring water that feeds the brewery and the camp.

James added to the enthusiasm telling of his purchase of four more stills to add to the brewery and the sugar and molasses production that would arrive from Nassau. "You could make rum if you want, but there is a tax on rum made from sugar coming from the British colonies in the Caribbean. What you are making is already better than the *rotgut* down on the river. You'll give the *moonshiners* a run for their money. But here is another idea; they could sell or barter their moonshine for lumber or food, and you could refine it in your brewery. I think in a year, you will be the main supplier for all the whiskey going west on the trails and have an excess to send east."

Irwin related that the ditch to the lake would be complete in another month. The level of the lake was going to drop three feet, and more than two thousand acres of the swamp that will dry up around it will be tilled and planted in corn and grain. "What else did you buy me in St. Louis?" he asked Aaden.

Aaden smiled his best devilish Irish grin and replied, "A machine shop."

Irwin looked amused. "Oh, really now! And who do you reckon is going to run such a thing?"

Aaden shrugged. "I've advertised in the Jefferson City paper for a machinist. If we don't have any takers, we'll send someone that shows some talent off for an apprenticeship. Either way, we will have a machinist, a bottle maker too."

Irwin raised his eyebrows, "A bottle maker, of course! Is there no end to your ambition?"

"No!" Aaden leaned forward and spread his arms wide. "We will control every operation it takes to make and bottle whiskey. Just think, our grain, our liquor, our bottles behind every bar in the West." He leaned back with satisfaction.

Irwin gave him an imaginary toast knowing it was useless to buck Aaden's resolve, "So here's to it."

Aaden clenched his fist in the air, "Indeed!"

Content with the *man talk,* Irwin turned to the ladies. "Anything else?" He was anxious to get Denise alone now that they finished the business end of the meeting.

Anna took Aaden's hand on one side, and Denise's on the other. She said, "Lily says I am pregnant again, and this time it's going to be twins!"

"How does she know?" Aaden asked incredulously.

"Trust me, she knows," Anna replied. Denise hugged her daughter, Aaden sat quiet, half joyful, half astounded.

That night the Callahans and the Sawyers had a simple reunion dinner in the kitchen. Irwin and Denise had a reunion of their own over in Irwin's cabin, and Ben was the only newcomer to the group that set out from New York over a year ago. Aaden asked Lily how she knew Anna was pregnant. More animated with her eyes flaring wide, Lily steepled her fingers. "I see you do not believe."

Aaden was a bit flustered at Lily's intense gaze and confrontation and tried to explain farther, "If it is not science or mechanical ...."

Lily cut him off and smiled, "I've missed you, Aaden," and then she stood up. "What if I show you?"

Fascinated despite himself, Aaden watched as Lily had Ben withdraw a case from his jacket and set up a miniature set of the guessing game that Lily used to train with Celeste while on Nassau. Lily said, "This isn't to show off; this is to prove to you that I can *see*."

One-by-one, Lily played the game with everyone. With Anna, Denise, and her mother, she was one hundred percent right on ten attempts each. Aaden was suspicious and suspected that the women had arranged some secret code or sign to tell Lily the colors of the disks. He asked if she would mind wearing a blindfold during the demonstration. With the blindfold, she repeated the exercise with Anna and again was ten for ten. She did her father and was down to eight for ten. Maybe she was getting tired. Aaden gave it a try, and Lily was down to seven. For some reason, she was reluctant to do James and a smile spread on her face when she got zero right. "Your mind is inscrutable, but it is not blank. What are you thinking?"

"I think that I will take you and Ben to Ireland and enroll you in college. Ben can be admitted to Trinity with no problem, but we may have to bend the rules a bit to get you in."

Lily scoffed at the thought of higher education, and she dismissed the topic and repeated the game with Anna, back to ten for ten. She ran her hand over Eli's forehead and smiled again, then put her hand on Anna's stomach. "They are boys," she said looking deep into Aaden's soul. You are going to be a fine father."

"I was hoping for girls," Anna said with a trace of disappointment in her voice.

Denise was also hoping for a girl and took Eli from Anna and said, "You, little man, will just have to wait for a sister."

"There will be a girl a little later, maybe in a few more years," Lily added.

"A family of four!" Aaden exclaimed. He was amazed beyond belief but had gained a great deal of respect for Lily. As they retired to their cabin, Aaden couldn't help but notice the men posting the first watch around the camp. He wondered how long the slavery issue was going to keep tearing Missouri apart. It seemed like an equal amount of trouble always accompanied the good. Like the Chinese *Ying and Yang,* there was always a balance.

The next morning Denise took Anna and Hannah aside; she had an announcement of her own. "Irwin and I are going to marry. These children to come, don't need grandparents with loose morals spoiling them. How do you feel about that, Anna?"

Anna started to cry. Was it the journey from New York and the trials and tribulations along the way that bonded her mother and Irwin, or was it fate? Maybe it was the freedom she finally realized in Vicksburg or her desire to keep Irwin in the family for a long time to come. She didn't care; she was buoyant with joy for her mother and looking forward to calling Irwin dad and grandpa. Choking back sobs, she said, "We're going to plan a wedding. It won't be like New York, but it's going to be fine."

And fine it was. Anna invited more than five hundred people, and five hundred more wanted to come. All were welcome. The town square in Independence was cordoned off for several days because there wasn't a single church or meeting hall in Independence big enough to host the event. Denise thought it would be a good idea for Aaden and Anna to renew their marriage vows at the same time. She always felt bereft over not being able to give her daughter a formal wedding, even though she fondly spoke of the ceremony aboard the *Blessed.* The town was engaged, building a new pavilion in the square. They also were busy removing all the manure and waste from the thousands of pioneers that gathered every week in the square to start their journeys west. Flags and banners flew around the square, and after an orchestra from Jefferson City arrived the morning of the event, the townsfolk moved wagons in to block the road. Guards took up positions -- armed men and women from *The Meadows*. Everyone expected trouble from the slaver's campaign building against Denise and her *Abolitionists*. "Hope for the best and prepare for the worst," was the mantra of the day, and all of Independence was solidly behind their heroine Denise and *The Meadows* community to the south.

About an hour before the ceremonies were due to begin, a small packet boat put to shore a mile down the river from Independence Landing. Isaac and Elizabeth were hiding in the rushes along the shore, and Isaac sent Elizabeth running to warn the security forces at the barricade. The name of the packet was *Slave Catcher,* and it was notorious for its raids into Missouri and up the Mississippi kidnapping blacks with no regard for human life that got in their way. Forty armed men disembarked over the gangplanks and made their way up to the east-west road from Jefferson City. They turned west and walked in a loose column towards the barricade. Jackson was there with more than twenty other armed men and women from *The Meadows*, sandbagged and entrenched behind the barricade. He said, "Hold up there, men, you're not invited to this party, and you're not coming into town."

"Says who nigger?" With that, the leader of the column started to raise his rifle, and Jackson shot him through the heart. A thunderous volley from both sides followed the single shot and more than half the men in the column fell. Only one of the defenders suffered a wound behind the barricade. The rest of the column started to reload, but as one, the men behind the barricade formed a skirmish line and moved forward, picking off the remaining column one-by-one with well-aimed shots from revolvers. One man from the column was allowed to run away to the east to carry the news back to the sponsors of the *Slave Catcher* that the attempt to disrupt the ceremony in Independence Square failed meeting fatal force at the hands of the men and women from *The Meadows*.

When the shooting started, Isaac lit the wick on a bottle of one hundred percent alcohol and heaved it about sixty feet onto the boiler deck of the packet. The pilot saw it coming, turned to the captain, thanked him for paying him in advanced, and dived into the river. The captain rang the bells for full reverse, but the engineer and boilermen were long gone, over the side. The captain left the pilothouse, ran down the side of the Texas, and slid down a pole to a lifeboat on the stern. He launched the rowboat and, as he picked his crew out of the river, cursed the Mercier widow and every black in

Missouri. He failed to notice that the boy who burned down his boat was white.   As the boilers aboard the *Slave Catcher* exploded, the orchestra on the pavilion struck up with Felix Mendelssohn's "*Wedding March*" in C major written the previous year.

With an air of normality, Denise and Anna walked up the back stairs of the pavilion to join the tuxedoed men in tails and top hats in the center of the stage. Denise wore a simple white shift, but Anna wore a flowing wedding gown with lavender flowers at her waist and in her hair. The vows for Irwin and Denise were read first as Aaden and Anna stood as their first man and maid of honor. Ben and Lily stood for Aaden and Anna, and when the formalities were complete, Hiram Young and James, decked out in the borrowed regalia of the *Knights of Columbus,* drew sabers and formed an arch through which the couples descended the front stairs of the pavilion into the welcoming arms of well-wishers.

The wedding party was on. Pork from *The Meadows,* cooked over barbeque pits since morning, fed the throngs; children played their games, and fine whiskey flowed freely. At dark, the party moved to the landing on the Missouri, and a grand display of fireworks worthy of a Washington D.C. Fourth of July lit the skies for over an hour. Slowly the party wound down, and the townsfolk returned to their homes reliving the wedding day that would never dull in their memories. Rufus loaded the married couples in the carriage along with Ben and Lily and drove them through the moonlight back to *The Meadows.*

Riders were on their way to Jefferson City after the ceremony. A full account of the event would appear in the Jefferson City News and the St. Louis papers. Mention of the demise of the *Slave Catcher* or its mercenaries was purposely absent from the news they carried. The riders passed by the security force finishing up the roadside graves and took note of the packet drifting down the river burning down to the waterline. The event would be told and retold in the bars along the waterfront after the riders delivered the newspaper articles to the editor of the Jefferson City News. *Hunting season* for slaves or abolitionists in Independence was over forever. Beyond that, the young men and women of the security forces from *The Meadows* would mature and play key roles in the black regiments that would form and fight on the side of the Union to make Missouri slave-free twenty years yet in the future.

James stayed another week and then left with Lily and Ben for New Orleans, where they would join with Connor, who would take them to Ireland.

The summer plodded on. Aaden and Irwin threw themselves into the expansion of the Brewery, and by the end of the summer, the brewery was making over fifty gallons of whiskey a day. The farming expanded, the young orchards continued to grow, and the spent mash from the brewery was feeding over five hundred very happy pigs. Almost every new house in Independence was going up with lumber from *The Meadows,* and every wagon heading west was built of wood and iron fittings made in the new foundry below the old camp. The great house for Aaden and Anna was complete, along with most of the homes and cabins on the homesteads. When Aaden took Anna up to her new home, she carried a wooden box with her. At the bottom of the stairs, she looked up, and the first board from the sawmill hung from the beam over the portico, and it bore the inscription in French *Château des rêves* – *Castle of Dreams*. She walked to the fireplace at the end of the great room, opened the wooden box and placed the alabaster horse with the silver knight in a cubby hole in the center of the mantel. So much had happened since that Christmas Eve in New York City. Aaden marveled at the statue; he had forgotten all about it. Anna would never forget, her knight in shining armor was right here by her side.

Anna was growing heavy with the twins as fall set in, and Eli was learning to crawl. Jessica brought Eli down to the mule stables and set him down where he could raise himself on the side of a water trough. She was watching Jackson in the round pen for a minute and then looked over to check on Eli. The little tyke was under the rails of the mule pen, heading out where he could be trampled. Jessica stifled her scream so as not to spook the mules, but got Jackson's attention waving her arms and pointing at the pen. By the time Ben got over the top rail of the mule pen, his big jack mule Blackie was standing over the baby, protecting him from the mulling hooves of the rest of the mules. Jackson walked up to Blackie, cooing, "Good boy." He picked up Eli and put him up on Blackie's back. Eli grabbed two handfuls of the coarse mane and Jackson clicked his tongue. Blackie walked around the pen several times with Eli smiling and laughing all the way. Blackie seemed to shine to a new master. Jessica was wringing her hands with worry and finally got Jackson to stop the mule and hand Eli back over to her. Eli didn't cry or fuss like other babies might have done when he was lifted off Blackie. He grabbed onto Jessica's neck and looked back at Blackie knowing he would be back. Jessica wondered to herself, "What will I do when you start to walk, and I'm too pregnant to run after you?"

THE PROFESSOR

With the festivities behind them, the folks of *The Meadows* settled into the intense construction season of summer. Denise and Irwin undertook the construction of a Victorian mansion that would become the headquarters of her growing newspaper conglomerate. Anna's school was expanded and was soon educating children of all colors. A nursery was included in the school and overseen by Jessica. Hannah lorded over the kitchen where breakfast and lunch were prepared every school day for all the students and evening meals for those staying in the modest dorms provided by the school. Teachers hired on when the fall semester opened; education spanned infancy through high school. It was more than Anna ever dreamed possible and brought quality education to people of all means, color, and creed. Tuition was minimal or waved for the poor. Children from *The Meadows* commuted daily, but some stayed in the dorms throughout the week. The women spent their weekdays in town to save the travel time back and forth from *The Meadows*, which would turn their workdays into nonstop twelve-hour days.

One Saturday after Anna had returned from town, Aaden was in the meadow below the sawmill when he saw a carriage pull up and discharge a passenger he didn't recognize. The man was portly, dressed in khakis with a full grey beard and a pith helmet crowning the hairy mass of his face. Aaden was working with carpenters and masons overseeing the construction of four large warehouse buildings. He huddled over drawings, discussing questions and answers in the patient manner that was the custom at *The Meadows*. The buildings would be used for corn storage and whiskey aging and serve as a shipping depot for the many items produced in the industries on the outlying homesteads. Salt pork and beef for the hungry pioneers on the burgeoning trails west was another windfall for the corporation. Aaden looked up from a set of drawings for the heating plant for the warehouse complex and finally recognized the man standing before him, Professor Charles Coryn. "Charlie! You're the last person I would expect on the frontier." Aaden pulled

Charlie into a crushing bear hug and heard the older man wheeze as his strong arms pushed the last of the air from the older man's lungs.

When he could draw a breath, Charlie said, "Easy son, you could stop an old man's heart that way."

They laughed, Charlie wasn't that old, but overeating and indulgence had taken its toll on his health. Aaden finished the meeting with his crew and turned towards the great house on the low rise on the south end of the orchards. As they walked up slowly and the lake came into view, Charlie was impressed with over two square miles of corn and grain growing around the lake. Aaden explained that the fencing wouldn't be complete this year, and they would have to share a good deal of the corn and grain with the deer. But the crop should start filling the warehouses and supply the brewery through the winter months. Corn and grain were always available at the trailhead in Independence to fuel the westward migration, and sugar and molasses were arriving steadily from Nassau.

"Aaden, you have built a remarkable industry here. I knew you were not cut out to be a history teacher the first time I met you. How did you get all this done in just one year?"

"It wasn't me. It was mostly Irwin Higgins who we took on board out of Bath, North Carolina. It's a long story. Irwin is a blacksmith and a genius mechanic. I am a figurehead and the administrator, and it was my vision to free slaves and provide them with the opportunity to become independent and more productive human beings. We now control over forty thousand acres, and there is a long list of applicants, both black and white, that want to join the corporation. There will be time to explain all this. You're staying awhile, right? By the way, why are you here, other than to take in my good looks and ogle the women?"

Charlie laughed, "James stopped with the young black couple on his way back to Ireland. By the way, the next time Connor crosses the Atlantic, he is going to bring your father and mother here for a visit. Reportedly, your father is rogue as ever and stirring the pot for Irish independence. The folks down in London will be glad to see him leave for a while. The House of Lords isn't pleased with him because the papers play him up to be a folk hero. I expect some money or some barrels of good whiskey has a lot to do with his popularity in the press. He is said to be funding resistance groups opposed to British rule and pushing for representation in the House of Lords. The Brits would love to hang him, but they fear it would cause widespread rebellion.

Both the Irish and the Brits would rather stop the bloodshed, so the situation is at a stalemate. America should expect a mass migration before long; conditions in Ireland for the common men and women are not good."

They were approaching the house. Aaden asked, "Do you know I have a son, and there are twins on the way?"

Charlie looked up at the great house and said, "That's one hell of a cabin for a frontier village." Anna was at the top of the stairs, one hand on the rail of the portico and one hand on her belly. She broke into a beaming smile and cried, "Charlie!" She wanted to run down but had to wait till the men ascended the stairs before she could be enveloped in Charlie's arms and kissed with tears of joy in her eyes.

They entered the great room, and Eli was up and staggering with the first steps of an infant towards Goliath. The big dog was Eli's constant companion now and endured the tugging and pulling affections of the toddler, with the patience and understanding of an experienced nanny. Charlie knew the parents were expecting praise for the child, but in his dry wit, he said, "Wow, you don't see a dog like that every day!"

Goliath was stretched out lying on his side, and Eli was making for the back of his neck. The toddler gripped two handfuls of hair and swung his leg onto Goliaths back as far as he could. The big dog knew his cue and slowly rolled onto his stomach then rose to his feet, Eli squealing with joy clinging to Goliath's neck. Goliath walked around the great room, and Charlie just watched, mouth agape in amazement. Aaden said, "He can ride mules too." They laughed together as only old friends could as if time and distance hadn't occurred. Aaden snatched the boy after several trips around the room and handed him to Charlie and said, "Meet Eli. Eli, this is your Uncle Charlie." Eli smiled and cooed and grabbed Charlie by the beard. The young boy probably thought Charlie was another St. Bernard to ride, and Aaden had to open Eli's hands to pull him away.

The men talked long into the night. Charlie told Aaden that he invested the money Aaden left him in New York with the young railroad companies of the nation. Aaden had wanted to invest in the Anchor Line, the St. Louis–New Orleans Riverboat Company. With examples and a rundown on the progress of railroad construction, Charlie pointed out that the steamboats were doomed. Railroads were connecting ports with inland cities daily, and everywhere the railroads reached, the railroads were replacing river transport with more efficient trains and safer trains. "Think about it Aaden; no floods, no snags or sandbars, and no massive tragedies with boiler explosions or wrecks ashore." Then he dropped his bombshell, "Besides, I bought you about twenty miles of rail, an engine, and some flatbed cars. Like it or not, you are going to be a railroad man now."

Aaden just looked at his friend in disbelief. Charlie softened the news. "I had a graduate student, who came to Columbia after graduating Rensselaex Polytechnic Institute, first in his class. His mentor was Amos Eaton himself, and the young man came to me highly recommended. He got bored with the curriculum for his master's degree because it didn't contain much about the impact of the Industrial Revolution on modern times. He left Columbia to go to work at the Baltimore & Ohio Railroad. The young man went with Ross Winans, who worked at the Baltimore & Ohio Railroad machine shop for some years before going out on his own; they were building locomotives in Baltimore. His name is John Gould; you'll like him. He's young and ambitious and will take up a homestead if you accept him. He is out to make his way in the world, but the railroad is in his blood; he is alive and as powerful as the steam in his engines."

Charlie went on, "John came back to see me shortly after James passed through New York. Winans wanted to raise money to build a bigger locomotive, one with four sets of drive wheels. I went up with John to see him. Winans was looking for money, and John was looking for an innovative application for a bigger engine. We talked about your timber business over here in Missouri, and by the time I left, I had agreed to finance the construction of a prototype with three sets of drive wheels, a horizontal boiler, and a steam winch to pull logs down out of the forest. It's not pretty, but it will do the job, and it's on the way. Oh, another thing, I used your money to invest in the engine; if you don't like that, I will buy the engine from you and sell it to someone else. The rails, engine, and cars were loaded on freight ships in the Baltimore harbor weeks ago and should be arriving in New Orleans within the week. It will take another month to get the parts and pieces up here, but I also hired the young engineer to put it all together for you.

"Charlie, what am I going to do with a railroad?"

"Connect everything out here! Connect the sawmill to the forests. Connect the farms to the storehouses and the brewery. Connect to Independence if you want. Run it down to the landing on the Missouri if you can."

"Was this James' idea?"

"It was James and Lily. She is a remarkable young woman Aaden. She told me I didn't have much time to get this done. She wouldn't tell me why, but my condition is pretty obvious. I'm old, and I am wheezing, I have a little time left, and I am going to make the best use of it on your behalf. I can't take up a homestead, but I can live in Independence or St. Louis and handle your investments from there. Did you read about Samuel Morse? He has invented a way for cities to communicate with each other using electricity."

They talked on and on until Charlie fell asleep in a comfortable chair. Aaden woke him and took him up to a guest room. Charlie already knew that the house had flush toilets, but hot water and a bathtub? "You've got to be kidding me! I'm not out in the frontier; this is uptown luxury at its best."

Aaden fell asleep with his arm around Anna with Goliath's tail making the occasional thump on the floor next to Eli's crib. It seemed all his life he was being pushed to the next level by people and events around him. He wondered when or if it would ever stop. With the wisdom that only comes with faith in the future, Aaden finally fell asleep thinking he would get Eli a pony when he was two. He would see to all his children's futures as his father had seen to his. With the last thought of his father and mother, he fell asleep wondering when they would make their appearance here at the camp.

The next day Aaden walked down to the stables to get a buckboard to tour Charlie around the homesteads and the fields. Jackson was in the stable nervous, and agitated. Jessica was in labor and Jackson was in the imposed exile of the father from the birthing room. Hannah and Jessica were in the small infirmary that had been completed in the summer, waiting for the baby.

Jackson and Rufus were in the stable, Rufus grooming the Belgian, and Jackson busying himself with chores. The familiarity of the animals, the gentle stomps, huffing, and the smells of feed and manure was comforting to the anxious mind of the expectant father. Jackson helped Aaden hitch up the buckboard and offered to come along. As always, the three men left the stable armed, Rufus and Aaden, with revolvers and Jackson with his long rifle. They headed up to the great house to pick up Charlie, and the four men spent the day touring the entire forty thousand acres.

Each time they passed through the camp; they drove past the clinic. Isaac and Elizabeth were sitting on the front porch and would shake their heads *no,* and the tour would continue. Charlie was much impressed with the facilities. Everything exceeded his expectations far and beyond James's report. They finished at the brewery with a drink of the oldest whiskey produced to date.

Charlie commented, "That's already smooth and better than many brands I have tasted over the years." They finished with a drink of apricot brandy that was in the making. "That's going to be good too. I'm impressed, especially with the machinery. I have toured several breweries in Kentucky and from what I saw there, you are way ahead of your time."

They passed by the clinic again and then went down into Independence to visit Denise and Irwin at the mansion. Even though it was fall, the town square was full of wagons ready to head west the next day. Since grass would be scarce on the prairie soon, almost all the teams were mules. Oxen were the draught animals of choice in the spring because they could eat grass and pull better in the mud. You had to feed mules, so there was always a freight wagon loaded with bags of corn or grain with each Conestoga or Conway. Mules could average fifteen miles a day and make the almost eight-hundred-mile trip to Santa Fe in two months, but one had to put up with the cantankerous nature of the animals along the way. There were other disadvantages for mules. Indians would try to steal them, and they were less than desirable to eat than oxen if the owners ran out of provisions. The town square was a cesspool of animal and human wastes. Sewers carried a good deal of the waste to the river, and sweepers did their best to keep the animal manure to a minimum. However, it was always a relief to get to the upwind side of the square.

North and west towards the river were the favored areas. Throngs of travelers were set up cooking their last meal in town for a good long time. Outfitters and vendors were making transactions and providing the last of the provisions needed for the trip. The faces in the crowd were full of ambition with intelligent talk in English, German, French, and Dutch. Expectations ran high, regardless of the language. Last-minute haggling filled the square with a never-ending banter. Arguments over the last sack of corn or a keg of nails filled the last restful evening for the westward bound. Charlie was amazed at the enthusiasm and vibrant energy of the people as they gathered around the square. Aaden was pleased to see a barrel of *Callahan Meadows* Whiskey bring a hundred dollars at an impromptu auction. "There's a lot of opportunities out there," Charlie said as they pulled up in front of the Higgins Mansion. The exterior of the Victorian wood and brick structure stood complete and elegant, but the workdays rung with an army of workers finishing the interior. Wares of the craftsmen littered the yard, but only a few men remained taking care of details after the close of the workday.

As usual, Denise was writing for the papers, sitting on a hard-back chair, diligently penning the conclusion to her latest series of editorials on slavery and human productivity. She and Charlie had been casual acquaintances in New York through their mutual acquaintance of Aaden, and she was thrilled to welcome the *Professor* to her home. Denise apologized for the construction mess, and they quickly settled into the subject of Anna's school. The new school was to open the coming Monday, Denise invited Charlie to address the opening assembly. "I know this is a long way down from Columbia, but would you please come and talk to the children and the parents?" Denise implored and her charms aside, Charlie said he would be honored to speak and asked to see the school.

It was an easy walk to the school. Contractors were working late painting and putting on the finishing touches. Almost all of the teachers were there too, unpacking books, going over the curriculum, and looking forward to teaching in a progressive private school, unbound by politicians, school boards, or meager state budgets. Charlie was impressed by the staff. It was obvious that great care had been taken in the selection of the personnel. There was a good mix of older, experienced teachers well regarded in their specialties. There was a solid core of educators in the middle of their careers and several new teachers eagerly awaiting their first students. Several Ph.D. men and women augmented the staff here and there, particularly in the science and math areas.

As they made the rounds through the nursery, the dormitories, and the dining hall, Denise started to talk about Anna. "My daughter will be here on Monday, but she won't be able to do much until the twins are born. I will stand in as administrator until she can return to the school full time, but I am no educator. I'll do my best, and there is a lot of wisdom here in the staff that will help me, but I am really worried that I could mess this up for her."

Professor Coryn transformed from the personality of the friendly, fatherly façade of Charlie, and emerged as the experienced educator; he reassured her that the hard part wasn't the teaching. "The hard part is the politics of the outside world versus the underlying philosophy of the institution and the interface to the parents that were the challenges. You will do just fine with both of these. You can count on some backlash from the Slavers. You and Anna have made quite a name for yourself. There is a column in the *New York Times* that follows your activities from time to time, and I even read about your school in the Chicago paper on the way out here."

"For me, it will just be a temporary position. I am more worried about Anna over the long haul. I watched just what you are talking about destroying teachers and complete schools in New York. Just look at Aaden, and what happened at Columbia?"

Charlie knew a sweet and cunning manipulation was afoot, but he was retired from Columbia, and he could think of no better way to spend his remaining time than to help with this cause. "Why don't you let me handle that job until Anna is ready to take back the reins? I'm not going back to New York, and this is the most exciting place I have seen in my travels west. One condition though; there has to be a boarding house for me to stay in."

"You'll stay with Irwin and me at the mansion. Rufus and Hannah are moving down too. Rufus will see you over to the school every day, and I will guarantee that Hannah is going to take on your disregarded health as serious as the reconstruction of Washington D.C. after the War of 1812."

Charlie held up his hands, "I am perfectly capable of taking care of myself, at least for now. But if you and Hannah don't mother me to death, I'll take the job."

With that, *The Independence Freedom School* gained years of experience and the leadership of the eminent Dr. Charles Coryn from Columbia College as its regent, superintendent, principal, and friend. Denise was excited to get back to her desk and write a news release on the new addition to the staff for a run on the front page in the morning.

It was dark by the time they started back to the mansion. Aaden, Denise, and Charlie were walking the short distance back to the mansion, taking it slow on Charlie's behalf. Rufus and Jackson joined them at the edge of the square; while the others were at the school, Jackson spent his time tutoring the new *mule skinners*. As they walked toward the mansion, there were several resounding bangs back in the square. It was a favorite pastime of some of the young boys among the permanent residents of Independence to harass the pioneers in the square. It was easy with mules. Half the species were usually mild and easily trained into their roles as draught animals. The other half operated as independent contractors and would only yield to the harness under the constant curses and cajoling of the owners. The biting, kicking, cantankerous nature of half the mules was only part of the problem; most of the owners were from the city, and most had never owned or even touched an animal until they arrived in Independence. Outfitters loved these immigrants; they could easily sell the worst of the mules to the first-time buyer, mules that had been passed over many times by the more experienced. None of the pioneers were *teamsters* in Independence, but all would be "wagon masters" by the time they reached Santa Fe or Fort Laramie.

The young scallywags could pick out the green handlers easily. They would crawl under the wagons and unhitch teams or unlatch the gate on a makeshift corral. A few large firecrackers later and the mule melee was on. If the noise and commotion didn't produce the desired stampede, a few well-placed pebbles from slingshots onto the rumps of the lead mules would do the trick. One unfortunate fellow who fell asleep on the driver's seat of his Conestoga had wrapped the reins around his hand; he intended to be ready to leave early and be first on the trail. He woke flying through the air and hit the ground hard, trying desperately to free himself as the team of eight mules thundered west.

Without question, he would have been the first out of town on his way west without his wagon if it wasn't for Jackson. He watched the team barreling down the street, terrified eyes wide and white in the dim light of the campfires. He waited in the street for the team to reach him, then grabbed the harness on the lead animal and swung up on the back of the big mule. He reached down and slipped his fingers into the side of the mule's mouth and turned him to the side. The rest of the team followed, and as they plowed through the ditch and empty field on the side of the road, Jackson kept turning the team until they finally settled. Aaden and Rufus ran up and released the bedraggled owner from the reins. He sported bruises and road rash, but his fashionable buckskins, newly purchased for the trail, saved him from serious cuts and scrapes.

Jackson helped the man take the team back to the square, and as he expertly backed the mules up to re-hitch the drawbar, he heard the man's wife ask from her bed up on top of the loaded supplies, "Elmer, where did you go?" It was funny, and Jackson would bet a fortune that the man would never wrap a rein around his hand again. He also suspected that the young boys getting paid a dollar here and there to round up the stray mules were the same boys behind the stampede in the first place. He would have accosted some of them, but he was anxious to get back to the clinic. He ran back to the mansion to join up with the rest of the men.

Denise put Charlie up in a stately room on the first floor of the west wing where he wouldn't have any stairs to climb, and Aaden, Rufus, and Jackson started back to *The Meadows*.

When they arrived, there was still no baby. "Get some sleep, Jackson. Your wife is only in her first day," the experienced fathers advised wisely, and Jackson went over to the clinic and fell asleep on the bench outside the door. Around one in the morning, Hannah came out and found him on the bench. She went inside and got a pillow and a blanket, and as she covered him up, she said, "You got what it takes, son, you are going to make a great father." That is exactly what happened the next afternoon, as Thomas Jackson made his début with Jackson and the children waiting outside for the first cries of the newborn.

Monday morning, more than five hundred people arrived for the opening of the school. Parents from town, parents from the outlying areas with modest luggage to install their children in the dorms, and a good number of military families from Fort Leavenworth; organized with footlockers for the dorms and neat packages of notebooks and other school supplies. The crowd gathered in the courtyard and Aaden was there to help Anna up the stairs. Dr. Charles Coryn joined the proud founders on the stairs, and Denise had artists making sketches and was taking notes, ever the publisher, ever the reporter.

After an affectionate introduction from Anna, Charlie was polished and eloquent in his speech. He stressed the importance of a well-rounded education and stressed history and science as the key to producing young men and women to assume their roles in the rapidly changing world on their doorstep. By the time he finished his speech, every parent listening intently to every word in the morning sun believed that their sons would be president one day, and their girls would become prominent women like Anna and her mother.

As the students found their classrooms and the parents from the outlying areas installed their children in the dorms, Irwin took Anna and Charlie aside and said, "You have done something remarkable here – and you are going to need a bigger school."

Irwin was right. When the articles Denise wrote about the opening, which included Charlie's speech word-for-word, appeared in the papers all over the east coast and down to New Orleans, support in the form of endowments, scholarships, and donations for expansion started arriving in the mail daily. Denise hired an accountant and business manager to help Charlie run the school.

Anna's simple effort of teaching Ben and the children at *The Meadows* to read and write was on its way to play a significant role in the lives of thousands of young adults, one of the great resources of the rapidly expanding west

THE CHRISTMAS HORSE

The days of fall started slipping away. The lush green of the forest gave way to the brown colors of winter, and the symphony of the night turned toward the white-quiet cold of winter. The young fruit trees in the orchards were covered with sailcloth to protect them from the freezing air. Men from the sawmill stocked firewood and supplies at all the homesteads, and the first warehouse was nearly full. Aaden was in his office in the corner of the whiskey aging warehouse, working on completing his inventory of the barrels and noting each numbered barrel's position in the warehouse racks. He was working at his desk, comfortable in the warmth of a wood stove in the corner blazing and crackling with pine pitch. The aging warehouse was appropriately called the *Rackhouse*. There was a steam-driven elevator that hoisted a rick of four barrels up the nine-tier rack. Irwin had designed the *Rackhouse,* and all the barrels moved with the elevator and steam winches. When Irwin completed the racks, the warehouse would hold two million gallons of bourbon; it would take two years to fill it.

Aaden was finishing his long day, and it was nearly dark when a young man in a canvas jacket with a multitude of pockets stepped into the light of the office. "You have to be Aaden Callahan; I'm John Gould," said the young man extending his hand over the top of the desk.

Aaden jumped up to shake the young man's hand. "I've been expecting you. How did you get here? I didn't hear a horse or carriage."

"I walked up from the river. I wanted to see the road I'll bring the engine up, and I made a lot of notes on the way. Sorry, I am so late. It's cold out, that fire feels good."

Aaden poured a glass of the best of the whiskey for the young man and asked him to bring him up to date on the railroad. They walked over to the dining hall to get John fed and talked for several more hours into the night. The engine would arrive at the landing on the river in a few more days. Getting it off the packet and onto shore was the biggest challenge, but the young engineer had a good plan and was confident that his preparations would bridge from the riverboat to the shore with no problem. He took out his notebook in its metal cover from a pocket on the front of his jacket. With a fervent intensity, he started to draw a map of the road from the landing to the machine shop. "Why the machine shop?" Aaden asked.

"It's the most logical place for an engine shed," was the reply. "These four turns on the road up from the river are too tight for the engine. We will have to work on them or find a straighter route around them."

"Let's go up to the house and call it a day. We'll take the buckboard in the morning and pick up Irwin in town. We can start at the river and work our way back."

As they entered the great room, Goliath met them at the door. He had been waiting patiently for Aaden to let him out for his night business. John took a quick step back from the door, "Wow! That's some dog!"

"Don't come up here alone at night. That is why we talked on the way up. He is a gentle soul but ferocious when he sees his territory or his loved ones threatened." Aaden put the young man up in a guest room and let the big dog back in. He went into the master bedroom and saw Anna lying on her back asleep, her enormous belly rising in the middle of her body made her look like a giant snail with blond hair in the dim light from the embers in the woodstove. He snuggled Eli up in his crib and noted that he would get the carpenters building the infant a bigger bed soon. Aaden got undressed, gently kissed his wife not to wake her, and fell asleep wondering about twins and the railroad. Goliath took up his guard position at the bedroom door. While instinct told him the visitor seemed like a good man, the young man was a stranger in the house, and the big dog slept lightly, ready to respond to the smallest out of place sound.

The next morning Aaden got the young engineer up early, and they hitched up the buckboard and drove into town for breakfast at the mansion. Charlie greeted John like the old friend he was. He saw him last up in Baltimore when he financed the locomotive. He knew John was the right man for the job at hand out here in Independence, and he was thrilled to see that the young man finally arrived.

Hannah was up *doctoring the Professor* as she called it. Charlie sat at the kitchen table with Rufus and had a lot to say about the diet. "Oatmeal and unfermented fruit juice," he complained. "Cows, pigs, bacon, and eggs as far as the eye can see, and she has me eating like a goat. Oatmeal for breakfast, lettuces for lunch, lean meat, or fish for dinner, and can you believe this, **NO BOOZE UNTIL CHRISTMAS**!" Everyone laughed as the older man nearly shouted this last vituperation through clenched teeth, and his hands curled into tight claws like he was ready to strangle Hannah; to say the least, it was a commanding performance. Hannah just cocked her head and looked at him with a loving, but disapproving smile.

Despite the discontent, Charlie had already lost more than twenty pounds under the strict regimen and was looking better and breathing better every week. Irwin came down the back stairs (they didn't call them the *servant stairs* in the mansion) and piped up with, "Come on, Charlie, you know she is saving your life. Quit complaining; you're going to thank her for a good many years to come."

Aaden introduced John all around, and the engineer and the blacksmith embarked on the first day of a lifelong friendship. What the young engineer lacked in experience; the blacksmith bore with the confidence of many accomplishments. What the blacksmith lacked in math and science; the engineer could calculate to the nearest millimeter over the girth of the planet. Charlie looked over at Aaden and gave him a smug nod of approval. Charlie listened, his diet a forgotten item as the conversation turned to the railroad, the weight of the engine, the size of the track, and how to get the heavy machine off the riverboat. John assured everyone that he had it figured out, but the engine with its modifications for the lumber industry weighed twenty-five tons, and it would be a challenge to get off the boat safely. There were no wharves in Independence, just the landing suitable for riverboat gangways. A trestle would have to be built on the soft soil of the river bank with closely spaced bents to support the weight of track sections and the engine with its tender.

Rufus took the professor in hand and said, "Time for your walk to school, Charlie." Hannah handed Charlie his mid-morning snack in a small metal box and gave him his daily admonishment to not cheat on his diet while in town. Rufus had become interested in the *Mormon Wars* that took place in the previous decade in the northwestern corner of the state. There was still property in Independence that was owned by the Mormons. The Professor and his *tender* had many discussions about this recent history on their walks to the school. Both had read all the accounts of the battles and massacres that were written during the time of the conflict. Few Mormons remained in Missouri; most had fled to Nauvoo, Illinois. Tensions were building up there against their sect, just as they had in Missouri. History was repeating itself, and Rufus brought up the important question -- where would they go next? The

Mormons could bring their troubles to Independence, and they were not a bit good for the whiskey business.

Aaden, Higgins, and Gould were leaving in the buckboard to go down to the landing to start their recognizance of the route down to *The Meadows*. The landing was too steep for the engine to climb on its own, but it was outfitted with the strong cable winch on the front and could pull itself up the bank once they had it down on tracks. John had three sections of track; each forty feet long built on heavy skids. The skids keyed together, and when the engine was advanced, the last section of track was moved to the front of the engine, coupled to the front of the leading skid, and the engine and its cars could advance forty more feet. It was a laborious process, but the engine would make the fourteen miles up to its new home – once it was off the boat.

By the end of the day, Irwin had heavy timbers moving down to the landing to build a trestle from the riverboat to the shore. The gannons and ox teams that had been used to drain the swamps were lined up to start taking the kinks out of the road the next day. With everything in place, the trestle construction itself would have to wait for the arrival of the packet to match the elevation of the trestle to the rails on the deck. Many eyes were turned to the river as news about the locomotive arriving for *The Meadows* traveled around town. Independence didn't have a mayor or a town council as yet, and ownership of the landing was nebulous at best, so building on the landing didn't require any landowner approvals or permits or oversight by the town. John picked out the most favorable spot on the bank to offload the locomotive. The work teams under John's planning and Irwin's direction started preparing the groundwork for the bents that would support the track skids to bridge the locomotive to shore.

All eyes were turned toward the river, waiting to see what Aaden was bringing to town. The morning of the second day after John's arrival, a rider came up the road from the east at breakneck speed, yelling, "It's coming! It's coming." Outfitters, shopkeepers, and the bartenders closed their doors and walked down to the landing. Gamblers had been making bets on such trivialities as how many wheels the engine had, how much it weighed, and how much it could pull. One would-be bookmaker was even giving odds on getting the engine off the riverboat without dumping it in the drink. The smart money went with Aaden's young engineer on that one, but there were always the naysayers playing the odds. All betting ceased as the riverboat came into view. The speculation raging for days was to end in a few more moments with winners counting their money and losers moaning their losses.

The packet was laboring heavily against the current with the weight of the locomotive and the track skids. It pulled abreast of the landing and turned in to ground the front of the boat as solidly as possible on the bank, directed in by John to line up with the groundwork for the first bent. The gangplank lowered, and blacksmith and engineer walked onto the packet, looking the engine over. "It's bigger than I thought," Irwin said as he ran his hands appreciatively over the thirty-five-inch drive wheels and the 17x24 inch steam cylinders that drove them. There was a massive winch mounted on the front of the engine where a *cowcatcher* would typically be on a more standard locomotive. A thousand feet of oiled cable wound around the drum. The scent of oil and grease pervaded the atmosphere, and the smell of wet ashes from the last fire in the boiler used to drive the engine aboard the packet, wafted through the air as John climbed onto the control platform. Irwin stayed on the deck studying the mechanics of the steam control system and the *reversing lever* that was used to run the engine backward. He was particularly interested in the steel cable wound on the winch; this was going to make a major difference in how they dealt with the big trees. John joined him, and they walked down to measure the elevation to the rails on the packet so they could get the crews sawing the posts for the trestle bents.

Hiram Young was at the first bent. He took Irwin aside and said, "You know, that engine is one ugly son-of-a-bitch." It struck Irwin odd that anyone would even care how it looked. All he saw was twenty-five tons of iron that could pull five-hundred tons of cars on level ground at twenty-five miles per hour. But Hiram was right; the locomotive was ugly. It was a brute, built for heavy work and not some fashionable streetcar business moving well-dressed citizens around a city. Everything on the engine was a dull black except for two nameplates, one on each side of the control platform fastened to the handrails that told the world the name of the engine was **ANNA**. The nameplates were fashionably a deep green with bright gold letters and gold stripping that lined the edges.

The boiler was a horizontal model and covered most of the back half of the forty-foot chassis. There was a deck behind the boiler where a fireman would stoke the firebox with wood from a trailing tender. Ahead of the boiler was the control platform where the reversing lever and brake handles rose through the floor. Valves to control the steam and a pressure gauge that was redlined at 85 p.s.i., were mounted on a plate in front of the boiler. Ahead of the control platform sat the winch. It looked massive with a set of gears in between the drum and the steam engine that geared the winch down to overwhelming mechanical advantage. John claimed it was strong enough to raise the entire engine off its track; in fact, spars that would attach to the sides of the chassis and turn the engine into a small track crane were due to arrive with track and barrels of spikes. There were three sets of drive wheels and a small four-wheel truck, similar to the wheels on a boxcar, under the winch on the front of the engine. Two heavy cylinders powered the center drive wheels, and a strong bar hooked the other two drive axles to the drive wheels.

John was alive with energy, and his enthusiasm infected everyone around him. He ran a string line from the bottom of the skid to the bank and set the crews to sawing the posts and building the bents. Ten bents would be needed, and there were ten teams of men from *The Meadows* and Hiram's shop to build them. The noise of saws and hammers rang out through the day, and Jackson showed up with twenty mules to pull the heavy skids off the boat. There were two empty skids on either side of the one the engine sat on. Jackson hooked on with his heavy chain and pulled the first skid off the boat. It made a heavy thwack as it hit the ground. The mule team pulled it up the bank and got it positioned in front of the last bent. It took the rest of the day, but as evening fell, all was ready to pull the first skid onto the trestle. John was anxious to get the locomotive off the boat, less the river rose, or fell unexpectedly and upset the careful planning of the elevation of the trestle. He built a small fire in the boiler about an hour before the last of the sway braces, stringers, and diagonal bracing was complete on the trestle. He was checking and topping off all the oil cups lubricating the many bearing surfaces and moving parts of the engine, and waiting for the pressure in the boiler to reach at least 50 p.s.i.

One last inspection of the work and the young engineer climbed up to the control platform and released the brake and clutch on the winch. Jackson and his mules pulled the cable out to the skid at the end of the trestle and hooked the cable into a heavy eye on the skid to tow it along. As John engaged the clutch and fed steam to the winch engine, the cable drew taught, and then the skid was pulled effortlessly back to join the skid under the engine. Jackson looked on and knew that the days of the mule were threatened, if not over, for good. What took him all day to accomplish, the steam winch accomplished in minutes. The heavy skid moved back to the front of the riverboat. The second skid was pulled down the trestle and joined to the first. Another inspection and this time when John climbed onto the platform, he gave a pull on the shrill whistle and slowly drove the locomotive off the boat. Much to the relief of the Captain and pilot, the riverboat rose a full foot without the weight of the heavy machine.

Cheers went up from the bank, and again money changed hands among the crowd. People started to drift back to town. The exhausted crews didn't want to work around the strange equipment in the dark, but there was still freight to be unloaded from the riverboat. Rufus arrived with a whole roasted pig and a barrel of whiskey, and the long workday and the tired muscles quickly lapsed into forgotten issues. The last skid was pulled backward to un-key it from the forward ones where the engine and tender sat. Using a snatch block tied off to a dead-man on the bank and the cable from the locomotive, moving the skids was easy. Till then, no one paid any attention to the heavy sheave on the front of the locomotive that allowed the cable to turn back under the machine, but now they marveled that the engine could pull in both directions without having to be turned around. Jackson maneuvered his team down the bank and pulled the freed skid off the trestle. He took it up the bank, and the cable was run out to pull it back to the front of the engine. With the trailing skid now in front, John moved the engine forward another forty feet. Moving the engine forty feet at a time was a slow process that would be repeated many times. The three miles to Independence and another ten or so down to the engine shed on the farm would take many days. With the last move, half of the heavy machine was now on solid ground, and John was satisfied that it was safe from the whims of the river for the night.

He wasn't the only one relieved. The pilot moved the riverboat away from the trestle and landed again a little downstream. He set the roustabouts to unloading the rest of the freight. More than half of them were slaves and enlightened with the spirit of freedom in Independence; they wouldn't be on the riverboat when it left at first light in the morning. Some of them would hire out and go west on the trail. The rest of them just joined into the work crews preparing to move the skids and take down the trestle. Hiram smiled and gave each of the new men a reassuring nod as a silent welcome as he noticed them among his men. So much was communicated among the Ne-groes with simple nods, expressions, and body language; many people that worked with the blacks every day thought someone needed to write a book similar to a dictionary about it. The Captain of the riverboat wouldn't even miss his slaves until it was time to take on his next load of cargo. He rarely left the comfort of the Pilot House or the Texas, the upper deck of the riverboat where the Captain and crew cabins were.

John was the first at the landing the next morning; it was still dark. He started the fire in the boiler and walked down to strike up a conversation with the guard Hiram had left there overnight to ensure his tools would be safe. As dawn broke, John looked up at the engine and saw that ornate wooden signs were hanging over the handrails covering the name **ANNA** with, **THE BRUTE.** John asked the guard about the sign change, but he replied, "I didn't see nutin sar." *Brute* it was, John left the signs in place. The name was fitting. There was no other locomotive like it in the world, and after meeting Anna, he doubted that she would appreciate an engine that looked like a brute and bore her name.

The work crews arrived, and the process of moving the skids and advancing the locomotive began. John pushed the trailing skid back with a specially designed bar from the back of the engine. The bar fit between the ties of the skid, and the force of the engine pushed the skid back about two feet to uncouple it. The bar was then swung over to the side of the skid, and the end of the rear skid was pushed sideways until it cleared the skid in front of it. John explained that on land, the engine would then be used to pull the skid forward using a dead-man or a tree for an anchor for the snatch block. It was faster to use Jackson's team, though, and Jackson swung the skid perpendicular to the trestle and pulled it down to the ground and around to the front of the engine. As soon as the skid was off the trestle, disassembly of the trestle began; the bents were moved down to the south where they would become trestles needed to cross the small streams and creek bottoms on the way to the engine shed.

Moving the first skid took about thirty minutes; the second only twenty and once off the trestle, the crew was advancing the engine once every fifteen minutes. In work from dawn till dusk, the engine advanced almost a half-mile a day. In a week, it was sitting on River Road west of the town square. Many a traveler wished the train was heading west instead of south. It would be years and many improvements in the locomotives before anyone would even dream of crossing the nation on a railroad. Few of the spectators even had faith that the engine sitting next to the square could even go that far without breaking down. Those familiar with boiler explosions kept their distance.

Anna was walking to the square with Rufus and Hannah. She had Eli in a pram, but he opted out and was in front of the group riding Goliath down the street. A man was loitering on the side of the walk up ahead, and two more mounted men held the reins of the sidewalk man's horse. Rufus was uneasy and felt for the handle of the revolver at his waist. Goliath looked warily at the man as he walked up next to him, and his mistrust proved to be worth his weight in gold. The man reached down and snatched Eli off the back of the big dog. He broke for the street, but Goliath, in one of the fastest moves Rufus ever saw, lunged and hit the man with both feet in his back. Eli went rolling out of the kidnapper's hands as he hit the dirt with a whoosh of breath leaving his lungs and a cloud of dust billowing up around him. Eli's little buckskin outfit prevented anything other than a few scrapes on his hands and face; a mouthful of dust was the worst of it. Anna could see he was unhurt.

Goliath lunged forward and with a huge paw in the middle of the man's back, bit down on his neck, breaking it and puncturing his jugular vein with his canines. The two men on horseback looked on in horror as their plan for kidnapping and ransoming the infant fell apart before their eyes. They kicked their mounts cruelly and broke for the west side of town. Rufus had his revolver out and was going to take a shot at the fleeing men, but thought better of it with the backdrop of carpenters and masons working on house construction down the street. The men were never seen in town again; the dead man in the street was one of the big losers in the betting on getting the locomotive off the riverboat. Goliath was standing over Eli; he looked at Rufus for either approval or forgiveness for biting the man. Rufus stroked the big dog on the head and told him he had done well. Goliath thumped his tail in the dust.

Hannah picked Eli up out of the dust, and the little guy was no worse for the wear. He clung to Hannah, though, and looked longingly at his mother, who was too far along to carry him. He didn't cry, he was angry; an odd reaction Hannah thought for an injured child. The constable, now called the *Town Marshal*, was summoned, and a reporter from Denise's paper came running back from the square to find out what happened. He wrote up the story and had the artists draw a picture for the front page of Goliath lunging at the kidnapper's back, jaws agape. Goliath was a hero but was humble in the limelight, more content with a whole hindquarter of hog off of Hiram's grills in the square for a reward than the many pets and praises he received for the rescue. The reporter's story appeared in the Independence paper the next day and made its way back across the nation with the paper to paper couriers. Everywhere the human-interest story was printed, sales of Saint Bernard dogs peaked. A wealthy family in Boston even sent an endowment to Anna to add a guard dog kennel to her school.

All Aaden said about the incident was, "I guess the little guy just wasn't ready to head west yet." Anna looked at him with a raised eyebrow, but she also wondered if the draw of the trail would someday take her sons from her as it did so many other mothers.

As the week wore on, the shrill whistle blast every time John moved the engine, grew dimmer and dimmer as the engine moved further south. Two more riverboats arrived, carrying disassembled flat cars and rails. Load after load was removed from the landing and moved to a marshaling yard below the warehouses at *The Meadows*. Rail construction wouldn't start until the crew was finished moving the locomotive to the engine shed, but Irwin was already busy with the ox teams and gannons building the roadbed to the upper end of the forest. The first spur would be over five miles long and connect the sawmill to the southeast corner of the holdings. The railroad bed was graded so that all the log hauling would be downhill. There was a ridge to the south covered with live oaks that must have been hundreds of years old. Irwin couldn't wait to get the engine and winch busy, pulling down the big trees.

Fall deepened, and the inevitable winter set in with the snow and ice. Anna was the only one happy to see the colder weather. Sitting by a wood stove reading with her feet up and a blanket across her lap was her favorite way to spend the day; reading and napping were all she could accomplish. She was bigger than when she delivered Eli; she knew there would be twins. She ran the names Jacques and Roland around in her mind over and over again until even images of the twins started to appear in her dreams. She let herself become housebound in the mansion, where she would be close to Hannah when her time came. Everyone in the household checked on her constantly, and the overzealous attention was starting to make her anxious. She wanted to deliver but knew the babies would come when they were ready. Every day Charlie would give her a full report on everything that happened at the school. They had received endowments sufficient to provide for the first year of college for the senior class that would graduate in the spring. Aaden was helping with the planning to expand the school, and like Charlie, he would tell his wife all the day's events each evening. As usual, Denise was constantly writing; she was on a mission to make her daughter and her school nationally accredited.

The men at *The Meadows* were laying about one-hundred yards of track a day. They had advanced about halfway to the southeast corner of the holdings by the time Christmas week rolled around. The train delivered ties from the sawmill, rails, and barrels of spikes to the railhead every day, and then would return to the camp with a load of logs. The forest rang with the ring of the spike hammers and the songs sung by the workers as they labored with the heavy rails.

It was obvious that they were going to need a bigger sawmill soon, and the brewery was gaining acclaim throughout the world. Orders for bourbon and brandies regularly came in the mail from both coasts. Aaden's dream that people on Fifth Avenue would be drinking liquors from Missouri had come true. Money was flowing plentifully into the accounts of the corporation and its shareholders. Charlie kept them well invested in the growing railroad companies and delivered a report at monthly meetings of the shareholders up in the community hall on *The Meadows*.

A letter from Ireland arrived on the day before Christmas. Rufus brought it to the house, but Anna decided not to open it until the get-together for Christmas Eve. She had a copy of Douglas Jerrold's essay on Christmas traditions and his boyhood experiences with Christmas in England. She was going to read it to the gathering that evening. She also had written a Christmas story and was mulling over reading it to her friends and family that eve. She couldn't do any shopping for the holidays. It didn't matter, a lot of baby clothes were expected to show up offered by the well-wishers around her. She saw Aaden sneaking a double baby carriage into the house earlier when he thought she was asleep in her chair. She reflected on how much faith everyone had in Lily's prophesy, including herself. Would Lily be right? Would she have twins?

Evening came, and her family gathered. Jackson and his family and the Greens arrived. Denise and Irwin welcomed everyone at the door and gave their usual apologies for the under-construction condition of the house. If there was construction, it wasn't evident. The great room was simply, but nicely decorated. Irwin had imported a live-medium-sized fir tree from New England. It took six men to carry it into the house, and one of the men was a lumberjack from *The Meadows* who laughed at importing a tree when they lived in a forest. The tree draped heavy with garlands of popcorn and candy. The children flocked to it and were delighted to see presents under the tree with their names on them. John Gould arrived with a young woman on his arm he introduced as Mary Jackson. She was a fair looking young woman and was a little overwhelmed and shy on her first visit to the mansion. She blushed as John walked her around finishing the introductions in a more personal way. Denise sensed her unease and took her by the arm to steer her away from the men and into the woman's circle around Anna. Mary was amazed at Anna's size and asked when she was due. "Now," was the only reply necessary.

Aaden poured a round of brandy for the men, and Charlie looked wistfully at Hannah. Hannah said, "Tomorrow, doc, break your fast, and I'll quit feeding you. You'll be dead within a week." Hannah made a mysterious little wiggle of her fingers while holding an ominous and foreboding gaze on the Professor. It was just enough to get Charlie thinking about Lily's West African religion. He knew Lily was on the side of the good, but he also respected the other side, the evil doings of the voodoo masters on the lower end of the Mississippi. Not out of fear of voodoo but respect for Hannah and the gratitude he felt towards her mothering him, he passed on the liquor. The men hoisted their drinks in a toast to the unborn twins and downed their drinks. There was nothing but admiration on their faces. The liquor wasn't just fine brandy; it was the best they ever tasted. All opted for a second drink. Aaden was proud to serve it; he had a warehouse full of it up the road, all would drink their fill; overindulgence and hangovers be damned.

Anna said they should open presents next. She remembered her agonizing waits at the Christmas Eve parties in New York while the grownups idled away their time in useless chatter. The children flocked to the tree. Eli just settled down against Goliath and fell asleep. His time would come. The children tore into the presents. There were the usual groans as clothes and school supplies were set aside for the more interesting gifts. Each child received a game. They included *Whirli-Gigs* and *Skittles,* bags of clay and glass marbles, and a set of *Battledore & Shuttlecocks* that would have to wait for spring. The children retired to a far corner with their new treasures and settled into what was occasionally noisy contention over the rules of *Skittles.*

Anna announced that it was time for her to read. "I was going to read some essays from a French writer, but I would like to read you a Christmas story I wrote, inspired by his essays. The name of my story is *The Christmas Horse*. But first there is a surprise, there is a letter from England."

Mouths opened in surprise, Rufus and Hannah rushed over to Anna, and both gave her admonishing looks for not opening the letter the minute it arrived. Anna started to read. Lily had been admitted to Trinity College as a *Provisional Student*. Aaden was thrilled she was studying the history of world religions and was going to make it her major. Ben was studying politics and mired in the math and science that the College required of all freshmen. Aaden's family was in good health, and his father and mother would travel to the Americas at the first sign of spring. There were several newspaper clippings about Aaden's father and the movement he was funding for Irish independence.

Anna handed Aaden the letters, and Aaden handed her a hand-written manuscript. Anna started her story *The Christmas Horse*. It was about a French girl, age eight, who had lost her mother earlier in the year during childbirth. Her descriptions of the winter forest in France and her father who was a farmer were as rich as the soil of the farm where they lived. The girl longed for her mother, but as the headstone on top of the little hill behind their farmhouse testified daily, that would never be. The father was afraid to ask her what she wanted for Christmas because he knew she only wanted one thing in the world and it was too painful for both to revisit his wife's death.

She related much about the farm and several trips into Paris the father used to distract his daughter from her ever-constant brooding about the loss of her mother and the unborn child. There was a single woman close by on a farm, and the young girl could sense with some fear that her father would bring her into their family of two. She didn't want more change. She clung to her father for strength; she didn't know how he bore the empty loneliness around them.

The story moved on to Christmas Eve; a simple meal, some prayers and then the father took the conversation on a different tact:

> "Suzette, I think you missed feeding an animal out in the barn on your rounds tonight."
> "I did not. I never miss, every single animal got fed; even that smelly old goat."

"You better check anyway." And with that, Suzette bundled up against the cold, lit a lantern, and made her way to the barn.

The night was well below freezing, the forest soft and beautiful with the moon shining on the hoarfrost in the pines. In the distance, a lone wolf howled, hoping for a return answer from a mate. Suzette opened the barn door. There was a single lantern burning inside for meager warmth to keep the hard freeze off the animals and the ice off the inside walls. The milk cow was chewing her cud, content with her evening meal of hay and oats. The draught horse was leisurely finishing his meal. Two pigs were rutting; they always ate voraciously and were always the first to finish. The evil goat looked at her with meanness in his eye. Why did her father keep the loathsome animal? The last stall on the left was usually empty; her father kept it for a birthing stall. She heard a stomp that came from the birthing stall and couldn't understand. The stall was empty earlier when she made her rounds.

Standing on the bottom rail and hoisting the lantern up so she could see into the pen, her heart almost stopped and then leaped for there was a weanling mare; black with white socks and a white mane and forelock. The young horse came over and nuzzled her stomach through the rails of the pen. Suzette got down and noticed a nameplate on the gate, Né de Nouveau. She got a pail of water and oats and fed the young animal. Her father was right; the weanling was hungry. She got her milking stool and sat watching the young animal eat.

She sat there for an hour, and then her father came in and put his hand on her shoulder. Suzette looked up with tears in her eyes and said, "Je t'aime père. Merci père. Merci, merci beaucoup".

A horse couldn't fill the emptiness of a lost mother, but the hollow place in Suzette's chest was a last filled a little bit. It gave her father great joy to see the young girl smile again.

There wasn't a dry eye in the audience, and Mary was weeping openly. Anna wasn't finished reading the story, but she dropped the manuscript and leaned to her left trying to stretch out her body as an agonizing pain wracked her womb, and she cried out in pain. Like a fire drill at the school, Rufus rushed to a closet and returned with a wheelchair. Aaden and Rufus picked Anna up, one on each side, one hand under a leg, and another under an arm. They put her in the wheelchair, and Hannah wheeled her to the birthing room she had prepared in the back of the east wing with the other women in tow. The serving girl from the kitchen picked up the manuscript and put it up on the mantel then rushed back to the kitchen to boil water. She hoped it wouldn't be long labor like the first one. The stories of Eli's birth didn't have the young girl looking forward to motherhood; in fact, she thought she might just remain single.

Lily's prediction turned to reality shortly after midnight. Jacques was born, and shortly after that Roland. Both babies were big, like Eli when he was born. Compared to Eli, it was an easy birth; the first child is always the most difficult. Denise walked out to the great room and woke Aaden. She took Eli from his arms and said, "It's time for a drink."

Aaden jumped up and ran back to the birthing room. Anna was there with a baby on each breast. This time she wasn't exhausted; she looked at her husband and said, "They're here." Aaden fell to his knees at the side of the bed and took her hand. His relief was palpable; his somewhat petite wife carried two robust boys to term and delivered safely.

Out in the great room, Denise found the manuscript up on the mantel and read the finish of the story. She was going to set it in print and send it to the Copyright Office in the morning. She was pleased to discover that her daughter, who had written many articles about the school, had a flair for storytelling.

Aaden returned and woke all the men, handing each a glass of rye whiskey. They toasted the newborns and gave thanks that Anna was safe. Charlie cherished his first drink in four months. The rye went down smoothly, and he knew he was going to have a hard time staying away from it, but for the moment, he didn't have a craving for a second drink, and he was surprised.

Anna was up late the next morning. She was pushing the twins around the great room singing to them as she rocked them back and forth in the buggy occasionally, to a particularly catchy phrase in her tune. She had found the men asleep and hung-over in the soft chairs. John held Mary in his arms, the couple asleep on the couch. Charlie had retired to his room shortly after the toasts to avoid not the evils of overindulgence, but a lecture and censure from Hannah that drunkenness would be sure to bring on.

Denise came out of her office. She had recopied Anna's story and was taking it down to the newspaper office for printing. She wouldn't publish it until several weeks after she was sure a copy arrived at the Copyright Office in Washington, D.C. She admired the twins and told Anna what a tremendous job she had done on the story. She was going to make her daughter even more famous than she already was. Little did she know; *The Christmas Horse* was going to make a pony the universal Christmas request of nearly every boy and girl in America for many years to come.

The days drifted away, and soon it was New Year's Eve. Rufus drove Aaden, Anna, and the boys out to the community center on *The Meadows*. When they arrived, Rufus jumped down, and Aaden handed him the twins, one at a time. Rufus walked into the community center, beaming like the proudest uncle in Missouri, if not the entire United States. Goliath walked up to Rufus and sniffed at the newborns. Aaden carried in Eli and set him down to run around. Goliath left Rufus to follow the boy around the room, ever watchful, ever alert for the slightest danger. There were more than a hundred people there; *The Meadows* was steadily growing. The women flocked around Rufus to see the twins and hugged Anna and told her what a good job she did. Anna was glad to be home and was looking forward to a night in her own bed.

Irwin and Denise stayed in town and hosted a party in the Mansion that rivaled galas at the governor's mansion. The chamber orchestra that played at the wedding was better than ever, regularly practicing with encouragement and financial support from Denise. At the stroke of midnight, they played *Auld Lang Syne*. The men kissed and danced with their wives, and all was well ushering in the year 1845.

SUZETTE

Winter gave way to spring, and the first leaves appeared on trees. The men were stripping the sailcloth covers from the fruit trees as the young saplings sprang to life. The forest again filled with the sounds of the timber operation, big trees smashing to the ground, steam slash saws cutting the trunks into sawlogs, and the locomotive moving up and down the tracks. The railmen were running rail sidings to each warehouse, and Aaden was looking for more track to run a permanent line down to the landing on the river. Upon news of a major fire in Hamburg that caused great loss of life and property, Irwin had the masons buttressing the sides of the warehouses with limestone façades for fire protection. The noise of carpenter hammers and saws were a constant backdrop to the warming days, and the slosh of mortar and the occasional break of limestone blocks was walling the outside of Aaden's office.

Aaden wondered if Connor had set out from Ireland with his mother and father. More than ten years had passed since he last saw them. He was concerned about their health over the long journey. His father and mother would now be almost sixty years old. Settling into a relaxed, quiet life, was more typical of people their age and station, than world travels on the open seas. He doubted that his father would ever retire, he enjoyed what he did, and when Aaden left Donaghadee, his father told him he would never quit. Whiskey and smuggling were his way of life and the constant angst that Irish independence wove into the history of the times, was second nature to the cunning family patriarch.

It seemed like every week, news of a new invention or the biggest of something ever built dominated the headlines. Aaden read of Isambard Kingdom Brunel's iron steamship, the SS Great Britain, an ocean-going craft with an iron hull and screw propeller, the largest vessel afloat in the world. Charlie was constantly looking for innovations and inventions; he was shifting some of the investments in the railroads to the young telegraph companies on the east coast. Samuel Morse was innovating how cities would communicate with each other and promised to cover the entire nation with telegraph within ten years. Charlie was one of Morse's original backers, and all involved would become even wealthier as the electrical signals carried millions of messages from breaking news to good wishes from town to town and across the nation. Aaden was watching the development of Thurber's typewriter as soon as he saw the announcement of his patent. Denise and Anna were writing almost constantly. They had already changed the world with handwritten pages, Aaden could only dream about what they could accomplish with a machine that would write for them just by pressing keys.

As promised, Aaden bought Eli a purebred Welsh Pony for his second birthday. Every day Jessica would take the boy to the stables, and Eli would feed the small horse a carrot. Jackson started training the horse when he fully developed at age three but had Eli up on his back long before that. Anna sent away for a small saddle, a toddler-saddle it was called. The saddle sat like a box on the horses back and had its own pommel and stirrups. They looked forward to Eli and the horse to mature a little more before they would let Eli out of the pens. They knew that as soon as Eli and the pony were turned loose, Eli would disappear into the forest with its miles of logging and game trails until the horse got hungry and returned home. The w*anderlust* was strong in Callahan men, as evidenced by Eli disappearing several times for hours among the buildings of the camp and the thousands of hiding places in the warehouses. The little boy was a *loner*. Anna hoped that would change when the twins got big enough to provide him some playmates.

Anna desperately wanted to get pregnant again, wanting to add a girl child to the Callahan household. She constantly sought Hannah's help and advice, but the wise *Doctor of Independence*, as she was becoming known, would tell her to relax. Another baby would come when her body was ready. Anna wrote to Lily asking if she could tell her anything about another baby; Lily wrote back with the sage advice to listen to her mother; all would be well.

Entrepreneurs constantly approached Aaden for money to back a new idea or some grandiose scheme. He would refer inventors to John and the schemes to Charlie. They had quite a lot of fun listening to other men's dreams for success. One of the few investments Aaden did make was to back a blacksmith, William Ray, to take a land position in what was known as *The Lost Township*, a township west of Independence; a township inadvertently not included in the sale of land in the other townships of Jackson County in 1827. Hiram Young recommended William Ray to Aaden. Hiram was working to establish a series of supply stations along the trails and make his wagon parts and staples from *The Meadows* available as far west as Lawrence, Kansas, and eventually beyond.

Aaden settled into the monotony of the day-to-day operation of the corporation. He was working at bookkeeping on a warm summer day in June when Elizabeth came running into his office, terrified. "Isaac is snakebit," she cried out. Aaden knew there was a lot more to tell about this bite because he was constantly lecturing the children about the dangers, in fact, kept a specimen of each poisonous critter in cages up behind the sawmill to add reality to his lectures. That would come later, for now, he hurried out to have Hannah summoned from town.

Jessica already had Isaac settled in the clinic. There was no specific treatment for a copperhead bite; Aaden was thankful that the bite was on the boy's shoulder where there was some muscle mass to absorb the poison. Considering the many hours the crews worked in the woods, snake bites were relatively rare; smashed fingers or a broken arm or leg was much more common. On a grown man, a copperhead bite was a painful experience but never fatal. Aaden was concerned because Isaac was still smaller than a grown man. He was thankful that it was a copperhead and not a rattlesnake bite. One of those could prove fatal to a grownup or a child.

By the time Hannah arrived, Isaac was already in considerable pain and already had emptied his stomach and was wracked by dry heaves as Jessica cradled his forehead over a pail on the floor. Isaac laid back, his whole body in pain. Now the watch for the symptoms to subside started. If Isaac's condition carried on to shock, Hannah was prepared to give the boy laudanum to ease the pain. On the bench outside the clinic, Aaden got the rest of the details. Isaac and Elizabeth had been playing up above the sawmill. They loved watching the train pull in with a load of logs and would often ride up the line with the engine crew and spend their day in the forest. Both were wary of snakes, so Aaden wanted all the details, especially why was the bite was on the shoulder? They had been playing, and Elizabeth pushed Isaac backward over a log. One of the rules was never stepping where you could not see your foot. The snake was on the other side of the log and struck when Isaac fell on him. "How big was the snake?" Aaden asked the sobbing girl.

She held out her hands about as far as she could reach. It was a mature copperhead; Aaden was hoping for a smaller snake and a smaller amount of venom. Isaac was in for a bad time. The boy would recover, especially under Hannah's watchful eye, but he didn't think Elizabeth would ever get over the emotional trauma of nearly getting her brother killed. Had the snake been a timber rattler or a Mississauga rattlesnake, Isaac wouldn't just be in pain; he would be fighting for his life. Isaac's nausea had passed, and the area around the bite was still inflamed. Isaac constantly moaned from the pain in his limbs. Jackson returned from a freight run to Fort Leavenworth to find Aaden on the bench with his arm around Elizabeth. He heard Isaac's moans inside the clinic and ran in, but Hannah shooed him out. She and Jessica had everything under control. Elizabeth fell into her father's arms and sobbed her tale of guilt. Aaden left them together on the bench and walked back over to his office in the warehouse.

We've been lucky so far; he was thinking to himself as he noticed it was already evening. He would go into town and spend the night with Anna and bring the mansion up to date on Isaac's condition. He hitched up the buckboard, and it was relaxing to roll along to the clop of the horse and the forest critters starting up their nightly symphony. It was a clear night with a full moon, and Aaden could easily see to navigate the road. Suddenly the horse dug in and stopped, frightened and tensed up as he would bolt; the horse was trying to back up. Aaden almost pitched out of the driver's seat from the sudden stop. Ahead about fifty feet, a large mountain lion jumped into the road. In the bright moonlight, Aaden saw the large slender cat. He had a small head with rounded ears, and his eyes glowed yellow in the pale light. The lion only paused a second and then, with a swish of his long tail, leaped straight up to a limestone ledge about eighteen feet high on the right side of the road. Aaden murmured, "You better hide big guy, you won't last long if the farmers see you." That was one change in Missouri Aaden didn't like. The big cats were being killed off, and the deer were disappearing from the forest. He was sure that soon, there would be nothing left but snakes, ticks, and chiggers as the trend played out. He waited for about ten minutes on the road. The horse settled down, his brief encounter with the lion already forgotten. Aaden clicked his tongue, and the horse and the driver finished their trip to town without further incident.

The next morning Aaden set out to return home. He was coming up behind a north corner of the square where he saw travelers waiting for rides to the outfitters. Among them were two older people sitting on enormous steamer trunks. The man was dressed in a light brown suit of clothes with an Irish derby on his head and had a cane with a brass cobra on top for a handle. The black cane with the heavy brass cobra brought an image of the cudgels in the duel in New York to Aaden's mind, an unwanted memory intruding on his study of the travelers. The woman wore a long blue dress and carried a matching parasol. These were not pioneers. He was going to look them over when he passed, but then he saw Connor and James across the street haggling with the only Hanson Cab driver in town. He pulled up short, set the brake and walked up behind his father and mother. "Welcome to Independence," he said in Gaelic. His parents spun around and were swept with relief, rescued from the hustle and bustle of the busy pioneers in the square.

Aaden, Sr. was a big man, an older version of his son. His mother's name was Caireann; her once shiny black hair now turned an elegant silver. The three embraced with long hugs and kisses from the mom. Connor and James came back across the street, glad they didn't have to pay the outrageous fee demanded by the Hansom Cab driver to make two trips down to *The Meadows*. Aaden helped his mother up onto the seat of the buckboard and put his father up beside her. James and Connor settled in the back sitting on the trunks, and Aaden stood behind the seat and took the reins. "Push that lever forward," he instructed his father, and he turned the horse around and headed back to the mansion.

As he pulled up under the portico, his father's eyes were full of astonishment and admiration. "Is this your house?" he asked.

"No, this is Anna's mother's house. Anna and I live down on the farm." Rufus came out to meet them, and with introductions complete, Aaden asked him to get the carriage ready. As usual, Denise was in her office writing, Anna and Charlie were already at the school. Aaden settled his parents in the great room and went to extract his mother-in-law from her stacks of papers and books. Denise had taken Rufus's obsession with the Mormon Wars to heart and was writing a detailed, chronological history of the recent events in northwestern Missouri. Brigham Young was now the head of the Latter-Day Saints, and Joseph Smith was mayor of Nauvoo and running for the presidency of the United States. Public sentiment in Illinois ran heavily against the prophet just as it had in Independence, and it was obvious to all who followed the news that something was likely to happen soon. Joseph Smith's policy of polygamy for the elders of the church only fanned the fires of hatred and inflamed Denise's zeal for women's rights.

Denise welcomed Aaden's parents effusively; she was as excited about their arrival as Aaden and sent her helper from the kitchen for some cool refreshments. Aaden Sr. opted for something stronger, and as Aaden poured out his best Missouri bourbon, asked his father, "You want ice?"

"You've got ice?" his father asked incredulously with his eyebrows raised.

"Of course! We have everything modern, a steam generator behind the house and an icehouse down on the farm." Aaden was showing off now and pushed a button switch at the side of the bar, and lights illuminated the back-bar. Only Callahan liquors were on the shelves, and Aaden, Sr. took each down in turn and inspected the labels and the bottles.

Aaden toasted the safe arrival of the travelers, and Aaden Sr. was amazed at the smooth quality of the bourbon. "This is a fine whiskey, maybe better than any I have ever made. What you need now is whiskey taxes so you can assume your role as the family patriarch and a smuggler." All laughed, but whiskey tax was something no brewer in the states wanted, and Aaden Jr. was a heavy contributor to the lobby in Washington, D.C., that was against such measures.

Denise was busy with Caireann, telling her that her daughter-in-law Anna and the twins were at the school, and Eli was down at *The Meadows* with Jessica. The women bid the men a farewell and walked arm and arm to the school, two guards falling in behind. Caireann was uncomfortable with the armed men following until Denise explained the security measures around herself and Anna.

Rufus had the carriage ready, and his big Belgian was ready for a run in the country. Aaden, Sr. said, "That's some horse!"

Rufus replied, "Wait till you see the dog." The four men loaded into the carriage, and again, Aaden Sr. was impressed with the ornate trims and the comfortable leather seats. With Rufus at the reins, they toured around town, visited Hiram at the bar, and went down to the landing. Everywhere, Independence was teeming with activity, vibrant and alive feeding pioneers to the western trails. They started down the road to the south and had to pull over to let wagon after wagon carrying lumber and other wares to the town square and the riverboat landing.

When they arrived at *The Meadows*, Aaden excused himself and went over to the clinic. Rufus ushered Connor and his father into the dining hall and gave the kitchen their lunch order. They were going to feast on rice pilaf made with Grey Partridge and Bobwhite Quail. Everything now served in the dining hall came from the fields and homesteads, including the rice and the flour in the bread. Aaden was explaining that *The Meadows* now had a grist mill, and produced a good deal of the flour going west. Aaden, Sr. was distracted by the steam whistle on the locomotive, but Rufus assured him he would want to eat first, seeing everything was going to take some time.

Aaden found Isaac sitting up on the bed, eating some chicken soup, Hannah's standard prescription for the infirm. The boy was past the worst of it, and Hannah assured Aaden that he would be back to complete health in a week. "I'm sorry, Mr. Callahan," Isaac said as he finished retelling the story as to how he got bit.

"What are you sorry for, Isaac? Did you bite yourself?" The boy laughed, and Hannah shooed Aaden out of the clinic. She had an issue of the *Boston Medical and Surgical Journal* open on the table and was making notes in the margins and adding text to the article. She was writing a manual for snakebite for the clinic, and Isaac's treatment and recovery from the copperhead bite added to what she was studying about rattlesnakes. Somehow it seemed there should be an antidote for the venom, but in all her inquiries around the country, the answer was always, *no*.

Aaden joined the rest of the men for lunch and then had the locomotive take them to the end of each spur. Aaden, Sr. had never ridden in the locomotive of a train before. He was having the time of his life working the levers and controlling the heavy machine. The nameplates on the engine were polished and shiny, a sharp contrast to the appearance of the rest of the machine. *The Bruit* had given way to *Anna* after Anna didn't object. When they got to the active logging spur, the cable was run out, and the son let the father pull down one of the biggest live oaks they had ever encountered. Aaden had ordered a new sawmill, one with six-foot blades. Parts of this tree would have to wait for it to arrive before it would be milled into lumber. Aaden had also purchased a large horizontal boiler that would become the central steam plant for the complex; his planning and building dominated his tour guide conversation with the Irishmen. It suddenly hit Aaden that he wasn't like his parents anymore. Their Irish lilt even seemed a little strange to his ear.

When they settled back in Aaden's office after the long day of touring, Senior commented on how hard it was to take in all that Aaden had accomplished. Then he asked, "How much money do you have now, son?"

"I don't know. The corporation is in the black several million dollars, and that is after the dividends to the shareholders. Charlie, you'll meet him back at the mansion, takes care of our investments. I have no idea where we stand, but it is considerable. We'll ask him later. I want you to taste the brandies, and then we'll head back into town."

Rufus brought the carriage, and everyone helped Senior into the driver's seat next to Rufus. Aaden collected Eli from the clinic and handed him to Rufus. Rufus sat the boy in his massive lap, and Eli clicked his tongue, and they left for Independence; the Belgian knew his way home and wanted his evening meal. Amazingly, Senior had never talked one-on-one with a black man before. He was impressed with the big man's perfect English and his depth of knowledge on human rights. Rufus addressed not only freedom for all blacks, but also the history of the Irish Independence movement and Senior's involvement with it. He looked on as only a grandfather could as Rufus handed Eli the reins. The boy took the reins and talked to the horse as they clopped along. Senior swelled with pride and tears welled up in his eyes as he thought of his boyhood and his own father's farm and racehorses. He reached over and gave the boy a loving stroke on his head. Senior regretted that he wouldn't play a bigger role in Eli's upbringing, but he could see that horsemanship was in the boy's blood, and he had no worry that the boy would do well on his own.

On the way back to town, the sunset was spectacular. As they pulled into the square, over five hundred wagons were waiting to head out on the Oregon Trail in the morning; the sheer mass of the wagon train would make history and reporters were circulating among the pioneers collecting stories to fan the fervor of *Westward Ho* in the newspapers back east. The square was alive with enthusiasm, cook fires, and last-minute transactions and preparations. Again, Senior couldn't take it all in. He did wish for another lifetime, however. He wanted one he could spend as a young man with wilderness to conquer like his son. He wondered where he would fit into this crowd. Would he be a pioneer, a supplier like his son, or would he choose a darker profession, the likes of which was obvious among the carpetbaggers in the square? As Eli slowly threaded his way through the wagons, gamblers and hucksters gave them a wide berth, slinking into the shadows and curtailing their efforts to swindle the pioneers until the carriage passed. Aaden's reputation was well known and most dishonest people avoided him whenever possible. The Belgian and elegant carriage sent a strong signal for the low-life to fade into the shadows. Aaden's reputation around town for dealing with dishonesty encouraged many a scam artist to take their wares elsewhere after even a brief confrontation with Aaden.

Back under the portico, Anna met the carriage. She wanted to know about Isaac, and Aaden assured her he was going to be fine as the rest of the men got Senior down from the driver's seat. Rufus pulled away to put his Belgian up for the night, and Aaden introduced Anna to his father. Senior kissed her hand and said, "You, lassie are every bit as *dathúil* as your mother. I be pleased to meet you." Aaden squeezed his wife to his side and told her *da-thúil* meant good looking, a pleasure to the eyes. Anna blushed and took Senior by the hand and led him up the stairs. She decided at that moment that she was going to enjoy Aaden's parents immensely. After the day with her mother and Caireann, the three women were as comfortable as old friends and glad that they had finally met.

Senior entered the door first and drew up short as Goliath rose in the foyer and greeted him with a deafening deep woof. "My God, is that a dog or some prehistoric creature yet undiscovered out here on the frontier?" He was trying to make light of his instinctive fear of dogs that had his body full of adrenaline and his heart beating a lot faster than normal.

"Rufus likes his animals large. This St. Bernard is Goliath, and he is Eli's pet and guardian."

"I read the story of him killing the kidnapper. How many men has he killed?"

"Only that one, but he has a few years left to improve his record," Aaden answered.

Aaden put Eli down, and he went to his dog. Caireann was pushing the twins around the room in the tram, singing an Irish lullaby in Gaelic. Senior looked on admiringly and sat down in one of the leather chairs, showing quite a lot of fatigue from the day's outing. Caireann put her hand on his shoulder and gave Senior a gentle look that could only mean – you've overdone it again, *old man*, but we will take care of you. The smell of roast turkey wafted through the great room, and the table in the dining room was set for a feast. They set Senior down next to Charlie, and the two older men had a lot to discuss. Aaden was pleased; he too had a lot to talk to James and Connor about and was glad his father was busy with Charlie.

Aaden listened in from time to time, and the conversation went from Irish Independence to slavery in America and the ins and outs of the smuggling business and the tax structure of England that made smuggling such a lucrative business. When they finished the meal, Senior told the story of how he sent Aaden to America. It was obvious to Aaden that his father was trying to steer the conversation to the subject of Aaden's success, so Aaden stepped in and addressed Charlie. "My father asked how much money I had today, and I told him he would have to ask you."

Charlie didn't like being put on the spot, but he looked at Senior and said, "Somewhere a little north of thirty-four million dollars. But that pales when compared to Anna's share of the Mercier fortune. Why? Do you need a loan?"

Everyone laughed, but Senior was impressed. He wanted Aaden to assume the leadership of Callahan Seas, but after seeing what Aaden had accomplished here, he knew that Aaden would never leave. What he and James had seen through the day was equal to or better than Senior's empire in Ireland. Connor was a nomad and would never leave the seven seas; James would have to look to yet another brother or a cousin to keep Callahan Seas together in Ireland after Senior passed. He wasn't looking forward to the transition and impressed with Charlie; he was going to ask him for his advice on the matter before he left here.

Senior piped up, probably feeling his liquor, "Charlie, how much money do you have?"

"That's hard to answer without some current stock quotes. Maybe a couple million, maybe more, maybe less. I'm a lot better at managing money for other people than myself." Caireann shot her husband a hard look, and it was obvious that she wanted Senior shut down for the night.

After dinner and the sumptuous dessert of apple pie and vanilla ice cream, Charlie raised his glass in a toast. "To the Irish!" he said, standing up, "And to the Callahans."

Senior chimed in, "To hell with the Irish; they will be fighting among themselves for another millennium. To *Callahan Meadows*, Missouri, and the pioneers." All stood and repeated the toast; even the women joined their voices with enthusiasm and quaffed a brandy.   It was time to put Senior to bed. Denise showed her visitors to their guest rooms. Anna stayed and fed the babies then helped the kitchen staff finish the cleanup before she turned in. She thought how lucky Aaden was to have a father that loved him dearly and wasn't ashamed to show pride in his son. Compared to her father, it was like looking at an angel on the one hand and an abusive demon on the other. Irwin finally arrived from a hard day's work at the farm, and the two of them sat up talking for a long time. Irwin was the only real father she ever had in her life, and he loved Anna like she was his daughter. She didn't need the memories of Mercier and his evil games. They finally retired for the night, both exhausted from a nice fulfilling day.

The parents stayed for several weeks. Anna tried to talk them into staying permanently, but Senior insisted that he had to live where he could hear the foghorns and watch his schooners come and go. James, Irwin, and Aaden spent most of their days going over plans for the central steam plant and visiting the numerous projects, commenting, and making changes as good suggestions presented themselves. The masons were building about twenty feet of fire-wall a day, and the plan for the new steam plant and sawmill were modified to be all stone construction. The brewery was expanding yet again and needed steel and a bigger boiler. James suggested that Aaden buy a used packet boat and some barges for Hiram and build the packet into a salvage vessel. The Missouri River was full of steel on sunken riverboats. Once the heavy boilers and engines were removed from a sunken riverboat, the rest could be salvaged for firewood. Aaden had the charcoal, building a melting furnace was not that complicated compared to smelting iron from its raw ores. "A steel mill melting salvaged iron seems possible," James said.

"What would we make?" Aaden asked.

"Anything you want, but I would suggest cannons," James replied. John Gould was getting bored with the railroad. Aaden thought a steel mill would be just the thing to keep John around, but Mary more than likely would have a bigger say in that. Regardless, the young engineer looked thoughtful and said he would talk to Hiram about the idea soon. John had already studied up on steelmaking and had a small melting furnace down in Hiram's wagon factory, pouring out small billets that were the feedstock for a myriad of wagon parts. The military at Fort Leavenworth was a big customer for the billets. John wondered what the Army needed so much steel for, but it seemed that all over the country, the Army and the Navy in the coastal states were always preparing for war.

As the day for the traveler's departure dawned, everyone was up early and dined heartily on fresh bacon and eggs. At the table, Senior took the lead and reminded Aaden that, in his opinion, the slavery issue was pitting the South against the North, a situation that could only end badly. Aaden listened but was sure the democracy of the young United States was not going to repeat the history of the past. Senior was adamant though, the things he saw while traveling through the North and the South, only reaffirmed his convictions that it would eventually end in war. "Be prepared," was how he let the discussion lay.

As they hugged and kissed goodbye under the portico, Rufus had the carriage ready to take the travelers down to the landing. Senior pulled Anna into a fatherly hug and said, "By the way, your Lily told me before we left Donaghadee that you would have one more child. She was pretty sure it would be a girl, but that wasn't certain yet." Anna took the news to heart. Lily was never wrong; she felt a wave of relief now that she knew that her most fervent dream would eventually come true. She couldn't wait for the travelers to be off so she could take Aaden aside and tell him.

June ended with the news that Joseph Smith and his brother Hyrum were killed in Carthage, Illinois. Brigham Young assumed leadership of the church and was planning to move his flock west. From Independence through the northwest corner of Missouri, citizen militias were formed to keep the Mormons out if they chose to return from Nauvoo. Independence even built blockades that could close the road from Jefferson City. The blockades would be fortified if necessary, to keep the unwanted sect out. Lookouts were posted on all the riverboat landings to search every vessel coming up the river for unwanted passengers. Toward the end of summer, it was becoming evident that all this effort was in vain. The Mormons had chosen Brigham Young to lead the church, but there was dissent among the ranks because many thought that Joseph Smith, the third, should be the leader. Young's plans on taking his church west the coming year would not bring the Mormons back to Independence. They weren't interested in Missouri anymore. They were looking to go somewhere remote, somewhere they would be left alone.

Fall came all too soon, and Aaden and Irwin were working furiously to finish projects before the onset of winter. Anna walked down to his office on the first of October, took his hand, and said, "Aaden you are working yourself to death. Let's go up to the house and make a baby." As usual, Anna was right, and Aaden once again had the feeling that his wife was always one step ahead of him. Anna was eating what Hannah dubbed a *woman's diet*, exercising daily with long walks, and getting plenty of rest. She was determined to have another child and took special pleasure in seducing her husband when he least expected it. Jessica kept the children that night, and after a walk in the forest in the early evening, Aaden and Anna returned to the house and conceived their fourth child.

The season turned to winter, and the winter plodded slowly on to Christmas. Charlie dispensed the toys for the kids. He had bought four electric telegraphs and several miles of wire and batteries for the children to set up out at *The Meadows*. Aaden was still watching for a typewriter to appear on the market, but his vigilance was yet to produce results. It was finally a quiet Christmas Eve. Isaac and Elizabeth and the Green children were busy studying the manuals for the telegraphs. Denise and Irwin just sat content; Jackson and Jessica did the same. Aaden was content too. He held Anna's hand as she rubbed her tummy. The baby was starting to move. She had what she wanted for Christmas and was looking forward to the early summer when the baby would be born. Life was good, and for once, there were no wars, no local conflicts, or a crisis to manage. There was news that Mt. Rainier had erupted in the northwest corner of the country, but that was very far away and only a news item of minor interest on the winter streets of Independence.

Winter turned to spring, and in May, war broke out between Mexico and Texas. California declared its Independence from Mexico, and it was apparent to all that the Santa Fe Trail was going to become a vital avenue of supply to western forts. Many young men from Independence left with Army units heading west. Some left as teamsters and some as soldiers. Many wouldn't return, either fallen in the war or victims of cholera or malaria on the long march west. Irwin finished the steel foundry and was casting cannons for the Army at Fort Leavenworth. There was a never-ending demand for everything produced at *The Meadows*. The army took everything and paid fair prices for the goods. Food was the main necessity. It was a challenge to ship enough food to keep the troops fed. Aaden was glad to see the fields come alive and start to produce. The warehouses were nearly empty, the grain and corn supply already exhausted.

It was June 4, 1846. Aaden was busy as usual, filling orders and carefully watching his dwindling inventories. Isaac came to the office and told Aaden he better go over to the clinic. Mrs. Callahan had something to show him. Aaden immersed himself in his work every day and wouldn't think of Anna being due, sometimes for hours. He jumped up and ran to the clinic. Anna was sitting in a rocker with a baby at her breast. Hannah was rocking the chair with the tip of her toe. Anna just looked up at Aaden as if childbirth was the easiest thing in the world and said, "Suzette, say hello to your father." She handed Aaden the baby, and he took his little girl in his arms with tears in his eyes. She was tiny compared to Eli and the twins. She rested easily lying in the palm of his hand, her arms and legs draped over the sides and her head at rest on his wrist. To Aaden, she was already the most beautiful girl in the world.

Fatherhood would be different with a girl. No ponies to fall back on for easy gifts. Raising a girl was going to be a new challenge and take some thought to provide her the best of everything. He sat for an hour holding the baby properly after an admonishment from Hannah as to letting the newborn sleep on his hand was no way to hold a baby. Aaden held Anna's hand and was thankful that he had the best partner in the world to help raise this one. Despite the troubled times, his optimistic confidence returned, and his faith in the future bolstered with the arrival of the baby. He wasn't worried. He would continue to do his best, and all would be well.

FAREWELL BROTHERS

Fourteen years had passed since Suzette was born. Aaden still considered the United States a young nation. The growing pains turned to cancer as the issue of state rights, and slavery turned the one nation into what was now known as the North and the South. Two separate entities pitted their philosophical differences against one another every day in Congress, in the media, and with bloody conflicts in the states and territories. Conservative leaders struggled to temper the firebrands, but over the years, even though an even balance of free and slave states remained the norm, the emotional cancer of the division grew to the breaking point. The South threatened succession as the trump card in the debate to preserve their economy and their way of life. The Slave States and the Free States; the North and the South, Missouri was in the middle, and there was constant violence between the slavers and the abolitionists. A civil war was imminent, flowing through the veins of the citizens, poisoning the very fabric of the nation.

Many changes also came the way of Aaden and Anna as the years slipped by almost unnoticed in the intense activity of their daily lives. Aaden's father and mother perished at sea in a steamship disaster in the Straights of Magellan. Connor was a captain in the British Navy, and James had retired to Nassau, where he married a black woman, contentedly living out his life on the sugar empire he built out of swampland and the Uruguayan gold. Aaden sat in a porch swing under the portico of his great house in deep contemplation of all that had happened over what now seemed like a short time. The frantic pace of their daily lives lulled them into a passive observance of their children getting older. Aaden looked down into the fields below the house, and where children used to play, he saw only young men and his beautiful daughter walking up to the house.

There was a family gathering that evening to see the boys off on their new adventure. The commanding officer at Fort Leavenworth had argued with great effect for Anna to let him put the boys into the Quartermaster Corps as civilian employees -- teamsters. The boys would make short deliveries of ammunition and supplies to outposts on the trails, keeping the endless flow of supplies west to support the Army engaged in the Indian Wars. Working for the Army, they would not be called upon to serve in the front lines, given that the growing tensions between the North and South escalated to separate nations at war. The *Think Tank*, known as the *Rookery* at Fort Leavenworth, was predicting war. Jefferson Davis had been arguing for years in the US Senate for state's rights with the slavery issue and the economy of the South continuously fronting every argument. Anna argued that the twins were too young, but the Commander countered with the fact that the boys were bigger than most of his drivers, and he would handle the problem of their age by adding a couple of years when he filed their applications. The Quartermaster needed wagons and drivers, and Eli and his brothers were the best teamsters in the area.

It was Aaden who tipped the scales in the argument. He had seen the Mexican American war drain the resources of men and stores from his warehouses. The California Gold Rush drew many more of the original homesteaders west, some of which never returned. If America fell into civil war, he hoped that the conflict would be short and quickly decided. But the history of civil wars in Europe taught there was never a short conflict and devastation, and tremendous loss of human life was the rule; there were very few exceptions. History also taught that in war, the first objective of the individual was to survive. He didn't want to see his sons fall in battle at the hands of slavers, so with great trepidation, he agreed to let the boys go. As a parent, he knew he would not be able to hold them back if war started. Ely already wanted to join the army and was influenced by the many officers and sergeants he befriended on his deliveries to Fort Leavenworth. All over America, and especially in the slave-free North, boys as young as fifteen were lying about their age and training with front-line infantry units. Whatever happened, the boys would be caught up in the melee of the times. The best he could hope for was to see them in the safest position possible. He hoped the outcome of his decision would not cost him his marriage. Anna didn't want any of it. She treasured the peaceful life they had built out of the wilderness, despite the years of hard work and the constant demands of her school.

The carriage was coming up the road from the old camp, which had been called *The Complex* for the last ten years. Aaden noticed that the carriage wasn't as elegant as before, its plum paint and gold trim was peeling here and there, and a young Belgian mare pulled it. He would have to get Rufus some help with the stables at the mansion soon. Rufus and Hanna rode inside with

Jackson. Thomas was walking up from the complex; he was the engineer on the railroad now. John Gould and Mary went on the California Trail in the gold rush of 1849. Their son Jefferson returned to *The Meadows* when he was old enough to travel back on his own and was full of stories about his father's engineering feats equipping the hard rock mines with steam hoists and compressors along the Mother Lode. As the placer gold mined from the rivers and streams of the Sierra Nevada disappeared, deep lode deposits continued the gold rush. Within a decade, all of the operations had moved underground save for several huge hydraulic mines that were sluicing millions of tons of mud and silt down the rivers and into San Francisco Bay. John now was the owner and chief engineer of *Motherload Mine and Mill*; his company headquartered in Sacramento, and his work was in great demand. Aaden would always remember him as the eager young man unloading the locomotive *Anna* from the riverboat. He doubted that he would ever see John and Mary again.

Rufus was suffering from a number of the ails of aging large men. He had pains in his limbs, and the muscle mass that made him a man among men was now heavily carried along on aching legs supported by a sore spine. Rufus liked to walk and sometimes hunt on the Mormon property not far from the mansion. Shortly after the Mormons left Missouri, Denise had fenced the site before Joseph Smith's polygamy policies turned her sympathies elsewhere. She preserved the site as a wilderness area in the middle of the growing city and cordoned off the area where Smith had laid the cornerstone of his temple. She also enjoyed walking in the seclusion of the site occasionally and would check the fence and the cornerstone on her rounds.

Hannah was still healthy and was a chief nurse at the hospital Denise founded in Independence. When the Women's Medical College of Pennsylvania opened in 1850, Denise enrolled Jessica in the first freshman class. Jessica and her family moved to Philadelphia for the years of medical college. Jessica graduated with honors and then worked at *The John Hopkins Medical Institute* to learn surgery. Denise was a little worried that her *doctor* would want to stay in the east, but Jackson and Jessica were very much a part of Aaden's family, and their loyalties ran deep. Jessica returned to Independence as an accomplished surgeon and took on the job of Chief Surgeon and Hospital Administrator. There were now several doctors on the staff and an emergency room that ran on endowments and donations. The operating room was state of the art using ether and chloroform to sedate the

patients. The surgery was kept as sterile as possible, wiped down with a solution of chlorine bleach after every use. Like doctors and surgeons worldwide, Jessica was watching and waiting for a way to combat the infections
that killed more patients than the surgeries employed to save their lives. Her
surgery was gaining a reputation for being the safest in the country. Suzette
worked side-by-side with the nurses in the surgery during the day and studied
medical journals at night. Anna constantly admonished Suzette's poor grades
in general studies. Even though she ran the school, her daughter was far from
the top of her class. Here was a girl with a photographic memory that could
only focus her camera on state of the art medicine. It rankled the educator
that was the essence of Anna's character and life's work.

Lily and Ben would be missing from the gathering. They were finally married and at the moment in West Africa, tracing the origins of the West African
religions and the unfortunate turn of the ancient practices to voodoo in the
West Indies. Lily and Ben would write often and visited Independence every
couple of years. Anna wanted her to stay, but Lily and Ben were becoming
renowned authorities on voodoo. Her last letter reported that she had traced
the ancient religion back to one area in Niger, where witch doctors claimed
their ancestors were the first to use the Yoruba god *Petro Loas* against their
enemies. There seemed to be over twenty Yoruba gods, each with specific
duties concerning the spirit of all living things and the powers of nature. Each
time Lily encountered another god in her travels, she would trace it to its
roots and document its role in the stewardship of the universe. She had also
found that the names of the gods had evolved many variations, and Lily and
Ben had been to Haiti and the Spanish, French, and Dutch countries and colonies in South America several times to sort and classify the names used by
different sects. Haiti was the focal point for the dark side of the religion prac-
ticed in New Orleans. Lily wrote biographies of each god and drew maps for
each of them from their roots in Africa along their travels to the Western
Hemisphere and recorded the many name changes along the way. Aaden
wondered if she traveled the wilds of Africa with the Bowie Knife still in its
sheath on her back. Ben and Lily were due for a visit soon; along with Rufus
and Hannah, everyone was anxious to see the world travelers again.

Denise and Irwin would arrive later. Denise was looking at retirement, and
Irwin had already passed the day to day operation of the complex to younger
managers. Denise was discouraged and sometimes even depressed. In 1849,
the riverboat *White Cloud* caught fire at its moorings in St. Louis. It burned

loose of its mooring and drifted downstream, catching twenty-two other packets on fire. The fire spread into town and burned for several days destroying all the wood structures in the Northeast sector of the city. The city fought the fire to a standstill at Market Street; however, a contingent of slavers took advantage of the opportunity and set fire to the school behind the *Black Freedom League*. The heat from the intense flames ignited fires in the rear rooms of the headquarters across the alley, and all was lost; only the shell of the outside brick walls was still standing, a silent sentinel guarding the ashes of thousands of legal records and active court cases. Despite the massive loss of property, only three lives perished in the epic fire, one of them the fire chief while setting out black powder charges to take down wooden structures to create a fire break.

The headquarters and school were never rebuilt; Denise didn't have the energy to take on the struggle anew. One-by-one, the offices she started in other cities were deeded to the core lawyers of each group and transitioned to individual law firms. Offers came weekly for *Missouri Publishing,* and Denise was of a mind to sell. Most of the good offers came from pro-slavery newspapers that wanted to shut her down; offers from abolitionist groups were just too low to be considered. Her years of working for the cause of freedom for all people of color still left Missouri a violent hotbed of discontent between the abolitionists and the pro-slave block. At times she felt as she had gotten nowhere and had spent a considerable amount of her fortune to no end. Irwin talked about moving to San Francisco, where, like Aaden's father, he could hear a foghorn and smell the salt air. They would have gone by now if it wasn't for their close ties to family and friends.

Aaden wished Hiram was closer, but his salvage operation had grown, and he was working in the Mississippi below St. Louis. He now had four salvage boats, three in the Mississippi and one working its way up the Missouri, clearing snags and charting the channels. Hiram was becoming one of the Army Corps of Engineers' most important contractors. He would visit every time he passed through on his way up the Missouri River. He always would arrive with a full load of steel scrap for the foundry. Aaden and Hiram were like brothers, and Aaden missed him dearly when he was away.

The one person Aaden missed most was Charlie. Hannah had kept him alive for ten more years after his arrival in Independence. He never left his newfound city and worked tirelessly at Anna's school till his dying day. Charlie had taken an interest in astronomy and Aaden, and Irwin bought a state-of-the-art telescope and built a tower at the college to house it. Aaden and Charlie spent many nights in the observatory looking at the universe and arguing theories about its origin. Anna now sat at the desk where Charlie spent his last hours. It was a bit spooky for Anna; Charlie had died at the desk writing one of his many articles for the astronomy journals around the world. After Charlie's death, Aaden turned control of the investments over to the banker Denise first worked with in St. Louis. Things were still in good hands, and the corporation and the family's investments kept building a foundation of wealth as solid as any old-wealth family in the east.

The children reached the bottom of the stairs. Aaden looked down at three strong young men that looked like younger versions of himself, but stronger than he remembered himself to be. Suzette took after her mother and was tall for her age, a girl full of vitality and love of life like her mother. Eli had a St. Bernard at his side, one of the many descendants of Goliath. There was never another Goliath; Eli always wanted to remember the big dog just as he was, and he didn't want or need a surrogate named to remind him of the best dog he ever had. Aaden shook hands with each of the boys and embraced them in the manly way fathers did after sons were too big to kiss. However, he enveloped Suzette in his arms and kissed her on the forehead and told her in Gaelic that she was more beautiful every day. Suzette was the only child who took the time to learn the language of the Emerald Isle along with French, German, and Dutch – her mother's languages. The boys moaned with the *here we go again* look painted on their faces. It was obvious to them that Suzette was the favorite of the four children, and when father and daughter reverted to Gaelic, they were outsiders of the secret world their father and daughter shared. There were other reasons for their jealousy; Suzette was a better shot with pistol and rifle and her good looks always made her the center of attention in any crowd. Aaden was trying to get Suzette to look at the universities back east, but Suzette was adamant that all the education she needed was right here in her mother's school and Jessica's hospital.

Irwin and Denise arrived. She had several more offers for the newspapers in her bag, and she wanted Aaden to read them later and render an opinion as to which one looked the best. Money wasn't the most important issue. She wanted the abolitionist foundation of *Missouri Publishers* to remain intact after she sold it. Aaden, with his political ties to the state legislature, knew most of the newspaper owners in the state. Aaden was her anchor of reasonability, helping with the difficult decision. Denise was aging gracefully, her blond hair silver, and her trim figure only slightly heavier. Irwin was well but the years of hard work showed. Like Rufus, he hurt worse in the winter but even some in the summer months. Aaden constantly reminded him that San Francisco was cold and damp most of the year, but Irwin wouldn't listen. He wanted a small sailboat in the bay and a house on Rincon Hill where he could watch the ships come and go. Aaden didn't argue, Irwin deserved a good retirement; he should be wherever he wanted to live out the rest of his days.

Through the evening, the family recounted stories of their travel to America, the duel in New York, and the sea battle with the Argentine frigate off the coast of Cuba. Rufus laughed at being in jail in New Orleans and told some interesting stories he heard while posing as a fireman on the mail packet that carried them north from the city on the delta. Rufus was a good storyteller, and when he told of the little Indian they threw out of the window of the stage after they left Clinton, he had everyone in stitches. It was time well spent. Roland, the family poet, and musician entertained them into the night with ballads of the west and some instrumentals that he composed for his guitar. Anna looked over her children with great pride; Eli and Jacques, the rugged teamsters, her poet, and the linguist. She often wondered where the years had gone.

The boys would go out on the trail and return home only every two months or so when their treks brought them back to Fort Leavenworth. Anna still wasn't convinced this was the best or safest path for the boys because the trails were still bereft with disease and peril even though from Leavenworth to Santa Fe, the route was supposedly rid of Indians and thieves. Abraham Lincoln's acceptance speech after his nomination as a senator in Illinois, made him famous for his, "A house divided against itself cannot stand." Now Lincoln was the Republican nominee for president; if elected, Anna was sure that his administration would polarize the nation even further and possibly push it into the civil war that everyone feared. She didn't have a better option to keep the boys safe, so she quietly acquiesced to her husband's decision.

Jessica never arrived at the small farewell party. No doubt she was tied up with an emergency at the hospital; the boys would stop by and see her on their way to Leavenworth the next day. Hannah quipped that she had the same disease as Anna and her mother. Anna asked, "What disease is that?"

"Work," was Hannah's answer. "You women wouldn't recognize a day off if it ran you down in the street and clubbed you in the head while you were down."

"Come on, Hannah, when was the last time you took a day off?" Hannah was caught short, she couldn't remember. Everyone laughed and said their goodnights. One-by-one the family retired, only Roland and Anna remained to lounge in the easy chairs in the great room.

Anna brought up a subject that was on her mind to discuss with Roland. "You children have never been separated. It is going to be very hard on Suzette when you leave. I'm worried about you out on the trails, but I am also worried about Suzette and the loneliness that she is going to feel. It could push her into bad decisions about her education, marriage or any number of problems that arise in lonely young women. I'm even afraid she will run away and head west to find you."

Roland thought for a while and responded with the wisdom of a much older man. "If the nation turns to war, we will all be separated for God only knows how long. Suzette has to finish growing up in the times we now share. I am not sure what we can do about that."

"Just come home as often as you can and write often. Don't let your brothers drive themselves into the ground. Each of you is wealthy in your own right. There is more money than you will ever need in the bank in St. Louis. When it's time, promise me you will take care of your sister and make sure your brothers know where they are going every time they start in another direction. Don't let the lure of the trail or any weak breeze be your master; always have a goal and always above all else, stay together. That is all I can ask."

Mother and son sat quietly for a while. Roland sought the solace of his guitar and played soft ballads until Anna fell asleep in her favorite chair. Roland covered her up and went up to bed with a lot on his mind. His mother just gave him a leadership role he wasn't sure how to handle concerning Eli and Jacques. Eli, the oldest and strongest, was the natural leader among them. Roland followed Eli's every move like the rest of the current behind a leading ripple in the river. He never perceived Suzette as someone he would have to look after as a parent. He was bewildered as to the *what and how* of fulfilling his promise to his mother. He finally slept uneasily and still awoke with everything on his mind when Eli knocked on his door long before dawn to leave for Fort Leavenworth. The boys tiptoed past their sleeping mother and walked down to the stables. They were quiet, as men are when danger is about, or something weighs heavy on their mind. They spoke little as they rode north. Their lives had just changed, and the direction was less than certain. When they stopped for lunch in Raytown, Eli asked Roland what Mom had said the night before. Roland just replied, "Nothing important." He was already resigned to his role as an agent rather than a leader. A time-honored role learned by younger brothers worldwide since the beginning of time.

Aaden awoke to find his wife still asleep in the great room. He made coffee and oatmeal, and Suzette wandered in bleary-eyed, another victim of a sleepless night. Anna awoke to the smell of coffee, and Aaden was trying to get his daughter to talk to him. Anna sat down at the table; Suzette was idly stirring a bowl of oatmeal. The closest Anna had ever experienced someone leaving was when her father alienated her and her mother in New York, or perhaps when Charlie died. Anna sat next to her daughter and covered her free hand with her own as Aaden put her coffee down. At her mother's touch, Suzette's expression turned from pensive to distress and her eyes filled with tears. From young woman to child, Suzette laid her head on her mother's shoulder and whimpered, "They're already gone."

Aaden sat with his coffee and was glad that his daughter was opening up a bit, but Anna started cooing to her daughter in German, the one language that left Aaden a deaf-mute. Anna told her daughter that they were all going to miss the boys. The times were changing now, and soon many a man and woman they knew would leave and never return. Her childhood was over, and now womanhood was all that was left her. In a time of war, women wait and pray. Suzette started to cry, and Anna put her arms around her and went on, "That is what we will do; we have to have faith that the boys will be safe and that they will come back to us." Anna rocked her daughter back and forth and looked over at Aaden. He gave her an understanding nod; the German was signal enough that he should leave the two women alone. He got up quietly and went to his study. When he looked into the kitchen after a while, they were working together to clean up the mess from last night's party, babbling back and forth in four languages, something they often did to practice. Suzette caught her father's eye and said, "Tá mé ceart go leor." (*I'm okay*).

Weeks passed, and then the first month was behind them. The Quartermaster would send a note letting the family know where their young men were on his schedule board whenever he had someone coming into Independence or sometimes with children returning to the dormitory after a weekend home. The boys were due home the very next day, their first rotation off the trail and the never-ending back and forth routine of supplies moving west. Anna worked late into the night at her desk at least two, sometimes three nights a week. On those evenings, Aaden would spend his time in the observatory finding faraway galaxies and studying the crevasses, mountains, and plains of the moon. He wasn't the scientist Charlie had become, but he knew the intricate instrument as well as the mechanic that maintained it. He had a special surprise for Anna when she came to gather him up for their walk back to the mansion. He heard her footfall on the metal stairs up to the observation deck and withdrew the eyepiece from the instrument and inserted one of his makings. He worked the switches that controlled the pointing mechanism of the scope towards the full moon to backlight his handy work. Anna always wanted to look through the telescope at whatever Aaden had it trained on without fail every time she arrived. "There is something special to see tonight," Aaden said in a bored tone as he lowered the observation chair and lifted his wife into the seat.

Anna looked through the eyepiece and saw an image of three wagons pulled by mules crossing in front of the Independence Town Hall. She choked up a bit and marveled at the many ways Aaden could come up with to soften the absence and worry about her sons. Her love for this man only deepened as the years wore on. Aaden lowered her down and held her close. "They are supposed to be here tomorrow. You'll see that they are fine. Suzette wants to go fishing in the morning, let's walk home and get some rest." Hand in hand, they left the campus. The early summer night was warm and clear, and the owls and insects filled the night with their sounds as the couple walked a little way north to avoid the square. The paved streets, concrete sidewalks, and manicured front lawns and gardens adorned their way home. The scent of honeysuckle and wisteria hung heavy in the air. Tomorrow would be a fine day; it would be Suzette's fourteenth birthday. Besides being smart as a whip, she had grown up fast and tough with three brothers to wrestle with as she grew. Anna was pleased that her family would all be together for the occasion.

RUNAWAY

As the wild African night gave way to the early dawn in the upper Niger River valley, Lily stirred in her half-awake dreaming state and an overwhelming feeling of dread settled on her spirit like the noonday sun on the sand wilderness of the Sahara. Lily and Ben had traveled up the Niger River and camped in a village on the outskirts of Ségou, one of the ancient cities in the region. They were in search of an old Mandingo, said to tell the tales of the Yoruba that spanned millennia back to their ties to Egypt. At sunrise, a young man who knew the way to the old man's village would guide them north, up through the savannah of the lower Sahara, and act as their translator. Lily and Ben slept naked in their tent. The air was always hot, even at night. Now she rolled over and cuddled Ben with her leg across his body. Her feeling of dread had turned to a feeling of deep loss. Ben asked, "What's the matter?"

"I can't tell exactly, something bad is coming, something in Missouri." Because she couldn't *see* what it was, she knew it would involve someone close to her, someone whose loss would impact her deeply. This time she wouldn't be there to push Anna aside from the assassin's bullet or save someone else from danger. Whatever brought these unwelcome feelings was going to happen, and she wasn't going to be able to stop it. She would have to accept things as they wove their way into the fabric of time. Lily knew the feeling of loss was going to settle deep in her soul until they returned to America and found out just what happened. Everywhere their skin touched, sweat would well up almost immediately. They would have sex and then wash in the river before heading north. They loved the blue water of the Niger and the open savannah as compared to the jungles farther south.

In Independence, Aaden and Anna had just fallen asleep in their room at the mansion looking forward to tomorrow. The night air of the early summer was still cool, and they slept soundly with the French doors to the veranda opened; the familiar sounds of the night breeze rustling leaves, and the soft hoot of owls lulled them into a deep sleep. In the morning, they would gather up Suzette and go down to *The Meadows*. If it was a nice day, Suzette wanted to go fishing and have a meal of fresh fish to feed her brothers when they arrived. Everyone was anxious to see the young men who should have returned to Fort Leavenworth the previous day. They would leave their wagons there and ride down on their horses if everything was in tune with the Quartermaster's schedule. There was always the unexpected; a thousand mishaps could occur on the prairies interrupting even the impeccable planning of the US Army.

Anna rose early and was surprised to see Suzette at the kitchen table dressed in her buckskins. Suzette tried to close and push aside a map of the Santa Fe Trail, but Anna saw it and said, "We love you Suzette, and I know you want to run away with your brothers, but tell me, how will that solve anything?"

Suzette was a little mad at herself for being so transparent but said, "I was planning to ride out with them a little way and then come back home. Would it be alright if I rode *Patches* down to the complex, this morning? The boys will be on their horses, and I want to ride around the lake with them. I promise I won't run away or go anywhere without telling you. I love you, mother, and I wouldn't do that to you."

Anna accepted that for the moment. *Suzette is getting older*, she thought. Anna knew it would soon be impossible to tell her what to do. For now, she was happy to be still able to influence her daughter. Suzette was a Callahan and blessed with the same fierce independence of her father and brothers. Anna worried that her time to influence her daughter might have already passed. For the boys, that time came when they were eleven. Roland, her poet and artist, was a little slower to develop his independence. Suzette was fourteen, about the age Anna's troubles started with her father. She picked up the map from the table and handed it to Suzette, "Don't lose your map," was all she said as she turned and walked up the back stairs to wake Aaden.

Aaden hitched up a two-seat buggy and brought it around to the front of the mansion. Anna was waiting under the portico; she prepared a picnic lunch and had a basket on her arm and a bottle of wine in her other hand. On their way through the square, Aaden bought a newspaper from a straggly young lad and gave him an extra nickel hoping the lad would find a good meal soon. The headline read; **OREGON ADMITTED TO THE UNION**. The follow-up article said the South finally agreed to allow Oregon statehood as a free state. He imagined that many of the pioneers assembled to leave later that morning were pondering their three choices; Oregon, California, or the wild west of Santa Fe and the New Mexico Territory. The lower-left corner of the front page reported on Arkansas, where a bill forcing free blacks to choose slavery or exile was being argued hotly in the state legislature. Aaden questioned the constitutionality of that one. Just one more issue to further divide the nation.

Aaden put the buggy and mare up in the stable at *The Complex* and got the handcar out of the engine shed. The children loved the handcar, and almost daily would have races down around the lake and back. The downhill run was always fast, but coming back was slightly uphill, and many a young fellow was developing a strong back working the rocker arm that propelled the car. Even the girls had organized into teams of two for the older girls and four for the younger ones and competed with the boys for the fastest time. Even lads from town would come out and try their hand at the race, but few were as strong as *The Meadow's* children. Aaden loaded Anna onto the front of the handcar, stowed the lunch in the toolbox on the rear, and threw the switches to get them onto the track down to the lake. "All aboard," the shout startled Anna, and she laughed when she saw Aaden had donned the engineer's cap that always hung on the inside of the shed's door. She thought that despite the worries for their sons, they had to be the happiest couple in Missouri.

Suzette was already down at the fishing shed, getting three long bamboo poles ready and digging through the worm box on the shady side of the little house for bait. Fishing was one of their weekly activities since the boys left. They had a tradition, the person who caught the most fish just got to eat, the one who caught the least had to do the dishes, and the other was the cook. Suzette was down on the end of the pier and already had her line in the water as Aaden pulled the break on the handcart and slid to a stop with a loud screech of the wheels on the tracks. He had pushed himself on the trip down from the Complex. Anna had to hold her hat and was yelling, "Faster. Faster," as he pushed the handcart up to about thirty miles an hour on the downslope to the lake. On their way back, Anna would be on the other end of the rocker arm, and the pace would be much more sedate.

The morning was turning hot, and by the time they broke for lunch, the temperature was easily hovering around a hundred degrees. The sun was still bright, but a low cloud cover was slowly moving east and would provide shade soon. As usual, Suzette was ahead in the fish derby, but the bass were either lazy today or well-fed. The fishing was slower than usual. Anna was on a campaign that she shouldn't have to cook because even though she only caught one fish, it was the biggest one yet in the morning catch. Aaden was watching the clouds. All seemed calm except over the west side of the lake, the low mist was rotating, and the trees in the forest to the south were starting to whip back and forth as if caught in a wind unable to make up its mind on a steady direction. Suddenly the low clouds were swept aside, and almost right over them, a large black funnel cloud was swooping down from the bottom of a much bigger system. The air was dry, there was no rain blanket, but the ominous roar was building. The bottom of the funnel reached down to the surface of the lake and sucked millions of gallons of water up into the funnel.

They left the dock at a dead run, but Aaden caught Suzette as they passed the handcart, threw her onto the deck, and tied her to the rocker arm stanchion with his belt. He got Anna onto what he judged would be the downwind side of the stanchion and was reaching around Suzette to shield the two women as best he could with his body. The front of the tornado was on them in seconds. The roar of the wind was deafening, but the crack of lightning broke through the impossible roar with ear-splitting intensity and eye-blinding flashes. Aaden saw the dock shred and disappear into the wind front and then the shed. He was being hit hard with debris and put his head down and closed his eyes waiting for the funnel to pass over them. His resolve to keep the women safe turned to terror when he felt the handcart start to rise. He was thrown into the air as the handcart tipped over. He caught a glimpse of Anna falling in front of the cart as it tipped, but he lost consciousness as he was carried hundreds of feet into the air, just another piece of living debris among the thousands of fish sucked out of the lake. The handcart tumbled over several times and then came to rest upside down. The rocker arm stanchion kept Suzette from being crushed, but she was bruised badly and couldn't reach the buckle on Aaden's belt to free herself. She finally gave up and just slumped against the belt, crying and calling for her mother.

Eli and his brothers were about a mile north of *The Complex* when the tornado touched down. They watched in horror as the angry storm tore through *The Complex*. Their horses were ready to bolt, but Eli kicked his mount hard, and the big gelding covered the last mile in record time. The other two horses followed. Horrific devastation was waiting for them at *The Complex*. The roofs of two warehouses were gone. Only bare ground remained where the community hall, dining hall, and clinic, once stood. The church was a shattered mess, and the brewery badly damaged. Towards the lake, there was a dirt scar a half-mile wide where not a single tree or blade of grass was left standing. They could still hear the tornado off to the east, leveling everything in its path, wrenching trees from the ground and scouring the earth with the swirling debris. Looking south to their home, they could only see the stonework of the foundations and the chimney standing in defiance against the force of the storm.

People were emerging from storm cellars to find their world gone. Thomas pointed at the lake, and Eli caught his arm and spun him up onto the back of the horse as he galloped by. When the four men reached the lake, they leaped down from their mounts and ran to the handcar. Suzette was underneath whimpering; the belt so tight Eli couldn't unhitch it. He drew a knife from his belt and cut Suzette free. He drew her out gently, and Roland stepped in to carry her away from the handcar. He didn't want her to see the mangled body of their mother lying on the other side. Anna was dead, having been rolled under the heavy handcar several times and crushed. Their father was nowhere in sight. Suzette struggled to walk about twenty feet, supported by Roland, and then passed out. Roland caught her before she fell, and he had Jacques hand her up to him, and he put her in front of him in the saddle. He walked the horse back to the remains of *The Complex*. He had one of the teamsters hook up the tram. The man asked him about Aaden and Anna as he handed Suzette up to Roland, but taking his sister in his arms, he just shook his head *no*. The teamster drove them into town, and Suzette woke up in Roland's arms when they were about two blocks away from the hospital. Jessica had the emergency room prepared for the worse. It was obvious even from town that the tornado had passed through *The Meadows*.

Eli and Jacques were going crazy, looking for their father. They organized the people at *The Complex* to search the tornado path to look for their father. Amazing as it was, no one else perished in the storm. Five shrill whistle blasts from the sawmill had everyone hurrying to the shelters before the tornado arrived from the lake. Several homesteads were leveled, but again the people were safely sheltered. The tornado cut a swath more than twenty miles long and more than a half-mile wide. It had been bad enough when it tore through *The Complex,* but the path was over a mile wide before it suddenly disappeared. The searchers never found Aaden; the search was called off when darkness fell. A casket was retrieved from the homestead that made them, and Anna lay inside it in Aaden's office. All the men, women, and children looked on as her mangled body was cared for as good as could be managed. An unexpected and unwanted future had arrived for them and fear and dread showed on the faces of everyone.

Eli and Jacques got fresh horses and rode into town. They found Irwin and Denise at the hospital. Jessica had moved Suzette from the emergency room to a regular room, and she was sitting outside the room with Irwin, Denise, and Roland when Eli found them. Denise ran to Eli, she wanted desperately to know about Aaden and her daughter but was afraid to ask. Eli sensed this and like Roland earlier, just shook his head *no*. Denise broke down, and Jessica took her in hand. Suzette slept the deep sleep of the drugged, and Denise was soon to join her. Jessica was hardened to death, it was part of life, and she saw it almost every day. Irwin and the boys stayed in the hall all night. The boys gave him a full report on the damage to *The Meadows* and Irwin didn't know where he was going to find the energy to put it all back together. It wasn't just Aaden's youth and enthusiasm that built up the corporation. It was his leadership and fairness that was the glue that held the people together, all working for a common goal. Aaden, the man who vowed he would never leave, took that with him forever when he was swept away by the storm.

Denise woke first the next morning and for that first waking moment, escaped the horrible memory of the previous day. Suzette moaned in her sleep, and the weight of the memories returned. Denise held her granddaughter and told her that her mother was dead, and her father couldn't be found. Suzette knew without being told. She saw her father swept away and saw her mother fall under the handcar as it tipped off the track. Suzette was bruised badly on her limbs and torso. Jessica was concerned that the hematomas could turn infectious. She didn't want to administer any more laudanum; depression and pain together was a proven pathway to addiction. As an alternative, Hannah arrived with the chicken-soup cure at hand. Suzette didn't want to eat. She could hardly lift her arms, let alone hold a spoon. Hannah fed her as she had when Suzette was an infant. Hannah knew the young woman would recover. The physical injuries passed by quickly in the young. The trauma was the hard part. Suzette would never be free of the memory of those last moments with her parents.

A week passed, and the search for Aaden was finally given up. It was time to bury Anna. Denise had a gravesite prepared on Anna's campus, and two large marble headstones had been finished and delivered to the site. Only one grave stood open, waiting for Anna. Thousands of people were gathered around the grave and overflowed onto the street. Eli and his brothers, along with Thomas, were slowly bringing Anna into town in an ornate funeral hearse pulled by the Belgian. More than four hundred people followed the freight wagon into town, the entire population from *The Meadows*, walking slowly, heads down, and black armbands on every arm. Suzette sat with her grandparents and Rufus and Hannah as the young men carried the casket and placed it on the straps that would lower it into the grave. There were thousands of flowers; the sweet smell of roses was strong. Pastors and priests were standing by, but Denise had not called on any to deliver a eulogy.

Everyone sat quietly for about twenty minutes, and then Suzette labored to her feet. She had a small box that Roland had given her. He had climbed the chimney at the great house, and the silver knight on the alabaster horse was safe in the nook above the mantel. He gave it to Suzette thinking she would want to keep it. Suzette walked up to the casket and asked Eli to open it. They had kept the casket in the ice house, but the smell of decay was already strong and thankfully was softened by the sweet smell of the flowers and dissipated in the breeze. Anna lay in folds of satin dressed in her white wedding dress. Suzette opened the box and placed the figurine under her mother's hands laying crossed over her breasts. She touched her mother's face and then bent down, kissed her, and straightened a lock of hair. Tears flowed down her face as she turned to return to her seat; most everyone, even the priests, and pastors cried openly.

The casket was closed and sealed for the last time, and the ratchet mechanism lowered it down into the grave. Denise and Irwin got Suzette back up, and each picked up a handful of dirt, and in the symbology of the last farewell, threw the dirt down on top of the casket. Covers were pulled off to unveil the headstones. Each had their full names and dates of their births and deaths. Aaden's had a simple inscription that flowed with an elegant script that said, "Aaden, the best of men." Anna's said, "Wife, mother, and founder of the Independence Freedom School." The date of their death inscribed on the tombstones, June 4th, 1860, would never be forgotten.

Irwin and Denise turned and walked to the mansion with their grandchildren. The people stayed on the campus, and Anna's beloved chamber orchestra played at the graveside well into the evening. So many had thrown their handful of dirt into the grave that little had to be done to fill the rest of the grave. By morning the grave was overlain with sod, and an ornate iron fence surrounded it.

The school closed for the rest of the week, and as the children were leaving the dormitory, Eli handed the Quartermaster's son a letter and a contract that he and his brothers signed for them to take a massive load of ammunition, rifles, and cannon to Fort Moore in Los Angeles. They wouldn't leave for another week, but this time they would be gone a very long time. That night, Eli and his brothers told their grandparents that they were leaving and going to California. Denise was disheartened, and Irwin tried to make the case that the people at *The Meadows* would look to Eli for leadership and guidance. Already some of the families had left, and Irwin didn't know if the corporation would even survive. The boys were adamant, though; they couldn't stay. Especially Eli, he simply said, "I'm not like my father. I want to go west and make my own way for a while."

Denise thought, *Odd, that is exactly what Aaden wanted years ago.* After arguing back and forth for some time, Denise gave in and told the boys that she would transfer their trust funds to the Bank of San Francisco. Some months before, she had started the process of transferring Irwin's and her funds out west for retirement. She would have the St. Louis banker do the same for her grandsons.

Suzette broke into the conversation, "What about me?" she asked incredulously.

"Suzette, Irwin, and I will take you to San Francisco on a clipper. We'll get you enrolled in a good school, and when the tension between the states settles down, Eli can send for you." Suzette said nothing, but going to San Francisco on a clipper was definitely not in her plans.

In the morning the boys were making ready to leave for Fort Leavenworth, Suzette hugged each of them and said her goodbyes and quickly left out for the school. Denise thought her demeanor somewhat strange in light of how long it would be before Suzette saw them again but dismissed her concerns thinking that Suzette was in denial and didn't want to suffer another loss. The boys saddled their horses and noticed that *Patches* was missing from the stable. The young mare had survived the tornado by running ahead of it back to the stables. The tornado spared the stables, or *Patches* would have died there. Eli and Jacques thought nothing of it, but Roland suspected that they would see Suzette again soon and not in San Francisco. Before he left, he retrieved an extra feedbag from the rack on the stable wall. Like his father, he was always planning ahead, anticipating the future. The young men stopped at their mother's grave before they left town. They stood silent, hats in hand, and then mounted up and rode west on their way around the bend of the Missouri River, to Fort Leavenworth.

The day passed, and when Suzette didn't return from the school, Denise asked Rufus to send someone over to look for her. Rufus had some of Denise's newspaper staff organized that wanted to help find the girl. He sent one lad to the school, one down to *The Meadows* and several others to look around town and check some homes of Suzette's close friends. By nightfall, all had returned empty-handed. A sense of dread settled into the pit of Denise's stomach. She went up to Suzette's room and found her granddaughter's buckskins and her 9mm Lafourche revolver that her father gave her when she was twelve, missing from the closet. She pulled open the drawer of the small writing desk, and a few other items of Suzette's personal things were missing along with her map of the Santa Fe Trail. Her worst fear was confirmed. Suzette had run away. She was already with her brothers or out on the trail or waiting somewhere for them to pass. Denise almost fell, running down the stairs to Irwin's study. She was frantic and choking back sobs but finally blurted out that Suzette was gone, runaway trying to join her brothers. She wanted him to take her to the Constable's office to convince him he had to hunt down her missing granddaughter. Irwin was skeptical the Constable would do anything before morning, but he went to the foyer and lit a lantern for the short walk up to Town Hall anyway.

As Irwin predicted, the constable proved sympathetic but wouldn't send anyone west until morning. He had already had a long day looking for the girl. His men had gone home, and he wasn't going to roust them out for a ride west in the dark of night. When he returned home, Denise asked Irwin how many men the constable would send, and the answer was two.

"You need six at least, two to go up towards Leavenworth, two to search Olathe and two to ride further west. She will be out there somewhere."

The lawman was still reluctant, and Denise reminded him that he was due for re-election, and he would be running without her support unless he made a decent effort to find her granddaughter. He reluctantly agreed to her request and sent a runner around to notify the men he wanted to send that they would be leaving out at dawn. He hoped that would placate the frantic woman. He didn't want to find another job come the election in November.

Irwin walked Denise home. She was still distraught. She wanted to get Rufus to hitch up the buckboard and go looking for Suzette herself. Irwin squelched that idea. They could step on Suzette in the dark and never see her. Denise started to calm down on the walk through the warm night back to the mansion. In the morning, she would post a reward of ten thousand dollars for the return of her granddaughter. Irwin squelched that idea too. The last thing they needed was to have dozens of bounty hunters and slave catchers after Suzette. She wasn't going to come home quietly. The girl knew how to ride hard, and she was an expert shot with the Lafourche, any pursuit by dishonorable men could only end badly. She could end up arrested for murder, or worse yet, wind up dead herself. "Let's let the Constable and his men do their work." With that, Irwin put an end to the desperate ideas and hoped Denise would sooner or later accept that Suzette might be better off with her brothers. Denise wasn't going to accept the rejection that she felt with what she perceived to be Suzette's abandoning her and all the plans she had for the young woman. Denise had many sleepless nights ahead of her and for the first time in her life, didn't welcome the future.

EPILOGUE

Eighteen years seems a long time for the young but passes as fast as a comet for the middle-aged and is marked with amazement by the elderly that they are still here to see the next day. Denise was no exception. She watched Aaden and Anna build a frontier empire in those eighteen years. Sometimes it seemed not only like a long time but also the best of times. Then it was swept away in a few moments, and it seemed like only yesterday since she fled New York. She dwelt heavily on destiny and the path from her childhood in France, to her marriage to Mercier, to Independence, Missouri, and the tragic loss of her only child. She was a wealthy woman who couldn't have the things in life she wanted most.

The *Black Freedom League* and *Missouri Publishers* were gone. *The Meadows* was in decline without their leader. Her beloved daughter Anna lay in her grave, and Anna's husband Aaden was gone forever. Her grandsons were on the Santa Fe Trail, and she prayed that Suzette was with them. The nation that she loved was on the verge of war with itself, state against state, brother against brother. Denise remembered that Aaden taught that there never was a civil war all through history that was over quickly or ended with anything else than a massive loss of life. It was always the young that died; the average age of the US Army was now less than twenty-three.

Every night she prayed that the next decade would spare her grandchildren. Every night she tossed in fitful sleep with the feeling that God had forsaken her. Irwin was her only anchor now, her rock. Irwin would take her to Los Angeles to wait for her grandsons to reach Fort Moore. Irwin encouraged Denise to finish writing the story of her coming to America and the house in New York. He missed Ben and Lily terribly, but his concern for them was a mere shadow of concern compared to his wife's anguish over her grandchildren, especially Suzette.

Denise had Rufus take her to Fort Leavenworth, and she got the schedule for the grandson's wagon train crossing the prairies and mountains on its way to California. The Trail, with all its dangers, was alive with the constant stream of pioneers headed west. If she were younger, she would have gone on the trail herself, but common sense and the many stories of the arduous crossing had her looking forward to the trip around the horn on a steamship with first-class tickets. They would leave soon to backtrack down the Mississippi and then travel around the horn on the *SS Coloma*, on her maiden voyage to the Pacific Coast. If they chose to cross Panama on the Charges River, the trip would be shorter. But around the horn was safe from the marches and mosquitoes of the isthmus. Neither of them had been to sea since they left New York. There would be many changes compared to their voyage on the *Blessed,* and both anticipated the trip to California with the enthusiasm of the pioneers. There was no hurry. They would reach California long before their grandchildren could cross America on a wagon train.

The only regret was that Rufus and Hannah were in their *Golden Years* and wouldn't be coming with them. They would stay in Independence and wait for Lily and Ben to return from Africa. They would move to quarters in the hospital and live out the rest of their days working with Jessica and doing what they could to keep the hospital running smoothly. Rufus and Hanna took them down to the landing in the carriage. The carriage was showing its age, and the Belgian's grey mane and tail had turned as silver as Rufus's hair. More than a thousand people gathered at the landing to see the couple off. Denise and Irwin stood at the rail of the Texas, as they waved their last goodbye to the people onshore. Rufus and Hannah stayed on the landing until the smokestacks of the side-wheeler were out of sight. Hearts heavy, they went back to the hospital knowing they would never see Denise and Irwin again. The future now belonged to the young; it was theirs to shape and mold to meet their dreams. The young United States, the hope of millions who came to her welcoming shores, was poised for division and civil war. A battlefield would prove a difficult place to shape a dream for many.

End of Volume I

Volume II – Pioneers, sees the young Callahan adults across the Kansas grasslands to the California Coast. Wrought with Indians, renegades and the perils and pleasures of the Santa Fe trail.

Volume III –Paydirt, they settle on the hill that becomes The Red Mountain Mine and where the dragon awaits discovery.

For more about the author and Dragon Tooth Gold, visit the website

https://dragonstoothpublishing.com/

To contact Kent McGrew

kent@dragonstoothpublishing.com

9 781733 665001